The Eagle and the Analyst

Bryan Neville

Table of Contents

Introduction

Recent news report from the major news outlets:

The North Korean state news service, Korean Central News Agency, reported today that the Democratic People's Republic of Korea had successfully launched a new rocket, and that it landed in the North Pacific, 500 miles east of Midway Island, just as planned.

The News Agency indicated that the successful launch of this new rocket signaled a new and glorious day for North Korea, as it demonstrates the military's claim that they are capable of attacking U.S. soil.

A White House spokesman said that while a rocket launch from the Tonghae launch facility had been observed by satellite, the rocket never achieved a trajectory that would allow for true transcontinental travel.

Chapter One

I glance at my watch and grimace when I see it's about 4 AM, and yet I'm unable to sleep. What's keeping me awake, I suspect, is wondering how I even got here in the first place. *Here*, by the way, is on the side of a small hill in North Korea overlooking a missile launch facility at Sohae, on the west coast of North Korea really close to the Chinese border. The launch pad itself is just about three quarters of a mile away, and except for a solitary light shining midway up the gantry, is completely invisible at this time of day.

My name is Robert Johnson, and I'm a Lt. Colonel in the United States Army. I'm supposed to be assigned to a desk in the Pentagon, but here I am on a cold, dark February night in North Korea. But at least I'm not alone. Hiding with me is an Army sniper team consisting of Master Sergeant Paul O. Parker, "Pop" to his friends, recognized as the Army's top sniper. Next to him is his spotter, Sergeant Paul Harris. In their unit, they are referred to as "two Ps in a pod."

Also with us are four Navy SEALS whose job it has been to ensure we arrived here safely. After our task is completed, it will also be their job to see that we arrive back at the submarine rendezvous point on Korea Bay so we can go home. They also provide perimeter security for us while we are hiding here on the side of the mountain. I'm not sure how effective four Navy SEALs may be, because if we are discovered, it won't take long for the North Koreans to put the bulk of their million-man army between us and Korea Bay. Whose idea was this anyway? Oh wait, I'm the brains of this outfit!

As I think back, it occurs to me that the report I prepared regarding the capabilities of the North Koreans to launch a ballistic missile toward the United States was the catalyst. In that report I made a strong argument that the North Koreans had finally developed a rocket that could reach at least as far as Hawaii, if not the West Coast of the United States. And I had to go and state my opinion that they would want to test it in front of the world media. Although my commanding officer told me I was crazy, he must have forwarded my report to his CO, the Pentagon general in charge of U.S. Army military intelligence. Heaven only knows who *he* sent it on to!

And wouldn't you know it, now it's starting to snow. With the wind blowing up the hill, the solitary light below is no longer visible. This will be a real problem in the morning because we won't be able to see our target. During our predeparture briefing, when the Navy meteorologist told us that his forecast for snow at Sohae was 50-50, I was praying for no snow. Well, at least it will cover the trail we made to our present hidey-hole. The bad news is, if there is snow on the ground when it's time for us to leave, we will leave a trail that even a fuzzy-chinned second lieutenant could follow.

Sohae is one of two rocket launch sites that North Korea maintains. We have another sniper team on a mountainside near Tonghae, the other North Korean launch site, on the east coast of North Korea. That team consists of a Marine Corps sniper duo and four additional Navy SEALS responsible for the safety of that team, all under the leadership of a Marine Corps major.

Our intelligence was pretty certain the North Koreans would be launching a ballistic missile, but it wasn't clear from which site the launch would take place. That's why we have sniper teams at both locations. Because I felt strongly that the launch would take place at Tonghae, I assigned the Marine Corps sniper team there. Even though I'm an Army officer, I had to admit that during the mission training, the Marine Corps sniper team performed marginally better, so they were assigned to what I considered the primary target.

It also occurs to me, as the snow continues to fall, that the weather will make it harder for any North Korean patrols to find us here while we wait for morning. Feeling somewhat more comfortable in my surroundings, I turn slightly so that the wind and snow are not blowing directly into my face.

Chapter Two

Sitting on that dreary cold hillside, with very little to do right then, my mind wanders back to an earlier time – the time this whole thing got started.

One morning, I was sitting nice and comfortable in my office in the Pentagon looking at satellite pictures of a missile launch site in North Korea. Most people would be surprised to learn that the photographs I was looking at had been provided by a commercial satellite firm rather than from a military satellite. I'm sure they make a ton of money with their government contract, but I have to admit, the pictures are excellent. The stream of events that ended with me on that hill started when my secretary, Master Sergeant Estelle Garcia, knocked on my office door. Sergeant Garcia is more than a typical office secretary; she is the major reason I appear to be so well organized. As is her custom when there's no one else in my office, she entered without waiting for me to answer and told me she just received a summons from Colonel Jacobs, my commanding officer. Colonel John Jacobs is an old-fashioned, by-the-book kind of guy. He could have sent me an email or even texted me on my cell phone. But instead, he called my secretary and asked her to give me a message to report to him immediately.

I hustled to his office as quickly as I could. Being only five doors away, it didn't take very long. He met me at the door, invited me in and closed the door himself. He was obviously anxious to get to whatever it was he wanted to talk about. After he sat behind his completely empty government-issued desktop, he asked me what I've been working on. Since I'm a senior intelligence officer with a tested IQ of 135, and I give him regular reports about my activities, I knew something was up.

I started to tell him about my work in reviewing intelligence reports from my South Korean contacts, when he interrupted and said, "I just received a telephone call inviting you to a meeting at the White House." He leaned closer to me and said, "What is this meeting about?" Since this was the first I'd heard about such a meeting, I shrugged my shoulders and said, "Sir, I haven't the foggiest idea." His expression clearly told me he wasn't happy about this answer.

Now, you have to know something about my commanding officer. He is what some would call a hands-on type of officer. In the business world he would be known as a micromanager – a really serious micromanager. He is always businesslike in the office, at least his version of businesslike. Plus, he is a West Point graduate, while I am an ROTC officer. I think he automatically assumed I wasn't as serious as he was about an Army career. Getting a phone call inviting one of his staff to the White House must have driven him absolutely up the wall. But there's nothing to be done for it, because I didn't know why I'd been invited to the White House, either. When I told him that again, he did something really unusual for him: He stood up and came around and sat on his desk right in front of me.

I had to turn away and cover my mouth and give a small cough to hide what was going to be a chuckle. The thought occurred to me, rude as it might be, that his big butt must be the only thing of substance that's been on the top of his desk in the last six months.

He sat there a few moments, as though he was thinking, and then said, "Bob, it's not every day that our office is asked to attend a meeting at the White House. Since you were invited, and I'm your commanding officer, don't you think I should know what the meeting is about?"

He finally gave me a chance to say something, and I repeated, for the third time, "Colonel, I have no idea why I've been summoned. Do you have the details, like what time I'm supposed to be there and with whom I'm going to meet?" He was clearly frustrated as he jumped off the desk, walked around to his chair, opened his top middle drawer and pulled out a sheet of paper with handwritten notes.

After he made a pretense of reviewing the notes, he looked up and told me, "You are to report to the office of the National Security Advisor at 1 o'clock." As it was already midmorning, I realized I had just enough time to rush home and change into my Class A uniform, which seemed a better choice than the Army Service Uniform I was wearing. At this point Colonel Johnson leaned forward and said very clearly, "After your meeting, you will report directly back to me and brief me on the meeting. Is that clear?" What else could I say but, "Yes, sir." His only response was, "Dismissed." So I stood up and left his office.

I hustled back to my office and told Sergeant Garcia I'd been invited to a meeting and didn't expect to be back until late afternoon. She reminded me of two meetings I had on my calendar, but I told her I had to leave right away because the word "invited" is not as accurate as "ordered," and would she be kind enough to invite my deputy, Major Green, to attend in my place. Major Green is a competent intelligence officer who will be okay in these two meetings. I continued by telling Sergeant Garcia the meeting was at the White House, but she didn't necessarily need to tell anyone that. When she raised her eyebrows, I told her I didn't know what the meeting was about but asked her to stay near her cell phone in case I needed to text her for information. You see, unlike Colonel Jacobs, we both live in the 21st century and enjoy our modern technology.

As I sat back in the taxicab on the way home, I wondered about the possible reasons I'd been summoned to the National Security Advisor's office. Since the major part of my assignment deals with the Korean Peninsula, I was pretty certain it would have to do with events that happened there recently.

Let me give you a little background about why I'm assigned to what we might call the Korean desk at the Pentagon.

When I was younger, I volunteered to be a missionary for the Mormon Church. My family and I were surprised when I was assigned to Seoul, South Korea. After attending language training in Provo, Utah, I spent nearly two years in South Korea, primarily in the capital city of Seoul. Although I struggled with the language initially, I eventually learned to speak more than just the language of proselyting. In fact, after my mission I continued to study and practice the Korean language. Although I grew up in Arizona, I attended Brigham Young University after my mission.

There was a small Korean community of students there, so I was able to practice my new language skills on an almost daily basis.

While at BYU I joined the Army ROTC program and was happily looking forward to serving my country. To make a long story short, when the Army discovered I spoke Korean almost fluently, I was immediately assigned as a military intelligence officer, after I was commissioned a second lieutenant that is. And yes, I've heard all the jokes about the phrase "military intelligence" being an oxymoron!

My goal of traveling the world as an Army officer would have to wait until after my first assignment. After graduating from BYU, the Army sent me to Fort Huachuca, Arizona, where the Army school for the training of professional military intelligence officers is located.

The familiar hills in Arizona where we practiced our military intelligence skills were never as cold and windy as this hill in North Korea.

Chapter Three

My thoughts are interrupted as the cold wind blows snow into my face. What's an Arizona boy doing with snow in his face! I pull the hood of my parka to cover more of my face, and my thoughts return to that first meeting in the White House.

The lunchtime traffic made the trip from the Pentagon to my condo seem frustratingly long. I didn't want to have to call for another taxicab, so when we got to my condo, I told the cabbie to wait while I ran upstairs to change. That may seem extravagant, but how many times do you get invited to a meeting at the White House?

I changed quickly, and because I was then dressed in the formal uniform of a U.S. Army officer, I *walked* back to the taxicab. When I told the taxi driver that our destination was the White House he asked which gate? It dawned on me that I had no idea how to get into the White House. I asked the cabbie to start toward the White House while I called my ever-able assistant. As usual, Sergeant Garcia knew the answer, so I told the cabbie to head for the west gate of the White House.

The taxi wasn't allowed inside the White House grounds, so I had to walk from the gate. I didn't mind because the walk allowed me to compose myself for my first meeting in the White House.

After I passed through the metal detector, the Secret Service guard asked if I knew my way to the National Security Advisor's office. When I said that I did not, he called for someone to escort me. Just a few minutes later, a young woman appeared, a presidential intern I discover later, and lead me to the proper office. She left me as I entered the outer office door.

The current Assistant to the President for National Security Affairs, Sarah Richardson, is your typical National Security Advisor. She has a PhD in national security studies, and before coming to the White House, she was a full professor at Georgetown University. Before that she was a civilian research professor at the Strategic Studies Institute, located in, of all places, south central Pennsylvania, specializing in national security research and analysis. She speaks four other languages – French, German, Spanish and Italian. She also served as the U.S. ambassador to Italy under a previous administration. To say she was accomplished and qualified would be an understatement.

Although she does not attend many social functions, she is considered the most eligible single woman in the current administration. I remember a rumor circulating about a year ago that suggested she may not be interested in men, if you know what I mean. However, she quickly put that to rest; in response to a reporter's brazen question as to whether she was hiding in the closet, she said, "I'm not hiding anywhere, especially in some silly closet." That was the end of that rumor!

As I entered her office, she stood and walked around her desk to shake my hand, even though she outranks me by more than a dozen levels. My admiration for her as a person went up a notch or two. "Welcome," she said, "I'm happy you could meet with me." To one side of her office was a small sofa and two cushioned side chairs. She invited me to sit on the sofa as she sat in one of the chairs.

Without any further small talk, she got right to the point. "The President is concerned about North Korea's recent statement that they are close to launching a rocket capable of hitting the U.S. West Coast with a nuclear weapon. We understand you have a reliable contact in South Korea's intelligence community. What can you tell me about their capabilities?" It suddenly became clear why I had been invited to meet with her. Her question left me unclear, though, whether she was asking about South Korea's intelligence capabilities or the capabilities of the North Koreans to launch a rocket as far as the U.S. West Coast. She saw my hesitation and said, "I mean, how reliable is South Korea's intelligence?"

I began by telling her that my contact was Major Kim Jin-ho, an intelligence officer in the South Korean army. I explained that I first met Major Kim while we were students at Brigham Young University. When I graduated and went to the Army intelligence school, he returned to South Korea and attended their intelligence officer training program. My first assignment after training was to South Korea, where we renewed our friendship. We were both married at that time, and our wives, Beth and Soo-jin, became close friends as well. I explained that we have maintained our close association over the many travels our military careers have taken us. "In short, ma'am, I have great respect for the South Korean Intelligence Service, at least as far as it concerns North Korea capabilities.

"It's clear the North Koreans have a new rocket, and we don't know much about it. Major Kim has been assigned to learn more about their rocket program, and although our official relationship is fairly formal, he has told me privately that he is concerned they may have received sufficient aid from China to enable them to build a new rocket that does have the capabilities they've announced."

She responded by saying, "I've been led to believe, Colonel Johnson, that you are the preeminent authority on North Korea's capabilities. What have you been doing to confirm your friend's informal fears?"

I wasn't quite sure where she was headed with that question. As the National Security Advisor, she certainly had access to a much higher level of intelligence than I did. In fact, she has the authority to order satellite surveillance over North Korea to see what they're up to. If our commercial satellites have the capability to watch a man dancing in a parking lot, certainly the military satellites can track essential rocket materials around North Korea.

I told her, "We have a rather sizable budget for commercial satellite imagery, and I've been closely reviewing the imagery of the two rocket launch locations in North Korea. It is clear to me that something new is going on, but it's hard to determine what that is. In fact, the same commercial satellite imagery has been made available to the South Koreans, and they are also wondering what the North Koreans are up to.

"It would be nice to have someone on the ground there, but it's difficult to insert a spy into North Korea because they have such a regimented society. I raised this question with Major Kim, and he indicated their leadership is hesitant to take any overt action that would exacerbate the current poor relations they have with North Korea. He reminds me often that they are still at war with one another."

Then I go out on a limb, and tell her, "If I had the authority, I would task the National Reconnaissance Office with very specific assignments over North Korea. With access to this more recent and detailed satellite imagery, I might be able to learn a bit more about their capabilities."

She had been listening intently, even leaning forward as I spoke. "Interesting you mention the NRO. At the President's direction, I have formed a working group to address this challenge from North Korea. Can you join us in a meeting here tomorrow at 7:30 AM?"

"Of course. I'll just let my CO know that I'll be back here in the morning."

"There's no need for that," she said. "Colonel Jacobs will get a call to let him know we're going to borrow you for a while. In fact, it would be best if you didn't say anything to anyone about your meetings here in the White House. Are you okay with that?"

At that point I knew there was more to this than just the attention my intelligence analysis might have brought.

Chapter Four

It suddenly occurs to me that the snowfall has increased in intensity while I've been reminiscing. Since I'm not really a field soldier, I decide to ask the SEAL team leader for his assessment of the snowfall and its potential impact on our exfiltration plan. As the officer in charge of this team, I'm carrying two radios. All the team members are carrying short range tactical radios so we can keep in touch with each other. In addition to that, I'm also carrying a satellite radio with its heavy-duty battery so I can communicate via satellite with the special ops headquarters operations center in Florida, and I can also talk to the other team at Tonghae, the other rocket launch facility. Our radios use burst technology, so hopefully the North Koreans will not be able to find us by triangulating on our radio transmissions.

The operational plan we discussed and practiced back in Florida placed two SEAL team members to my left and two to my right, with the sniper duo and me, the officer in charge, in the middle. The thinking was that the SEAL team members could maintain a good lookout and warn the sniper team and me if anyone was coming our way.

Even though I can't see more than about 3 feet, I turned to my right as I called Lieutenant Carrollton on the tactical radio. He assured me, with what I thought was a slight lilt in his voice, that it didn't matter what the weather was, at least the SEAL team could get out. Ha, ha, I thought to myself, a little SEAL team humor. After a pause, he assured me that we would all make our submarine pickup deadline.

Getting off this hill and back to the submarine could prove to be the most challenging part of this assignment. We left the submarine after the sun had already fallen and were able to get into our present position while it was still dark. Because we're not certain when the North Koreans plan to begin the countdown on their missile launch, we may find ourselves with several hours of daylight left after we take our shot. Ideally, we would stay hunkered down until dark and then hike back to our rendezvous with the submarine. On the other hand, if we have to leave our hideout immediately after the shot, we may have to hike to the shoreline during daylight hours. That is Plan B. I don't like Plan B.

During the hike in, we found two places that might serve as temporary hideaways if we have to leave our current spot during daylight hours and wait for darkness to fall. My preference would be to stay where we are and begin our hike back to the submarine after dark. Although we surveyed more than a few escape routes by satellite during the mission planning and selected the most desolate path, you never really know who you will run into during daylight hours.

We also don't know what the North Koreans may do tomorrow prior to the missile launch. Their standing army is so large they may just decide to surround the missile launch facility with thousands of soldiers. As good as our hideaway is, a determined brigade of soldiers would eventually find us. And Plan C is . . . Well, there is no plan C.

So while the snow is helping to hide us now, if we have to hike out during the day tomorrow, our trail in the snow would be a dead giveaway to even the dimmest foot soldier. As an Army officer I know that even the greatest of plans only lasts until the first shot is fired; nonetheless, I'm still praying that Plan A works.

As I turn my attention back to the snowfall, I remember the first time our daughter Susan played in the snow. She was just two years old and tried to catch every snowflake. While our son Jacob was busy making snowballs, Susan was trying to catch a snowflake so she could examine it. Even though they are twins, they are so different. As they grew older, Jacob seemed to accept that everything was just as it was, while Susan wanted to know why. I'm not surprised that Jacob wants to attend the Baylor School of Medicine, while Susan wants to attend Georgetown and get a degree in philosophy.

If Beth were alive, she would be so proud of both of them. In fact, she used to say that Susan was the spitting image of her mother and that Jacob was the spitting image of his father. As my mind wanders in the past, I remember another occasion when Susan looked just like her mother.

I was sitting in the living room one autumn evening with the latest Reader's Digest when Susan came home from her piano lesson after high school. Although she didn't slam the front door, she certainly closed it firmly! Without greeting me, she walked quickly to her room and closed the door.

Jacob heard her come in and went out of his way to walk by Susan's bedroom and sang, "Susie lost her boyfriend! Susie lost her boyfriend!"

She opened her door and loudly said, "Don't call me Susie; my name is Susan!" It was not a family secret that when he wanted to dig at her he called her Susie and when she wanted to return the favor, she called him Jakey. Just one of those teenager things.

At this interchange, I left the living room and knocked on Susan's door. She knew it was me because I had a special knock for each of them. I heard her say, "Go away. I don't want to talk right now."

Using a father's prerogative, I peeked around the door and said, "I think I heard you say, come in, Father. I'd like to explain why I'm in such a bad mood."

She gave me one of those looks only a teenager can use on her father, but didn't say anything. I took this to mean that I was welcome to enter, so I closed the door and sat next to her on the bed. As she focused on some particle of dust on the carpet at her feet, I said, "Care to explain?"

"Dad, you wouldn't understand." After a short pause she continued, "I wish mom were here!"

I put my arm around her and said quietly, "So do I, sweetheart; so do I." And then using my normal voice, "But I'm the best you're going to get for now. So, what's up?"

Leaning her head onto my shoulder, she began to share her story. "Boys are so stupid!" Wow, only 17 years old and she has us all figured out! "I've been out with Barry four times and I thought he liked me."

I interrupted and said, "You mean that football player you brought home a few weeks ago?"

"Yes, Daddy, he's the star quarterback for our team. Anyway, we've been meeting at the bleachers after our last class and then we walk home together. Today, I got out of class a little early and when I got to the bleachers I saw him with his arm around another girl. I was so humiliated! I couldn't even concentrate on my piano lesson."

"So you didn't even talk to him?" She shook her head, so I continued. "How do you know he wasn't just consoling her over some misfortune?"

She jumped away as though I were a hairy spider! "Dad, I'm not stupid! And the smile on her face was not because of some misfortune, that's for sure."

Feeling as though I was wading into quicksand, I quickly changed tactics and said, "Sweetheart, what do you say we have dinner at Bertucci's, your favorite Italian eatery? We can even leave your favorite brother at home to fend for himself."

Apparently the hairy spider was gone, because she jumped back and gave me a hug and said, "Yes! Give me just a few minutes to change my clothes and brush my hair."

True to her word, she was ready in under five minutes. As I turned at her approach, I was surprised at the metamorphosis which had taken place. She was no longer the despondent high school teenager in ragged jeans and sweatshirt; instead, she appeared before me as a smiling and confident young woman in a brightly colored skirt and blouse. My voice caught as I recognized so much of her mother in her appearance. Then the teenager returned as she said, "Bye Jakey; enjoy your tuna fish sandwich! If Barry calls, tell him I'm not home."

If Barry calls. This thought rings a bell. I glance at my watch and see that I've almost missed our check-in time. So I call Lieutenant Carrollton on the tactical radio, and sure enough the others check-in immediately. Using the SatCom, I say "Ranger" and hear "Tonto" from the team at Tonghae in response. If either of us were under duress, we would simply begin talking without using the security word. So, both teams are still in place and waiting to see what tomorrow, I mean this morning, brings.

Again, my mind turns to that first White House meeting. After I left Dr. Richardson's office that afternoon, I called Sergeant Garcia to tell her that I would not be back to the office and that I would not be in the office tomorrow. Before I could brief her, she told me that Colonel Jacobs was on the warpath. She told me he had come charging into her office asking if she had heard from me. She told him no and after he left, called his secretary and asked what was going on. She learned that Colonel Jacobs had received a phone call from the office of the chief of staff of the Army, and that's all she knew.

That phone call happened so fast I knew it had been arranged before I even showed up in Dr. Richardson's office. Now I really was curious to know what was going on; I remember thinking that I could barely wait for the next meeting. In fact, that evening I called Major Kim and asked if he had any new information pertaining to the North Korean development of a long-range missile. His answer completely surprised me.

He told me that someone named Admiral Harrison, who is apparently a staff officer in the office of the Joint Chiefs of Staff, had called his counterpart in the office of the South Korean Joint Chiefs of Staff. That Admiral had called Major Kim directly and asked for the latest information regarding the North Korean capabilities. Major Kim told me he'd given Admiral Cho the same information that he'd given me two days before. In other words, the North Koreans had most likely not only designed and built a long-range missile, but were planning to test it in the very near future. Their intelligence had detected increased activity at both rocket launch facilities, so they were unable to determine at which facility the new rocket would be launched.

After the conversation with Major Kim, I changed my mind and decided to return to my office so I could review the latest intelligence we had available. I waited until I knew Colonel Jacobs would be gone; it was a pretty simple determination because he left the office at 5 PM sharp every day. On the way into my office, I left a note on Sergeant Garcia's desk asking her to have Major Green call me on my cell phone as soon as they got in the office at 0700 the next morning, so he and I could discuss the most current North Korean intelligence.

I spent a couple of hours in my office reviewing the available intelligence, and that's when I noticed the NRO photographic intelligence had diminished in quality and quantity over the last several days. I chastised myself for not noticing that difference sooner. After examining the intelligence photography with a new perspective, it was now easy to see that someone had carefully edited the photographic feed to our office. With this new perspective it was easy to see that the continuity of the photography was not as seamless as it had been before.

I went to bed that evening wondering why someone would want to keep the Army in the dark.

Chapter Five

I arrived at the area outside the west gate of the White House the next morning at about 6:45. I found a relatively quiet spot where I could take the phone call from Major Green. When my phone rang at precisely 7 o'clock, I was curious to hear Major Green's report. Not unexpectedly, he had nothing new to report; what I had looked at the night before was the latest. As I walked away from the gate, I asked him to re-examine the photographic surveillance we had received from the NRO for North Korea over the past week and to look for discontinuities in what they had provided in previous weeks. I asked him to look specifically for any apparent trend or pattern to any issues that he discovered. I told him I would call him later in the day, after my meetings were completed.

I hung up and hightailed it back to the west gate of the White House.

I walked up to the gate and showed my ID to the guard, and after checking the list of approved visitors for that day, he pointed to the door I should enter. Even though I now knew how to get to the National Security Advisor's office, they asked that I wait for an escort. It turned out to be the same young intern I met the previous day. She escorted me to Dr. Richardson's office and left me without having said a single word.

Her secretary looked up and greeted me with a smile and a pleasant greeting. "Good morning, Colonel Johnson. Please go right in, they're waiting for you." I thanked her, knocked on the inner door and walked in. Dr. Richardson was on the phone so she motioned me in with a wave of her hand and pointed to the only empty chair. I looked around at the other guests while waiting for her to complete her phone call. The only person I recognized was the White House Chief of Staff, Jefferson Jackson. As I listened to Dr. Richardson on the telephone, it was obvious she was talking to someone higher up in the food chain. In her case, that could only mean the President.

While looking at the other individuals, I heard her say, "Thank you, sir, we will keep that in mind. Goodbye, sir." As I turned back to her, she said, "Good morning, Colonel Johnson. Thank you for being on time. Let me introduce the others.

"This is Jefferson Jackson, White House Chief of Staff, who is here representing the President. Marty Packard is from the CIA, Admiral Harrison is here representing the Joint Chiefs of Staff, and Dr. Vivian O'Brien is from the National Reconnaissance Office."

She looked back at me and told the others, "Lt. Colonel Robert Johnson is considered the Army's preeminent authority on North Korea. He is here to help us understand the situation we face with this new information about North Korea's announced intent to launch a missile with a nuclear warhead toward the West Coast of the United States." That was the second time she referred to me as a preeminent authority. If she wanted to make points with me, she had a good start!

Her phone rang again, and after looking at the caller ID she held up her right index finger and answered the phone. While she was talking with whom I expected was the President again, I more closely examined the others in the room.

Without consciously doing so, I started with the national reconnaissance officer, Vivian O'Brien. She dressed conservatively and even sitting down, it was obvious she was tall, probably 5'9" or so. She also had what appeared to be a permanent and engaging smile on her face. But what really stood out was her bright and curly red hair that hung down almost to her shoulders. Because of a sprinkling of freckles across her nose and under her bright green eyes, I surmised the red hair was all natural. It also seemed obvious from her lithe appearance that she maintained some kind of workout regimen. I remember blushing as I had these thoughts; I hadn't really noticed other women in that way since Beth's death.

Although I could've looked at her all day long, I moved my vision to the somewhat roly-poly man from the CIA, Marty Packard. Sitting next to

Dr. O'Brien, it was clear he was only of medium height, maybe 5'7". What little hair he had was swept across his head in a vain attempt to not look bald. Curiously, he looked bored.

Admiral Harrison on the other hand looked alert, bright and well aware of his surroundings. The top of his head was covered by silver gray hair that gave him a sophisticated appearance. He was obviously tall, probably 6'4" or so, and looked ready to begin the meeting. He also looked like he belonged on the bridge of a mighty warship, not in a small office.

Last was Jefferson Jackson, who was about 5'8" tall with just the beginnings of a potbelly. His hair was probably too long for his position and obviously colored. His eyes were constantly bouncing back and forth, reminding me of a ping pong ball. I smiled as I noticed he clearly did *not* have a workout regimen. I remembered that Time Magazine recently described him as "an obviously politically motivated man in all he does."

I wondered what my role would be in this politically charged and obviously high-level meeting. Without consciously doing so, my eyes wandered back to the NRO officer. She threw a smile in my direction as Dr. Richardson was hanging up the phone. I was a little embarrassed when I realized that even though I call myself an intelligence officer, I did not hear one word she said while on the telephone. This bothered me for two reasons: first, because normally I hear every word spoken in a room, and second, I knew exactly what, or who, to be more precise, had diverted my attention. That hadn't happened in a long time!

"Sorry everyone," Dr. Richardson said, "That was the President again with another question about our current situation. But we'll get to that in a minute."

She continued, "Let me start with a brief statement of the President's primary concern. Colonel Johnson, the recent intelligence analysis you drafted concerning North Korea's boast that they are close to launching a nuclear missile toward the West Coast of the United States has caught the attention of everyone who sits on the National Security Council."

I pondered this statement as I remembered that my report had been toned down at the request of my commanding officer. I wonder what the

National Security Council would have thought if I had not softened my original and somewhat stronger language.

"The President has asked me to chair a small working group, which is what we are," as she pointed to each of us, "and asked that we develop a plan to minimize the threat to the United States."

She paused for a moment and allowed us to consider what she had just said. Then, "The President has made it clear that we are to develop recommendations for action that will hinder their ability to launch that long-range missile. On the phone just now he was even more emphatic; he wants a plan that will ensure they cannot launch that missile for a long time, if ever. His question was, can we do that without risking a new war?

"Mr. Packard from the CIA is a Senior IT manager, specializing in what the CIA calls "IT warfare." He suggests the CIA is capable of inserting a virus into the North Korean missile launch software that will ensure the missile cannot be successfully launched. While this may be true, the President is concerned because the proof of this approach cannot be ascertained until launch. If that approach fails, we will not know until it is too late.

"Admiral Harrison, who represents the Joint Chiefs of Staff, brings their recommendation that B-2 stealth bombers be sent over North Korea to bomb both of their missile launch sites to oblivion. Clearly, the President does not want to commit an overt act of war. Their alternative, to bomb the missile on the launch site near launch time, is also problematic because B-2 bombers, although nearly invisible to radar, would be clearly visible in the daytime."

Turning to me, she abruptly asked, "Colonel Johnson, is it true you have been to North Korea?"

This question caught me by surprise because no one was supposed to know about my little escapade to North Korea when I was but a lowly Captain. I looked at the Admiral, who smiled expectantly, and then back to Dr. Richardson.

"Dr. Richardson . . ." I started, hesitantly, but she interrupted me.

"Colonel Johnson," she said, "let me explain. While researching everything we know about North Korea, we found a reference to a certain Captain Robert Johnson in an old CIA report. We just want to ascertain if that was you. Was it?"

I looked at the Admiral with what I'm sure was a plaintive expression.

He looked at me as he raised both hands and shrugged his shoulders. "Colonel, the Korean Peninsula did not explode into open warfare back then, so whatever you did could not have been openly aggressive. Besides, there must be a statute of limitations on youthful recklessness! We just want to know where you went and how you got there. It may have a bearing on another plan that has been proposed."

"Well, in that case, do you want the short version or the long version?"

Dr. Richardson answered for the group. "The short version will do for now, but we may have questions."

"I served two tours in South Korea; both with the Eighth Army as part of the 501st military intelligence brigade. Before that, I graduated from Brigham Young University, where I met a fellow student who was from South Korea. During my first tour in the 501st, I renewed my friendship with him. He had joined the South Korean Army and was in their intelligence command. We were both young and we both thought we were kings of the world.

"I learned that they maintained open communications with a dissident group just over the border into North Korea. Periodically, his unit surreptitiously sent officers across the border to meet with this group, and often as not they would bring back a North Korean soldier who wanted to defect and live in South Korea.

"One time he had been selected to go across the border, and in a light moment, he asked if I wanted to go with him. I hesitated because I knew that if I got captured in North Korea all hell would break loose. He told me that I spoke Korean well enough that if we got stopped and questioned I could pretend to be drunk as I responded to anyone's questions. He also said that they, meaning his office, were routinely able to create realistic North Korean travel papers. When I reminded him that my appearance was definitely not Asian, he said that we could dye my hair and put lots of dirt and makeup on my face and hands.

"So long story short, I went with him as we traveled aboard a small ship about 125 km, that's about 80 miles, north of the border and then just a few miles into North Korea from the west shoreline. Just as my friend had explained, we met with the radical group on the outskirts of a small town and they introduced us to a corporal in the North Korean Army.

"After about two hours of questioning, my friend decided we would take him back to South Korea. He was cautious because some who had been brought back had turned out to be spies. We took a different route back to the shoreline where we were met by two operatives who took us out to a small boat just offshore. We didn't meet anyone going in nor coming out, and I never told anyone in my command about my excursion. I found out later that one of the operatives we met on the shoreline was actually an American CIA agent of Korean ancestry. I didn't realize until just now that he even knew my name."

Dr. Richardson asked, "Was that friend of yours Major Kim?"

"Yes, it was. But I hope we don't have to use his name anywhere. He could get in a whole heap of trouble at home."

Admiral Harrison said, "We believe he is your primary contact for intelligence information about the North Korean Army; is that correct?"

"I have several useful contacts in South Korea, but yes, he is my primary source of information."

Dr. Richardson continued, "In fact, Admiral Harrison spoke with an admiral in the South Korean office of their Joint Chiefs of Staff and learned that Major Kim, who by the way is soon to be Lt. Colonel Kim, is considered one of their best intelligence officers. As you might imagine, their primary focus is what's going on in North Korea."

I responded, "Major Kim lives in a suburb of Seoul, and I've learned from him what it feels like to be just a few minutes away from the demarcation line, and how close renewing the war really is for South Koreans. So you might say he is really motivated to do a good job!"

I turned to Admiral Harrison and said, "Admiral, when you say that my previous experience may have some bearing on a proposed plan, please understand that the South Koreans no longer go into North Korea by using a small boat off the west coast. I believe they still go into North Korea, but I haven't asked Major Kim how they do that."

Dr. O'Brien looked right at me and said softly, "I know how they do it."

Everyone turned from me as we all looked directly at Dr. O'Brien.

Chapter Six

Dr. O'Brien turned to Dr. Richardson, and began to explain. "After I was assigned to this project, I began to look at the old satellite imagery of North Korea for the past year or so. Although I did not notice initially, I eventually saw in one photo a man standing in the middle of no man's land just north of the DMZ. I looked at the preceding image in the sequence and he wasn't there. Then on the next image, all of a sudden he is there.

"I now focused on this area on every passing satellite image. Sure enough, after I started looking, I once again noticed an image where a man was standing in the exact same place as I previously noted.

"I continued to watch this series of images. Four days later in the sequence I saw two men standing in that spot, and on the very next image they were gone. It was like they had simply disappeared. I believe the South Koreans have excavated a very small tunnel into North Korea.

"As time went on, I began to wonder why the tunnel hadn't been discovered by the North Koreans. And I also wondered how the South Koreans were able to move into North Korea without being discovered.

"I did a little bit more research and discovered that every time I saw a man standing in that spot the South Koreans had created a very visible and probably noisy distraction just a few miles east of that position but right on the demarcation line.

"I was able to see in the satellite imagery that the North Koreans in that area had moved to the east in response to the South Korean distraction. It was just about a mile, but that was enough to allow the South Korean agent and the presumed defector to disappear without being seen."

Dr. Richardson turned to me, and asked, "Colonel Johnson, can you call Major Kim and confirm what Dr. O'Brien has just shared with us?"

"I can, but I don't think I should be asking that kind of question on a telephone line, and even if I did, I don't think he would answer."

Admiral Harrison then spoke up in an animated voice, "Why wouldn't your friend answer that question?"

I had been pondering this train of thought, and responded, "Do we really care if the South Koreans are doing that? It's a long way from that point near the DMZ to either of their launch facilities. Besides, I don't think we should put them on the spot with that kind of a question. After all, we don't always share our methods with our allies."

As Admiral Harrison was beginning to respond, Dr. Richardson quietly interrupted and said, "I agree. Let's table that discussion for another day."

Although we were ready to move on to the next point, I noted that both the CIA technician and the White House Chief of Staff had made brief notes. In my opinion, it's never a good thing when a politician knows something as sensitive as the topic we've just discussed! And one can never know what the CIA might do with that new information.

Dr. Richardson continued, "The other question the President asked me was this: Can we destroy the rocket as it sits on the launch facility and at the same time cause significant damage to the facility itself?

"The unspoken assumption is the President's previous requirement that we do all this without being discovered and without the North Koreans being able to point any fingers to the United States."

At this point, Mr. Packard, the CIA technician spoke up. "Dr. Richardson, I must remind you of the significant capabilities we have in attacking North Korean technology. If we can cause the rocket to be destroyed right at the point of launch, certainly the launch facility would be partially if not totally destroyed. This seems like the right answer to the President's question."

Dr. Richardson leaned back in her chair and asked, "Can you guarantee that your IT attack will destroy the rocket?" She smiled as Mr. Packard appeared uncomfortable with her question.

He responded, "There is no guarantee with any plan we come up with."

Mr. Jackson, who had not appeared very interested in our discussions up to this point, now spoke up and said, "With an election year coming up, we certainly don't want anything to happen that would have a negative effect on the President's reelection chances. With all the challenges we face in Iran, Libya, Afghanistan, the Ukraine and Syria, we certainly don't need more saber rattling in Korea."

Admiral Harrison commented, "And we certainly can't launch any cruise missiles; they would be easily identified with the United States. And for the reasons already discussed, sending bombers would not make sense."

Glancing around the group, Dr. Richardson said, "All good observations." Then she looked at me and said, "Colonel Johnson, as the man with the most experience in Korea, and because, as you implied earlier, telephone lines are not very secure, I'm going to recommend that you fly to South Korea and visit with your friend Major Kim. He is likely to tell you more if you are on his home turf. We want to know all they know."

She turned to the admiral and said, "Admiral Harrison, can you arrange military orders and appropriate transportation so that Colonel Johnson can fly to South Korea?"

"Yes, ma'am."

She then turned to me and asked, "Colonel Johnson, how soon can you leave?"

I knew the correct answer to her question, so I said, "I can leave as soon as arrangements can be made. The flight is long and I can organize myself and make preparations for the meeting while *en route*. I would, however, like clarification on some of the issues we raised today."

Our small workgroup spent the next hour discussing other options, including the questions I would ask Major Kim, emphasizing to him the sensitive nature of our discussions. When Admiral Harrison specifically ordered me to ask Major Kim if the South Koreans had any plans to sabotage the new rocket, Mr. Jackson spoke up.

"Wait a minute, I disagree. We cannot afford to give away our plans, and asking this question will imply that we have plans to sabotage the new rocket." His argument made sense, at least in my mind. He continued, "In fact, I'm not sure we should send Colonel Johnson to South Korea at all. His presence may be noticed by the North Koreans, or even the Chinese who will pass that information to the North Koreans. In fact, I strongly recommend that we develop plans without including the South Koreans at all."

All eyes turned to Dr. Richardson as she said, "We've never done anything on or near the Korean Peninsula without informing the South Koreans of our plans. Do we really want to do something there without letting them know, at least in general, what we're doing?"

"We can always let them know at the last minute," said Mr. Jackson. "If nothing goes wrong, why do they need to know at all? Our recent operations with the Navy SEAL teams have been very successful. Why should this project be any different? I'm afraid I'll have to get the President in on this decision."

While we all pondered his statement, I for one knew that he was more concerned about any potential impact on the President's reelection chances. But as I continued to think about it, why didn't our little workgroup have a representative from the Navy SEALs? They certainly have more experience with this kind of mission than any of us. I kept thinking there's more to this little workgroup than meets the eye!

Dr. Richardson looked at the White House Chief of Staff for a few moments and then said, "Alright everybody, let's meet back here at 1:30 after lunch. Mr. Jackson and I will meet with the President and have the benefit of his input when we meet again. So that we can meet back here on time, I recommend you all eat in the West Wing cafeteria."

I heard Marty Packard, the CIA specialist, turn to the Admiral and say, "I have to make a quick phone call; I'll meet you in the cafeteria in a few minutes."

So I joined Admiral Harrison and Dr. O'Brien to make a threesome as we walked to the White House Mess, as the cafeteria was formally known.

Chapter Seven

Awakened from my reverie by a click in the radio, I hear the SEAL team leader, Lieutenant Carrollton, who is down the hill on my right, say "Two-man patrol coming up the hill!"

I can't believe the North Koreans are out in this snow storm. We've been here about five hours, and this is the first hint of any North Korean activity. I'm hoping these two soldiers ticked off their sergeant in some way, and he sent them out for a little walk, and thus they won't be very observant. When I hear two clicks on the radio, I remember I'm supposed to give a single click to acknowledge the warning from the SEAL team leader. If I'm not more careful, those Navy SEALs are going to think I'm sound asleep! I pull the radio out of my pocket, press the transmit button with my gloved forefinger and immediately release it.

Although it is difficult to know how far I can see through the falling snow, I'm pretty certain that if I cannot see them, they cannot see me. At least that sounds like something my father would've taught me. Just as I have that thought, the falling snow to my right takes on a gray appearance. Sure enough, although I cannot make out any details, two gray blobs move slowly to my left. As they draw closer to me, I can just make out the crunching sound their boots make as they take each step.

My heart begins to race as the gray blobs stop just in front of me. As one of them turns toward me, I can barely discern the outline of his face in the hood of his parka.

After a moment, they continue their journey along the hill to my left. Although I don't remember holding my breath, I start breathing again. I don't know why they stopped, but I'm sure glad they kept going! I wonder whether they will continue down the hill and return to their barracks by crossing our position at the bottom of the hill, or if they will come back up and go across at a different point on the hill. If it hadn't been for this snow that I had earlier found so annoying, I'm sure they would've discovered me. I hope they just keep on going!

After a few minutes, I decide to check on their progress. "Lieutenant Williams, if you can talk do so, otherwise send a single click." I hear a single click, so I check my watch and wait another five minutes. Then I send the same message, "Lieutenant Williams, if you can talk do so, otherwise send a single click." After I hear another single click from the radio, Lieutenant Carrollton calls me and says, "Colonel, be patient; they will call you when they consider it safe to do so."

I'm suddenly aware of the sessions I missed while both teams were practicing for this operation in the hills of West Virginia. I'm embarrassed as I realize I really am better suited to a desk in the Pentagon.

While I'm waiting for the SEALs on my left to check in, my mind wanders back to that lunch in the West Wing of the White House.

It was just the three of us walking over to the West Wing cafeteria – me, Admiral Harrison, and Dr. O'Reilly – since the CIA operative had excused himself. Looking around to be sure we were alone, Admiral Harrison said, "What do you bet the Director of the CIA knows about our meeting before the President does?" It turns out he was wrong, as we learned later, but it was a good guess.

The cafeteria was crowded, so our conversation during lunch was truly just social chit chat, and not even much of that. Although I was no longer awed in the presence of flag rank officers, I was still the junior officer and Admiral Harrison was not very talkative. Dr. O'Brien seemed to focus on her salad, so I was left to my own thoughts.

This was all right with me because I wanted to give some thought to what I had learned so far in our meetings. It was obvious that Dr. Richardson's little group had been meeting prior to my being invited to join them. Evidently, some decisions had already been made. I wondered how long it would take them to bring me up to speed or if, indeed, I would be brought up to speed. It was obvious there was more to their discussions than what they've shared with me so far. I don't know why, but the

Iran-Contra affair popped into my head. I hoped I was not to become the modern version of Oliver North.

Other than a lack of much conversation, lunch was excellent. Admiral Harrison had a steak, Dr. O'Brien took a pass at the salad bar, and because it was Thursday, I elected the Mexican special. Their meat tacos were delightful! Admiral Harrison told us the White House Mess has been run by Navy personnel ever since it was established in 1951. He said it only serves breakfast and lunch, but nothing is prepackaged; all the food is prepared in the cafeteria kitchen.

He proudly pointed out the uniformity of the tables, each one round with four place settings and a Lazy Susan in the center holding a single red carnation, making for a cozy meal. The china was cream-colored with bands of blue and gold and carried the Presidential seal. Keeping with the other Naval decorations, such as royal blue carpeting and naval paintings and seascapes on the walls, the placemats were also Navy blue.

On the walk back to Dr. Richardson's office, I found myself next to Dr. O'Brien. Well, truth be told, she was in the middle as the three of us walked back to the office, but she was next to me! It was hard not to notice that she was almost as tall as I was, and she had no trouble at all keeping up with us long-legged men. I'm guessing, though, based on my previous observation, that she would have run us both into the ground had we been on a track.

As we approached Dr. Richardson's office, we spotted the CIA spook approaching from the opposite direction. He apologized for missing lunch by telling us that his phone call took longer than he anticipated. His lopsided smile did not seem sincere.

Settling into the same seats we had before, the team listened as Dr. Richardson told us that Mr. Jackson, the White House Chief of Staff, would be joining us shortly. He and the President had a few things they wanted to discuss privately. "Meanwhile," she said, "let me tell you about our meeting.

"First, since everything we discuss in this meeting is considered top secret, he has authorized me to tell you that in a rare piece of diplomacy, the Russian ambassador told him that their intelligence services have come to the same conclusions we have. They *also* believe the North Koreans have developed, built and are ready to test fire their first truly long-range missile."

She continued, "They believe the test will take place in early February. Apparently the North Koreans have purchased a specialized rocket transporter from the Chinese. Their first attempt to move the rocket from its production facility was a disaster. That problem precipitated the request for more substantial rocket-handling equipment from the Chinese. The President told us the Russian ambassador informed him the new equipment would be delivered to Pyongyang in early January. So the earliest they could launch the rocket would be in early February."

Admiral Harrison asked, "Why would the Ruskies tell us that?"

Her response was, "The President thinks the Russians are now worried that if North Korean's new rocket can reach our West Coast, then it can also reach into their territory. So it just makes sense that they'd like us to take care of that problem so they can still be the good guys in the bad guy's eyes."

I spoke up and said, "We truly live in a convoluted world! So what is the bottom line?"

Dr. Richardson looked at me, smiled, and quietly said, "He wants us to develop a plan that will ensure the rocket never takes off. And he re-emphasized that any damage to their launch capabilities would be icing on the cake."

Admiral Harrison now spoke up, and said, "You've already told us that we cannot send bombers and that an IT option would be 50-50 at best. And it is my opinion that the South Koreans are not able, and even if they were able, they would not be willing to participate in any direct action. And I doubt the Chinese will want to get involved. So where does that leave us?"

As he asked that question the door opened and Mr. Jackson walked in. After he sat down, he looked around and asked, "Where does what leave us?"

My memories are interrupted again by a radio call from a SEAL team member on my left. He tells me, well, he tells everybody on the radio circuit, that the Korean patrol had continued down the mountainside. I ask everyone on the circuit if anyone has seen any indication that they are aware of our presence. The response is a clear negative from everybody. I ponder for a moment, wondering if we should do anything different. If we move, we would leave a clear trail in the snow, so that option is not a good one. Is there anything else we could do?

I key the radio and ask, "Lt. Carrollton, is there anything else we should be doing, anything that would keep us from being discovered?"

He immediately responded with, "No sir, not at this time." No hesitation. No questions. Just a simple statement. I wish I felt as confident as he did.

Chapter Eight

Satisfied that we are doing all we can do here on the mountainside, my thoughts return again to that fateful meeting in the National Security Advisor's office.

I remember Dr. Richardson responding to Mr. Jackson's question. "I think it is safe to say that everyone is wondering how we can meet the President's demands. How *do* we stop that rocket from being launched with all the president's restrictions attached?"

Everyone looked at Marty Packard as he said, "I still think that an IT attack is the safest and best plan."

"Sorry Marty," said Mr. Jackson with a stern look on his face. "The President simply does not have confidence that such an attack would be successful. He hopes to carry California's vote in the next election, and if they are reeling from a North Korean rocket attack, even if it landed in the ocean, he wouldn't stand a chance of getting their vote."

Although I disagreed with the political motivations behind this statement, I agreed that an IT attack just did not have the level of certainty the president was looking for. There was a thought forming in the deepest reaches of my brain but it wasn't quite ready to come forth. So I was quiet as Admiral Harrison spoke up. I remember smiling as I listened to his Texas twang, which apparently was more obvious when he was frustrated.

Looking at Dr. Richardson and then Jefferson Jackson, he said, "Y'all are not being very subtle. It sounds like you want us to come up with a military option. We've already discounted the possibility of bombers, cruise missiles, and a direct attack by the Marines, so what does that leave?"

We all looked at Dr. Richardson as she spoke up. "With the recent successes that SEAL teams have had, the President was hoping for a surgical strike by one of the teams. There, now it's out on the table."

I immediately spoke up. "Dr. Richardson, I've been studying for some time the satellite imagery of both launch facilities in North Korea. Over the past several months, I've noticed a subtle but steady buildup of security around both facilities. Plus, I've looked at the surrounding terrain, and between mud flats and snow covered mountains, there is no way a SEAL team can get close enough to destroy the new rocket." I pause as it occurred to me that she already knew this because she has been reading my surveillance reports. "But you already know this." She didn't even smile.

I then looked at Dr. O'Brien and said, "And you are the one they asked to confirm my observations, aren't you?"

She actually blushed as she looked down at her hands in her lap.

"And you," I said as I looked back at Dr. Richardson, "ordered the NRO to stop sending me all of the satellite imagery. You only gave me what you wanted me to see. Why did you do that? And why am I here today?"

Without hesitation, she said "Colonel, today is not our first meeting on this subject. In fact, even as we sit here, a team of military experts are working on the same question; what do we do about that rocket? To answer your second question, you are here today because Dr. O'Brien told us that you were the best analyst of North Korean satellite surveillance.

"As far as the imagery goes, you are correct; we didn't want the Army to make any premature announcements about your findings."

I turned toward Dr. O'Brien, who spoke up and said, "To clarify, I am better at interpreting raw satellite imagery, but you have the advantage of understanding North Korean intentions. Plus, I don't speak Korean. That's what I told Dr. Richardson. I also told her we would make a great team as we try to understand their intentions regarding their new rocket." This time she did not look down at her lap; her big green eyes looked right into my baby blues.

Without looking back at her, I could hear Dr. Richardson talking, "Colonel, we decided to add you to our little task group because of your experience in South Korea, your grasp of their language and the contacts you have developed there. I must say that your brief excursion into North Korea, once we discovered that information, is what tipped the scale in your favor for joining our group."

She looked at her watch and said, "We have a video meeting scheduled in 30 minutes with the tacticians down at the Special Operations Command. Let's take a short break and then meet in the Situation Room, say in 20 minutes." Looking directly at me she said, "Does everyone know how to get there?"

Pulling my eyes away from Dr. O'Brien, I spoke up and said, "I have no idea how to get there."

Before anyone else could respond, Dr. O'Brien said, "I've been there before, Colonel; I'll show you the way."

I turned back to her, smiled and said, "That would be great. Thanks."

"Before we break up, there's one more item of business." Looking to her left, she said, "Admiral Harrison?"

He turned and looked at me and said, "Lt. Colonel Johnson, the paperwork to officially transfer your duty station from the Pentagon to the White House is being processed even as we speak; it should be signed by the end of the day. You may consider that, effective immediately, you work for and report directly to Dr. Richardson. If you need to return to your office in the Pentagon to retrieve personal items, please do so after normal working hours. We prefer that you did not have to explain yourself to anyone in your office. Colonel, do you understand these orders as I've explained them to you?"

"Yes sir, Admiral. Uhm, ah . . . Admiral, with respect, sir, are you in my chain of command?"

Turning his body toward me, he said in a most commanding manner, "Those orders, Colonel, come directly from the Chairman of the Joint Chiefs of Staff. And the last time I checked, he was the highest-ranking Army general we have. Is that good enough for you, son?"

Right then, I felt like I should stand at attention to answer his question. But instead, I remained in my chair and said, "Sir, yes sir!" Maybe I was still awed in the presence of flag rank officers!

With a huge smile, Dr. Richardson then said, "Colonel Johnson, in case I forget to mention it later, I'll be right here at 7 o'clock tomorrow morning to continue our discussions." She then looked at everyone and said, "Now we can retire to the Situation Room. See you all in 18 minutes."

As I was standing, Mr. Jackson turned to me and quietly said, "Colonel, may I speak with you a moment?"

He pointed with his hand, so we walked outside and I followed him up the hallway for several steps. Turning so quickly that I almost ran into him, he looked directly into my eyes and said, "Although you may report to Dr. Richardson, please remember who her boss is." And then he turned and I watched him disappear down the hall. Still standing there in the hall, I couldn't help but wonder what that was all about?

I heard a soft step behind me, and as I turned, Dr. O'Brien asked, "Do you want to take the elevator or shall we walk to the Situation Room?"

I may have been born at night but it certainly wasn't last night! Should I spend two minutes with this beautiful woman in an elevator, or 15 minutes walking the back halls of the White House with her? The only correct answer was, "Yes, er, um, I mean, let's walk."

And then I wondered what I was doing. I haven't even looked at another woman since Beth died. And here I am all tongue-tied with a woman I just barely met. Shaking my head, I rushed to keep up as she had already started down the hall. That's when I noticed for the first time that she was not wearing heels; though still feminine, her shoes were very practical for walking the halls of the White House. So much for being an observant intelligence officer!

Normally I walk at a pretty quick pace, and I noted earlier that she also walks at a good clip. But somehow it took us the full 18 minutes to walk a distance that would normally have taken us half that time, or less. What did we talk about? I don't remember. But I know that I felt at peace when we arrived at the Situation Room.

When we arrived, a Marine NCO asked for identification. After Dr. O'Brien and I displayed our identification cards, he pointed to the door and snapped to attention. It was then that I noticed he was carrying a side arm and as such, a salute would be inappropriate.

I held the door for Dr. O'Brien, and when I entered after her, I once again became an observant intelligence officer. There were others in the room, so I glanced at each in turn. Across the table was sitting the entire Joint Chiefs of Staff, and I noticed Admiral Harrison sitting behind them in the staff seating. The President was there, as was his Chief of Staff, and Dr. Richardson was sitting at the table to the President's immediate left. Dr. O'Brien sat in the staff seating behind her, so I sat next to her. I noticed another civilian next to Dr. Richardson, and when he turned slightly I could see it was the Director of the Central Intelligence Agency. There were others in the room I did not recognize and who were not introduced.

As I turned back to look at the President, I noticed that the five highest-ranking military officers in the country were staring at us. I felt a warm feeling rising from my neck into my face as I realized they had all been waiting for us to arrive. What a great way to start out a new assignment!

The President pointed to an officer at the opposite end of the table and said, "Tell them we are ready to start the meeting now." That officer, a Navy commander with the Navy SEALs emblem on his uniform, spoke quietly into a telephone, so quietly in fact I could not hear a word he said. As the screen behind him came alive, he hung up the telephone.

I heard someone call "attention" and was about to rise when I realized it came from the person whose image was being projected on one of the six large LCD screens in the Situation Room. The President said, "At ease gentlemen, and carry on."

I could see a small group of men and one woman sitting around a table, and the person speaking was a Navy commander. I noticed the gold device on his uniform, which indicated he was also a Navy SEAL.

"Sir, we have been reviewing options since receiving your orders five days ago. We started by putting all options on the table, no matter how wild the suggestion might be, and then discussing each as we considered its pros and cons. Sir, we have to tell you that your first requirement is the toughest one to meet. We are not comfortable telling you that any of the plans would be 100% effective. With that in mind, we have the beginnings of a plan that we think carries the greatest chance of success."

At this point the President interrupted and said, "Commander, before you present your number one plan, would you be kind enough to review the other proposals and tell us why you excluded each plan from consideration."

"Yessir. Several of the plans had a similar reason for excluding them from consideration, that of the certainty of identifying the United States as the instigator. For example, using Air Force bombers to drop a bomb, even discounting the possibility of detection, leaves the problem of bomb fragments being identified as belonging to the United States. Using a bomb from another country creates technological difficulties, as well as procurement problems.

"For the same reason, we excluded launching a cruise missile because its components could be identified forensically as belonging to the United States. Furthermore, the launch could potentially be detected by other countries and we have no way of ensuring they wouldn't broadcast that news.

"We discussed at great length sending in a SEAL team to destroy the rocket. That type of mission generates a whole slew of difficulties; for example, transportation in and out of two locations, possible detection by their security forces, and the difficulty of actually getting close enough to the launch facility and rocket to carry out the mission.

"We even considered asking the South Koreans if they had the capability of sending a team to the launch facilities to destroy the rocket and facility. The information you sent us from a report generated by an Army intelligence officer clearly indicated that their political situation wouldn't allow such an operation." I perked right up when he referred to what I assumed was my report.

"We also talked at length about an IT attack on their systems, including a long conversation with a CIA operative who specializes in that kind of work. Although he insisted such an attack would work, he could not convince us that, first, an IT attack would be 100% effective, and second, that an attack on their infrastructure would not be traceable back to us."

Now I know why our CIA specialist, Marty Packard, did not join us for lunch. He wasn't talking to the CIA Director; he was on a long telephone conversation with this Navy commander. It is interesting to learn how the decision-making process works – and the politicking involved.

"As we started looking at the satellite imagery of the terrain surrounding each of the two sites, we began discussing the possibility of using long-range snipers to take out the rocket just as it was being launched. This would have the effect of not only destroying the rocket but also of severely damaging the launch facility at the same time. And the bullet fired would be impossible to trace back to the United States, even if it could be found.

"Without revealing why we wanted to know, we asked around about long-range snipers, and found out that while we Navy SEALs like to think we have great snipers, the best out there aren't ours. It seems to be common knowledge among those who know that at the present the best long-range sniper is in the Marine Corps and the second best is in the Army.

"While there are still a lot of details to be worked out, we believe this is the best option for success. Our primary reason for this is that a sniper does not have to get close to the launch facility, relatively speaking. A sniper can take a shot, a successful shot that is, from about 1,600 yards, almost a mile away. Of course, we still have to determine how to get the sniper in the right spot. However, having looked at the terrain features from the satellite imagery, we believe it is possible. And this is true for both launch facilities. This is our first choice. Sir, do you have any questions?"

"Standby, Commander; I'm going to talk to my National Security Advisor." He turned to Dr. Richardson and asked, "Dr. Richardson, what does your working group think?"

"Mr. President, we agree with Commander Throckmorton as far as his reasons for excluding the itemized proposals as he explained. We also believe the sniper scenario is the best choice."

This last statement was a surprise to me, because I had not heard that proposal before.

Dr. Richardson continued, "If you approve, Mr. President, I'd like to send two of my staff to meet with Commander Throckmorton's group and participate in the planning."

"That's a great idea, Dr. Richardson. I'd like to have White House involvement in the planning. Who do you plan to send?" Now I understood why I was transferred to the White House today. I turned to Dr. Richardson as she said, "Dr. O'Reilly is an NRO officer on loan to my office; she is an expert in analyzing raw satellite imagery and has recently been reviewing satellite imagery of North Korea. And Lieutenant Colonel Johnson, a U.S. Army intelligence officer who just joined my staff today, is considered our leading expert on North Korea."

"Excellent! And you'll keep me advised of their progress, right?"

"Of course, Mr. President."

Shifting his gaze to General Underhill, Chairman of the Joint Chiefs of Staff, the President asked, "General, do you have any thoughts or observations on their plan?" Without even looking at the other admirals and generals in the room, General Underhill said, "No sir, Mr. President. We've been briefed on that plan and agree with Dr. Richardson and Commander Throckmorton."

Turning back to the screen, the President once again spoke to Commander Throckmorton. "Commander, you have my authorization to begin detailed planning of your proposal. I will be sending two people from the White House down to join you in your planning sessions."

Before the President could continue, Commander Throckmorton interrupted, "Mr. President, we believe we have the necessary staff to complete our planning."

Although it may not have been visible to Commander Throckmorton, I could see the President was not pleased with his interruption. What was apparent to everyone, including Commander Throckmorton, was that the President's voice was somewhat elevated as he responded. "Commander, do you speak Korean?"

"Uh, no sir, I do not."

"Then you will be pleased to learn that Colonel Johnson does, and I have been given to understand that he speaks it fluently. He will be joined by an NRO officer who is an expert in analyzing raw satellite data. She has been examining the area for several weeks now. Any questions, Commander?"

"No sir, Mr. President, we look forward to your people joining our team."

"Thank you Commander. Any other questions?"

"No, sir."

The President gave a clearly visible cutting motion with his right hand and the video screen went dark.

Turning to his National Security Advisor, the President said, "Dr. Richardson, make sure your people get down there as quickly as possible."

Turning back to the Chairman of the Joint Chiefs of Staff, the President said, "General Underhill, make sure that Dr. Richardson has everything she needs to ensure this plan is a success."

"Yes sir, Mr. President."

Since I was looking at General Underhill, I noticed that Admiral Harrison sitting behind him was making a note. He passed it to General Underhill, who turned slightly and nodded to Admiral Harrison. Admiral Harrison saw me looking at him and gave me a wry smile. I was thinking that it wouldn't be long before I was standing in the JCS office being reminded that I was a serving officer and even though I was presently assigned to the National Security Advisor's Office, I still "belonged" to the Army.

A man at the other end of the table, who I now recognized as the Secretary of Homeland Security, spoke up and asked the President, "Mr. President, should we begin contingency planning for the West Coast in case this plan doesn't work?"

"Hank, let's not get in a panic yet. I don't want anything leaving your office about this. If you and your assistant secretary want to give this some thought, okay, but I don't want anyone else to know about it yet."

Henry "Hank" Williams nodded but did not say anything.

"Okay everyone, we will meet one week from today for an update. Dr. Richardson, be sure your people keep you informed. If any questions come up, see that Jeff brings them to me right away." Jeff, of course, was the President's Chief of Staff, and reading between the lines, it was clear to me the President wanted a political assessment as part of his briefing on any questions. I noticed that Dr. Richardson hesitated slightly before responding, "Will do, sir."

The President closed the meeting by standing up and saying, "Thanks everyone. Have a good afternoon."

We all stood as the President walked out. After the President left the Situation Room, Dr. Richardson turned to Dr. O'Brien and to me and said, "I have some things I need to take care of this afternoon, so let's meet first thing in the morning. Shall we say 7 o'clock in my office?"

Dr. O'Brien and I said "okay" at the same time, then looked at each other and smiled, and then slightly embarrassed, looked away from each other.

Sure enough, Admiral Harrison hurried over and invited me to visit with General Underhill, who was still sitting on the other side of the conference table. Once I stood before him, it was quietly but clearly explained to me that I was a U.S. Army officer, not a White House staffer. Blunt but clear.

I jump as my thoughts on the snow-covered hill are interrupted by a buzz on the satellite phone. I glance at my watch and see it is time for our regularly scheduled check-in to assure one another that all is going as planned. I hope it is!

Chapter Nine

As we left the Situation Room, Dr. O'Brien and I waited until all the higher ranking individuals had left and then walked out together. We were quiet as we walked upstairs together, and as we approached the White House exit, we looked at each other and I said, "Well, I'll see you in the morning." After a short pause, I added "Have a good afternoon."

Yes, I know this would have been the right time to pick up a conversation with this strikingly beautiful woman, but I had other things I needed to do. And beauty does not always win.

I could see that she started to say something and then changed her mind. She ended up saying, "Okay, I'll see you in the morning. Have a pleasant evening." She turned around and walked away as I watched her until she disappeared around the corner. Shaking my head, I followed after her, because I needed to catch a taxi and get to my office at the Pentagon as quickly as I could.

I remembered that Admiral Harrison had warned me not to go to the Pentagon until after normal working hours, but I needed to get there before Major Green left for the day. I also wanted to visit with Sergeant Garcia on a couple of items. Although Admiral Harrison and I worked in the same building, the chances of him seeing me were remote.

Unless you've been there, you have no idea how really big the Pentagon is. I suppose everyone knows the Pentagon is the largest office building in the world. But do you really know how large 6.5 million square feet is? It is called the Pentagon because it has five sides, but it also has five floors. There are over 17 miles of corridors, 131 stairways, and 284 restrooms, and the parking lot alone covers 67 acres! The possibility of us meeting was so remote as to be nonexistent.

The other reason I wanted to get back to my office was so I could make a secure phone call. If I waited to make my call until about 6 o'clock, I knew I would catch Major Kim as he started his day in Seoul. I had a lot of questions, and I hoped he had a lot of answers.

Meanwhile, I needed to catch a taxi! After I spent several frustrating minutes waving at several taxicabs, one finally pulled to the curb. I said "the Pentagon" to the Pakistani representative of the D.C. taxi system. It's only about 3 miles from the White House to the Pentagon, and if there was light traffic it would be about a 10-minute drive. However, traffic was anything but light. I was beginning to feel frustrated as we were only half-way there after 10 minutes had passed. You just have to love the traffic in Washington, D.C. Twelve minutes later he dropped me off in front of the Pentagon. A full 22 minutes after we left the White House!

To ease congestion, the Pentagon uses a rotating beginning and end-ing time schedule for staff. Those who started at 7 o'clock this morning were now streaming through the exit, and although the exit lanes were jam-packed, the entry area was virtually empty. After showing my ID and passing through the metal detector system, I almost sprinted to my office. I did not want to miss Major Green! It still took me almost five minutes to get to my office.

Sergeant Garcia looked up with a quizzical expression as I made a Kramer-like entrance to my office. Without so much as a howdy-do, I asked, "Is Major Green still here?"

Her response politely put me in my place, "Good afternoon, Colonel; yes, I'm well, thank you for asking. And yes, Major Green is in his office."

I stopped and took a deep breath. Sergeant Garcia was still looking at me, so I smiled and said, "You are looking well, Sergeant. Has it been a good day for you?"

Smiling at me, she said, "If you ever want to be a successful full-bird Colonel, you may want to learn the art of polite social chitchat. I under-stand it's a requirement as you continue to climb the command ladder of the Army."

"Thank you, Sergeant. If I ever decide to climb that ladder, I'm going to drag you along to keep me out of trouble. By the way, are you in a hurry to leave tonight?"

Her response, "No, not really," meant she really would like to leave on time, but she would wait at my unasked request. "Thanks," I said, as I headed into Major Green's office.

I knocked, opened the door, and headed right in to discover Major Green looking through a magnifying glass at a photographic image on his desk. As he looked up, I said, "Hello David." And then remembering Sergeant Garcia's gentle reprimand, I continued with, "How are you?" Although impatient, I waited for his response.

Surprised at my question, he responded, "I am unbelievable, Colonel. How are you?"

Thinking I've had enough of this polite chitchat, I ignored his question, moved closer and asked, "Have you been able to discover anything from your review of the satellite imagery of North Korea?"

"Ah, there now, that's the boss I remember!" With a Cheshire cat smile on his face, he continued, "Yes, as a matter of fact I have. You were right. After a review of the recent satellite imagery, it's clear that we haven't re-ceived a linear progression in that imagery. In fact, the photographs we've not received would have given us vital information about the progress the North Koreans are making with their new long-range rocket. In other words, they are probably further along than we were able to discern with the photographs provided us. In my opinion, someone has cut us out of the loop."

Nodding, and looking at a blank spot on the wall, I softly asked out loud, "Why would someone do that?" Knowing it was a rhetorical ques-tion, Major Green remained silent.

Remembering that Dr. Richardson had addressed that question, when pressed, I still wondered why withholding those images from my office would be beneficial to anyone. Shaking my head, and after a mo-ment's thought, I decided to disobey my instructions and brief both Major Green and Sergeant Garcia about my upcoming activities.

Looking back to Major Green, I said "Major, call Sergeant Garcia in. I want to brief both of you on my new assignment."

As he invited Sergeant Garcia into his office, I wondered how much trouble I was going to be in if Admiral Harrison found out about my briefing them. I knew them both and had complete trust in their discretion. I had always been open with them in the past and did not see why I should cut them out now. I suppose I was also irritated at being cut out of the information loop and then being invited to be part of Dr. Richardson's team only to discover essential information and conversations had been happening around me but without my knowledge. It just didn't seem right.

First swearing them both to secrecy, I briefed them on my upcoming trip to the Special Operations Command to assist in planning an operation, the general instructions from the President, and my concern that we needed more information to proceed rationally. I told them both that I had been transferred to the office of the National Security Advisor in the White House. I further told them that if anyone asked them about me, they were to say they were surprised when they reported for duty to find my office cleaned out, and they were to act surprised when Colonel Jacobs gave them the news of my transfer. I told them both that I would be in touch occasionally to ask for favors.

In the Army, competent officers quickly learn that Sergeants know things before officers ever hear about them, so I told Sergeant Garcia that I wanted her to keep her eyes and ears open for any talk or conversation about me, my assignment, or North Korea. With that, I told them I had several things to do in my office and they could head for home.

It was still too early to make the phone call I wanted to make, so I started to gather my personal possessions, few as they were. As I was looking around my office, it occurred to me that even though I'd been here nearly two years, there was very little that was uniquely mine. In fact, there was nothing in the office I would miss if I simply walked out.

I walked to the fireproof safe where I kept classified items. In addition to my secure laptop, there were several things in there I wanted to take with me in my new assignment. I could always argue that my new assignment was temporary in nature, plus I had personally signed for everything in the safe; therefore, they were all my responsibility.

One of the items in my safe was a Glock 17, a 9 mm handgun. As a serving officer in the Intelligence Corps, I was authorized to carry a handgun when it was appropriate, even in the United States. Although I was issued a Beretta M9 as a standard issue handgun, I preferred the Glock. This preference resulted from a nasty firefight in Afghanistan during my tour there. Why they sent a Korean-speaking intelligence officer to Afghanistan, I'll never know!

As the brigade intelligence officer there, I decided to go with a squad to find a tribal leader who we were told had information about an Al Qaeda unit operating in his area. We parked our Humvee and were walking up a mountain trail when we were surprised by several men with AK-47s as we rounded an outcropping. I was still reaching for my Beretta when the shooting started. By the time I had it out and was fumbling to flick the safety off, I'd already been wounded. Probably because I'd fallen to one knee, the terrorists were concentrating on the soldiers with the M-16s, so I started shooting at them with my Beretta. They told me later that I had shot five of the terrorists and probably saved the squad. Although several of us were wounded, no one died.

After I returned from that tour of duty, I replaced my Beretta with the Glock 17 as soon as I could. Maybe if I was a line officer, I would get used to the Beretta, but with a Glock, all I had to do was point and shoot; I didn't have to think about an external safety switch.

Now that I thought about it, my annual qualification was due next month. I took the gun out of the safe, set it on my desk, and sat back in my chair. As I looked at it, my thoughts turned to Beth, who did not like me to have a gun at home, especially after one particular incident.

One day our young children were playing in our bedroom and Susan walked out with my gun hanging from her right index finger. She said Jacob had found it and pointed it at her. She told us she took it away from him and brought it out to me. Ever since that day it's been locked in my office safe; it didn't matter where I was assigned, I never took it home again. As I looked at it sitting peacefully there on my desk, a voice in my head told me to put it in my briefcase. I had two extra clips, so I put them in the briefcase as well. I also put a copy of my last North Korean surveillance analysis report in there. I wanted to review that report to see exactly what in it might have been the catalyst that generated my reassignment to the White House.

It was almost 6 o'clock, so I picked up the phone, dialed the secure operator and gave him the direct telephone number for Major Kim's office in South Korea. I listened to the clicks and buzzes as an encrypted connection was being made.

"Sir, Major Kim speaking." Because he answered in English, I knew the caller ID on his end was working properly. I heard the Pentagon operator tell him, "Sir, this is a secure connection. Please confirm that your system is in encrypted mode." Being a man of few words, Major Kim simply said, "Confirmed."

The operator then said, presumably to me, "Sir, a secure encrypted connection has been confirmed. Please continue." And then I heard the click as he went off-line.

"Jin-ho, I understand congratulations are in order."

"Good morning Robert, or should I say good evening? And, how do you know about that?"

"Well, I am an intelligence officer. Now that you've confirmed it, congratulations!"

"I too am an intelligence officer! I understand you are on the selection list for Colonel. So congratulations to you, as well."

"I didn't think that list was public knowledge yet."

"We also have our ways. Regarding my promotion, I've been told it will be effective later this year. It most likely means that I get the opportunity to do more paperwork."

"You were always good with paperwork. Remember that senior project we worked on together? We couldn't have done it without you!"

"Oh, you would've gotten it done, and enjoyed your B grade. My efforts merely raised our project to an A grade.

"By the way, in this morning's briefing we were told that the Americans were up to something and we should pay extra attention to our areas of responsibility. So, putting two and two together, as intelligence officers are occasionally called upon to do, I speculate that one of your generals called one of my generals and asked a question that got them thinking about what you guys were up to. Care to share?"

"Actually, one of our admirals called one of your admirals. He probably shared that our President is concerned about the new long-range rocket that your friends to the north have announced." Although he is a friend, and we share a common enemy, I did not want to say too much on a telephone line, even though it's supposed to be secure. Who knew who was listening, both on his end and on my end. "In a spirit of cooperation, perhaps we should get together and discuss our common enemy. I have a new assignment, and I've been ordered by my new bosses to go to Seoul for an in-person assessment. Are you planning to be around over the next few weeks?"

"At present, I have no plans to be anywhere else. The paperwork, you understand! And what new assignment do you have?"

"I'll get into that when we meet. I'll take care of details here and let you know when I will be arriving. Just to pique your interest, do you remember that little thing we did when we were lowly captains?"

Hesitating just a bit, he replied, "Yes, I remember; but I am no longer a young and foolish captain, and neither are you."

"So true! That's why we should talk. I'll call you when I have the details worked out. Say hi to Suzie for me."

"I will." And with that we closed the connection. I hung up the phone and sat back in my gray, government-issue desk chair. I had a lot to think about.

Chapter Ten

My focus returns to the mountainside, and I notice the snowfall has diminished. It is not quite dawn yet, so visibility is still poor. After a few moments though, I once again see the single light shining from the top of the gantry below us. If our intelligence is correct, in just a few hours there will be a great deal of activity around that gantry.

With the information the Russians had shared with us, we knew it would take most of a day for the Chinese transporter to convey the assembled rocket from the assembly building to the gantry. We believe this is the reason the North Koreans purchased the Chinese transporter; previous rockets would take most of three days to make that trip. That travel time has now been reduced to one day.

We knew a rocket had been in the assembly building because the North Koreans could not hide that from our satellite surveillance. We had watched in almost real time as the components of the new rocket were delivered to the Sanum'dong missile research factory, and that's where the new Chinese erector transporter was delivered. In fact, the last satellite image Dr. O'Brien shared before we embarked on the submarine was of the transporter sitting on the railroad track waiting for the rocket to be loaded.

We still did not know whether the new long-range rocket would be going to this facility or at the Tonghae facility on the East Coast. The North Koreans had to be aware of our satellite surveillance, because similar trucks were delivering components both to this facility and to the facility at Tonghae. We also did not know and could only speculate about how long it would take the North Koreans to get the rocket ready for launch. We had talked to an engineer at NASA who told us that it would take at least a day and probably two days to prepare a rocket for launch once it had been erected in the gantry.

Because of this uncertainty, we placed a sniper team at both potential launch sites and made the decision during our planning sessions to arrive a day early at our location overlooking the gantry. Although this increased the risk of discovery, it was the only way to absolutely ensure the rocket was not launched before we arrived.

I shift my rump to get more comfortable, and think about how my friendship with Major Jin-ho Kim had developed.

After my church mission to South Korea, I returned home to Arizona. In the fall of that year I moved to Utah to attend BYU, where I discovered there was a small Korean community. I was still gung-ho about Korea at that time, so I started attending church with a Korean congregation. My language skills were good, but they became much better as I also began to mingle with a group of Korean students. Jin-ho was part of that group, and he and I became good friends that first year. The following year Soo-jin started her freshman year at BYU and consequently joined the group. Jin-ho and Soo-jin became friends almost immediately and were married the following year during spring break.

Jin-ho and especially Soo-jin enjoyed American cuisine, but shortly after they were married I was invited to dinner at their apartment for a Korean dish of bulgogi. Jin-ho explained that bulgogi (roughly translated it means fire meat) is made from thin slices of sirloin that have been marinated with a mixture of soy sauce, sugar, sesame oil, garlic, pepper, and mushrooms. Even though I had eaten bulgogi before, he assured me that his mixture of ingredients was special and a family secret!

The meat was served with Korean mandu, which is a filled dumpling; the dumplings that evening were filled with minced meat, tofu, green onions, garlic, and ginger. The other side dish was chapchae, a vegetable dish made from sweet potato noodles, carrots, onion, spinach, and mushrooms, flavored with soy sauce and sweetened with sugar.

Jin-ho was right, and the bulgogi didn't disappoint. The memory of being rather full after that main course is still quite vivid! My contribution

Chapter Eleven

Again my reverie is interrupted by the crackling of the tactical radio and then the message, "Heads up, a two-man patrol is coming back up the hill from the north."

Apparently their sergeant of the guard appreciates variety, sending them up the opposite direction from before. Although snow is still falling, its intensity has decreased significantly and there is now the real possibility we could be discovered.

I look over to the sniper team and am startled to discover they aren't there. Before I make a call on the radio, though, it dawns on me that a sniper team is supposed to be invisible. But even though I know they are there, I still cannot pick them out of the snowy terrain. I hope the North Korean patrol has the same difficulty.

After several minutes, the patrol passes by my spot, and as long as I have them in sight, they never turn their heads to the right or to the left. They walk right on past and keep going. In just a few more minutes, the SEAL team on my right report that they had continued down the hill. It seems their Army has the same problem every Army has-soldiers get bored pretty quickly when nothing is happening.

Then it occurs to me that we have not seen any patrols all night, and now we've seen two patrols in the last hour. Since our satellite surveillance did not show any patrols this high on the mountainside for the last couple of months, this may be a sign that they really are going to launch the new rocket tomorrow, or rather today.

I am curious to know the significance of these patrols. It is close to our normal check-in time, so I pull out the satellite phone and call Major Denton at Tonghae. When he answers, I ask, "Major, have you observed any increase in North Korean patrols on your mountain or any of the other mountains around you?"

"Sorry Colonel, we haven't seen any patrols up in the mountains the entire time we've been here. There are patrols, and I mean really regular patrols, around the perimeter of the launch facility below us, but nothing up this high."

"Have you seen any increase in activity at either the launch facility or the assembly building?"

"Everything seems pretty normal here, based on the briefing we had back home."

"Everything is normal here also, except for the increased patrol up on the hilltop where we are. Let's stay in touch."

"Sounds good, Colonel. We'll let you know if anything new happens. Denton out."

"We'll do the same. Johnson out."

Just as I turn off the satellite phone, the tactical radio chirps. "Colonel, something is happening below at the assembly building."

Although the sun has not yet popped above the horizon, it is becoming easier to see below us. Sure enough, there is increased activity around the assembly building. I remove my night vision goggles and raise my high-powered binoculars to my eyes; though it is hard to see details, it is clear that people are working on the erector transporter. Just as I'm shifting position to get a better view, the radio chirps again. "Another patrol on its way up from the south."

Now I'm certain the increased patrol activity indicates something significant is about to happen. I make certain I am still hidden in the scrub brush on the hillside as I wait for the patrol to wend its way toward me. This time it's different! There are three soldiers instead of two, and their rifles are in their hands and not on their shoulders. And they are walking three abreast about 10 yards apart. The soldier nearest me is going to walk right past the scrub brush I am hiding in. I almost miss the downhill soldier and only see him because his helmet is slightly above the top of the hill to the southeast. I consciously hold my breath.

They are walking more slowly than the previous patrols had been, and their heads are on a swivel, just as they would be on soldiers who were ordered to be more alert. This is clearly the varsity team! Then the radio chirps again, "Another patrol on its way up the hill. Three soldiers." But this is from the SEAL team on my left. The North Koreans are serious this time!

Now I really am grateful for the snowfall, light as it was.

The six soldiers cross in front of me and do not stop nor say a single word to each other. As they continue their patrol, though, I wonder why they had not checked each of the brush areas where someone could be hiding. Good soldiers, certainly more attentive than the previous patrols, but within a few minutes both SEAL teams transmit that they had continued their patrol down the hillside without incident.

I bring my binoculars back up on the scene below and see that the assembly building doors are almost fully opened. If our information from NASA is correct, that means the rocket will be erect on the gantry about suppertime. That means we have to stay in our hidey hole all day and be ready to take our shot any time after that.

I key my radio. "Sergeant Parker, you there?" He is only a few feet away, but I want everyone to hear what I have to say.

"Yes, sir."

"It may be a night event."

"Roger that, Colonel."

We had briefed that if it appeared we would be taking our shot in the evening, Sergeant Parker would be responsible for his own rest. Since we had hiked most of the night, the briefing called for him and Sergeant Harris to rotate sleep periods during the daylight hours. Sergeant Parker assured us that he would wake at the slightest noise. With the radio earbud in his ear, making a noise that he could hear and that would be silent to a patrol would be easy. Let's hope it works out that way. Besides me, Parker and Harris would be the only two to get any sleep between now and the time we are picked up by the submarine. The four Navy SEALs would be on constant alert and would get no rest until we are on the submarine.

On the Air Force flight over to Japan to meet up with the submarines we used for transportation to North Korea, the SEAL team guys told me they routinely go without sleep for as long as three days at a time. This will be new for me, because ever since I started working at the Pentagon, I've been in the habit of going to bed at 10:30 and getting up at 6:00. That's what working at the Pentagon will do to you.

As things settle back to normal here on the mountainside, my thoughts return to that evening when I cleaned out my office at the Pentagon.

Chapter Twelve

After I locked up my office to go home, I dropped my keys on Sergeant Garcia's desk. As I walked out, I thought back to my meeting with the President in the Situation Room and my telephone conversation with Major Kim. I still had questions that needed answers. For example, how long ago had the planning team been formed at SOCOM, and thus how long had they been considering alternatives? Was it just five weeks as Commander Throckmorton indicated? It was clear from the Commander's remarks that they had been together long enough to research and consider several options, review the impact of each, and settle on a recommended solution.

But then I started thinking about the date I had submitted my analysis of the increased activity discovered by satellite surveillance of the two rocket launch facilities in North Korea. It was only about 10 days before I was invited to the meeting with the National Security Advisor. In addition, the conversation I had with Major Kim regarding his assessment of the South Korean intelligence on the new rocket was at about the same time.

I was beginning to think that someone else had come to the same conclusions I had.

It was dark and past the normal evening commute time, so the plethora of taxicabs normally waiting in the parking lot were all gone. I did not want to go back through the metal detectors to use my office phone, especially since I now had a loaded Glock in my briefcase, so I pulled out my iPhone and called for a cab. It was then I noticed I had a text message from Dr. Richardson. How did I miss that?

It was a message telling me and Dr. O'Brien that we should plan to spend three to four days at SOCOM, and that we should come to the 7 AM meeting already packed and ready to go. The message said we would be flying on military transport. Well, at least I had some idea of what I would be doing tomorrow. Though in reality, other than the appointment with Dr. Richardson in the morning, I had no idea, except for a long and probably uncomfortable flight, what the rest of the day would bring.

At home, I ate a late dinner with Jacob and Susan. I smiled as I remembered the old days when I would have to rush around at the last minute to find an ATM so I could get some cash for traveling. Now with the wonders of technology, all I needed was my trusty iPhone. It was quite a coup when Apple convinced the Department of Defense that all military facilities should install new point-of-sale technology so soldiers, sailors and airmen could make electronic payments simply with their phone.

Thinking ahead, I called the taxicab company and ordered a cab for 6:30 in the morning. I got up from the kitchen table and walked to the refrigerator, and after looking inside I decided that what little there was in there would be okay for three or four days for the kids. I'd also leave some cash on the kitchen table, like I usually did when I was going to be out of town. Although I don't travel as much as I used to, I occasionally go out of town to meetings, so the kids have become rather self-reliant. In any case, cell phones make it pretty convenient to check in.

While I was thinking about things to do, I called our neighbor and left a message saying that I would be out of town for a few days and asking if she would mind checking in on the twins. She was a widow and had become a good friend to Susan and Jacob. Even so, they both hated it when I did this – they insisted they were old enough not to need any looking after – but I was more comfortable knowing that someone would at least give them a call to be sure they're doing okay.

After dinner, Jacob and Susan wandered off to their rooms to work on their homework as I wandered over to the sofa and turned on the TV. It was Thursday night and my favorite team, the Denver Broncos, was playing the Seattle Seahawks. I can't tell you anything that happened in that game because my mind was filled with thoughts about all the planning that was going to take place during the next few days. I finally turned it off and headed for bed.

I awoke at 5:55 the next morning with an active mind still wondering what my role would be during this mission. I wanted to be able to provide all the support the SEAL team commander would need as he completed the detailed planning for his mission. I knew that Dr. O'Brien would be there to provide analysis of satellite imagery, and I would be there to share my insight of the North Korean Army.

It never dawned on me, even for a moment, that I would be in North Korea with them. But I get ahead of myself.

I finally jumped out of bed, completed my morning ablutions, and wolfed down an English muffin and a glass of orange juice. I checked to be sure that Jacob and Susan were getting ready for early-morning seminary. As I finished packing my bag, I threw in several protein bars; you never know when you might get hungry at 30,000 feet! I transferred the contents of my briefcase to a soft sided computer bag, said goodbye to the kids as I gave each a hug, locked the door and headed down to catch the cab.

Although traffic was heavy, I still arrived at the White House with a couple of minutes to spare. As I passed through the side door of the West Wing, I spotted Dr. O'Brien already going through the metal detector. I hurried to catch up, when it suddenly occurred to me that I would not be able to go through the metal detector. Remember the Glock?

A brief conversation with the guard standing outside the metal detector solved the problem. It turns out the White House has a small storage closet for just such occasions. I cleared the metal detector and hurried to catch up with Dr. O'Brien.

She must've heard my footsteps because she stopped and turned and then displayed a big smile when she saw who it was. The only other place I've seen a smile like that was at the Miss America pageant – and on Beth. And because I am a professionally trained intelligence officer with keen observation skills, I couldn't help but notice that her travel clothes were conservative yet clearly feminine. While I was making this observation, the thought occurred to me whether a woman ever gets used to men noticing her figure.

We walked together to Dr. Richardson's office without saying much more than good morning to each other and arrived just as Admiral Harrison was walking into the office. Already seated was the CIA guy with the unruly hair, whose name I momentarily forgot, and the White House Chief of Staff.

Dr. Richardson was all business. "Because Colonel Johnson and Dr. O'Brien have an airplane to catch, let's cover the material we need to and send them on their way. Mr. Jackson, I believe you have something to say."

"Thank you, Sarah." An observation my father taught me was that men and women in powerful positions tend to use first names when they wish to impress upon the audience that they are the most powerful person in the room. He continued, "To be brief, the President has decided it is necessary for him to inform the Senate and House select committees on intelligence regarding the upcoming operation. He plans to name you, Colonel Johnson, as the officer in charge. Because this will be a military operation, and not a White House foray into the field, you will, in turn, report directly to Admiral Harrison in the JCS office. Admiral Harrison will keep the Chairman of the Joint Chiefs informed and will, as necessary, brief Dr. Richardson, who will keep the President informed. You will not report your activities to anyone else. Is that clear?"

I consciously kept myself from shaking my head as I thought about how convoluted that organizational structure was. But all I said was, "Yes, sir; perfectly clear."

Admiral Harrison jumped into the conversation, "It has been my experience that as soon as the President briefs one or both of the committees on intelligence, the JCS gets a phone call from the committee chairmen. We will handle those phone calls, but if you get a phone call, Colonel, just tell them you're busy and refer them back to the JCS. Is that understood?"

"Yes, sir." Then another thought occurred to me. "Pardon me, I do have one question. Since Dr. O'Brien will be there with the planning group and not here, who will direct her activities?"

Admiral Harrison looked at Dr. Richardson and indicated it was her decision. "Vivian," she said, "do you have any problems taking direction from Colonel Johnson?"

After a short pause, she said, "I'm just thinking out loud, mind you, but I theoretically report to a lieutenant general at the NRO, who is considerably higher in rank than a lieutenant colonel." Another short pause. "But on the other hand, since I am temporarily assigned to your office, Dr. Richardson, I am supposed to take orders from you. So if you tell me to take orders from Colonel Johnson, I guess that fits in with the general scheme of things."

Again, I thought how convoluted everything seemed to be.

As Dr. Richardson gave Dr. O'Brien a forced smile, it occurred to me that Dr. O'Brien was also thinking about how convoluted all this is. What have we gotten ourselves into? Then it dawned on me that if she reports to a lieutenant general, she must be higher in the hierarchy than a simple analyst.

Before I could consider this thought further, Dr. Richardson turned to me and said, "Colonel, it will be vital that we determine the timeline under which the North Koreans are operating. We cannot afford to let them get ahead of us on this! How accurate is your estimate that early February is the soonest they would be ready to launch a rocket?"

I looked at her and paused a moment and then said, "Based on my conversations with a NASA engineer and the information the Russians gave us on the new Chinese transporter vehicle, it seems pretty accurate." I shifted my gaze to Dr. O'Brien as I continued, "Nothing in the satellite imagery, at least what I had access to, would indicate otherwise."

Dr. O'Brien nodded and said, "I agree with that assessment."

We all looked to Dr. Richardson as she continued, "Very well, then. Dr. O'Brien, until this mission is successfully concluded, please report to and take instructions from Colonel Johnson. But I'm always available if you have a question." The chain of command is so much easier in the military world! This last comment by Dr. Richardson essentially gave Dr. O'Brien the privilege of questioning anything I might ask her to do. I'm not sure I could work in the White House very long with that kind of ambiguity.

Before anyone could say anything else, the CIA expert, Marty Packard, whose name I suddenly remembered, spoke up and said, "I've been led to believe that intelligence developed by the Agency indicates they won't be ready to launch until at least March, if not April. That certainly gives us time to consider alternative plans. I understand the Director is meeting with the President today to suggest that we re-examine the IT alternative."

The President's Chief of Staff said, "Marty, we've had two groups look at that IT alternative, and both groups said they could not guarantee a successful outcome. There's no way we can allow the President to be embarrassed by a failed attempt. Now if you'll excuse me, I have another meeting to get to."

I don't know about anyone else in the room, but I was pretty certain Mr. Jefferson Jackson would shortly be in the Oval Office discussing this with the President.

As he was leaving, I spoke up and said, "While we believe early February is the soonest a launch could take place, it is true the North Koreans could theoretically delay the launch to another time of their choosing. But based on their previous history with rockets, it is more likely they will launch sooner rather than later."

After Mr. Jackson left the office, Dr. Richardson turned to me and said, "Colonel Johnson, would you share with us please, what you believe the likely scenario will be."

"Yes ma'am." I paused just a moment and then said, "If the North Koreans have truly developed a long-range rocket, and I think they have, I believe they will aim it on a trajectory that takes it directly toward the West Coast and then crash it in the ocean between Alaska and the West Coast. That will allow them to make several assertions regarding their capabilities. First, by passing over the Aleutian Islands, they clearly demonstrate they can attack U.S. territory. And second, by crashing it into the ocean shortly after passing over the Islands, they can then claim that if they had wanted to they could have sent the rocket all the way to the mainland. And we would never be able to positively know whether their rocket had that kind of range. The Pacific Ocean is pretty deep, and I suspect we would not be able to recover the rocket for analysis. And to make matters worse, Japan has already expressed concern about an overflight of Hokkaido by a North Korean ballistic missile. Tensions would definitely increase in the area."

And after a short pause I continued, "And I think I agree with Mr. Jackson regarding the effect of such an event; the American people would never reelect a President who allowed the North Koreans to threaten our homeland.

"An alternative might be for them to launch the rocket toward Hawaii and have it crash in the ocean before it gets there, and then boast that they could have sent it the rest of the way but did not because they had proved their point about launching a long-range missile to American territory. Again, we would never know if the rocket had the range to reach Hawaii or not.

"In my opinion, if the North Koreans were able to launch a hitherto unknown rocket *anywhere* into the Pacific region, tensions worldwide would rise exponentially. But I also think the President is caught between a rock and a hard place. He's definitely in trouble politically if they launch a long-range rocket, but he is also in trouble if he takes military action to stop the launch."

Dr. Richardson glanced at her watch and abruptly said, "We best bring this meeting to an end so that Dr. O'Brien and Colonel Johnson can get on their way." She looked at Mr. Packard and said, "Good to see you again, Marty; thank you for attending our meetings." She stood, and even Marty figured out that was his cue to leave the office! After he left she turned to Dr. O'Brien and said, "Vivian, why don't you wait outside just a moment while the Admiral and I talk with Colonel Johnson."

After she closed the door, Admiral Harrison turned to me and smiled, and then said very quietly, "Here's why you are on the team Colonel, and why you are on your way to SOCOM to oversee the planning. We want you to ensure the plan not only stops the rocket launch, but also effectively destroys their launch facility. An action, by the way, that cannot be traced to the United States!"

As he stood up, he said, "You will discover that Commander Throckmorton, who you saw in the President's briefing, is accustomed to thinking outside the box. I'm sure he will already have several suggestions for consideration by the time you get down there."

He continued as he walked to the office door, "We know we are asking the impossible, but the President has come to expect that from our military leaders. Your instructions should be clear that we want to seriously impact their ability to launch transcontinental rockets, but of utmost and overriding importance, leave no evidence that points to the United States.

"You and Dr. O'Brien should be on your way. There's a staff car waiting outside to take you to Andrews Air Force Base. Good luck and stay in touch." And with that statement he was gone.

I stood and turned to Dr. Richardson. She smiled and said, "It seems like a lot, doesn't it?" As she looked at me she cocked her head to one side and said, "But then, I've been told that you are a pretty bright guy!" Again, she's making more points with me!

She walked around her desk and, shaking my hand, walked me toward the door. Then she turned to me and said, "Just one more thing. You do your job and leave the politics to me." And with that I was out of her office and standing in the hallway.

Dr. O'Brien, or Vivian, or whatever it is I'm going to call her, was leaning against the wall opposite Dr. Richardson's door. As I looked at her she smiled and said, "Now I presume you know all the secret stuff!"

"You are right about one thing; there are secrets. But I don't think I know any of them!"

With that, we both turned and walked toward the exit. It turns out she also had a bag, or to be more precise, two bags, stored in the closet outside the metal detector area. We gave our receipts to the guard, grabbed our bags, and sure enough, there was a Navy staff car waiting for us in the parking lot. Thinking back to the first time I came to the White House, it occurred to me that Navy staff cars must have privileges that city taxi-cabs do not.

Chapter Thirteen

As we surmised later, while we were engaged in our meeting at the White House, another early morning meeting was taking place less than two miles away. The meeting was attended by only two people – Congressman Paul Singleton and his Chief of Staff, Michael Fontana. They were sitting in old but comfortable side chairs in front of the congressman's desk. Because Singleton was a first-term congressman, his office was in the basement of the capitol building. Offices in the capitol basement consist of a private office for the congressman, a really small office for his Chief of Staff, and a large reception area divided by cubicle walls into small workspaces for his congressional staff. Again, because he was a freshman congressman, his personal office was relatively small; there was only room for his desk, the two side chairs, and a small sofa. If there had been anyone on the sofa, the coffee table between the chairs would have made it very awkward.

Paul Singleton was from Palisades Park, New Jersey, and had run a hard-fought campaign for the seat held by Republican Jackie Keenen, whose wife, unfortunately for him, had chosen an election year to divorce him, allegedly because of an affair with a younger woman. It seems that people are generally forgiving of such indiscretions by congressmen, but only when the wife is! Even so, he lost the election by less than one half of 1 percent of the vote. Although a last-minute effort by the Tea Party made up some lost ground, it just wasn't enough.

Although his election was a closely fought surprise, the Democratic Representative from New Jersey's Fifth Congressional District was only halfway through his first term, and already news reports indicated he was lagging in the polls.

The generally Republican Bergen County was swinging away from Paul Singleton's liberal agenda. He was doing everything he could to appeal to the voters, including the over 10,000 Korean Americans living in his district. To bolster his image with that ethnic group, just three months ago he had hired Julie Park Endicott as a legislative assistant. She was a Korean woman whose marriage to a businessman living in Bergen County had ended with his sudden death during a mugging gone wrong in New York City. Singleton was hoping her high profile position, just one level below his Chief of Staff, would garner more of the Korean American vote.

Although doing so was technically illegal, the Congressman was sharing with his close friend and Chief of Staff what he had learned from the President just the evening before. "I tell you, Mike, the President is really between a rock and a hard place this time. With the North Koreans bragging they have developed a long-range ballistic missile that could reach the West Coast, and his promise to withdraw United States troops from all the little regional wars going on, he has to do something that reassures Americans of their safety. His promise to bring home half the troops from South Korea has stalled because of this. He's going to have to pull a rabbit out of the hat if he expects to retain his popularity, especially since next year is an election year. An election year for both of us, I might add.

"When he told the intelligence committee last night that he had formed a group to develop a plan to counter the North Korean capabilities, we were dumbfounded. And to compound this rash action, he's put an Army Lieutenant Colonel in charge! Mike, I want you to find out all you can about a Lieutenant Colonel Robert Johnson. Apparently he's an intelligence officer based in the Pentagon. Try to stay under the radar, though; I don't want the President's people to find out we're snooping around. In fact, the committee chair cautioned all of us to keep this closely held. I shouldn't even be telling you this, but you're my closest confidant and advisor. I rely on you to keep me out of trouble.

"Don't worry, Paul, I know how to keep a secret."

The congressman continued, "The President said they were looking primarily at the possibility of inserting a virus into the North Korean IT system. The reason his briefing was so unbelievable was because he also told us he was not ruling out putting boots on the ground, probably in the form of a SEAL team. But he reassured us that all this was in the early planning stages, and he would keep us advised of their progress."

His friend commented, "I have to wonder if he wouldn't get more support from the American people if he just bombed the heck out of the North Korean launch facilities with the B-2 bomber."

The congressman responded, "He might initially, but I doubt he wants to run the risk of North Korea either attacking or invading South Korea as a reaction. If they invaded, he would be compelled to send more American soldiers into harm's way; that would not go over well with the voters.

"In any case, while you're finding out what you can about Colonel Johnson, let's figure out a way to use this to our advantage with the voters back home. Remember, keep this conversation to yourself."

As he rose to leave the office, his Chief of Staff and friend said, "Yes sir, just between the two of us."

"Oh, and Mike, I'll be leaving in a few minutes for that breakfast with the businessman's group from Palisades Park." Shaking his head, he continued, "I don't know what the Founding Fathers were thinking, making a congressman's term only two years. Almost as soon as we are elected we have to start running our next election campaign!" They both chuckled as Mike left the office.

True to his word, the congressman left for his breakfast meeting just a few minutes later.

Shortly after that, the rest of his congressional staff started showing up for work. Last to arrive was Julie Park Endicott, one of the Congressman's legislative assistants. Twenty-eight years old with raven black hair, and rather tall for a Korean woman at 5'8", she could have been a model.

She had met the congressman during one of his infrequent visits to his home office in Bergen County, where she was working as a volunteer.

She had made it clear that she'd love to work for the congressman in Washington, D.C., but a position had not been available at that time.

At a fund-raising dinner that evening, she had been seated next to Mike Fontana. Mike's wife had not made the trip with him and was still at home in Virginia. They seemed to get on well at the dinner, and it was apparent to observers that Mike did not mind sitting next to a beautiful Asian woman.

A month or so later, when a position did open up in the congressman's Washington office, Mike suggested they hire Julie, for several reasons. First, she had made it clear she was willing to move to Washington, D.C. Second, after being asked, the home district manager said she was intelligent and got along with everybody. And third, her full name was ideal for reelection purposes. She had kept her maiden name as her middle name, and it would be obvious to the Korean community that she was Korean; at the same time, it was not obviously Asian and so would not be off-putting to the white and Hispanic ethnic groups which make up the bulk of Bergen County.

Even though a proper background check had been completed before she was hired, it failed to discover that Julie Park Endicott was not who she said she was. The background check showed that she had been in the United States for 15 years, since she was about 14 years old, but the truth was that she had sneaked across the Canadian border just 17 months ago. Her real name was Pak Ji-woo, and she was from Nampo, a large city southwest of Pyongyang in North Korea. Her family was well connected, and she was now a captain in the intelligence branch of the North Korean Army.

She was not the only spy from North Korea in the United States, but she was the only one currently considered a hero at home because of her successes. Having obtained work in the office of a U.S. congressman who was a member of the House intelligence committee was considered quite a coup by her superiors. Not only was she able to collect a ream of sensitive information simply by being observant in the office, she also used one of the oldest methods of intelligence gathering known to man – the honeypot.

Although one might jump to the conclusion that she had compromised the congressman, it turns out that for all his other faults, the Congressman was faithful to his wife. Captain Pak Ji-woo was very subtle, in fact almost too subtle, in plying her trade as a spy. While she was concentrating on getting closer to the congressman, she hadn't been initially aware that Mike Fontana was attracted to her.

One night he asked her to stay late and complete a project to be presented at a congressional hearing the next day. While there were no attempts at intimacy that evening, it was soon clear to her that the Chief of Staff was interested in more than her legislative prowess. Soon, working late together became a habit. She was initially surprised by his attention; she had met his wife on several occasions, and she was good-looking and intelligent. But not one to question his motives, she slowly cultivated the new relationship. It wasn't long before they were exchanging more than just emails.

Falling victim to one of man's greatest weaknesses, he was soon telling her all the little secrets the congressman shared with him. Whether he was boasting of his special knowledge to impress her or simply wanting to share secrets with someone, he probably felt it was safe to communicate with a fellow staff member. He shared with her on one intimate occasion that his wife told him she did not want to know his secrets. After that first time alone together, their pillow talk became so sensitive that he insisted a radio be played in the background to mask their conversations. Ji-woo could hardly believe her luck; she had literally fallen into a spy's most popular dream.

Ji-woo was also talented at using modern technology in her work. Using a commercially available encryption program on her computer, all the little secrets he shared were soon emailed to her bosses in Pyongyang. Some of his comments, when taken alone, seemed innocuous and unimportant, but when placed with other intelligence gathered from around the world, including news reports from dozens of well-meaning but liberal journalists, they allowed the North Koreans to develop a rundown of American intentions not only for the Korean Peninsula but in other sensitive areas of the world, as well.

Unknown to Mrs. Endicott, the FBI had, after painstaking hours of mind numbing work, discovered one of her emails in an NSA report on suspicious communications. Although they had not yet traced the origin of the email, they knew that someone was sending sensitive information to North Korea.

The most popular propaganda posters during World War II in the United States contained the phrase, "Loose Lips Sink Ships"; that caution is still true today. If Congressman Singleton knew that everything he said to his Chief of Staff would be on the desk of a North Korean general in just a day or two, he would've had a heart attack! And if he knew the FBI was conducting additional background checks on his staff, as well as the staff of all the members on the two intelligence committees, he would have been surprised. After all, hadn't all the members been sworn to secrecy? It never occurred to him that his discussions with his Chief of Staff were a serious violation of that trust.

Chapter Fourteen

On the way to Andrews Air Force Base, there were questions I wanted to ask Dr. O'Brien, but I didn't think the Navy staff car was the most secure place to talk. So the ride to Andrews passed in awkward silence. When we arrived at Andrews, it was clear this staff car did have unusual privileges, because the gate was opened and we drove right out on the ramp and parked next to a Gulfstream G550 in U.S. Air Force livery.

It looked like our ride to MacDill Air Force Base near Tampa, Florida, where the Special Operations Command, better known as SOCOM, is headquartered, would be in high style. As we climbed the stairs, an Air Force chief master sergeant in dress blues appeared at the top. "Welcome aboard, Colonel Johnson, Dr. O'Brien. Y'all are the only two aboard for our flight to MacDill, so please sit wherever you'd like. You can leave your bags here and I'll move them to the baggage area before we take off."

I glanced at the ribbons on his uniform and saw that he had a Bronze Star and a Purple Heart, mixed in with a whole bunch of others. I also saw his name was Mitchell. He saw my glance and said, "I have some buddies who didn't make it; they're the ones who really deserve the medals."

"I know what you mean; we'll do our best not to be a burden for you today."

He smiled and said, "At least you're not a general! They can be pretty demanding!"

Dr. O'Brien and I looked at each other and I stepped aside allowing her to precede me into the aircraft. There was a small galley just inside the entry door, and as we turned to the right we saw that the forward part of the aircraft was furnished with four facing leather seats, two on either side of the aisle, followed by two facing white leather sofas. Beyond that, through a curtained divider, was a miniature conference room. There was a small conference table between four luxurious leather seats and a credenza across the aisle against the bulkhead with a large LCD screen.

I turned to Sergeant Mitchell and said, "This is pretty luxurious for an Air Force aircraft."

"It's my understanding the IRS confiscated this aircraft from some high roller running a Ponzi scheme and we were next in line to get a confiscated aircraft. By the way, y'all must be pretty important because you're the lowest ranking officer we've ever had on this ship; we usually carry high ranking generals and department heads. That's why we wear dress blues instead of flight suits."

His Texan accent was now pretty obvious, so I asked, "Where you from, Sergeant Mitchell?"

"Little town in East Texas called Tyler. We're known as the Rose capital of the world cuz we have the largest rose garden in the United States in Tyler. We're also famous because the adopt-a-highway program started right there in Tyler." His face was just beaming with local pride!

"What do your folks do in Tyler?"

"My daddy worked in the oil fields; in fact, he worked every day 'cept Sunday in the oil fields. He'd come home every day just covered in dirt and grime and grease and oil. That's the reason I'm here today; I didn't want to be dirty every day."

"You said worked, past tense?"

"He's retired now, and he and mama sit at home watching the big-screen TV most of the day. They have more money than they know what to do with, but it doesn't help much. Mama spends most of her day taking care of daddy, because he's just plum worn out."

"Do you get a chance to talk to them?"

"I call ev'ry week to see how they're doin'. I served two tours in Afghanistan as a crew chief, so that's all they talk about with their friends; that and my medals. They're pretty proud of their boy! So I call 'em every week and let 'em know I'm okay." He smiled and then turned to close the entry door.

I smiled in return and turned back to Dr. O'Brien. "Where would you like to sit?"

Without hesitating she said, "Let's sit in the conference room so we can talk during the flight."

I looked at her and said, "Do you want to fly backwards or would you rather face forward?"

"I like to know where I'm going, not where I've been!" And with that she stepped into the forward facing window seat and sat down.

After I threw my soft sided bag in the credenza, I sat in the aisle seat diagonally opposite her so we both had room for our legs underneath the conference table.

Not long after, the pilots started the engines, and soon we were moving toward the runway. Sergeant Mitchell came by and said, "Them two majors up front are darn good pilots, but I still suggest you fasten your seatbelts. Best if you keep 'em fastened while you're sitting just in case we run into rough air. Major Guthrie said we might run into some rain and such over North Carolina, but otherwise it should be a smooth flight. Feel free to stand up, walk around, and use the restroom if the seatbelt sign is not lit up. I'm going to sit up front with the pilots, so if you need anything, just wander up and tap me on the shoulder. We've got coffee, we've got water, we've got soda pop, and we've even got some sandwiches if you get hungry."

Dr. O'Brien responded, "Thank you, Sergeant. That's very kind of you." That's when I noticed that Sergeant Mitchell had been directing his conversation to Dr. O'Brien the whole time; it's like I wasn't even there. She seemed to have that effect on people, especially men.

Sergeant Mitchell then wandered up the aisle and disappeared into the cockpit. After he closed the cockpit door, I wondered how we were going to tap him on the shoulder.

I turned back to Dr. O'Brien and said, "Dr. O'Brien, after we get up to cruising altitude I have some things in my bag that I'd like to discuss with you. I think we should also have an open discussion about what I saw on the satellite imagery and what you saw. Apparently you've been looking at it as long as I have, or perhaps even longer."

"Yes, let's talk. And since it's just the two of us, why don't you call me Vivian." As we began taxiing to the runway, I noticed her smile was made even brighter by the sunlight coming in the cabin window. That's when I saw that she had the greenest eyes I have ever seen. I must have hesitated because she said, "Are you okay?"

"Yes, I'm fine. I was just thinking. All right then, Vivian it is. And please, call me Robert." I don't know why, but I proceeded to tell her why I'm called Robert. "I was called Bobby or Bob until high school. In fact, my aunts and uncles still call me Bobby. In high school, there were three of us 'Roberts' on the baseball team. The coach made us draw straws and I pulled the short one. After that first practice, the first baseman was called Bobby; the shortstop was Bob; I played catcher and was called Robert from then on. And of course my parents always called me Robert."

Before she could reply, the engines spooled up and we were taking off. It was not as noisy as I expected, but the engine noise still made it difficult to talk while we roared down the runway and climbed to our cruising altitude. We did not speak, but I watched Vivian gazing out the window; her expression as she watched the earth recede was almost childlike.

In a few minutes the noise dissipated to a level allowing normal talk as the pilots reduced the engine power for normal cruise flight. I could see that we had climbed above the clouds and the ground was no longer visible. We turned our gaze to one another as Vivian asked, "Shall I tell you what I know first?"

"Yes, I will be interested to hear."

She paused a moment, as if gathering her thoughts, and then said, "The intelligence analysis you wrote eventually made its way to Admiral Harrison's office; it was he that recommended you join our group.

"Apparently the South Korean chairman of the Joint Chiefs of Staff and our chairman have an informal conversation twice a year. During their last conversation, he offhandedly asked General Underhill if we were aware of the North Korean intentions to launch a new rocket toward the United States. Since your report had not yet made its way to his office, he could only plead ignorance. Because of the sensitive nature of the intelligence gathered, they agreed that a courier would be sent to personally brief General Underhill. As a result of that briefing, and General Underhill's subsequent briefing of the President, our little group was formed.

"The NRO was tasked to review satellite imagery over the past several months. That's where I come in to the picture. I was invited because my assignment at the time was far eastern Asia and all of Japan, and of course that took in the Korean Peninsula. I discovered what appeared to be increased activity at their primary rocket manufacturing facility, and also increased activity at both launch facilities.

"With the intelligence provided by the South Koreans, and the increase in rocket building activity I discovered in the satellite imagery, the President ordered the JCS, the CIA, and Dr. Richardson's office to make recommendations. My role was as advisor to Dr. Richardson. I'm not even sure the National Security Council is yet aware of what we're doing. The JCS, represented by Admiral Harrison, followed up with their intelligence sources in the South Korean Army, but I understand they made some inquiries with the Japanese, as well.

The CIA, well, they did what they always do – they worked alone. Pretty soon though, they sent Mister "roly-poly" CIA guy who was introduced as a senior IT manager for them. It was his job to pitch to Dr. Richardson the IT solution to what we were coming to recognize as a major threat to the United States. And of course the CIA Director went straight to the President and made the same argument for the IT solution. Shortly after that the President ordered the Special Operations Command to form a working group to analyze the available intelligence and offer a workable solution."

I thought it curious that she referred to the CIA technician as "roly-poly" just as I did when I first saw him, but kept that thought to myself! I interrupted and asked, "How long has that SOCOM group been working?"

"About three weeks, maybe a little more, before you came on board."

"The recommendations Commander Throckmorton made in the briefing to the President is pretty fast work, then. Or, should I say, the negative recommendations."

"In my opinion, the negative recommendations are pretty easy. I think the reason we're headed to SOCOM is to confirm the one positive recommendation – in other words, the solution that has the best chance of working."

That gave me pause; then I said, "Okay; since we're the analysts, let's analyze. I've been looking at the satellite imagery over the last year, and you just said you were tasked to look at the same material but over a much shorter time period. So what did we see?"

After pausing just a moment, to organize her thoughts I suppose, Vivian began to tell me about her analysis. "I organized the relevant available imagery into three stacks and in chronological order. First was the rocket manufacturing plant near Pyongyang, then the Tonghae launch facility on the east coast of North Korea, and then the Sohae launch facility on the west coast.

"In addition I pulled out some old satellite imagery from their annual military parades and reviewed the appearance of the missiles displayed on their large carrier trucks. This proved to be nothing more than a distraction, however, because those missiles still appear to be mockups, just like they have been in the past.

"As you know, in August 2013 the North Koreans discontinued construction projects at the Tonghae satellite launching facility and began several construction projects at Sohae. And then in February 2014, our satellite imagery detected an additional level on that gantry tower. That additional level far exceeds the needs of any rocket known to exist in their inventory. The NRO has been paying particular attention to Sohae, and I've been the primary analyst.

"At the same time, another analyst was assigned to watch the Tonghae facility. Although those construction projects were halted, the facility is still large enough to launch long-range missiles. When increased activity levels were noticed there, she and I began to work more closely together. In our estimate, it appears the North Koreans now have two launch facilities for large missiles, and the Sohae launch facility has far outpaced the ability of the Tonghae facility. It was my initial opinion that if they were developing a new long-range missile it would be launched from the Sohae facility. However, there were some at the NRO at that time who believed that because of the significantly greater experience of the launch crew at Tonghae, that it would be used to launch the new missile.

"It was at about this time that someone at a much higher pay grade than mine decided to reduce the frequency of imagery provided to your office. I'm not sure why they did that, but as I said, that decision was made by someone way above me. In fact, I only learned that was the case after I had been assigned to Dr. Richardson's office."

I had been listening patiently, but so far I hadn't learned anything I didn't already know or had surmised. It was nice to know she had not been involved in the decision to reduce the frequency of satellite imagery provided to the Pentagon.

She moved to the aisle, and as she stood up she said, "I'm going to get some water; would you like some?" As she moved away from the window, I couldn't help but notice that her eyes were still bright green and her smile was still brilliant, even without the bright lighting from the sun.

"That would be great!" That's all I could think of to say. Before I could catch myself, I turned to watch her walk forward and then embarrassed, turned my eyes back to the report on the table. I was determined to concentrate on our discussion, but when she returned, I just looked at her.

She took up the discussion just as though she had never left. "We pretty much know where the North Koreans manufacture their rocket parts, so we monitored in more detail the traffic to and from those facilities. And sure enough we noticed increased activity. It was interesting to note, however, that shipments away from the facility were pretty much evenly divided between Tonghae and Sohae. That's the reason many at the NRO will not say for certain which facility will be launching the new rocket."

I interrupted again, and said, "You have hit on a point that I made in my report to the JCS. Because of the many failures of previous launches, the higher level of experience at Tonghae could prove to be the deciding factor. In fact, unless I see additional and contrary intelligence, I'm prepared to say that Tonghae will be the launch point."

She smiled and pointedly said, "I'm not prepared to choose between them at this point." She noticed that I glanced down to my report and said, "And yes, I've read your report and cannot disagree with anything you've said, except for that."

I looked at her and, changing the subject slightly, said, "Do you anticipate that we'll see additional satellite imagery that will help us make that determination?"

"They know we are watching them, and although they are an awkward people and in some respects backward in their views, they are not stupid. I believe they are purposely trying to confuse us about which launch facility will be used. That's another reason I believe they actually are going to do something of significance."

I thought for a moment and then said, "I agree they are not stupid; arrogant maybe, but not stupid. The increased activity levels you refer to are truck and rail transportation for the most part, right?"

She cocked her head to one side and said, "Yes, that's right. They are both inbound and outbound from the manufacturing facility. That usually indicates an increased level of production of something."

"True, but consider this. We don't know what's in those boxcars and we can't see what's in the trucks. What if there's nothing in them? What if the increased traffic is a ruse to get our attention? What if they allowed the leak of that information the South Koreans gave us? What if what they really are trying to do is to invite us to do something stupid? In recent years, we've had a pretty good record of taking action on inaccurate or incomplete knowledge. And now the President wants us to stop the launch of a rocket whose existence we haven't even confirmed. And with the constraints he's given us, it almost certainly requires boots on the ground. Something about all this just doesn't feel right!"

"I think you're right about that last part. What do you bet the planning group at SOCOM is made up of Navy SEALs? Commander Throckmorton certainly is. They seem to be our go-to special ops people."

"Commander Throckmorton and I are the same rank, and he certainly has more experience with special operations, yet the President gave me command of this mission. There has to be more to it or I wouldn't even be involved!"

Before she could answer, the cockpit door opened and Sergeant Mitchell stepped out and came our way. "I hope you're enjoying the smooth flight. We climbed way over those rain clouds above North Carolina. The pilots are ready for their lunch, so I thought I'd see if you wanted some sandwiches."

Vivian and I looked at each other and nodded. I turned to Sergeant Mitchell and said, "That would be nice, thank you."

"All righty then, I'll be right back!"

And he was! He juggled two boxed sandwiches and two bottles of water as he came back to the conference table. Setting them on the table, he said, "When we were notified we had two high priority passengers, the major sent me over to Fairfax to Jason's Deli. They make up a fine lunch box. We do that a lot for our generals. Enjoy!" And he turned and headed back to the cockpit.

The box I opened had a chicken salad with almonds and pineapple, and her box contained a roast beef on croissant sandwich. We looked at each other and laughed as we traded boxes across the table.

We were both quiet as we enjoyed our lunch break. I was thinking about why the President gave me command of this mission; it was the second time I had considered this question. As I was pondering this, a little nagging question that had been hiding in the back of my head finally jumped front and center. I needed to call Major Green with a new assignment, and I wanted Dr. O'Brien to call her fellow analyst with the same assignment.

Even though I'd only finished half my sandwich, I excused myself and walked to the cockpit whose door Sergeant Mitchell had closed. I tapped and in a quick moment it opened. Sergeant Mitchell looked up as I asked, "Can I make a phone call to the Pentagon from here?"

He answered, "Of course! Let me come back and show y'all where the phone is."

As he was showing me the panel that covered the phone, I turned to Vivian and said, "I'm going to make a phone call and then I want you to make a similar call. You can listen to my call and then you'll know what I want you to do." I turned to Sergeant Mitchell and said, "Thanks Sergeant, this is great. The Air Force is very accommodating!"

"No problem, Colonel. Just let me know if you need anything else."

As he walked away, Vivian turned to me and said, "I've been doing some thinking also. If we can get our associates to re-examine the photographs that have trucks in them, we might be able to discern discrepancies between previous trucks that we know carried rocket parts and the trucks we are now watching. And we might even be able to compare satellite imagery of them actually loading and unloading the trucks. That might be very instructive!"

I smiled and said, "Great minds think alike."

So I made my call to Major Green with the new instructions to check out the trucks, and she made her call to her NRO associate. I told Major Green I would call him in about three hours and Vivian made a similar comment to her associate. By then we had less than an hour to MacDill. Three hours would give them time to review the appropriate satellite imagery and give us time to get our feet on the ground at SOCOM. At least that's what I assumed. Oh, what a dreamer I was!

Chapter Fifteen

Although it hadn't been in the forecast before we left Andrews Air Force Base, it was raining lightly when we arrived at MacDill. We said our good-byes to the flight crew and Sergeant Mitchell, who had already pulled our bags from the forward baggage closet, and climbed down the board-ing stairs. There to meet us in a camouflaged Humvee was Commander Throckmorton.

We shook hands as he said, "Lieutenant Colonel Johnson, good af-ternoon." He turned to Vivian and said, "Dr. O'Brien, it's good to finally meet you in person. We look forward to hearing your interpretation of the satellite imagery that's been made available to us."

I hoped that his addressing me as Lieutenant Colonel rather than the informal and more typical greeting of Colonel did not indicate a turf war was already taking place. Even in the Navy, it's commonplace to ad-dress an officer holding the rank of Lieutenant Commander simply as Commander as an informal greeting. On the other hand, his warm greet-ing of Dr. O'Brien was not unexpected. As I noted before, she has that effect on men.

"Throw your bags in and let's get moving!" Since it was just the three of us, I took Vivian's bags and threw them on the seats in back. I motioned her into the front passenger seat as I climbed in back with the bags. As we started to move, Commander Throckmorton said, "I need to brief you before we get to the conference room. Just under an hour ago, Admiral Harrison and CIA Director Sanders arrived." As he said this, I realized that Admiral Harrison must've caught a flight right after he left our early morn-ing meeting with Dr. Richardson. He continued, "They apparently have information to share but wanted to wait until you arrived."

"There's more," he continued. "Ernie Hansen is with them." Ernie Hansen was the Director of the FBI. I wondered what new twist he was bringing to the party.

"They've asked to meet with you first, Colonel Johnson, before you meet with the whole planning group." Now I understood the Commander's less than warm greeting at the airplane. I remembered Dr. Richardson's parting comment about leaving the politics to her, and wondered what kind of trouble I could be getting into here. He glanced into the rearview mirror and then said, "I hope we are all on the same team here."

As his eyes in the mirror lingered on mine, I said, "Commander, I was as surprised as you when the President named me to head this mission. My only goal is to meet the mission requirements and not get anyone hurt doing it!"

He smiled as he turned into a parking stall next to a nondescript building with a sign in front that said Building 121. Sure enough, as we walked into the building a Navy chief petty officer walked right up and said, "Colonel, if you'll follow me this way please." I turned to Vivian, gave a shrug, and followed the chief.

He led me down the hall and stopped in front of a door with the number seven next to it. He knocked, opened the door, and stepped aside as I entered. Seated at a small conference table was Admiral Harrison, Director Sanders, and Director Hansen. Admiral Harrison pointed to an empty chair and said, "Take a load off, Colonel."

Without preamble, Admiral Harrison said, "After I left you this morning in Dr. Richardson's office, I went to a meeting with the President. Director Sanders and Director Hansen were both there, as was the President's Chief of Staff, Jefferson Jackson. The meeting quickly became intense, but let me give you just the bottom line.

"First, and I'm sure this came from Mr. Jackson, the President reiterated his strong desire that whatever action we take cannot be attributed to the United States. I assured him this was uppermost in our planning. Second, Director Sanders convinced the President that we should take another look at the CIA's suggestion for an IT solution. As he is our Commander-in-Chief, I told him that we would do so."

Without waiting for any questions or acknowledgments from me, he went on, "And third, Director Hansen is here to brief you on a new development. Go ahead Ernie."

"Colonel, what I'm about to brief you on is top secret, need to know only." After a pause, he continued, "We don't believe anyone on your planning team has the need to know. Is that understood?"

"Yes sir, Director Hansen." Well, what else could I say?

"Good. Today, the FBI was briefing the President on the results of an ongoing espionage investigation. During that briefing he told us that just the previous evening he had informed the two intelligence committee chairmen of your mission. Unfortunately, the reason for our ongoing investigation is that top secret and very sensitive information about certain Air Force black ops missions was discovered in a briefcase during a routine background check some months ago. While following up on leads, our agents learned that that information had also been made available to the two intelligence committees.

"We don't know where the leak is yet but we hope to shortly. Meanwhile, the President wanted you to know that one of our leads points to North Korea as the recipient of that information."

I interrupted at this point and asked, "How much information did the President share with the two committee chairmen?"

"When we asked the President that question, and as he was about to answer, Mr. Jackson interrupted and said that any communication between the President and the intelligence committees was privileged information. This was one of those times when our meeting became more intense!

"After some haggling about who knew what and when, we eventually learned that he told the two committee chairmen he was concerned about the North Koreans bragging about their new long-range rocket and that he was officially notifying them that he had ordered a team to consider possible options, including the likelihood of interrupting the launch of any new missile. I can tell you, Mr. Jackson was beside himself with the President giving us even that much information!

"Based on information collected during our investigation, we are concerned with the possibility that one of the committee staff members might be leaking information, although we are early in our investigation and that may prove not to be the case; we simply won't know until we finish our investigation. However, this is one of the reasons the President has ordered you to re-examine the possibility of an IT intervention. Can you imagine the international uproar there would be if North Korea discovered a SEAL team inside their national boundaries?

"Since the President gave them your name, there is a strong possibility that someone may get in touch with you. If you get any inquiries from Senate or House intelligence committee members or staff, you are not to share any information about your mission.

"But if they do call, you can help us in our investigation. We want you to give them a piece of information which is true but not critical to your mission. We want you to give a different piece of information to anyone who contacts you from the House and a different piece of information if someone from the Senate calls you. That way if the information is leaked, we'll know where it came from. Can you do that for us?"

I sat back and thought for a moment, and then, looking him squarely in the eyes, quietly said, "I'm not fond of people who betray their country."

"Thank you, Colonel." He reached into his jacket pocket and slid two small envelopes across the table to me. "Admiral Harrison has drafted two possible scenarios for you to use; one for the Senate and one for the House."

Admiral Harrison spoke up at this time. "It's vital you do not share these scenarios with anyone on your team. That way if one of them shows up, we can eliminate anyone from this group as a suspect. You can understand why we wanted to visit with you alone. Do you have any questions for us?"

"Just one, sir; do you want me to give you a heads up if I get any inquiries?"

They each looked at one another, and then Director Hansen said, "Let's save any contact until you're back in D.C. I think that would be best."

I nodded and said, "All right, I better meet with my team. Thank you for the briefing."

Admiral Harrison said, "Just one more thing before you go. The President agrees that your personal relationship with officers in the South Korean Army can be useful, so he approved our plan for you to go to Seoul. He feels they may be more willing to talk to you in person rather than over a telephone. Once you have the planning group running smoothly here, you will fly to Seoul and talk personally with your friend, Major Kim, and others in their intelligence community about their recent intelligence discoveries. They may know more about this ballistic missile threat, but you may also be able to discover their thoughts on the North Korean effort to shrink their nuclear weapons to a size that will fit on top of a rocket."

Without waiting for my response, he added, "To that end, I've ordered the Air Force crew that brought you here to be ready to leave tomorrow night. It's a long flight from here, so plan accordingly. When they land at Elmendorf Air Force Base in Alaska to refuel, call me before you fly across the Pacific – just in case there's any new information we need to share with each other."

After a short pause, he then said, "Thank you, Colonel, and God speed in all your endeavors."

And with that, I left the room to look for my new team.

Chapter Sixteen

My thoughts are interrupted as I change position again to renew the circulation in my legs. If the North Koreans are keeping to a rigid time schedule, it's about time for their patrols to walk our way once more. I glance at my watch, and key the tactical radio, and say, "Let's be on our best behavior; it's almost time for them to pay us another visit."

It is still snowing lightly, and with dawn almost upon us, visibility has improved considerably. I am still hopeful the scrub brush and snow will keep us concealed, and it will unless the North Korean patrols start to examine the hillside more closely.

Sure enough, in just a couple of minutes the radio screeches and the words, "Here they come, two soldiers from the west," are whispered. And a minute later, the words, "And now two from the east." Once again the soldiers pass before us without stopping and without noticing they have interlopers on their hill. A few minutes later the radio screeches again with the words, "They're out of sight on the east, going back down the hill." And immediately following, similar words from the west indicating the patrols have once again disappeared down the hill.

With the sun just peeking over the mountains, I clearly see a large rocket is on the transporter vehicle, and there's a beehive of activity in front of the assembly building. As I watch, a puff of black smoke climbs into the sky from each of the vertical exhaust pipes on either side of the transporter cab. The slow journey to the gantry is about to begin.

In our planning back at SOCOM, we had studied pictures of all the rockets that North Korea was known to have. The rocket on the transporter below, although similar to other rockets, is clearly larger than anything we were familiar with.

Just then the satellite phone vibrates in my pocket. After putting the earphone in my other ear, I press the mic button and say, "Colonel Johnson."

Major Denton's voice comes across clear as a bell. "Denton here. We have significant activity in front of the assembly building, plus they have just pulled a very large rocket out of the building on a transporter. It appears they are heading toward the launch gantry."

I respond, "I was about to call you; we have the same activity here, including a large rocket on a transporter headed for the gantry. I'm unable to match it up against our list of known rockets. How about you?"

"Same thing, we don't recognize it."

One of the nice things about an encrypted satellite phone is that you can call anywhere in the world, and I desperately want to call Vivian and ask if they have a satellite over North Korea right now. I end my call with Major Denton with a quick, "Let's keep the sat phones on and stay in touch with anything new. I'm going to call home right now. We'll talk later."

However unlikely it might be, the North Koreans have two big rockets several hundred miles apart on transporters each headed to a launch gantry. They were known to have used mockups in the recent past, such as during their annual military parade. The questions in my mind are, do they really have two new rockets? Are they both mockups? Is one real and the other a mockup? If one is real, which one? Because it had been easy to determine that the rockets in their military parade were only mockups, I am hoping we can get a good look at these two rockets and make a determination about them. This is why I want to talk to Vivian right away.

As I move around to more comfortably use the satellite phone, my elbow hits a medium-sized branch of the scrub brush in which I'm hiding and knocks snow all over me. What a doofus! Shivering from the cold snow, I punch in her number. It is approaching supper time there, so I hope she is still in her office.

No answer.

I redial, and this time she answers after the first ring. Without the social niceties that Sergeant Garcia picks at me about, I say, "Please tell me you're still in your office?"

I swear she must've been talking to Sergeant Garcia because she responds, "Yes, I am well, thank you for asking."

"Dr. O'Brien, Vivian, I'm on a freezing hillside in North Korea surrounded by a million unfriendly soldiers; please cut me some slack."

After a brief pause, she answers my question. "Yes, I am still in my office." Her voice is not very warm.

It is nice to hear her voice, despite the bit of tension. However, I'm keenly aware there's no time for anything but business on this call. I give up and use my most military voice. "Dr. O'Brien, both of our teams have just watched workers pull very large rockets out of their assembly buildings. The sun is just rising here so I'm hoping there will be a satellite pass so you can get some great pictures for analysis; it would be nice to know if these rockets are real or not."

As I say this, I look down at the transporter with the rocket sitting in its bed and notice additional activity taking place. "Dr. O'Brien, you're going to have to hurry because it appears they are pulling large covers over the rocket."

"I can hurry as fast as you want, Colonel, but I can't push the satellite any faster. They are obviously aware of our satellite schedule; it's due to overfly Tonghae in about 30 minutes and Sohae a few minutes after that. I think we're out of luck this time."

"Well, rats!"

"I presume that is a technical term from the Army intelligence community? In any case, on each pass of the satellite, we'll take pictures of both rockets on their journey toward the gantries. Maybe we'll get lucky and the wind will blow one of the covers off."

I lower my binoculars as I answer, "Not much chance of that happening; I'm watching them use very large straps to hold the covers in place. And now that I give it some thought, I bet the covers don't come off until after the sun goes down. They'll move the rockets in place in the dark and we won't know if the rockets are real until we see the engines fire."

After a brief pause, she asks, "Didn't our NASA contact say it would take a minimum of 12 hours to prepare the rocket for launch, including travel from the assembly building? If that's true, they won't be ready to launch until well after dark. They've never launched a rocket at night. Do you think they might launch this rocket at night?"

"That scenario generates all kinds of possibilities, none of them good for us. Vivian, I'll keep the phone on, so call me if you learn anything that would be useful. I need to work out some things here. Have a good night."

In a playful tone, Vivian says, "Well, lookee there! A few social words at the end of the conversation and I didn't hear your head explode!" And then the click of her signing off. I roll my eyes as I end the call and maneuver my arm around, carefully this time, to put the phone back inside my parka.

One thing I need to work out is how to ensure the sniper team is well rested when it comes time to take their shot. Back at SOCOM, both sniper teams had reassured us all that they could sleep at any time, allowing them to be well rested at all times. I hope that was true because it looks like they need to get their rest during the day, and then be awake and alert all night long. It would be just like the North Koreans to make their first night rocket launch on my watch!

I key the tactical radio and said, "Pop, are you there?"

"I'm here, Colonel."

"Based on the activity we see below, I recommend you and Sergeant Harris sleep during the day and then be available to pursue your trade after dark. They've never launched at night before, but we need to be ready in case they make the attempt."

"Roger that, Colonel. We'll keep the radio in our ear, so just call if you need us."

Without responding to the sergeant, I turn my attention to the SEAL teams and ask "Lieutenant, how do you guys want to handle sleep?"

"Just like we always do; one of us on each side will be awake at all times and both of us when necessary."

"Okay. Well, I'm beat, so I'm going to grab some shut eye." Thinking for a moment, I continue, "On the other hand Lieutenant, I think I'll wait until the next patrol has passed by and then I'll take my nap."

"Roger that Colonel. We'll call when we see them comin' up the hill."

And sure enough, about 20 minutes later the Lieutenant calls to say they are on the way. Five minutes after that, the master chief reports another patrol coming up his side of the hill. They cross in front of me, and a few minutes after that, both the lieutenant and the master chief say they are going back down the hill. And a couple minutes after that, I lay back and entertain memories of my first afternoon at SOCOM before falling asleep.

Chapter Seventeen

I left that first meeting with Admiral Harrison and his two very senior companions with mixed feelings. On the one hand, I understood the reason for the secrecy. On the other hand, I did not want the team members to learn they were not fully trusted by their civilian bosses.

I also appreciated, now that I'd learned the planning team had been together for almost a month, that it was technically possible one of them was the leak. But that just didn't make sense. If you can't trust a Navy SEAL team, who can you trust? And Dr. O'Brien was a senior analyst with the NRO, an agency where background checks are no small thing.

As I was pondering the ramifications of my new instructions, a Navy yeoman found me and led me upstairs to a large conference room. I was a little surprised to see two Marine guards at the door. After all, we were within the confines of one of the most closely guarded facilities in the United States. Nevertheless, they fulfilled their assigned duty. While one of them asked for my ID, the other carefully watched me while he held a Remington M870 shotgun at the ready. I couldn't help but notice that he took a couple of steps into the middle of the hallway so he would have a clear shot at me if it became necessary. The military version of the reliable Remington 12-gauge shotgun has been used by Special Forces for close-quarter engagement for decades. These guys were serious!

The Marine handed back my ID and said, "Thank you Colonel; you may proceed." All business!

As I stepped into the conference room, I stopped after only one step. Every flat surface, except the ceiling, was covered with satellite imagery, photographs, maps, and even Google Earth pictures. I doubt if North Korea even had this much detail about their own country.

I noticed the floor had two pathways, one around the large table in the middle of the room, and one around the outside of the room. This allowed individuals to see every display. Then I saw that one of the pathways led to another room. As I got closer I could see Vivian and six men seated around a small conference table in that other room.

Although I was their new team leader, no one stood as I entered. I suppose this was in keeping with the informal command structure of Navy SEAL teams. It didn't bother me because I'm not big on the formal niceties of the military, but I did notice. I am big, however, on every member of the team being a contributor. Therefore, I was happy to see that our planning table was round.

As I sat in the only empty chair, Commander Throckmorton introduced the rest of the team. "Colonel Johnson, let me introduce our planning team. To your right is Major Denton; he is assigned to the Marine Special Operations Command, what we used to call Force Recon Marines. They are like Navy SEALs, only not quite." After a chuckle from everyone, he continued. "Next to him is Lieutenant Williams, and next to him is Lieutenant Rogers; they are from SEAL Team 2. SEAL Team 2 is the SEAL Team that has full-fledged Arctic warfare capabilities.

"To my right is Lieutenant Commander Cromwell. He is from the SEAL Delivery Vehicle Team at Pearl Harbor. Of course, you know Dr. O'Brien. And next to her is Master Chief Petty Officer O'Shaughnessy. We call him Nessie because when he comes out of the water he's a real monster."

I could see what he meant. The Master Chief must've been 6'6" and 250 pounds. And his uniform barely contained his rippling muscles.

With a gleam in his eye, Commander Throckmorton said, "Now that you know a little bit more about our team, why don't you share your background."

Somewhere it says that you have 15 seconds to make a good first impression. So I said, "Yeoleobun, annyeonghaseyo. Naneun dangsin-ui jagyeog jeungmyeong-eul gamdong hassip-nida. Naneun uliga dae-tonglyeong-ui yogu sahang-eul chungjoghaneun gyehoeg-eul sulib hal su-iss-eul geos-ibnida midseubnida."

I paused for effect and then said, "I'm an Army intelligence officer recently assigned to the Pentagon, and even more recently assigned to the office of the National Security Advisor in the White House. As a young man I lived for two years in South Korea. I've served a combat tour in Afghanistan and two Army tours in South Korea as a brigade and division intelligence officer. And even though the North Koreans don't know it, I have traveled a bit in North Korea." Okay, I know this last statement was a stretch, but I was getting to the end of my 15 seconds! "And by the way, what I said in Korean was, 'Hello, everyone. I am impressed with your credentials. I trust we will be able to develop a plan that meets the President's requirements.'

"I don't know why the President put me in command of this mission, but like you, I follow orders. So, here I am. Let's get started.

"I appreciate everything that's been done up to this point. Commander, is there anything else I should know that you didn't share with the President?"

He smiled at me and said, "Nope, he heard it all."

"Okay, thanks." I looked around the table and then said, "You're probably wondering what was discussed in the meeting downstairs. I won't bore you with the details, but we've been ordered to reconsider the IT virus proposal." Before I could continue, there was general groaning around the table. "I feel the same way you do, but the President felt so strongly about this, he sent the Director of the CIA to relay his instructions."

Commander Throckmorton spoke up and said, "Colonel, you must . . ." I held up my right hand, interrupting him, and said, "If it's all right with everyone, let's say we've reconsidered the IT option and have determined the likelihood of success is not good enough to recommend it as a solution. Any comments?"

A general shaking of heads and a few smiles, but no comments were expressed.

"Along that same line of thought, is there any reason to reconsider the B-2 option or the cruise missile option?"

A few softly spoken "no" responses and more shaking of heads was the reaction around the table to this question.

"All right, then. Where does that leave us?" And I looked right at Commander Throckmorton.

He smiled and spoke up, "As you've just learned, we're all action oriented people here. We had supper in here last night, the beer was cold and the pizza was filling, and we stayed till the wee hours as we brainstormed several ideas. We discussed how to get a SEAL team in to blow up the launch facility with the rocket on it and then get everybody out. We're pretty confident we can get the SEAL team in and reasonably confident we could blow up the rocket, but we've been struggling with how to get the team out afterward.

"For example, we're pretty sure we could do a HALO jump right to the gantry and blow up the rocket. But we couldn't figure out how to get our guys out of the compound. They have a double security fence and lots of soldiers on patrol.

"Then Major Denton had an idea." He pointed to the walls and all the satellite imagery and photographs plastered everywhere and said, "We discovered as we looked at chronologically successive pictures of the facility at Sohae that the North Koreans have excellent perimeter security around the facility. We think they have a small brigade of regular Army soldiers bivouacked in the town nearby. They patrol inside the fence on a 24/7 basis; they use jeeps, walking patrols, and patrols with dogs. They have the same kind of control system outside the fence out to about 100 yards. But beyond that, they have only irregular patrols who climb up and down the hills surrounding the facility. And beyond about a mile, they don't appear to have any security in place.

"But we think we found a weakness. There's a hill southwest of the facility covered in scrub brush. It's about 1,300 meters as the crow flies from the gantry; that's about eight-tenths of a mile. Major Denton suggested we put a sniper team on that hill, and once the rocket is in place and ready to be launched, we simply shoot it. All that rocket fuel will make it go boom in a delightful manner!

"Then we looked at Tonghae and found a similar situation. The hill there, however, is about 1,600 meters from the gantry; that's about a mile."

I pondered what he said, and then asked, "How do you propose to get the snipers into position?"

"That same question last night generated a lot of controversy. SEAL team snipers could simply do a HALO jump, take the shot, and then walk out to the coast and swim away. But that would require perfect timing. After some discussion on this topic, we decided to call it quits for the night.

"With some good shuteye, we continued the discussion this morning before you arrived and came up with a possible solution. We're ready to discuss it with you now."

"I'm all for that, but let's take a short break first; where is the men's room?"

He smiled and said, "Go out the door and turn right. The head is down the hall and on your left." He looked at Dr. O'Brien and said, "The ladies room is just a little bit farther down the hallway on your left." Shaking my head, I thought to myself, apparently ladies don't use heads! He continued, "Be warned, if you go out the door and turn left, the guards will ask to see your ID all over again when you want to come back in here."

After a short break to stretch our legs and take care of physiological needs, we gathered around the table again and Commander Throckmorton shared their plan for getting the snipers into the proper position. As he explained their suggestion, I could see this was not going to be a simple mission.

He explained that since everyone agreed the best sniper team was in the Marine Corps, they should be assigned to what we thought would be the most likely launch facility for the rocket; in other words, Tonghae. The second best sniper team, the Army team, would be assigned to Sohae, just in case the North Koreans tried to pull a fast one on us. Each sniper team would be accompanied by four Navy SEALs for security and an officer in charge. It was proposed that Commander Throckmorton lead the team going to Tonghae and Major Denton the team going to Sohae.

Each team of seven would embark upon a submarine in Japan and travel to their respective landing points off the coast of North Korea, timed to arrive just after dark. The SEALs would then lead their team to the proper ambush point on the hill selected for them. He pointed out that there appeared to be sufficiently thick scrub brush on both hills to hide the sniper teams.

The plan was that after they took their shots, the teams would jog down the backside of the hill, travel to the coast, and meet up with an extraction team. This is where Lieutenant Cromwell will shine; his SEAL Delivery Vehicle pilots will be ready off each coast to carry the teams back to the submarine.

He ended with, "All *you* have to do, Colonel, is sell this plan to the President."

Chapter Eighteen

While I was sure the President would want to review any plan proposed, I was also certain that the Joint Chiefs of Staff would look at our plans first. With that in mind, I said to the group, "What I want you all to do tonight is this: Think about your contribution to Plan A. I want you to think about that tonight because first thing in the morning we start working not only on Plan A, but also Plans B, C and D.

"I also want you to think about the two sniper teams walking to and from their respective hillsides. We want to make sure they have enough time to do that safely; we cannot afford to lose or damage any piece of equipment, and we certainly cannot afford anyone breaking an ankle or a leg on a mountainside. Remember, Army and Marine sniper teams are accustomed to walking into their forward positions, so let's make sure they have all the tools to do that properly."

I looked at Dr. O'Brien and said, "Dr. O'Brien, I want you to review every piece of satellite imagery and confirm, or challenge, what they said about the two hills, including an analysis of the ingress and egress routes." I turned to Major Denton and said, "Major, I want you to review the North Korean security forces around both sites. I also want you to think about how we're going to get the best two sniper teams here." I looked around the rest of the table and said, "It appears the rest of you know what your areas of expertise are.

"Please keep in mind that we only have a limited time to finish our detailed planning, practice to the degree we can, and then move all the widely scattered pieces of men and equipment to an embarkation point.

"Also, from this point forward, I want the team to work without regard to rank or seniority. Every idea mentioned is to be considered by the entire group." I paused, because at that moment an important thought occurred to me. I looked up to Commander Throckmorton and said, "Commander, I have an idea. The best use of time for the eight of us is to focus on developing the plans. That being the case, I suggest we bring two people in to make notes and type up the final plan – plans that is. I have a sergeant in mind who can be trusted and would be ideal for this task. Can you find someone on the Navy side that would be a good fit?"

Without hesitation he said, "As a matter of fact I can. And he's right here at SOCOM."

"Excellent! I'll get Admiral Harrison to cut the orders putting them on TDY to us."

I looked around the room as I said, "Any comments or suggestions before we break for the evening? I want everyone to be well rested and sharp as a razor in the morning. Does 0700 sound okay to everyone?" A few shrugs, a few nods, and a couple shakes of the head, but only Master Chief O'Shaughnessy said anything. With a broad smile, he said, "Great! I get to sleep in!" With a few chuckles, we all stood and the meeting was adjourned.

I walked to Dr. O'Brien, smiled and said, "We have some phone calls to make; shall we find a quiet place?" Commander Throckmorton overheard me and commented, "Colonel, feel free to use this room. We're all going over to the officer's club. You can join us there later if you want."

I responded with, "That reminds me, how do we get around?"

"We reserved a staff car for you and Dr. O'Brien. The Navy yeoman downstairs can show you where it is." He paused for a moment and then said, "By the way, the Marine guards outside are the real deal. There are only eight names on the authorized list for access to this room, so always have your ID with you. The guards are there 24/7, and their instructions are simple: If anyone else attempts to gain access to this room, they are authorized to use lethal force." With a half wave and a cheery smile, he was gone.

I looked at Dr. O'Brien and said, "Let's make our calls."

Pulling out her phone, she walked to the other side of the table to make her call. I sat down and called Major Green, who was obviously still in the office because he said, "Three hours, huh? If I keep this up, my wife is going to think I'm seeing someone else." I laughed! He and his wife had been married 15 years, but they acted like they were still on their honeymoon. I doubt such a thought ever entered her mind.

"Whine, whine, whine; what have you got for me?"

With sarcasm in his voice, he said, "You always were a sensitive man. Seriously though, I just barely finished examining the satellite imagery. I looked at angles, shadows, shapes, and sizes, even tire shapes. Bottom line, there's nothing to indicate they are not what they appear to be. I think we could be looking at real rockets."

"And that's true at both sites?"

"Yes, basically true at both sites. However, I did make the observation that there were more ground crew at Tonghae. What significance that is, I couldn't tell you."

Thinking for a moment, I responded, "I don't know what that means either. Maybe their union is better there." We both laughed and I said, "Thanks David, that's a big help. And oh, by the way, tell your wife the other person is a man." He chuckled and said, "I've already told her all she needs to know about you! If that's all, have a good evening."

"Yep, that's all for now. But keep your phone handy just in case." And with that I hung up and looked at Dr. O'Brien. She looked at me and held up her right index finger, which I took to mean she wasn't finished yet; a pretty bright conclusion for an intelligence officer.

Then I set about making the other phone call I had to make. I called Admiral Harrison's office and got the after-hours operator, who told me that he was not available. I told the operator who I was and that I needed to talk to him right away. I said thanks and hung up. Not two minutes later my phone rang.

"Make it fast, Colonel, I'm in a meeting."

"Admiral, you said if I needed anything to give you a call. We need two additional people. Commander Throckmorton is going to arrange for one of them, but I need you to arrange for the other." He didn't say anything, so I continued, "There's a sergeant in my office, Sergeant Garcia, who we need down here to help us stay organized and to type up the final plans; can you get her down here tomorrow TDY for about a week?" I knew she was going to be mad, but I needed someone here I could trust and who knew how I operated.

The meeting must have been important because all he said was, "I'll take care of it." And he hung up.

This time when I looked at Dr. O'Brien, it sounded like she was finishing her phone conversation.

"Okay, thanks. If anything else shows up call me right away." She hung up as she turned to me and said, "Okay, you first."

I walked over and sat down in the chair next to her and gave a brief summary of what Major Green had told me. When I told her what he had said about the extra ground crew at Tonghae, she interrupted and said, "Melissa said the same thing. She told me there were 11 additional ground crew." She cocked her head, in that way I had noticed she does, and said, "What do you suppose that means?"

I wondered if Major Green had counted the additional ground crew and, after a moment, decided he had. If he had noticed a difference of only one or two, he wouldn't have mentioned it. But with 11 additional ground crew, it became part of the bigger picture, which is what he shared with me.

Vivian sat there with her head still cocked to one side while I pondered these thoughts. I looked at her, and said, "I can think of several reasons. First, Tonghae has been in business longer and they may simply have more staff on hand. Second, since the two transporters are exactly the same, the rocket on the transporter at Tonghae may be different, thereby requiring more ground crew. Third, they knew our satellite was passing over at that time, so maybe they are trying to mess with our heads!

"The bottom line is, both transporters appear to be carrying real rockets. I can't conceive of the North Koreans having two new rockets at two so widely dispersed locations, so somehow they've come up with an idea to make them look the same, at least under the tarps."

When she looked at me with a questioning expression, I said, "If a new rocket had been shipped in by China or Russia, I think we would've noticed it by now. We keep pretty good tabs on the ships that deliver goods to North Korea.

"So, if their public bragging is correct, that means they've built a new rocket, and I just don't believe they have the infrastructure nor the technical capabilities to build two at the same time. Besides, I think we would've noticed if either the Chinese or the Russians had sent scientists to both locations, and we're pretty certain the Iranians don't have the technical capability to build a large ballistic missile in North Korea."

"Well, you are the Korean specialist; I hope you're right. If you are, and they do have a new rocket, but just *one*, which one is the real one?" I didn't answer right away, and at that juncture she looked into my eyes and said, "I'm hungry."

I rose and bowed slightly toward the door and followed her out. We said good night to the Marine guards, whose expressions did not change at all. The same young yeoman was at the desk by the door. He stood as we walked up and smiled as he held out a set of keys. I took them and said thanks. He opened the door and said, "The Commander asked me to tell you both that you have rooms at the Bachelor Officer's Quarters. Turn left out of the parking lot, and you'll eventually come to a T in the road. Take the one on the right, and it will lead you to the main base where you can follow signs to the Officer's Club and the BOQ. If you turn to the left, you can follow signs to the main gate; the main road leads into town."

We grabbed our luggage from the lobby, and as we walked to the car I asked Vivian if she had a preference for supper. As I opened the passenger door for her, she said, "I'm sure the Officer's Club is nice, but what do you think about going into town?"

"That's okay with me; what did you have in mind?"

"How about something simple, but not fast food. A sit-down restaurant."

"That sounds good to me." I closed her door and hurriedly put our bags in the trunk. As I slid into the driver's seat, I pulled out my iPhone and said to Siri, "Directions to the nearest restaurant." Sure enough, the nearest restaurant was about seven miles away. It may not be fancy or romantic, but at least Denny's had good food.

We were both lost in our own thoughts as we drove off to find the left turn toward the main gate.

Chapter Nineteen

As my brain makes a slow journey toward wakefulness, I am momentarily confused by my hard and unforgiving bed. I turn to get more comfortable and am even more confused by the sight of snow in my bedroom. As it suddenly dawns on me where I am, I move my arm to get a look at my watch.

I can tell the sun is up in the east, but there is a thick fog covering the hillside; I can barely see 20 yards. Then I recognize that the reason I was disturbed in my sleep was because I had heard a voice talking in my head. Almost awake now, I realize it had to be one of the team transmitting on the tactical radio.

I look over at the sniper team and once again notice they are virtually invisible. As I become fully awake, I realize it had to be one of the SEAL teams on the radio, and they would only transmit if a North Korean patrol is making its rounds. As if on cue, I hear a crunching sound to my left. Pretty soon I could make out the hazy outline of a two-man patrol coming my way.

At first thinking they would pass by as the other patrols have done, I suddenly recognize that if they continue their current path, they will walk right over me! It's too late to say anything to alert Sergeant Parker, so I hold my breath and hope for the best.

I can't believe it! They walk right by the bush I was hiding in. Fortunately for me they never look down; in fact, it almost looks like they are in a hurry to get back to their warm barracks. I wait until they disappear off to my right before I start breathing normally again. Once again, Mother Nature has saved my bacon.

I'm sure it's only five minutes later, but it seems like an hour, that the SEAL team on the right announces that the patrol had disappeared down the hill once again. I glance down at the ground just outside the bush I'm hiding in, and in the snow I can clearly see the impressions of the soldiers' boots. I know I'm a soldier, but with the adrenalin pumping and my heart racing, I don't think I'm cut out for this kind of work!

As my heart rate begins to slow, I start thinking about the good luck that both teams seem to be experiencing. Here we are sitting on hills overlooking two of the most heavily guarded facilities in North Korea, and for all intents and purposes, they don't know that we are here. At least I hope that's the case. But it must be, otherwise they would be more earnest in their search for intruders.

I am startled when my stomach grumbles because it was loud enough that if it had happened when the two soldiers were walking by, they would've heard it. I decide it's time for breakfast. Although I would've enjoyed two eggs over easy, hash browns, wheat toast with grape jelly, and some orange juice, I'm happy to eat a couple of protein bars. It is clear I am not going to gain weight on this mission! I carefully put the two wrappers back in my pocket once I finish the not-so-gourmet feast.

I think back to my meeting with FBI Director Ernest Hansen and wonder if he is having any success in ferreting out the traitor. Even though he had mentioned it as a possibility, I was still surprised when I got a phone call from the Chief of Staff to a member of Congress who, it turned out, was on the House intelligence committee. The call came as Vivian and I were driving to supper that first evening in Florida. I was driving and only answered the call because I thought it might be Commander Throckmorton wondering where we were.

"Colonel Johnson, this is Michael Fontana. I am the Chief of Staff to Congressman Paul Singleton from New Jersey. You may be aware that he is a member of the House Permanent Select Committee on Intelligence. He asked me to call to discuss some important issues." I remember wondering why he thought it important I know the Congressman was a member of the intelligence committee; plus, by using the full formal name of the committee he was obviously trying to impress me. There must be hundreds of committees that keep the 435 members of Congress very busy. In any case, he went on, "I know this is your personal telephone, so when can we talk on a secure line? Will you be in your office tomorrow?"

Thinking back to my conversation with Director Hansen, I knew I had to talk to him. So I said, "I have a meeting at 7 o'clock in the morning; can we talk a few minutes before that?"

"A few minutes, Colonel, may not be enough time to complete our business." Yep, he worked for a Congressman and was letting me know who was more important. He continued, "Besides, I also have an early morning meeting that I must attend. I suggest we talk before lunch. How about 11 AM?"

Wanting to get this out of the way as soon as possible, I responded "Okay, I'll give you a call on a secure line. What number shall I call? Wait, better yet, just text me the number; I'm driving right now." Sometimes, even bright intelligence officers like me stumble into good decisions. I didn't know it then, but having his cell phone number would prove useful in the future. Anyway, he said okay and hung up.

I turned to Vivian and said, "That was the Chief of Staff to a Congressman on the House intelligence committee; he said he wants to talk about important issues. You heard me say that I'll talk to him tomorrow. Isn't it funny? Yesterday morning, nobody even knew I existed and yesterday I'm at a meeting in the White House and today I get a phone call from a congressman's office." I thought for a moment and then said, "I wonder how he got my cell phone number?"

I handed her my iPhone, and said, "While I'm driving, look up Congressman Paul Singleton and see what he's all about. The staffer said his name was Michael Fontana; see if the Internet knows anything about him."

She took my phone and said, "Yes sir, Colonel, sir!" and gave me my first salute of the day.

I gave her a wry look, but didn't say anything. We drove in silence for several minutes, and she was still reading as I drove into the Denny's parking lot. She looked up, handed me my phone and said, "I'm still hungry, so let's order first." Without waiting for me, she opened her door and started for the entrance. I ran to catch up, but she was inside before I got there. So much for trying to be a gentleman.

When the waitress came to seat us, Vivian pointed to a quiet section of the restaurant where no one was sitting. We sat down opposite each other and when asked by the waitress, we both told her we'd like water with a slice of lemon. She was back in a few minutes with two glasses of water with a lemon slice floating in each. Shaking my head, I reached in and squeezed the lemon. Vivian gave me a funny look, but didn't say anything.

She quickly glanced through the menu and then ordered country-fried steak with mashed potatoes and country gravy, with a side of broccoli; she asked for herb toast as well. I ordered a sirloin steak with mashed potatoes and brown gravy, and a side order of sweet corn; I also asked for herb toast. I guess I was hungry too! When the waitress left with our orders, Vivian began to brief me on what she had found on the Internet.

"It seems the congressman is a liberal Democrat who squeezed out a win in his district because the Republican incumbent was foolish enough to be caught in the bed of a woman who was not his wife. The very public divorce did not help his reelection chances! It seems the new congressman pretty much follows the party line when it comes to issues. Recent newspaper reports, however, do not give him much of a chance for re-election because the district he represents is a Republican district. He has a public education, including a bachelor's degree in philosophy from New York University; I wonder what he ever thought he would do with that?" Her disdain of his achievements was pretty clear. She continued, "To his credit, he's been married to the same woman for 35 years. They have two children, a boy and a girl, both grown and living in Colorado with families.

"His Chief of Staff, on the other hand, has a Bachelor of Science degree in finance and an MBA from Harvard. He grew up on the same block where the congressman's family lived. He married later in life; he's only been married seven years. Apparently his wife is a social gadfly. The article also said he was a volunteer on the congressman's first political campaign for only two weeks before he was promoted to be campaign manager. And, like they say, the rest is history.

"And I saved the best for last. Apparently there's a rumor going around that the congressman has been reprimanded at least once by the committee chairman for talking out of school. He denied it of course, but a corporation in northern New Jersey, with ties to the congressman, now has a lucrative government contract."

Before I could ask questions, the waitress returned with our food. As she set the plates in front of us and the aroma wafted above our table, I suddenly realized I was famished. I looked at Vivian and said, "I vote we eat first and talk later!"

She was already cutting her chicken-fried steak but looked up to say, "I agree," just before she put the first bite in her mouth. We both attacked our plates and it was several minutes before we looked up. She smiled and said, "I'm ready for a slice of apple pie; how about you?" Somehow the waitress was right there and said to me, "Shall I make it two slices?" I simply nodded.

Chapter Twenty

While we waited for our pie, she looked at me with her big green eyes and asked, "What would you like to know about me?"

To say that her question caught me by surprise would be an understatement. I wanted to say, "Everything since the day you were born," but instead I took a drink of water. Setting the glass back down on the table, I asked "How did you come to be a senior analyst for the NRO?"

She smiled and cocked her head in that bewitching way she does, and said, "That journey starts with my family. I'm the youngest of six; the others are all boys. So I grew up in Boston as a tomboy, really just one of the gang. One at a time, my brothers all went off to college – two are engineers, one is an architect, one's a cardiologist, and one is a lawyer. Dad made his money in arbitrage; he was a financial wizard and retired very wealthy at 47. He was disappointed that not one of his children developed a love for the financial world."

We were interrupted by the arrival of our dessert. After taking a small bite, she continued. "He was a proud father when I majored in finance at college. But I soon became bored; it just wasn't interesting enough. After I got my bachelor's degree in business finance, I saw an opportunity that was more interesting to me. My parents were disappointed when I told them I was moving to London to attend King's College and get a master's degree in international intelligence studies. Mom was disappointed because I was moving for two years, and Dad was disappointed because I was abandoning the financial world.

"After that, I moved to Arlington and began a PhD program in international intelligence at Georgetown. By then, I was no longer a tomboy, even though I didn't date much!

"While at Georgetown, and after I had written my dissertation, one of the professors introduced me to an Air Force lieutenant general, Kenneth Michaels, who was the Director of the National Reconnaissance Office. Still is, as a matter of fact. "She looked up and as she smiled, said, "That professor, by the way, was Dr. Richardson.

"I was able to avoid most social events simply because I was passionately working on my doctorate. And when I received my PhD, General Michaels offered me a position at the NRO. I suspect Dr. Richardson told him I had a keen analytical mind. In any case, it turned out I had a ready aptitude for not only analyzing satellite imagery, but also for knowing where to position the satellite for the next flare-up."

She paused for a moment to take a bite of apple pie, and then, as a pale pink color covered her cheeks, she continued, "We've kind of misled you about my position at the NRO; I'm actually the Deputy Director of the IMINT Directorate. IMINT is imagery intelligence."

I took another bite of my pie as I processed this new piece of information. Now I understood why she hesitated when Dr. Richardson asked her to report to me on this mission; she clearly outranked me, even though she was, like most NRO employees, a civilian employee of the Department of Defense.

I finally broke the silence by asking, "What do you do for fun? Do you have a hobby?"

She laughed and said, "I've always been tall for a girl, so my brothers encouraged me to join them in playing sports, which I did. To counteract my tomboy character, my mother insisted that I learn to play the piano. Although I hated the lessons at first, playing the piano is now a calming influence for me. And I stay in shape by jogging as often as I can; I don't run marathons but I try to jog about 30 minutes or so every day, usually in the morning."

She swallowed a piece of pie and then, in that disarming yet charming manner, cocked her head and asked, "What about you? What brings you here?"

I continued chewing for a few moments as I decided to give her the quick version of my life. "I grew up in Arizona as the oldest of seven children. Baseball was my favorite past time. When I was 18, 18 and a half, actually, because I had to finish high school, I was called to serve a two-year mission in South Korea for my church. That's where I picked up the language.

"After I came home from my mission, I moved to Utah and attended Brigham Young University. There was a small Korean community of students there, so I was able to practice my language skills nearly every day.

"While at BYU, I played baseball and, by the way, I still hold the NCAA record for the most stolen bases in a season! I met my wife, Beth, at BYU, and I also joined the Army ROTC program. I was looking forward to traveling the world as an Army officer. Of course, it's a long story, but suffice it to say that the Army soon learned I spoke fluent Korean, so after being commissioned a Second Lieutenant, I was assigned as a military intelligence officer.

"As far as my dreams of traveling the world as an Army officer, wouldn't you know my first assignment was to Fort Huachuca, Arizona. That's where the training school for intelligence officers is located. We practiced our military intelligence skills in the mountains of Arizona, where I had an unfair advantage because I was already familiar with them.

"We were stationed in Seoul for the second time when Beth and the children came home to spend some time with her parents at a family reunion." I paused for just a moment, then said, "She was killed by a drunk driver while she was driving home from the reunion." Vivian looked like she wanted to say something, but I was grateful she was wise enough not to add unnecessary words to a difficult subject. The kind look in her eyes was enough. I looked at those big green eyes and said, in a quiet voice, "It took me a long time to recognize it wasn't my fault she died."

"When I came home from Korea to attend the funeral, I was given a new assignment in the Pentagon, which is where I've been for the last two years. I learned just a few weeks ago that I'm on the short list for promotion to Colonel." I looked at her again, and said, "Assuming I don't mess up this assignment."

Moving on to a more cheerful topic, I said, "We have two children, Jacob, who wants to eventually attend med school at the Baylor School of Medicine, and Susan, who hopes to attend Georgetown. They are a delightful set of twins!"

Right then the waitress came by and said, "I'm going off shift now," as she slid our check on the table in front of me and waited. I can take a hint as well as the next guy, so I reached in my pocket for my credit card and handed it to her. As she went to the register, I turned to Vivian and said, "And that's the quick version of my life."

She looked at me and said, "So, why did you really join the Army?"

After a moment's thought, I said, "I was at baseball practice one day when I noticed a dozen young ROTC officers marching. I watched them for a while and noticed how polished and coordinated they were; they were clean cut and sharp looking, not grungy like the ball players around me. After practice, I went to the ROTC office on campus and asked lots of questions. The full-time Army officer assigned there, a lieutenant colonel, eventually asked me why I was interested.

"I told him I wasn't sure, but for some reason military service appealed to me.

"When he told me the Army would pay for my last two years of college tuition, I was hooked!"

My phone vibrated right then, and I saw it was Commander Throckmorton. I answered, and without a greeting he asked, "I presume you're not lost?" I laughed and responded, "No, we just decided to have supper in town." He was quiet for a moment and then said, "Well okay, we'll see you in the morning." From the tone in his voice, I knew that tomorrow's supper had better be spent in his company. I said, "Okay, we'll see you in the morning."

As I was putting my phone away, Vivian asked, "Any regrets? About the Army, I mean."

I looked up from my dessert and said, "No, no regrets."

The waitress came back with my card and a receipt to sign, which I did, adding a generous tip that brought a smile to her face. I almost, but not quite, missed the smile that gesture brought to Vivian's face.

It was a quiet ride as I drove back to MacDill; it seemed we were both lost in our own thoughts. I was still pondering Vivian's direct approach to getting to know one another when we arrived at the main gate. After a cursory glance at our IDs, the guard waved us through. We drove straight ahead and soon enough the BOQ appeared on our left.

It turned out the BOQ had a strict policy about mixing genders; I was on the fourth floor and she was on the third floor. When the elevator stopped at her floor she dragged her bags out and then turned to face me and said, "Meet you downstairs at 5:45 for a jog?" As the door was closing, I leaned to my left and quickly said, "Yes." And she was gone.

Chapter Twenty-One

Early the next morning, my internal alarm clock went off at 5:30. I lollygagged in bed for several minutes until I realized I had a 5:45 AM date, or rather a 5:45 appointment, or whatever it is I'm going to call this. So the question on my mind was this, how quickly could I dress and get downstairs?

As I was putting on my sweat pants, I realized I was in Florida and I had brought a sweat suit designed for the cold mornings in Alexandria, Virginia. I decided to wear the sweatpants and substitute a T-shirt for the hoodie. Rather than waiting for the elevator, I ran down the four flights of stairs, popping out into the lobby right at 5:45.

I stopped in my tracks when I saw Vivian standing before me in jogging shorts and a T-shirt; I'm clearly out of my class with this woman. I'll never criticize a woman again for bringing two bags on a trip! Before I could move, she was at the front door and holding it open for me. Embarrassed, I walked quickly outside, and as I did so she started running toward the jogging trail. I assumed she learned about the jogging trail the same way I did – there was a binder on the desk in my room that explained the amenities available to visiting officers.

She looked at her watch as I ran to catch up and began to jog as I fell in beside her. She turned her head and smiled at me and then turned back to concentrate on the trail. I soon recognized the pace she was setting would have me sweating like a racehorse at the end of 30 minutes! I was surprised when she didn't turn back after 15 minutes, but I stayed right beside her. After 20 minutes of jogging, she sped up and crossed in front of me and began to run back toward the BOQ. I say run because we had 10 minutes to cover the same distance it took us 20 minutes to jog. At least she smiled when she crossed in front of me.

Suffice it to say that I definitely needed a shower at the end of the run. Even though I exercised periodically over the last few months, it was obvious the desk in the Pentagon was not helping my physical condition. And I shook my head when I realized the intelligence part of my job description disappears when I was around her.

After a quick shower, I met Vivian downstairs and we walked across the Boulevard to the Officers' Club for breakfast. I had my usual two eggs over easy, hash browns, wheat toast with jelly, two strips of bacon, and a glass of orange juice. She had an English muffin and a small glass of orange juice. She looked at my breakfast and said, "A little hungry, are we?"

I smiled and said, "I always think better after a good meal."

During breakfast, I realized I had no idea how to get back to our planning building. As I finished my glass of orange juice I looked at Vivian and said, "I don't mind admitting I have no idea the best way is to get back to our building. Unless you have a better idea, I plan to drive to the main gate and look for the road that leads from there."

She looked at me with that permanent smile, and said, "Do you think they'll start without us?" I glance at my watch and realize that we're going to be late.

Without hesitation I responded, "Yes, I'm positive they will start without us!"

As we drove out, I saw a business jet on final approach and remarked to Vivian, "That looks like the same jet that brought us here." She looked out and shrugged her shoulders, as if to say that it didn't matter to us. I didn't say anything, but I had the feeling that it did matter to us.

We walked into the conference room, after once again having our IDs checked thoroughly, and we were, in fact, really late. I was reminded of an incident that happened when I was a young first lieutenant. I was ordered to make a presentation to a group of senior officers at a particular time and arrived two minutes late. The senior officer asked me if it was my habit to be late for meetings. As I started to explain that it wasn't my fault, he held up his hand and said, "Lieutenant, if you're not early and prepared at the appointed time, you're going to lose a war someday!" I've never forgotten that.

We walked through what I now thought of as "the map room" and into the small conference room. As we entered, Major Denton stopped talking and everyone looked at us. I looked at the group and said, "There is no excuse for being late, so I won't offer one; however, I do apologize for not being on time."

Commander Throckmorton looked at me and said, as he pointed to a new person in the room, "Let me introduce Senior Chief Aloysius O'Hara, who has been assigned to keep track of our needs and to make sure our resources are available when and where we need them. Senior Chief, this is Colonel Johnson, our commanding officer, and the lady is Dr. O'Brien, our intelligence analyst." The senior chief looked at me, so I nodded and said, "Senior Chief, welcome to the team." He didn't even smile.

The commander continued, "Major Denton was just beginning a discussion about the sniper teams. His first question was who has the authority to bring them here, since we're pulling teams from both the Army and Marine Corps? We had just decided his question applied not only to the sniper teams, but to all the resources we need to complete this mission successfully." Before I could answer, there was a commotion in the hallway.

As I cocked my ear to the sound, I recognized one of the voices. Now I knew why the business jet was flying back in. I smiled broadly as I walked to the door and opened it. Sure enough, there was Sergeant Garcia with her face right up in the face of the Marine guard. When she saw me, she turned her anger from the Marine guard to me. She said, somewhat loudly, "I might have known you were the one behind this!" I knew better than to interrupt.

"Last night, my phone starts to ring after my husband and I had gone to bed, and believe me, I was not ready to answer a phone call right at that moment! But it kept ringing every two minutes! When I finally answered the phone, some general tells me I've been assigned TDY and need to be on an airplane at Andrews Air Force Base at 4 AM; he didn't even tell me where I was going. Do you know what time I have to get up to be at Andrews at 4 AM? Then he tells me to plan to be gone about a week. Colonel, my daughter has a soccer game on Saturday, and if I'm not there, you're going to owe me big time!"

By this time, Commander Throckmorton had come out and was talking to the Marine guard. I overheard him tell the guard to add Sergeant Garcia's name to the approved list. He smiled at me, and said, "It's a good thing we decided not to pay attention to rank in here!" Shaking his head, he walked back into the conference room.

I motioned for Sergeant Garcia to follow the commander, and then I followed her back into the room. "Everyone, this is Master Sergeant Estelle Garcia." I turned to her as I said, "Her job is to write our mission plan based on our conversations. She will also keep us on track and make sure nothing falls between the cracks." I turned to her and said, "Sergeant, in this room rank is temporarily forgotten. So speak up if you feel the need. The only time rank is important is when I have to make a final decision."

I turned to Senior Chief O'Hara, and said, "Senior Chief, you and Master Sergeant Garcia are ordered to participate fully in our planning sessions and to ask questions whenever you have them. Is that clear to both of you?"

I received a "yes sir" from both of them. I turned to the whole group and said, "In case it hasn't been said before, everything we discuss in this room, and everything having to do with our mission, is classified top secret, need to know. In other words, you don't discuss this with anyone outside our little group without my specific approval.

"Just to be clear, let me give you an example. No one outside this group needs to know where we're going, when we're going, or what our target is. We'll brief people only as they are brought on board. Our cover story in Washington, as a matter of fact, is that we are going to collect intelligence about North Korea's capabilities in putting a nuclear device on top of a rocket. I'm told this is the story the President told the members of the intelligence committees in the House and Senate.

I paused and then said, "On a different but related topic, if there is anything you need and cannot get on your own authority, just let me know and we'll get the JCS to push it along. We have an admiral in the chairman's office who has been ordered by the President to give us anything we need to be successful.

"Speaking of orders, the President ordered me to fly to South Korea to meet with their intelligence community. I plan to leave sometime later today, meet with them as long as necessary, and then immediately fly back here."

Sergeant Garcia held up her hand, so I said, "During our planning meetings here, we're all equals, so no need to hold up your hand; just speak up."

"I forgot to tell you, sir, but the pilot told me to tell you that they wouldn't be ready to leave until after 1800. Something about they'd been up all night and needed to get some sleep."

I nodded to her and said, "Thanks." I turned back to the group and said, "Okay, let's get to work!"

And with that, the planning began in earnest.

It soon became obvious to me that they had already done a lot of thinking about this mission. As I thought about it, the men I had been introduced to were here because of their particular skills and experience. I listened intently to their discussions about different options and only occasionally asked a question.

I must admit, I was surprised at the depth these somewhat junior officers demonstrated at tactical planning. The basic outline of the mission, including a rather lengthy list of resources needed, such as personnel and equipment, was completed by about 10:30. At this point the discussion returned to the topic of the snipers. I was only vaguely aware of sniper competitions, but apparently the participants take it pretty seriously.

As they were discussing the results of this year's sniper competition, my cell phone vibrated in my pocket. Although inclined to ignore it, I remembered I was to talk with the Congressional Chief of Staff. I pulled the phone out, saw that it was Mr. Fontana, and interrupted the group by saying, "I have to take this call."

I walked into the map room and answered the call. "Good morning, Mr. Fontana."

His answer was brief and to the point. "I'll text you the secure phone number now. Call me in five minutes at that number."

So I followed suit and was also brief. "It'll take me 10 minutes or so to get to a secure phone; I'll call you as soon as I can." All I got in return was a click as he hung up. In a moment, my phone chirped to indicate receipt of a new text message.

I returned to the conference room, and of course my entrance interrupted their discussions, so I asked Commander Throckmorton a question. "Commander, where is the nearest secure phone I can use?"

He smiled and said, "Actually, Colonel, there is a secure phone downstairs. Just ask the yeoman at the desk." I thanked him and walked out. I patted my pocket as I walked past the Marine guards, remembering that I would have to show my ID again when I returned.

The yeoman showed me to a room that contained what appeared to be a large wooden box. It didn't quite reach to the ceiling, and I guessed it was about 8 feet on a side. As I entered, I could see that it was insulated and soundproofed. The yeoman flipped the light switch on and closed the door with a solid thunk. Inside were four chairs surrounding a small table, with an old STU-III encrypted telephone sitting right in the middle. Not the most modern of secure systems, but it still worked.

I waited seven more minutes, just on principle, then dialed the number Fontana had texted me. Playing his own form of one-upmanship, he let it ring four times before he answered. I heard the clicks and other noises as the encryption system was enabled. He then spoke, "Please confirm you have a secure connection."

"I have confirmation of a secure connection." What else could I say?

"Lieutenant Colonel Johnson," he started, "The President told the House intelligence committee that he has placed you in charge of an effort to discover the veracity of the North Korean boast that they have a new long-range ballistic missile with a nuclear warhead capable of reaching the West Coast of the United States. As you know, the law requires both intelligence committees be informed prior to initiating HUMINT operations in a foreign country. The congressman asked me to collect specific information regarding this new initiative."

He continued, "So that I may inform the congressman, and so that he may inform the other members of the House intelligence committee, please summarize your efforts to this point."

Being in the intelligence business, I was well aware of the law that he referred to. However, he left out the part that says the President, not anyone else, is required to inform the intelligence committees.

I was going to have to tread carefully here. If he was simply an overzealous congressional functionary, I did not want to offend him. On the other hand, if he was the source of the leaks, I did not want to give him information that could be detrimental to our mission. In addition, in keeping with my commitment to the FBI Director, I had to give him a false lead and make it sound real.

I must've hesitated too long for the Chief of Staff, because he continued, "We are aware of your background, Colonel. When I briefed the congressman, he was sad to hear of the loss of your wife. We know you served two different tours in South Korea as a staff intelligence officer." The way he said *staff* made it sound like a dirty word. "We also know that you spent a year in Afghanistan where you earned a Purple Heart and the Silver Star gathering intelligence on the front lines; I suppose that makes you a hero in some eyes."

If he was trying to irritate me, he was now succeeding.

"We also learned that your commanding officer is not aware of your new assignment, but he did tell us that you have been selected for promotion to full Colonel in the next promotion cycle. I hope your present mission does not have a negative impact on your promotion."

While I understand and agree with the necessity of a civilian directed military, in my short time in the Pentagon I had acquired an aversion to the meddling of politicians. If his veiled threats were intended to intimidate me, then he had not learned enough about me!

Nonetheless, it was necessary that I plant the misinformation discussed in the secret meeting yesterday. I responded, "Mr. Fontana, in brief, I can tell you that our planning meetings are continuing and we have not yet recommended a course of action for the President's consideration. You certainly understand that it is a matter of national security that we positively learn whether the North Koreans have in fact developed a nuclear package for long-range ballistic missiles.

"I will be speaking with my South Korean counterparts to ascertain if they have discovered new intelligence on this topic."

He interrupted and bluntly asked, "Will you recommend that a SEAL team be sent into North Korea?"

I immediately responded, "Sending Americans into North Korea would be a very dangerous proposition and should not be lightly entertained. That's the reason we have surveillance satellites that can take a picture of a man in a parking lot and read the lettering on his jacket. In any case, you know I am not at liberty to discuss that with you. However, we both know that Navy SEALs do not have the technical expertise to answer the question about nuclear capabilities, so you can draw your own conclusions.

"For the time being, my team will continue our planning and deliberations and eventually recommend a course of action to the President. I'm sure he will then share that with the intelligence committee."

In a more conciliatory tone the Chief of Staff responded, "Colonel, it's not our intent to go around the President. We simply want to ensure there is not another incident like in the past; you know, where the military does something and the President pleads ignorance of their actions. I'm sure we'll talk again." And then all I heard was *click buzz* as he hung up on me. Going self-righteous did not endear him to me at all.

I sat for a few moments and pondered our conversation. Then I picked up the phone and asked the operator to get me a secure connection with the office of the FBI Director. When I was told he was not in his office, I asked to be connected to him wherever he might be. When he came on the line, I briefly summarized the phone call and promised to keep him apprised of any additional conversations. He must've been in a hurry because he simply said thank you and hung up.

I turned off the light as I left the secure room and then waved to the yeoman as I passed the lobby to return to the meeting upstairs.

Chapter Twenty-Two

Unknown to us at SOCOM, there was another meeting taking place in the White House at about the same time. The participants included the President; his Chief of Staff, Jefferson Jackson; the Director of the CIA, Harmon Sanders; the Director of the FBI, Ernest Hansen; General George Underhill, the Chairman of the Joint Chiefs of Staff; and Dr. Richardson, the National Security Advisor. Also in attendance was Henry Williams, the Secretary of Homeland Security.

As he passed the secretary's alcove on his way to the meeting, FBI Director Hansen was told that he had an important phone call waiting. He excused himself, and went to take the call. It was a brief call, and he was back with the group in just a couple of minutes.

Although the meeting had not been generally announced, the White House rumor mill was already speculating about the reasons for a meeting of such senior government officials. What also made this meeting so unusual was that it was being held in the Oval Office rather than the Situation Room.

"Dr. Richardson, Gentlemen," began the President, "I've taken the liberty of inviting my Chief of Staff to join us for this meeting. To get right to the point, it's important we acknowledge the political implications of our response to the North Korean threat." From the reaction of the others, it was obvious to everyone but the President that not everyone agreed with his statement; nonetheless, he continued, "The House and Senate intelligence committees are aware of the threat and I have officially informed them that we plan to be more aggressive in determining if they, the North Koreans that is, have in fact developed a nuclear package that can fit on the top of a ballistic missile. Without saying so directly, I've let them believe that our options include putting Americans on the ground in North Korea.

"Jeff is of the opinion that I should inform the intelligence committees that we are sending a team of snipers to destroy the new rocket they have been bragging about recently."

Before he could continue, General Underhill, who was not known for mincing words, spoke up. "Mr. President, I think it would be a mistake to prematurely inform them; we are aware of certain leaks, leaks that I personally believe came from a member of one of the committees."

The President smiled, and said, "General, that's why Ern and Harmon are in this meeting. Let's hear their report." Turning to the FBI Director, he said, "Ern, why don't you tell us what you discovered."

"Yes, sir. But let me back up a little bit so everyone is aware of what's been going on." Nodding at CIA Director Harmon Sanders, he said, "Based on material the NSA discovered and provided to the CIA who then provided it to us at the FBI, we established a special investigative team at FBI headquarters six weeks ago which is looking into the leak of classified information. We've kept that information closely held because we didn't know where the leak was coming from. However, based on other information the CIA provided, we believe the leak is in one of four places: the White House, one of the two intelligence committees, or the Pentagon.

"We've taken steps that will allow us to more closely focus on at least the location of the leak. Once we know that, we can then begin in earnest to track down the traitor. In fact, I took a phone call as I was coming in to this meeting that should help us determine that."

Mr. Jackson interrupted and said, "We will need to know immediately once you determine the source of the leak." And before he could continue, the FBI Director interrupted.

"Mr. Jackson, the reason we've kept this investigation closely held is so we do not tip our hand to those responsible for the leaks. In case it's not clearly understood by everyone here, no one outside this room is to be informed of this investigation. The national security of the United States is at stake here; political implications will have to take back seat for the time being!"

The President spoke up at this time and said, "Gentlemen, let's not argue among ourselves. Ern, I'm sure Jeff understands the importance of not discussing this with anyone." The President emphasized his point by looking directly at his Chief of Staff.

Looking back at the group, the President said, "Moving on, gentlemen. George, I understand Admiral Harrison has a team at SOCOM working on a plan." He looked directly at the general, wordlessly inviting him to elaborate.

"Mr. President, the planning team has settled on what they believe is a workable plan, and we expect to have their basic outline of the mission sometime early tomorrow. My office is coordinating the efforts to bring all the resources together; in fact, Admiral Harrison is already signing orders on my authority. In keeping with the confidential nature of the mission, we will issue orders to individuals and units without telling them what the specific mission is. I'm sure that will generate some pushback from commanders in the field, but we're calling it a black ops training exercise, just to minimize questions."

Anxious to move the meeting along, the President said, "Thanks, General. Let me see that mission outline as soon as you can." General Underhill merely nodded.

Turning to the FBI Director, the President said, "Keeping in mind what we've already said about security, please let me know as soon as possible when you have identified our traitor." Taking his cue from General Underhill, Ernest Hansen also nodded.

Continuing, the President turned to his Secretary of Homeland Security and said, "Hank, the reason you're here is because if North Korea continues to make threats to launch a ballistic missile toward the West Coast, we will want you to assure the public that we have plans in place to ensure their safety." Turning to the Chairman of the Joint Chiefs of Staff, he said, "And George, we'll want you on the podium right next to him to confirm we have the capability to knock down anything they may launch."

"Now," the President continued, "Let's return to my original question. What should I tell the intelligence committees?"

After some hesitation, everyone turned to the FBI Director. Seeing he was on the hot seat, he spoke up. "Mr. President, I recommend you not tell them any more than you have already. At least not yet. Until we plug the leak, which I feel optimistic about, just tell them you're still in the planning stages. No details."

The President looked around to each of the men in the Oval Office, and with the exception of his Chief of Staff, everyone nodded or gave a sign of agreement. He turned to Dr. Richardson and said, "Since you like to keep the big picture in mind, do you have anything to add?"

She looked directly at the President, and after a short pause, said, "I think that's good advice, Mr. President."

He then said, "Okay. For now, we drag our feet!" Turning to his Chief of Staff, he said, "Jeff, when you get the inevitable phone calls from the committee chairmen, just tell them we're making progress but there is nothing new to report at this time."

Chapter Twenty-Three

Although it was after 9 o'clock in the evening in Pyongyang, Colonel General Kim Hyun-woo was still in his office. The Director of the North Korean intelligence service was a widower and had no specific reason to return to his spartan apartment. But tonight, the main reason he was still in his office at this late hour was that he was expecting another message from his most successful spy.

He still wasn't sure whether his niece was unusually lucky or extremely talented. Either way, he could hardly believe the report when he learned she was working in the office of a U.S. congressman who was on the House intelligence committee. He was further amazed when she reported the substance of conversations with the congressman's Chief of Staff. While he may have speculated where these conversations took place, her reports did not indicate a place. He smiled as he realized it didn't matter to him, one way or the other!

After a polite knock, the general's military aide entered his office. Looking up, the general quietly asked, "Is there a message?"

His aide bowed slightly and said, "Yes, General, there is a new message. It is a long message and is still being decoded. However, I can tell you that she used the special phrase indicating it is an important message. We should have it delivered in just a few minutes."

Although it was highly unusual for a senior general in the North Korean Army to ask a mere major to sit in his presence, he said "Please, Major, sit while we wait for the message." Although not related, General Kim found it difficult not to treat him as the son he never had. Accustomed to the idiosyncrasies of this particular general, the major sat in one of the side chairs, but he sat at attention!

While they waited, the general thought about his brother, the father of his favorite spy. Employed as a senior manager at the Korean Central News Agency, the state news service, he was under the impression his daughter was serving in a cyber-warfare unit based near the east coast. A female lieutenant on the general's staff preserved that façade by maintaining regular email communications with him.

A knock on his door interrupted his thoughts.

His aide jumped up and opened the door just enough to reach out for the envelope a courier was delivering. He closed the door and brought the envelope to the general, who nodded and smiled as he noted it was tightly sealed. It was rumored that he had sent a junior officer to military prison for violating his strict sense of security. That one incident had been enough to ensure compliance by others in his command.

He used a beautifully carved jade letter opener to slice the envelope and withdraw the two single-spaced pages. As he read, his frown became a smile, and as he read more his smile became even broader. Before he reached the second page, and without looking up, he said to his aide, "Major, call the Ministry of the People's Armed Forces and tell them I must speak with the commanding general right away. Tell them I have information the general will want to see before tomorrow."

As the major left his office, General Kim continued reading. He could hardly believe his good fortune. Not only was his niece working in the office of the U.S. congressman, but she now revealed that her most recent information came from her pillow talk with the married Chief of Staff to that congressman.

In this message, she reported that the Chief of Staff had shared the substance of a conversation he had with the congressman indicating that just the evening before, Washington time, the President of the United States had briefed the intelligence committee on his fears about North Korea's long-range nuclear missile capabilities. Her report further indicated that the President said he was going to authorize the U.S. military to undertake additional intelligence gathering efforts, even if that included secretly putting U.S. soldiers on North Korean soil.

She continued by reminding the general that U.S. law required the U.S. President inform the intelligence committee prior to ordering soldiers to enter another sovereign country. She was certain her source would tell her if that happened. She ended her message with a request to send a report more often than only once a week, as security protocol required.

Prior to leaving North Korea, she'd been told not to send a message more often than once a week, in order to diminish the chances of being discovered. She must have high expectations of learning more from her highly placed source if she was willing to expose herself to the risk of discovery.

As he was finishing the message, his aide quietly reentered his office. When he looked up, the major told him that the chairman of the Ministry would see him at his home in 30 minutes. "Excellent! Call my driver and tell him to bring my car to the front. Immediately after that, send a message to Captain Pak with just these two words: 'request approved.'" Looking up to the major and smiling, he said, "I shall not need you further today."

As the major departed, the general carefully placed the two pages of the message into a small briefcase. He then retrieved his hat and left for his meeting with the commanding general of the North Korean Armed Services.

Chapter Twenty-Four

Back in the conference room at MacDill, it was evident from the exhaustion displayed on our faces and in our voices that our decision to order pizza and work through lunch was taking its toll. However, we had made much progress. We had ironed out the basic framework that would allow us to successfully complete our assigned mission. I turned to Sergeant Garcia and said, "The basic outline we've given you of our mission is all we want you to send to Admiral Harrison; do not include any other details. I will hand carry the mission details to Washington and deliver them only to Admiral Harrison."

I turned to Chief O'Hara with a questioning look and said, "Senior Chief, as a matter of curiosity, where do you keep the notes from our discussions?"

"I leave them right here in that file cabinet," he said as he pointed to the far corner. I looked in the direction he was pointing and saw an old beat up, clearly obsolete, four-drawer fireproof file cabinet. I raised my eyebrows as I looked back at him, so he said, "The cabinet may not look like much, Colonel, but those two Marines outside are paid to keep this room secure. In my book, that's better than any secure vault." I smiled and nodded, satisfied that the need-to-know nature of our work was secure.

I glanced at my watch, and said, "It's time for me to head to the BOQ to get my gear so I can begin my excursion to South Korea. I'll be gone about three days, so let's plan a tabletop briefing on Friday afternoon. Since special ops is not my forte, I'm sure I'll have plenty of questions; we'll use Saturday morning for a Q & A. Then I'll fly to Disneyland East, as Washington, D.C. is sometimes called, to brief Admiral Harrison.

"I plan to carry with me on Saturday your recommendations for personnel and other resources, so please have those ready. Admiral

Harrison has promised to issue the appropriate orders under the signature of the Chairman of the Joint Chiefs of Staff as soon as he has our recommendations."

I looked at Commander Throckmorton as I said, "If I learn anything I think may have an impact on your planning, I'll call you directly, Commander." He smiled and nodded.

"Dr. O'Brien, why don't you drive with me so you can drop me off at the airplane and keep the car." She also smiled and nodded. With that, we both stood and left the conference room.

As she drove back to the BOQ, she asked, "Do you really think we'll have a plan put together by Friday afternoon?"

I looked at her profile, and answered, "Vivian, I think these men had most of the plan already in mind before we arrived. Now it's just a matter of working out the details and ensuring all the pieces are in place. So yes, I think you'll find a complete plan in place before I get back."

I pulled out my phone, and said to her, "May I have your cell phone number, please?" as I scrolled to Major Green's contact information. When she gave it to me, I texted his information to her and said, "I just texted you Major Green's information. What do you think about putting your contact in touch with him so they can work together at reviewing the satellite imagery?"

After we pulled into the parking lot, she turned to me as she smiled and said, "I was wondering how you were going to get my telephone number!" I actually blushed as I left the car and rushed upstairs to get my gear. When I returned, I saw that she had moved to the driver's seat and turned around so we could make an easy exit. We were both quiet as we drove to the airfield, until she said, "If something comes up at this end, how do we get in touch with you?"

I thought for a moment and then said, "When I get to Major Kim's office in Seoul, I'll call the commander on a secure line and give him the number. However, I think Commander Throckmorton would rather choke on a cherry pit than admit he needs my help." She laughed out loud as we stopped at the flight operations building.

As I started to get out of the car, I looked over at her smiling face and realized how natural it would be for me to lean over and give her a good-bye kiss. But I restrained myself and merely said, "See you on Friday." She simply waved. As I walked to the airplane, I wondered where that thought had come from!

The long flight to Seoul, the capital of the Republic of Korea, or as we refer to it, South Korea, went just about as anticipated. Although I had forgotten to ask about supper plans on the long eight-hour flight to Anchorage, Sergeant Mitchell had the foresight to bring some extra catering for me. We landed in Anchorage about 10 PM local time; the plan was that after refueling and a flight crew change, I would continue the next leg to Seoul, which was also about eight hours long.

While I was on the ground in Anchorage, I used the phone in base operations to call my friend Major Kim, and let him know I was about nine hours away. He told me that Soo-jin was excited to see me again and hoped I would have time to join them for a meal at home. He also shared with me that senior military officers were anxious about the President's plans in reaction to North Korea's taunts about its new long-range missile, and were very interested to meet with me. He told me that because of the late hour of my arrival, a car had been authorized to pick me up. Fortunately for me, I've long since mastered the art of sleeping on an airplane, so I expected to arrive well rested.

As I was walking back to the airplane, I remembered that Admiral Harrison had ordered me to call when I arrived in Alaska. I turned around and went back to the telephone inside base operations. Then I hesitated; it was almost 3 AM in Washington, D.C. But, orders are orders, so I dialed his number. He answered on the first ring. "About time you called, Colonel!"

I must've been tired because I answered, "Just following orders, Admiral!"

He paused and then said, "Okay, it's late so I'll make this short. I got the summary of your operational plan; thanks for that. I briefed the President and the chairman. I hope you know what you're doing,

Colonel, because if anything goes wrong, you can kiss your career goodbye."

I know I was brain dead, because my response was, "Admiral, I wouldn't be the first lieutenant colonel working in the White House to be abandoned by his superiors."

"Humph! Watch your manners, Colonel! On a brighter note, if you pull this off, you'll be able to name your next assignment." I chose not to respond to this, mostly because I couldn't think of anything intelligent to say!

"One last item, when you meet with the South Koreans, remember you'll be representing the White House, so don't do anything stupid. And don't make promises you can't keep." A short pause and then he asked, "When will you be back?"

"The plan right now, Admiral, is for me to be back at the planning table at SOCOM on Friday and back in D.C. on Saturday."

"All right, let's plan to touch base again on Friday. Good night and have a good flight." And with that he was gone.

◆ ◆ ◆

Such was the great working relationship between the U.S. and South Korean forces that a South Korean staff car was waiting for me on the parking ramp when I landed in Seoul. As I was leaving the airplane, I leaned in the cockpit and told the pilot to leave his contact information with the on-duty officer at base operations and that when I knew when I wanted to leave, I would contact him that way. I stepped off the airplane into a light rain and was met by a South Korean sergeant who grabbed my bag and led me to the car.

Imagine my surprise at this late hour (it was almost midnight in Korea) when I discovered Major Kim climbing from the car! He threw his arms around me and said in English, "Robert, it is so good to see you again!"

I responded, "It *is* good to see you, but isn't it past your bedtime?" And then I returned his manly hug.

"Yes, it certainly is! But Soo-jin insisted I meet you and bring you home; she rearranged the children so you can have a room of your own while you are here." Moving toward the car, he said, "Let's get out of the rain!"

The sergeant, of course, had already gotten out of the rain. As soon as we settled in the back, he started driving. We turned toward each other and Major Kim said, "I have to thank you for the official car; normally I ride a bicycle to work or, especially in inclement weather, Soo-jin drops me off. Because you are an honored guest, General Cho wanted to see that you were well taken care of.

"Even though it is late, he asked that we meet at 8 o'clock in the morning. Everyone is anxious that your American President is going to do something rash, something which will irritate the North Koreans and give them an excuse to create another incident. They want to hear from you as quickly as possible."

I turned to him and said, "Jin-ho, I had hoped to have some discreet meetings with you. I'm not sure how much I can share with your generals."

"Oh, not to worry, Robert! My generals, as you call them, can be very discreet. I can assure you there will be no leaks from our meetings." He laughed, and said, "In fact, our meetings tomorrow, or today that is, will take place in a hotel suite in downtown Seoul. We are all going to wear civilian clothes; it will look like another meeting of harried businessmen."

"I should've thought to bring a civilian suit."

"No worries. We'll stop in the morning and you can add to our local economy!" We both smiled!

Soo-jin must have been watching for us because she was standing in the door when we arrived at their home. I noted she was smart enough not to stand out in the rain! We removed our shoes just outside the door, and after we were inside, Soo-jin gave me a Western-style hug while Jin-ho frowned. He was still a traditionalist and preferred that women give men a simple bow. Although I knew she enjoyed being called Suzie, I was aware of Jin-ho's preference so I said in Korean, "Kim Soo-jin, it is good to see you again. You look well; in fact, you look great at this hour. How are the children?"

She smiled and bowed at the compliment. "Everyone is well! Thank you for asking. But enough of these pleasantries. I know you have important meetings early tomorrow, so let's not stand here talking." I looked at Jin-ho and raised my eyebrows; he said, "I cannot keep secrets from my wife!"

Their home was much as I remembered it; large for a Korean home, it had seemed small when all four children were at home. Now with two kids away at college, it was probably just right for a family of four. It was decorated in the Korean style, but I saw more evidence this time of Soo-jin's fondness for Western art. Jin-ho must be weakening!

We sat around their kitchen table for a few minutes and talked. I made polite conversation, including asking Soo-jin, "Now that the children are mostly grown, how do you stay busy?"

She surprised me with her answer. "I have taken up a Western hobby. I saw you looking at the walls as we walked through our living room; the oil paintings you saw came from my own hand. I've been studying European-style oil painting for almost a year now."

I remarked, "I did notice them and thought they had been purchased, probably without Jin-ho's knowledge!" She laughed, but he did not. "They are quite good!"

"Thank you, Robert." She was clearly pleased with my compliment. "Now go to bed so you can get some rest. My husband will be up at 6 AM, anxious to start his day. We moved the boys into one room so you can have a room for yourself; they are excited to see you tomorrow as well." She pointed down the hall and said, "I'm sure you remember where everything is. There is a light on in your room. I'll have breakfast ready in the morning." And with that we each went our separate way.

I fell asleep as soon as my head hit the pillow. The next thing I remember was Jin-ho at my bedroom door, loudly calling in Korean, "Wake-up sleepyhead! You can't save the world by sleeping in!"

As I rolled over, he said "Breakfast in 20 minutes!" I opened my eyes and looked at him, and saw that he was already fully dressed. I glanced at my watch and saw that he had let me sleep in until seven. I groaned and pushed the blankets off as I maneuvered to the edge of the bed.

Eighteen minutes later I walked into the kitchen in my sweatpants and T-shirt, as I pursued the pleasant aroma coming from that direction. Their high school boys were already at the kitchen table. Min-joon was a high school senior, and his brother Joo-won was a junior. I knew from emails that both were near the head of their respective classes. Their oldest sibling, a girl named Su-bin, was a senior at Seoul National University and living on campus; their older brother, Kun-woo, was attending Korea Advanced Institute of Science and Technology.

They stood as I came in and honored me with a bow, which I returned. Following their family tradition, we waited for Jin-ho to take his place before we sat down. He offered a simple prayer of thanksgiving and invoked blessings on us all. After he began eating, which was the signal that we could all begin, we dug into the mouthwatering breakfast.

Immediately after breakfast, the boys left for their high school; it would be a brisk 20-minute walk. Shortly after that, the sergeant showed up with the staff car for our ride to downtown Seoul where our meeting would be held. On the way, we stopped at a department store where I purchased tan slacks and a blue blazer, along with a white shirt and a raspberry colored tie. Not exactly a business suit but it would have to do.

As we approach the third floor conference room at the hotel, I notice several serious looking young men in ill-fitting suits outside both entrances. It looked like we would have adequate security for our meetings. There were only five men in the conference room, and I was introduced to each of them. Two generals and two colonels, and a civilian from the Agency for National Security Planning. The NSP in South Korea is equivalent to the CIA and FBI in the United States.

From my last tour in South Korea, I knew that General Cho, who was sitting at the head of the table, was the commanding general of the South Korean Army intelligence service, and General Chang was introduced as the deputy commander of the South Korean Army. I knew they were the same rank, but I wondered if General Cho reported to General Chang or if he reported directly to the Army commander in chief. The two colonels were introduced as senior aides to each general, respectively.

I still hadn't made up my mind what I would tell them about our plans when General Cho, speaking in the Korean language, addressed me directly, "Colonel Johnson, we welcome you to South Korea once again. We appreciate the effort you have made to meet with us in person. We understand your country's concern regarding the belligerent bragging of our neighbor to the north. We are interested to hear your report.

"As you can understand, we are concerned about the number of missiles they have aimed at our cities. We try not to upset them to the point where they might unleash their obsolete but effective missiles against us. It is of great interest to us then, to learn of any plans our allies may have that could disturb that delicate balance.

"We were surprised but pleased to learn from your Admiral Harrison that you represent the White House. Within the limits of your authority, please share with us how your President expects to deal with the unruly children to the north."

I hesitated just a moment, and then stood. I was not aware they knew I was representing the White House. I responded in his native language. "General, thank you for your courtesy. It is true that I am here under orders of the President of the United States. I will tell you that my orders from him include only three requirements. First, do nothing that would upset the delicate balance between the countries we call North and South Korea. Second, whatever we do in the field, leave absolutely no evidence that leads to South Korea or to the United States. And third, perhaps the most complex of all, it is the President's considered opinion that it is time to remove their bragging rights once and for all."

I paused as they looked at one another and then as everyone looked at General Cho. He addressed me without smiling, "How do you propose to meet all those requirements?"

Not yet wanting to share our detailed plan, I said to the group, "Another reason for my visit is to obtain from your intelligence services any pertinent information that may assist us in meeting those requirements and determining an appropriate course of action."

At this point the civilian from the NSP spoke up, "Pardon the interruption, but why do you believe we know any more than your own intelligence services? Besides, you have a dozen satellites that are so capable you can determine the value of paper currency being used to purchase from a street vendor."

I smiled as I turned to face him, "I believe that when a mechanic is faced with a challenge, he does not ignore any tool in his toolbox. Furthermore, we would be foolish to believe that we're the only ones capable of acquiring information on this topic. The enemy is at your doorstep, so you have a vested interest in knowing them better than anyone else."

As several heads nodded, I turned back to the general and said, "General, there are some things we know we will not do. We will not attack with cruise missiles or laser guided bombs from either manned or unmanned aircraft. We also know we will not make an attack by helicopter or by parachute. We also don't plan to march in through the DMZ or go in through a tunnel underneath. Those are all unacceptable approaches.

"However, we believe we have discovered a weakness in their security." I then paused before continuing. "Before I continue, there is something else I must discuss with you. And I would ask that you do not discuss what I'm about to say outside this room." I looked at each man before continuing. "We have discovered that certain sensitive secrets have been transmitted outside the United States and believe they have ended up in North Korea. We are pursuing reasonable steps to stop that leak, whether it be a traitor or a spy.

"With our national security at risk, the President has ordered me not to share our plans with anyone, either in the United States, or with any of our allies. Until we find the source of that leak, we're going to be very careful. And yes, I do understand the political implications of that order; it gives the White House plausible deniability should our plan go awry."

This statement generated a heated discussion around the table. I took my seat and quietly listened to the arguments being thrown to and fro. Finally, General Cho held up his hands, quieting the discussion, and turned to me and said, "You ask us to share sensitive information with you while admitting that you have a security leak in your own country; you also tell us that you do not trust us. How can we proceed?"

I look at him and quietly said, "I ask that you share your information with me, an individual you can hold accountable, and not a bureaucracy where no one is accountable." I looked at the NSP officer and said, "The fact that you have a large and active NSP tells us that you have your own security concerns within your bureaucracy." Another pause, "This also gives your President the ability to claim plausible deniability."

General Chang now spoke up, "The North Koreans, as you call them, do not care about plausible deniability; in their eyes, it is guilt by association. So, we understand your President wants to do something significant, but for now all you know is what you will not do." A short pause and then, "Do I understand correctly?"

"Yes sir, you do."

He looked to the other participants and then looked back at me and said, "Colonel, if you would be so kind as to wait outside, we will discuss your proposition and give you an answer shortly."

"Thank you, General; if it's all right with you, I will wait in the hotel lobby." He nodded, so I left the room and headed for the lobby. It had been quite a while since I had read a Korean language newspaper or magazine, so I thought I'd practice my reading skills. Imagine my surprise when, after a while, I looked at the large grandfather clock and discovered that two and a half hours had passed.

I heard the elevator ding and looked in that direction. I saw Major Kim walking toward me with a grim expression. He began speaking as I stood up; "Robert, you left quite a challenge for them. General Cho and General Chang are not in agreement about what we should do; the impasse was finally settled by a phone call to the Prime Minister's office.

General Chang does not like losing! Nonetheless, we have been discussing ground rules for opening up our intelligence files to you.

"Let us return, and those ground rules will be explained to you." With that, he turned and walked toward the elevators. I hurried to catch up. In the elevator, he turned to me and quietly said, "I hope you realize that my career could be affected by how you react to their requirements." What could I say? I simply nodded.

I was very familiar with the vagaries of military service at this level. Although my friend had been selected for lieutenant colonel, I knew that in the South Korean Army, a proposed promotion was just that; it was not a done deal until you had the actual written orders in your hand. Even a minor faux pas could have a major effect on the career of a senior officer. It was pretty much the same in the Army I served.

Back in the hotel conference room, it was explained to me that Major Kim would be my point of contact and that he was responsible for sharing top-secret intelligence with me. His orders had been made clear about what he could share and what he could not; if I wanted something outside his authority to share, he would bring the request to General Cho.

Furthermore, although I was free to use the information to comply with the President's demands, I was not to share the information, nor how it was received, with anyone in our bureaucracy nor with any other country. In other words, they were holding me to my promise not to share with the leaking American bureaucracy. In addition, they wanted my promise to notify Major Kim as soon as we discovered the identification of the spy.

As soon as I gave them my solemn oath as an officer of the United States Army, the meeting was adjourned. After the others left, I turned to Jin-ho and asked, "Now what?"

He smiled and said, "Now we go home for lunch and to change clothes, and then we go to my office."

Chapter Twenty-Five

Meanwhile, on the other side of the world, three people were in the Oval Office just after 7 o'clock at night – the President, his Chief of Staff, and the National Security Advisor. The President had just expressed his concern about his duty to brief the two Congressional intelligence committees. "Dr. Richardson, when do you expect to hear more about the mission planning?"

"Mr. President, since Admiral Harrison briefed us, I've learned that Colonel Johnson expects to be back from South Korea at the end of the week, and he plans to brief us in person sometime on Saturday." Looking directly at Jefferson Jackson, she continued, "I recommend we wait until we actually have the benefit of his briefing before you update the intelligence committees."

Jefferson Jackson interrupted, "Mr. President, Congressman Singleton's Chief of Staff has called several times, suggesting that you are stonewalling the intelligence committee and insisting on an update."

Dr. Richardson turned back to the President and said, "Mr. President, may I remind you that Director Hansen requested you not update the committees until they've had more time to ferret out the traitor or the spy. And you agreed to his request."

After a brief pause, she continued, "Can you afford to take the risk if the leak is coming from one of those committees?"

The Chief of Staff responded before the President could, "The real risk is that someone from one of those committees might suggest to the press that the President is not properly briefing the intelligence committees as the law requires. We have to say something to them, and the sooner the better!"

The President stood and walked to his desk and then upon reflection said, "Jeff, I think you're right. The political impact could be horrific." Turning to Dr. Richardson, he said, "Sarah, call Director Hansen tonight and tell him that late tomorrow I will be briefing the two intelligence committee chairmen. But you are right about what I should tell them. I will only tell them that we are making progress and that Colonel Johnson, who I told them about last time, is meeting with the South Korean intelligence people and won't be back until Saturday. That should keep them happy for a few more days."

Turning to his Chief of Staff, he said, "Call the two committee chairmen and invite them to a meeting here in the Oval Office at 5 o'clock tomorrow afternoon. If Congressman Singleton or his Chief of Staff calls back, you can tell him about the meeting, but remind him the meeting is for the committee chairmen only.

"Thank you both; have a good evening." And the President left his office for a late dinner in the residence with his wife.

Chapter Twenty-Six

Congressman Paul Singleton was at home spending a quiet evening with his wife; in fact, they were watching a rerun of *The African Queen* when his phone vibrated with a text message from Congressman Hoag, who was the chairman of the House intelligence committee. He squeezed his wife's hand, excused himself from their home theater, and stepped into his home office. She merely smiled at this very frequent occurrence.

The message was brief, typical of Congressman Hoag: *chairmen-only intelligence briefing oval office tomorrow 5 PM.*

He shook his head as he thought to himself, "Typical of the President to keep the intelligence committee in the dark. A meeting at 5 PM means the full committee won't meet until the next morning." Shaking his head, he decided to call his good friend and Chief of Staff, Mike Fontana.

Thinking he would be home at this time of the night, he punched Mike's home number on his cell phone and waited for it to ring. He wasn't surprised when Karen, Mike's beautiful wife, answered the phone. "Hi Karen, could I speak with Mike?"

"Oh, hi Paul, he's not home yet. He said he had a project to finish up at the office. Try him on his cell." Before he could respond, she laughed and said, "All these extra hours you're working him are wearing him out; you ought to give him a break!"

"Yes, I will. I'll give him a call on his cell. Thanks, have a good night."

Wondering what special project he might be working on, he dialed Mike's cell phone. It rang and rang and rang and finally went to voicemail. Almost hanging up, he decided to leave a message; "Mike, call me as soon as you get this; thanks, bye."

As he started to return to his wife and the movie, his phone vibrated again. He stepped back into his home office when he saw the call was from his Chief of Staff.

"Hello Mike, are you still at the office?"

After a brief pause he answered, "Well, I was, but I'm on my way home now. Did you need something?"

Dismissing the uneasy feeling he had, he said, "I just wanted to let you know that I've had a text message from Congressman Hoag. Apparently the President has invited him and Senator Bollinger to a meeting at the White House at 5 PM tomorrow." Senator Jack Bollinger was the chairman of the Senate intelligence committee.

After a moment's thought, Mike Fontana said, "Pretty slick scheduling; that means the two committees can't meet until the next day. Another delaying tactic! Our President is getting pretty good at that. Do you think he'll have anything important to share with them?"

"Since you told me that Colonel Johnson is still down at Special Operations Command, I would guess there will be nothing new to report." After a moment's pause he said, "Why don't you pretend we don't know about this meeting and give your friend Jeff Jackson a call to see what he has to say? His answer might be interesting." Before Mike could answer, he continued, "But don't call me back tonight unless he has something new to report."

There was another pause before Mike answered, "Sounds like a plan! I'll call him right now and then I'll see you at the office early in the morning. Talk to you later."

The congressman looked in surprise at his phone to confirm his friend had hung up on him! After a moment's thought, he shrugged his shoulders and returned to his movie. His favorite part of the movie was coming up soon; the part where they confront the German ship captain. He also knew he needed to be next to his wife holding hands while they watched Katharine Hepburn removing the leeches from Humphrey Bogart's torso and legs!

Meanwhile, the congressman's Chief of Staff laid his phone on the nightstand and turned back to face the beautiful woman who had just been in his arms. Julie Endicott had heard everything the Congressman had said during the brief phone call with her lover. She caressed his cheek and said, "You better make that phone call before you forget all about it!"

She glanced at him as he initiated the phone call. She was thinking that he was tall and physically attractive, and his smile was like a magnet as he looked down at her. She enjoyed the physical attraction, and almost enjoyed the physical contact – almost. She realized she could never love such a weak and vain man; a man who not only cheats on his wife but also betrays the trust his country had placed in him. Troubled by that thought for just a moment, she realized that duty required she smile back at him. And so she did.

She had previously discovered that he enjoyed her head resting on his chest as he made phone calls. She was surprised the first time he used the phone in bed because she could hear both sides of the conversation. She was astounded at his disregard of even the simplest security efforts. No wonder the President was unwilling to tell Congress anything!

She was further amazed as she lay listening to the phone call when even the President's Chief of Staff freely told him about tomorrow's meeting. When he laid the phone down, she said, "You told the congressman that you were on your way home; if he tries to call you there in a little bit, you don't want him to be curious if your wife says you're not there."

He turned and reached for her and said, "Another few minutes won't matter!"

Chapter Twenty-Seven

The scrub brush I'm hiding in, on this wretched mountainside in North Korea, does not allow me to stretch out fully, so I'm laying here in kind of a modified C shape, almost a fetal position. The SEAL team leader on my hill, Lieutenant Carrollton, told me back at SOCOM it's simply a matter of knowing how to relax. He smiled when he told me that at least we wouldn't have to worry about sand flies in North Korea.

I don't know how the snipers and the SEAL teams do it! Sergeant Parker and Sergeant Harris are only a few meters away from me, and I have neither heard nor seen a single movement from them. Even though I have a soft cushion on my chair at the Pentagon, I still bounce up several times during the day just to stretch my legs. Just a couple of laps around my desk would feel pretty good right now!

I flex and stretch as much as I dare and am satisfied when only a little snow falls on my parka. Because it would take all day to transport the rocket to the launch gantry, and thinking I might have to be up all night keeping an eye on the activities below us, I have been hoping to get some sleep during the day. I know the SEAL teams on either side of me and the sniper team are all accustomed to sleeping in rotation, so I was the odd man out.

I roll onto my stomach so I can use my binoculars to look at the activity below. Satisfied that everything seemed normal, I roll onto my side and, using my small pack as a pillow, try to sleep.

It's difficult falling back to sleep with so many thoughts running through my mind. I remember leaving the meeting with General Cho and General Chang in South Korea – General Cho with a neutral expression on his face and General Chang with a decidedly unfriendly expression. I knew that General Cho had gone out on a limb not only for me but for the United States.

Major Kim and I were quiet as we rode back to his house so that we could change clothes and have a quick lunch before heading to his office. Somehow Soo-jin knew we would be home for lunch, and it was already on the table when we arrived. We quickly changed out of our civilian clothes and into our military uniforms. At Jin-ho's suggestion, I had brought a Class B uniform with me to wear during our meetings.

The talk around the kitchen table centered mostly on their two oldest children; it was obvious they were very proud of Su-bin and Kun-woo and their achievements at college. We ate quickly and excused ourselves as soon as it was appropriate. There was much to be done and we both wanted to get started.

The same sergeant was waiting for us in the staff car as we left Jin-ho's home. I turned to him and said, "You must be pretty important to have a staff car and a sergeant assigned to you all day long."

He laughed and responded, "I told you already, as a major, I normally have to pedal my own bicycle to work! But you, as I mentioned before, are a visiting dignitary representing the President of the United States. Therefore, you are accorded not only a staff car but your own bodyguard. The sergeant is not just the driver; he is a member of one of our elite Special Forces units. If you look between his seat and the center console, you will see he has his pistol stashed there for quick use."

I looked at the sergeant with new eyes as we settled in the backseat. Before we started, I touched his shoulder and leaned forward to say in Korean, "Sergeant, thank you for your service." He gave a slight nod to acknowledge my comment.

After we arrived at Jin-ho's office, I thought it prudent to ask him to show me the recent intelligence they had gathered on the two launch facilities. I also knew they were following the developments surrounding the miniaturization of their nuclear weapons; I needed to learn all they had on this particular subject, as well. I would save my more focused questions until the morning. I still planned to leave at 3 o'clock Seoul time tomorrow afternoon, which would get me back to Tampa at 8 PM Thursday. Plus, holding my tough questions would give them less time to query me about our plans.

As it turned out, their clear and detailed briefings took the rest of the afternoon, and frankly, my brain was fried. I suggested we break for supper at about 6 o'clock and return in the morning. Although I could tell Jin-ho was surprised that I didn't want to work into the nighttime, he agreed to my suggestion.

I must have fallen asleep on the hillside, because the next thing I remember is jerking my head as a dollop of cold slushy snow hit my face. I really have to figure out how to keep the snow from my favorite North Korean bush from falling into my face every time I move. I carefully switch positions and try to catch some more sleep. But again, thoughts keep intruding on my attempt to return to my slumber.

I remember how irritated Jin-ho was when after supper Soo-jin and the two boys suggested we play Monopoly. I remember Jin-ho saying, "Soo-jin enjoys playing monopoly for two reasons. One reason is because it's a Western game. The other, perhaps more important reason, is because she always wins!"

So in fact we did play Monopoly after supper, and sure enough, Soo-jin beat us all! Because my visit was a special occasion, Soo-jin had made a desert called gangjeong, a tasty but not too sweet snack, which we enjoyed after the game. After the game pieces were put away, I said I was tired and would retire early. Again, Jin-ho raised his eyebrows. But he was a courteous host and said he would awaken me in time for breakfast.

Before I retired, I remembered to call base operations and ask them to notify my pilots that we would be leaving at 3 o'clock tomorrow afternoon.

The next morning, I was already awake when my host poked his head around my door. When he said he had changed his mind and that we would eat on base, I knew curiosity was finally getting the better of him. I was sure we would eat in a quiet corner of the officer's club where he could question me.

And that's exactly how it turned out. He ate quickly, and when I saw he was getting ready to ask some questions, I told him I would prefer to go to his office first. I can tell my attitude was beginning to irritate him, but I just smiled and headed for the door.

As we walked toward his office, I began speaking to him in Korean. "Jin-ho, I want to be able to tell my superiors that I absolutely did not tell you anything about our mission. They will ask, and as you already know, I would make a lousy poker player. So I will tell them that I volunteered nothing and I refused to answer your direct questions." I turned to him and said, "But if you listened carefully yesterday, you did learn a few things. And if you listen carefully today, you may learn even more about our plans." I smiled and continued, "You may have to put the pieces together, but I'm told you're a pretty bright guy!" I thought it curious that I used the same phrase to describe him as was recently used to describe me.

When we entered the restricted area that contained his office, we could see a Korean lieutenant colonel standing impatiently beside his office door. He was short, slightly overweight, and wore thick eyeglasses with black rims. He carried some thick folders in his left hand.

After we entered Jin-ho's office, he introduced himself as the commanding officer of the meteorological branch responsible for evaluating weather over North Korea. He told us he had received a phone call late yesterday from General Cho ordering him, and not one of his staff, to provide a more detailed analysis of the potential weather over Sohae and Tonghae for the months of February and March.

This was a valuable briefing. Even though we would get weather briefings from our own people, a briefing from an experienced meteorologist who worked only a few hundred kilometers away from the sites we were interested in would be of great value to us. It was almost an hour before he packed up his briefing papers and returned to wherever he worked. He promised to provide Major Kim weather updates as those months approached. I couldn't have been more pleased.

By midmorning, I was ready to begin asking the questions that were mission specific. I really raised Major Kim's eyebrows when I asked about highway conditions around both facilities. I specifically wanted to know if they had any information about security patrols and checkpoints on those highways. While we would gather satellite imagery for the sections we were interested in, I was hoping he would have additional information about the North Korean habits.

I also wanted to know if he had any information about maritime patrols during rocket launches, since both facilities were near the coastline, one on the east and one on the west.

By the time these and other searching questions had been asked and answered, I barely had time to get to the airport. My stomach was growling because we had worked right through lunch, so I hoped the flight crew would once again have something for me to eat in flight.

Jin-ho walked me outside to where the faithful sergeant was waiting in the staff car. My friend told me he would not accompany me to the airport because he had other matters to attend to that had been ignored during my visit. We shook hands, and then on what appeared to be a sudden impulse, Jin-ho stood to attention and saluted me. I was caught off guard but popped to attention and returned the salute. Military men have been showing respect for one another for many, many years by offering a salute; it was appropriate even for two good friends. I thought this salute summed up our years of friendship and mutual respect.

And then the good sergeant swiftly drove me to the airport; actually, true to my status as a VIP, he drove right up to the boarding stairs of the jet.

Chapter Twenty-Eight

The return flight was the exact reverse of the original flight. And yes, the crew had brought enough food not only for my missed lunch but also for our supper. When we stopped in Anchorage it was 5 o'clock in the morning and they told me we would have about a two-hour stop for refueling and breakfast. It was a pleasant surprise to find the original flight crew would now carry me to MacDill.

Sergeant Mitchell, who was once again the crew chief on the Gulfstream, smiled as I boarded after breakfast and welcomed me aboard. He leaned closer as I walked past and said, "You'll find an Air Force two-star sitting in the back; his ride has a mechanical and he doesn't want to wait for it to be fixed. PS, he doesn't seem very friendly." I nodded and walked down the aisle to introduce myself.

The general was seated in the first section and glared at me as I approached. When I reached him, he said in a very gruff voice, "Colonel, how can I help you?" It didn't sound like he wanted to help me at all!

Since he was hitching a ride on what I now considered my airplane, I decided not to play his silly games. "On the contrary, General; it appears I am helping you. There's plenty of room so I don't mind letting you ride along on my airplane." Before he could respond, I continued, "Now that I'm here, we can take off." With that, I turned to Sergeant Mitchell and made a big show of turning my arm in the air indicating they could start engines. He barely suppressed a smile!

I turned back to the general, whose face was now turning a bright red, and said, "It's a nice airplane general; enjoy the flight." And then I walked on to the second section. We didn't say another word to each other until after we landed at MacDill.

As we were taxiing to the ramp, he unbuckled his seatbelt and walked back to where I was sitting. I don't know what he expected, but since we were still taxiing I remained in my seat with my seatbelt fastened. He looked at my name tag and said, "Colonel Johnson, in case you haven't noticed, this is an Air Force airplane; it's not *your* airplane!" With a smug look, he asked, "What is your unit and your commanding officer's name?"

I thought, in for a penny in for a pound, so I looked up and said, "General, no disrespect sir, but I am not authorized to share that information with you." If I thought his face was red before, this time I was actually worried his head would explode!

In a slightly elevated voice, he said, "Colonel, you haven't heard the end of this."

As he was walking away, I said in a quiet voice, "General, I don't know who your boss is, but I do know he's not senior enough to go up against my boss." As he turned and listened, I continued, "Think about it; I'm a lowly Army Lieutenant Colonel flying in an airplane normally reserved for senior generals. There has to be a reason, don't you think?" And at that he turned and stomped off the airplane. I'm not sure, but I don't think I helped Army/Air Force inter-service relations that day.

As I walked off, Sergeant Mitchell said to me, "I thought you'd like to know that we've been tasked to take you to Washington, D.C., on Saturday." And with a wide smile, he said, "And by the way, you're now my favorite lieutenant colonel!"

I chuckled as I replied, "Thanks, Sergeant! On Saturday, can we leave at 8 AM?"

"Yes sir; I'll tell the major." And with that I grabbed my bag and bounded down the boarding stairs.

I walked through base operations and saw a familiar face. Vivian stood as I approached, and as much as I wanted to give her a hug, I restrained myself as she said, "Welcome home, stranger!"

"Why thank you, my dear! I'm glad to be back in the good old U.S. of A, but I'm not quite home yet. What brings you out at this time of night?"

I could see the question embarrassed her, so I asked, "Is there anything new to report from the satellite surveillance?"

"As a matter of fact, there is." She looked around and then said, "Let's go out to the car and I'll bring you up to date."

As she drove toward the BOQ, I turned to her and said, "Vivian, it is good to be back."

She paused a moment and then said, "The latest satellite surveillance shows a large railroad car, larger than normal, on the siding next to their rocket manufacturing facility; in fact, there are four of those new large cars on the siding. We also discovered that that particular siding leads to an intersection with tracks leading off in two different directions." She briefly turned to me and asked, "Guess where they lead?"

"Just a wild guess, but do they lead to our two favorite rocket launching facilities?"

She said, "Right the first time!"

As we approached the officer's club, she asked in a soft voice, "Are you hungry?"

I detected a subtle change in her voice and suspected there was more than just mere interest in my diet. I turned to her and said, "I'm not really hungry, but I would enjoy a chocolate shake!"

Without speaking, she turned into the officer's club parking lot. We found a table for two in a relatively quiet corner of the club; Thursday night is not as noisy as Friday night. As she took her seat, I asked, "Shall I get two chocolate shakes?"

She nodded and quietly said, "A small one, please."

As I returned to the table with our two milkshakes and sat down, she ignored her milkshake and said to me, "Robert, let me get this off my chest." Her green eyes were bright and alive, and they held my baby blues like a magnet! She continued, "Lots of guys have asked me out, and I've been on lots of dates; but I've never been on two dates with the same man. I guess I'm still a tomboy! I've never shared my emotions with anyone, much less a man. Robert, you were only gone two days, but I missed you! That's a new emotion for me and I'm terrified."

I reached for her hand and surprisingly, she did not pull it away. I wasn't sure what to say, so I said nothing. I did keep my eyes locked on hers. Finally she said, "Well, say something!"

"Vivian, I haven't been on a date since my wife died. I'm just as scared as you are!"

Right then, a voice said, "Am I interrupting something?" Our hands jumped apart as though they had touched a boiling pot.

We both looked up and saw Major Denton standing there with a beer in his hand. He smiled and said, "Don't worry, your little secret is safe with me." And then he turned and walked away.

Vivian and I looked at each other and both blushed. I spoke up and said, "Let's finish our milkshakes and go for a walk."

She said, "Let's take them with us." She stood and headed for the exit; I was close behind.

We walked across the parking lot as we drank our milkshakes. I thought the shake was pretty good, but she threw hers in the trash can at the edge of the parking lot. After a moment of indecision, I threw mine in after hers. We turned right out of the parking lot on to a sidewalk and continued walking, each of us contemplating our own thoughts.

A multitude of thoughts were bouncing around in my head. I had met and married the woman I thought was my soul mate. And she was rudely taken from me. Now those same warm feelings were happening all over again. Was this a betrayal to Beth? What would my children think? I didn't think I was ready to rush headlong into another relationship, especially with a woman I barely knew.

She was intelligent; she was witty; she had more common sense than most men I knew; she was certainly pleasant company! She had an attractive and seemingly constant smile, bright green eyes, deep-red curly hair that bounced when she walked, and a sprinkling of really attractive freckles. And though we had left the officer's club in a hurry, I noticed heads turn, both men and women, as we walked out.

We continued slowly walking around the headquarters area of the base. About halfway, she reached out for and held my hand. Neither of us said anything. I could tell she was still processing what was happening. Eventually, we completed our walk around the circumference of the headquarters area and found ourselves back in the officer's club parking lot.

She stopped next to our car and handed me the keys. She looked at me and said, "I have a lot to think about. I'll see you at 5:45 for our morning run." And with that she turned around and walked away.

I watched her walk away until she disappeared. I turned and slowly walked back to my room, with my own thoughts tumbling around in my head.

Chapter Twenty-Nine

Although I normally fall asleep when my head hits the pillow, I lay awake for a long time pondering what had happened. I don't know what time I fell asleep, but I must have because the alarm on my iPhone startled me awake.

No doubt in my mind about my morning routine this time; I quickly shaved, showered, dressed in my sweats, and rushed downstairs. I was three minutes early but she still beat me!

She seemed all bubbly and said, "Good morning, Robert. You lead this time." And she held the door open for me. I knew things had changed because as I walked past her, I noticed how close we were, and sensed the electricity between us. I let her catch up and then started jogging with her by my side. At the jogging path, I turned left. This half of the course was in the shape of an ellipse pinched on two sides and consisted of a series of short hills with nary a flat spot. The brochure in my room suggested the course could be completed in 30 minutes.

She must have read the same brochure because after just a few minutes she picked up the pace. Even with that increase it still took us 35 minutes to complete the course. We were both breathing hard as we walked back to the BOQ, but she seemed to enjoy it. "Nothing like a short energizing run to start the day, is there?" I just gave her a weak smile.

Another quick shower before I changed clothes, and then we met downstairs to have breakfast at the officer's club. This time I had an English muffin with grape jelly and a bowl of fruit, all washed down with a glass of milk. I ate quickly because I did not want to be late for our meeting.

I still had the car keys, so I drove; neither of us talked on the short drive. Although we entered the conference room a couple minutes early, we were still later than everyone else. Before I greeted everyone, a sudden thought occurred to me. I raised the palm of my hand and said, "I need to check something; excuse me for just a few moments." I walked back into the map room and walked around the circumference as I quickly glanced at each of the satellite images. When I satisfied my curiosity, I walked back into the conference room.

I greeted everyone and then asked each member of the planning group to give a brief report. I started with Lieutenant Rogers since he and Lieutenant Williams would be responsible for getting us into and out of the land portion of our mission.

"Sir, we've reviewed the geography of the two locations and we have no problems with the ground. The hills are small enough that hiking in and out will not be a problem, at least from that perspective. We also researched the weather we can expect during the mission. Tonghae will most certainly have snow on the ground and possibly snowstorms while we're there. On the other hand, the weather at Sohae could be totally different. While Sohae may also have snow during that time, it will be much lighter, and it may or may not have snow on the ground. There is a strong possibility of fog, however."

He turned to Lieutenant Williams, who continued. "We see two major problems that have to be overcome. The first challenge is if there is already snow on the ground, our tracks will be easy to follow – that's not good. The second problem could be even worse, at least from the hiking perspective. What I mean is, if the ground is soft or muddy, it could take longer than we anticipate to trudge into position. If it takes all night, hiking in the daytime, when there's a greater chance of being seen, could be a problem."

He turned back to Lieutenant Rogers, who picked up the conversation. "We've given our detailed resource recommendations to the commander, but we think it best that one of us be assigned to each team."

And that's when Master Chief O'Shaughnessy picked up the briefing. "Without a doubt, the discussion that took up the most time this week has been the composition of each team. Obviously, the smaller the team the more likely it is that we can get in and out without being spotted. But we need enough people to get the job done right.

"We finally decided that each team would consist of seven people, just as we discussed before; a team leader, the two-man sniper team, and four Navy SEALs. The first three are on the team for obvious reasons; the reason for the four Navy SEALs is to provide security on the way in and of course, on the way out. And because we're on one side of the hill, it will take a minimum of four SEALs to provide effective security to the left and right of the sniper team and on the back side of the hill.

"We also discussed personal weapons. We want to be able to move quickly so we are going to pack lightly. The snipers, of course, will choose their own weapons, but we anticipate they'll use a .50 caliber BMG round in an M107 rifle. For everyone else, we'll each carry a sound-suppressed MP5 and a silenced Glock 17 or 19, user's choice, so the ammunition is interchangeable. It'll be really cold up there and the bad guys will be wearing heavy coats or parkas, so nonlethal weapons won't work. Of course, the objective is not to find ourselves in a situation where we need to use our weapons."

Lieutenant Commander Cromwell was next, and his news was a mixed bag. The good news was that getting onto the beach at Tonghae appeared to be relatively easy. "It looks like we can have a SEAL delivery vehicle get really close to where the mountains almost come right down to the shoreline. This will be inside their maritime patrol areas. Everyone, and this goes for both teams, will wear a wetsuit with a change of clothes carried ashore in waterproof bags, along with their weapons, food and water. We'll have an extra man come ashore to collect the empty bags and wetsuits, and to erase any evidence of the landing. After properly attired, the SEAL squad will lead everyone to the hillside and then properly camouflage their position. That's the good news.

"At Sohae we have a different problem. The area around Sohae is covered with mud flats that would be virtually impossible to cross without leaving tracks; in fact, trudging through the mud would take more time than we have to get into position. We would definitely run out of dark.

However, there appears to be a small area just north of Sohae that could work as the ingress position. I suggest we send a SEAL team to that area right away to confirm that it will work for our sniper team. Without a direct observation of that area, we run the risk of not being able to get in. If it does work, it still means the team at Sohae will have a longer hike to get into position; we estimate it will take most of the night."

I remarked, "If your recon team gets spotted, it'll set off alarm bells all over the place and we'll never get in."

He chuckled and said, "Colonel, nobody sees us unless we want them too!" Bravado backed by the truth!

"All right; let's plan for that recon. And your unit has the capability to support two teams on opposite sides of the Korean Peninsula?"

"Yes, we can do that. Your challenge, Colonel, is to convince the regular Navy to let us use two of their submarines."

While I knew that inter-service rivalry would be an issue, I hadn't thought about intra-service rivalries. "I'll leave that to Admiral Harrison; after all, he is following orders from the Commander in Chief."

I turned to Major Denton and said, "Major, you're up."

"I've put some feelers out about sniper teams and got a few responses. Don't worry, they were pretty generic inquiries. What we'd like to do is bring six sniper teams here, three Army and three Marine Corps, and have them hold a shoot-out. That way if our number one choices have a problem, we know who our backup teams are. It's always good to be prepared! The sniper teams, by the way, are spread out all over the world so we'll have to get some orders cut pretty quickly.

"As far as security around the two launch facilities, it seems pretty basic. It looks like they have good security inside the fence line, but outside seems pretty sparse."

I thanked him and then looked to Vivian and asked, "Dr. O'Brien, what have our image analysts discovered?"

She looked at me with her professional face, and said, "Colonel, they've reviewed every day's surveillance for the past three months and haven't found any new activity or really anything of consequence we haven't already discussed. The big railcars coming out of the factory are probably to haul the main body of the new rocket to the launch facility building. We'll continue to watch that area for any new developments, should there be any.

"Now that we know where the teams are going to enter the country, I'll expand our surveillance area and let our two primary analysts know where to look." I made a mental note to talk with Major Green when I was back in Washington, D.C. She continued, "We'll maintain the extra satellite surveillance right up until we know the teams are back on the submarines." I gave her a smile before I moved on.

Finally, I looked at Commander Throckmorton. "Commander, it sounds like you and your team have done an excellent job of mission planning." Then I smiled and said, "But I guess that's kind of the norm for Navy SEALs, right?" Everyone smiled and there were a few chuckles as I paused.

I thanked everyone for their part in the mission planning and then started right in with a discussion of what I'd learned in South Korea. Things like meteorological patterns in February and March, littoral conditions off both coasts, security on the highways, especially patrols and checkpoints, and finally what support we could expect from the South Koreans.

That last point was especially important because we wanted to distract the North Korean army as we completed our mission. The last thing we needed was a million-man army chasing us in North Korea! It turns out they normally hold a winter military exercise and they've agreed to schedule it during our mission.

I also related what I'd learned about the North Korean Navy patrols in the waters near the two launch points. This information was critical to our success. While we had some idea about the patrols in these areas from our satellite surveillance, the South Korean naval expert gave us a different perspective, especially as it related to the North Korean philosophy on incursions in their waters.

I got everyone's attention and then said, "Based on what I learned in South Korea, I have a change I'd like to suggest." The room was suddenly very quiet. "I think we have a good plan for getting in-country, but I'm concerned about our extraction.

"If we chose a different point to be picked up, and had a plan to confuse anyone who may be chasing us, I think it would give us a better chance of escaping unnoticed." I turned to Dr. O'Brien and said, "Dr. O'Brien, will you make a detailed examination of the shoreline slightly north and south of each of our landing positions and see if you can't find a spot that would be ideal for pickup. Commander Cromwell, Lieutenant Rogers, Lieutenant Williams, would you work with Dr. O'Brien to find a new place the teams can walk to for extraction. Try not to make it a very long walk."

I faced Commander Throckmorton. "Commander, would you and Master Chief O'Shaughnessy and Major Denton brainstorm some ideas to distract and confuse anyone who might interfere with our extraction plans. Think outside the box, but keep in mind we mustn't leave anything behind that would identify either the United States or South Korea.

"I'll work with Senior Chief O'Hara and Master Sergeant Garcia to draft a formal summary of the mission plan that I can carry to Washington tomorrow morning. I want to cover the major points we've discussed, but I don't want to include any details yet." I did not at this time want to tell them that we had a critical security leak. "Commander, will you make sure that Chief O'Hara has all the notes that have been collected." He nodded as he reached for the file folders at his elbow.

I stood up and said, "All right, let's all get to work!"

As everyone started to gather into their individual groups, another thought occurred to me. I got everyone's attention and asked, "Are there any specific personnel requests that I will need to get Admiral Harrison working on?"

"I think everyone has given me their requests," said Commander Throckmorton, "I've put them in a folder. Just so you know, our Admiral has received orders to support our mission, so don't worry about assignments for Navy SEALs. We'll take care of that right here."

"Okay, thank you."

We all then worked the rest of the morning on our individual assignments, creating a constant buzz of activity in the room – about what I imagine a beehive sounds like.

Sergeant Garcia and Chief O'Hara were busy pecking away at their laptops, occasionally asking a question; it was a good thing we were all still in the same room. I told them I wanted no more than four double-spaced pages in the summary I was carrying to Washington. There could be an additional page for personnel requirements and one more for equipment requirements. I wanted my briefing for Dr. Richardson and Admiral Harrison to be clear, concise, and correct – but mostly concise.

As lunchtime approached, Major Denton called to me and said, "Colonel, will you be joining us for lunch today?" He had a curious smile on his face!

I caught myself before I glanced at Vivian and responded with, "Sure! Even better, why don't we all have lunch together? Commander, could we impose upon you to call the officer's club and try to get us a private room, a table for 10?"

I wanted very much to be alone with Vivian, but not only for social purposes. When I was in South Korea, I was shown some satellite imagery of the two launch facilities. When I went back to the map room earlier this morning, I saw the same imagery hanging on the wall. The images in South Korea had been wiped clean of the date and time stamp, but otherwise they were the same. I wanted to know more about what we were sharing with the South Koreans. But now I guess that would have to wait until later.

We carpooled over to the officer's club and had a convivial lunch; two chicken salads and eight steaks! The conversation was largely centered on tomorrow's football games. The Navy team at Annapolis was having a good year, so all the Navy guys were in good spirits. Although Sergeant Garcia attempted to throw in a plug for the Army cadets at West Point, their season was not going as well, and the consensus was that Navy would clobber them in the annual Army-Navy game.

Soon all the food had disappeared and the conversation was slowing down, so we all carpooled back to our own private building. There was still much work to be done, and I wanted to have a polished document to take with me when we left. Just before 3 o'clock, Senior Chief O'Hara handed me a folder with the six pages I would use for my briefing on Saturday. I reconvened the entire group to review the document.

There was some discussion about including too many details regarding the SEAL delivery vehicle team, so I asked Chief O'Hara to rewrite that paragraph to refer to the team but not describe their responsibilities. They also wanted me to recommend leaders for the two teams, so I asked that a new paragraph be added naming Commander Throckmorton to be in charge of the team at Tonghae, and Major Denton to be in charge of the team at Sohae.

I looked at Sergeant Garcia and with a stern face said, "Sergeant Garcia, I believe you have an appointment tomorrow! Be at base operations at 0745 or you'll miss your ride home!"

"Yes, sir!"

I don't know if earning points is a valid principle, but out of the corner of my eye I saw Dr. O'Brien smiling; I was pretty sure I just earned points.

I looked around the table and said, "Thanks for everything you've done so far; you are a pleasure to work with! I have everything I need for my briefing tomorrow, so take the rest of the weekend off. Plan to be back here at 0800 Monday morning, and hopefully we'll start on the detailed planning." I looked at Commander Throckmorton and said, "Commander, keep your cell phone on 24/7 and I'll call you as soon as I have the word."

And with that, the first planning stage was finished and I had a briefing document to present to those above my pay grade!

Chapter Thirty

On the cold hillside, I must've moved again because I have another dollop of cold, wet snow in my face. And of course when I react to the cold, wet snow by jerking my head, I bump the bush again and get another clump in my face!

I stretch my muscles and glance over at Sergeant Parker. Once again I am amazed at his ability to stay in one place without moving. The bushes that he and Sergeant Harris are in don't look like they've moved once; they are completely covered with snow. When we arrived, we looked around the side of the ridge line for a group of bushes where the two of them could be hidden; the clump they are in is in a more or less rectangular shape overlooking the gantry below.

My two little bushes are barely big enough to hide me. In fact, it occurs to me again that without the poor weather, one of those patrols would surely have seen me by now. So it's with mixed emotions that I welcome the misty fog. It's cold and wet, but it helps to hide us from those patrols.

I twist in my hiding place to look down the hill toward the launch site. Nothing! The ragged fog which drifts in and out of our hilltop location is as thick as soup down in the valley where the launch facility is. While I'm looking toward the valley, I'm startled by the appearance of two soldiers to my left; another patrol! Why wasn't I warned?

I reach into my parka hood to check the earphone in my left ear and discover it's not there! I need to stop moving around so much! The two-man patrol is drawing closer to my position and I realize all they have to do is look in my direction and they'll see my face looking back at them. Moving very slowly I lower my head so that if they do look in my direction all they'll see is the winter camouflage of my parka.

I remember thinking when I arrived at Yokosuka that it was fortunate Commander Throckmorton and I were about the same size, at least across the shoulders. He was an inch or two taller, but his winter gear still fits me okay. But more about this later.

Once again, the two soldiers walk past our lair and continue on down the mountain. Since I had replaced my earphone, I heard the report from the SEAL team on that side. I glance at my watch as it suddenly occurs to me that the patrols were now coming at random times. If they continue that routine, we won't be able to predict when they'll be back.

One concern raised during our mission planning was the uncertainty of the weather. Early in January, we brought a U.S. Navy meteorologist to SOCOM on a 30-day TDY assignment to forecast the weather in North Korea. We didn't tell him why we were interested, and we purposely included all of North Korea in our request.

At the same time, I asked Major Kim to request the same information from his South Korean meteorologist. If there was one job I wouldn't want to have, it would be that of a meteorologist. In the beginning the two meteorologists agreed about 50% of the time. We did notice, however, that as time progressed, our meteorologist produced a forecast that was closer to the forecast presented by the South Korean meteorologist. I'm glad we brought him on board in time to learn the winter weather patterns over North Korea. It turned out there was a significant amount of weather data available for that area of the world; it just took him time to pore over it.

Unfortunately for us, rain, snow and fog were eventually predicted by both meteorologists. In fact, they both warned of valley fog throughout the timeframe we'd given them, especially at Sohae.

When we asked Master Sergeant Parker, the Army sniper, and Gunnery Sergeant Patterson, the Marine Corps sniper, about hitting a target in fog or snow or rain, they both said that if they can see it they can hit it. On the other hand, if the target was hidden by fog or heavy weather, the chances of a hit were almost nonexistent.

On the practice range, when we hid the target and asked them to take a shot anyway, they hit the target about one time out of fifty. Then Master Chief O'Shaughnessy suggested we put a noisemaker on the target and see if they could hit it by aiming at the noise. The hit rate went up to one in five; still not very good.

Major Denton suggested that our only viable alternative in the case of fog or low visibility was to wait for the engines to start on the rocket and aim just above the bright engine exhaust. We knew from our discussions with the NASA scientist that the engines would fire a couple of seconds before the rocket moved. We eventually decided this would be an acceptable risk. I noticed the two snipers looked at each other with raised eyebrows, but they didn't say anything.

As my mind meanders through these thoughts, I notice that the snow had turned to a light drizzle. Even though the fog had turned to a light mist up on the hillside where we were, when I looked down into the valley, I could see that fog completely covered the gantry. I hope the NASA scientist was correct about the two second delay in rocket movement after ignition!

Chapter Thirty-One

My thoughts return to the end of the planning meeting at SOCOM. Vivian and I moved to the side of the room as everyone else was leaving to go their own way. When Major Denton walked by, he turned to me and winked as he quietly said, "Good luck, Colonel!" If it hadn't been for the wink, my first thought would've been that he was wishing me luck in Washington, D.C. I think the wink indicated he had another thought in mind!

When it was just the two of us remaining, I turned to Vivian and asked, "What's your preference for supper?"

She turned and answered, "Someplace that's quiet on a Friday night."

I smiled and said, "I have just the place in mind!"

She laughed out loud and said, "Yes, Denny's will be just fine!"

As we walked down the stairs, Commander Throckmorton came back in the front door. He looked up at us and said, "I forgot to tell you that if you leave the key to the car at base ops when you leave in the morning, you can still use it when you come back. If, on the other hand, you don't come back, we'll know where the key is."

"Thanks Commander; sounds like a good plan." He waved as he turned around and left to join his fellow SEALs.

Vivian and I walked to the car where this time she allowed me to open the door for her. I felt my face flush as she flashed her brilliant smile at me when she slid into her seat. I walked slowly behind the car as my brain started to work overtime on what the evening would bring. I still wanted to ask her about the satellite imagery I had seen in South Korea, but I didn't want to dampen the spirit. I made up my mind; it could wait!

As we drove toward the main gate and then into town, she turned to me and said, "I forgot to ask, how is your friend Major Kim and his family? Were they pleased to see you?"

So much for not thinking about South Korea! I kept my eyes on the road and said, "Major Kim was happy to see me, but it was obvious his professional curiosity was getting the better of him. Soo-jin, on the other hand, was clearly excited to see me! Her four years at BYU almost converted her to a Western lifestyle. I was surprised to see some decorations in her living room that were decidedly not Korean. In fact, she told me she had taken up oil painting lessons in the European style.

"Two of their children are away at college in Korea, and two live at home while they finish high school. They've made sure that all four not only speak Korean but are fluent in English as well." A short pause and then, "I was happy to see them as well; I haven't seen them since, well . . . I haven't seen them for quite a while." A vision of Beth appeared, smiling and waving goodbye when she boarded the airliner to leave Seoul that last time.

"You told us that you stayed in their home; did you remember to leave a thank you note for Soo-jin?"

I didn't know what to say! She was right of course; a handwritten note would have been the proper thing to do. It was what a wife would have reminded me to do. She knew my answer, so after a brief pause, quietly said, "You can hand write a note tonight and drop it in the mailbox in the BOQ before we leave in the morning." Yes, our relationship had certainly changed.

While the restaurant was doing more business than the last time we were here, there were still plenty of empty tables available. When the waitress came to seat us, I nodded toward the area we had sat in previously. We both ordered water with a twist of lemon and then studied the menus as though choosing required all of our attention.

When the waitress returned, we told her we were ready to order. Vivian ordered broccoli and cheddar soup and a slow-cooked pot roast. I ordered a Caesar salad without the cheese and anchovies and a T-bone steak and shrimp. I asked for herb toast and Vivian looked up and said, "Me too!" It seemed neither of us was going to go hungry tonight!

As we waited for our soup and salad, I smiled at Vivian and said, "Here we are, just the two of us; I'm an awkward widower and you're a self-described tomboy!" She nodded and waited for me to go on. So I fumbled onward!

"Vivian, I see how other men look wistfully at you as you walk across a room; I don't want to be one of them." I wasn't at all sure that came out quite how I meant it. I paused for a moment and then said, "When my son Jacob started noticing girls, I told him that you couldn't truly tell how beautiful a woman was until after you talked to her." I looked straight into her beautiful green eyes and said, "Well, I've talked to you, Vivian, and you are a beautiful woman!"

She blushed and said, "I've had other men tell me I'm beautiful, but that was different. Thank you."

The waitress walked up with my salad and Vivian's soup, so we were both quiet until she walked away. I poured honey mustard dressing on my salad as Vivian stirred her soup. In a moment she looked up and said, "Robert, I can't begin to tell you how disconcerting it is to be analyzing a satellite image and then all of a sudden be thinking about the two of us jogging together on a beautiful white beach somewhere. Look, I have a PhD and, by my own admission, one of the best analytical minds in the United States. But I don't understand how the heart controls the mind!"

"When you figure that out, a Nobel prize will be yours! I've discovered that some things can be over analyzed, so I find it best to take things at face value."

I could see the analyst at work in her mind. Finally, she looked up and said, "Robert, I have not been in love before, so I don't know what it feels like. I do know that my heart skips a beat when you walk into a room. I like listening to you talk. I enjoy jogging beside you. I thought about you while you were off in South Korea. I enjoy being with you, even here in Denny's!"

She paused, so I took a bite of salad and then she had a spoonful of soup. We continued eating while lost in our own thoughts. Pretty soon the waitress brought our main course. After the waitress departed, Vivian looked at me and said, "Robert, I'm really hungry; do you mind if we eat now and talk later?"

I laughed out loud and said, "The last time we were here, we agreed to eat first and talk later. I think that's a great idea!"

So we both dug in and enjoyed our supper while it was still hot.

Chapter Thirty-Two

About 900 miles north of us, another couple was having an intimate dinner. But they were not out in public. Mike Fontana and Julie Endicott were sitting at the kitchen table in her apartment enjoying a pleasant meal. When she learned he really enjoyed a T-bone steak with a baked potato, she decided to invite him for an intimate dinner in her apartment on a Friday night.

Wanting the evening to go well, she actually prepared the same meal on Wednesday evening as practice. That turned out to be a good idea because her Wednesday baked potatoes were not baked sufficiently; they were still hard in the middle. On the other hand, the steak turned out just as he liked it. She knew he liked his steak medium rare because she heard him order a steak during one of their fundraising dinners in New Jersey.

"Julie, you have outdone yourself! This dinner is absolutely scrumptious!"

"They say the way to a man's heart is through his stomach. In your case it must be true!"

He laughed and said, "My stomach is not the only way!"

She forced a smile and said, "Yes, I'm well aware of the other way." In an attempt to distract him from that line of thinking she asked, "How is it we are able to have dinner together? Won't your wife be suspicious?"

"Not at all! She knows the congressman is having a fund-raising dinner in Hackensack tomorrow as the last stop on a weeklong campaign fund-raising trip, so I told her I was going up a day early to make sure the arrangements were all taken care of." He gave her a silly smile and continued, "So, we can spend the night together and I'll take the train up tomorrow morning."

Although she smiled, her first thought was that he was a presumptuous so-and-so. How could he assume he could spend the night without even asking? His wife is probably glad to have him gone for a couple of days, she mused. She returned his smile and said, "When you called tonight and said you were coming over, I checked the satellite movie schedule. I noticed a movie with Angelina Jolie is on tonight – isn't she one of your favorites? Let's just stack the dishes and watch the movie."

"That's a great idea! We can snuggle on the couch."

She smiled outwardly for his benefit, but inwardly she cringed when she heard the word snuggle.

It would be impossible to talk about work during the movie, but it gave her time to consider the best way to get him talking about things he shouldn't talk about. She moved the dishes from the table to the sink with a grim expression as she realized there was only one way. And this thought renewed her desire to complete this mission as quickly as possible and return to her homeland.

Later that evening, he bragged about *his* congressman having been notified of a full committee meeting scheduled for Monday afternoon. He had to rearrange all of the Monday appointments for later in the week so the congressman could attend the committee meeting. He then shared that, in his opinion, the President was going to brief the committee on his plans to address the North Korean missile threat.

"Although I'm not supposed to know, I've learned that an Army lieutenant colonel by the name of Johnson has been ordered to draft a plan. I even talked to him earlier this week! He told me that his team is continuing their planning. What's interesting is that he's not in his office at the Pentagon, and his commanding officer did not know where he was. Army intelligence; what a laugh!"

And with that, he rolled over and went to sleep.

Captain Pak lay there pretending to be asleep for several minutes until she heard his rhythmic breathing. She carefully slid out of bed and tiptoed to the kitchen to retrieve her computer from a kitchen drawer. She opened the lid and waited for the system to boot up. She then opened her email program and selected an entry from her address book labeled "Father." Except in this case, the email would be routed to Colonel General Kim Hyun-woo, Director of the North Korean intelligence service.

Although it looked like a normal Microsoft Outlook program, as soon as she hit send, her message would go to an encryption program before it was transmitted. As she finished typing the message containing everything she had just learned from the loose-lipped Congressional Chief of Staff, she heard a noise behind her. She quickly hit send and turned to see him standing there.

Rubbing his eyes, he asked in a groggy voice, "What are you doing?"

She wondered how long he has been standing there, but said, "I couldn't sleep so I got up and sent a brief note to my father. It's just after lunch there and he'll enjoy hearing from me."

He glanced over her shoulder to the computer screen and saw that her address book was still open to an entry labeled "Father." He looked back at her and said, "Well, I missed you. Let's go back to bed!"

She put her arm around him and had the uncomfortable thought that if he had appeared just five seconds sooner he would've seen the unencrypted message. She remembered something one of her trainers had told her: "Excellent planning is vital to the success of any mission, but don't ever discount the effect that luck has on your success. When you plan well, you create your own good luck!"

Chapter Thirty-Three

Vivian and I were both either very hungry or at a sudden loss for words because we didn't say anything while we finished our meals. The waitress had come by about midway through our meal and asked if everything was okay, and then returned just as we were finishing our main course. She asked, "What dessert would you like tonight?"

I thought that was a good approach for a waitress. Instead of asking if we wanted dessert, she asked what dessert we would like. Vivian spoke right up and said, "I'd like a slice of apple pie, please."

I looked up and said, "Make that two!"

We looked at each other for a moment and then I said, "Here we are, Vivian; two adults having dinner together and wondering what tomorrow brings. Well, I can tell you how the next few days are going to go. We're going to finish our dessert and then drive back to the BOQ and go to bed." I blushed and stammered, "I meant, of course, that we'll go to sleep in our individual rooms." I stammered on, "Then we'll get up in the morning and go running, come back and have breakfast, and then get on the airplane and fly back to Washington, D.C.

"I would wager that Admiral Harrison will have a car waiting for us and will either drive us to the Pentagon or to the White House. If it's to the Pentagon, they'll ask me to brief the JCS and then we'll go to the White House. The alternative is to go directly to the White House Situation Room and brief everyone there."

With a broad smile on her face, Vivian held up her hand and said, "I agree with that but want to add one modification. There's just way too much left brain in your plan. Let me add a bit of right brain thinking. First, after we finish our dessert and while we walk out to the car, we're going to hold hands and you're going to open my door for me again.

"When we get back to the BOQ and while we're in the elevator up to our rooms, you're going to hold me in your arms and we're going to have our first kiss!"

I didn't know what to say, so I was glad for the arrival of the waitress with our dessert. I looked to Vivian and said, "You did say that we were going to finish our dessert, right?"

She laughed and said, "I'm going to eat my apple pie; you can do whatever you want with yours."

This time we carried our check to the register and paid for our meals there. I left a good tip for a good waitress!

I held the restaurant door for Vivian and then as I caught up with her, her right hand reached for my left. I liked that!

The drive back to the base was filled with inconsequential conversation about our supper, the dessert, the full moon overhead, the fact that we both had laundry to do when we got back to Washington. The only subject we did not discuss was – us!

Once we passed through the main gate, our conversation suddenly ended. I don't know about her, but I was suddenly thinking that I hadn't kissed a woman in a long time; I hoped I remembered how!

In the elevator after the doors closed, I pulled her gently toward me and held her in my arms as I kissed her lightly on the lips. Even though my eyes were closed, I had the impression that she had raised her right foot while kissing me; it was then that I remembered kissing was designed for two people. We held each other after with her head on my shoulder until the doors popped open on her floor. She slowly walked out, and as the doors were closing turned back and said, "See you at 5:45!" And the doors closed!

I slept like a baby that night!

In the morning we jogged for 30 minutes, changed out of our sweats, enjoyed a leisurely breakfast together and headed for base operations. We were not in a rush because I had scheduled the departure time for 8 o'clock in the morning. We arrived at base operations at about 7:45 and found Sergeant Garcia already there. It was obvious she was anxious to get home as she greeted us with, "Let's get this show on the road!"

I pulled one of Vivian's bags as we walked out on the ramp. Sergeant Garcia gave me a questioning look as I waited for Vivian to board first. I returned her look and said, "I thought you were in a hurry, Sergeant!" She smiled as she jumped on the boarding stairs.

Sergeant Mitchell was back at his station and welcomed us aboard. He greeted the ladies and then said to me, "Welcome back, Colonel. Major Guthrie says thanks for keeping us gainfully employed!" He then leaned closer and said, "You know that general you had words with?" When I nodded he continued, "It turns out he's just been appointed deputy commander of the airlift command. That's why he was in such a hurry to leave Alaska. Just thought you'd like to know."

"Oh, great, I'm just getting used to the luxury travel you provide! Do you suppose he'll remember me?"

"I don't think he's going to soon forget you. For what it's worth, we've been told to be ready for a flight back here sometime after supper on Sunday. You wouldn't know anything about that would you?"

Shaking my head, I replied "Sergeant, just like you, my travel plans are managed by someone else. Someone, I might add, whose pay grade is way above mine!"

He chuckled as I walked back to get settled in for the flight.

I told Sergeant Garcia and Vivian to sit wherever they wanted to, but after we leveled off at our cruising altitude, we would all get together around the conference table to review and practice the briefing I would be giving in just three or four hours. Vivian elected to sit at the conference table, and Sergeant Garcia sat across from her in the aisle seat. When I noticed, she gave me a wicked smile! I smiled right back, and sat down in the last row of the first section facing forward.

Sergeant Mitchell strolled down the aisle to ensure our seatbelts were fastened, and when he confirmed they were, he wandered back up to the cockpit and sat in the jump seat.

We were soon lined up and rolling down the runway for takeoff. With nothing else to do, I pulled the passenger briefing card out of the seat pocket in front of me and learned more about the Gulfstream G550 aircraft, one of the nicest airplanes in the business world.

It didn't take long to get up to cruising altitude, and as soon as the pilot turned off the seatbelt sign, I walked back to the conference table. The two women looked up at me and smiled, completely aware that they had provided me a dilemma by sitting across from each other. How would I choose who to sit next to? Well, I wasn't going to play their reindeer games!

I looked at Sergeant Garcia and said, "Sergeant, I think it best that you sit next to Dr. O'Brien so I can spread my papers out on this side of the table along with my laptop." She didn't move right away so I said, "Sergeant, just move, will you!"

I pulled my laptop out along with the draft of the briefing document. I looked at both of them as Sergeant Garcia settled in, and said, "Since both of you were there for all of the later planning meetings and heard all of the discussions taking place, don't hesitate to correct me if I say something that's not correct.

"First I'm going to read the briefing paper out loud so that I can hear the words; I'll probably make some handwritten notes as we go along so that when I'm finished reading, we can go back and clarify any questions. Feel free to make notes as I go along, but allow me to read the entire document before we try to clarify something.

I looked at Sergeant Garcia and said, as I held up a USB drive, "Sergeant, when we're finished I'll have you make the corrections on your laptop and then copy the file to this flash drive. That means after landing we'll go to your office in the Pentagon, make copies of the briefing document, and lock your computer in the classified safe." With a smile I then said, "Then you're off-duty. But keep your cell phone handy!"

She gave me a grim look so I said, "Relax, you'll still be on time for your daughter's soccer game at 1 o'clock."

It took us just over an hour to read and then reread the briefing paper with all three of us making suggestions to improve it. Sergeant Garcia took the flash drive from me and quickly had all the modifications made and copied to it. The biggest changes made were to reduce even further the details of the mission. If someone wanted more information, then I would answer their questions during the briefing, or better still, tell them we hadn't finalized those details yet.

I hadn't heard anything from the FBI on the progress they might be making in discovering who the traitor was. And since I didn't know who would be in on the briefing, I wanted to keep some things closely held. Although they were following dozens of leads, including several in the White House, the Director had a strong feeling the leak was coming from either the House intelligence committee or the Senate intelligence committee.

It wasn't long before the seatbelt sign came back on and we began our descent into the Washington, D.C. area. A glance out the window confirmed that it was a beautiful fall day.

Chapter Thirty-Four

On the other side of the globe, and several hours earlier, it was a brisk and windy 3°C in Pyongyang, although it was a sunny clear afternoon. General Kim was sitting at his desk trying to make headway on the voluminous stack of papers in his in-basket, when his aide, Major Yuh, knocked and entered.

While waiting for the general to look up, Major Yuh remembered the first time he had knocked on that door. He had been polite and waited for the general to invite him into his office. The invitation never came! When he knocked again after several minutes of waiting, the door exploded open and the general stood there with a grim look. His first day as the general's aide was inaugurated with General Kim severely and loudly reprimanding him for not entering his office immediately, thus requiring the general to get up from his chair to see who was at the door.

The general had told Major Yuh that if his business was important enough to interrupt him, then it had better be important enough to enter his office immediately after knocking. Other unimportant business could wait until the evening briefing or even overnight until the morning briefing the next day.

In this case, Major Yuh had been instructed to bring any message from Captain Pak to the general's immediate attention, no matter the time of day. When General Kim motioned to him, Yuh walked quickly to the general's desk and with a slight bow handed him the envelope from the communications room. He stood quietly while the general read the message.

Finally, he looked up and said, "Major, we have more news from our hero in America. The American President is going to brief his intelligence committee about his plans for addressing our threat to send a rocket to his West Coast." He was reflective for a moment and then said, "Major, don't you find it interesting that we can place a Korean woman in a United States congressional office without raising any suspicions. The Americans are so naïve!"

"They are a trusting people, General, but we should not underestimate the capabilities of their FBI. Although she is a skilled agent, this is her first undercover operation in America. I wonder if we should remind Captain Pak to be very careful?"

The general took a moment to respond. "It is my hope that we can welcome Captain Pak home as a hero." Another pause and then, "I don't want to send another message to her so soon. Send orders to her handler to deliver our message and to be careful, and at the same time, see to it that she is given an American handgun. I know that is dangerous, but the time may come when she may be required to permanently silence her source."

"As you wish, General." And with another slight bow he departed the general's office.

After just a moment's hesitation, General Kim lifted his secure phone and called General Gae, who was the commanding general of the Ministry of the People's Armed Forces. When the phone was answered, he said, "This is Colonel General Kim Hyun-woo; connect me with General Gae."

General Gae soon came on the line and abruptly said, "Do you have anything of substance this time, Kim Hyun-woo?"

Inwardly seething at the lack of courtesy, he nonetheless politely responded, "We have another report from our agent in America. Next week we should know the plans of the American President."

"When you have more than expectations, General Kim, please notify me immediately; otherwise don't waste my time." And he abruptly hung up!

General Kim slammed his phone down and said out loud, "If it weren't for me, you pompous cow, you wouldn't have any news at all!"

Chapter Thirty-Five

At about the same time back in Maryland, Harmon Sanders, the CIA Director, was on a secure telephone call with Ernest Hansen, Director of the FBI. Although both Directors were home in their comfortable beds, they had each left instructions with their duty officers to be notified immediately if any additional messages were intercepted.

Although he had just hung up from his duty officer, Director Hansen groggily answered his phone when Director Sanders called, "Ern, another message has been intercepted and we should have the decrypted message available shortly. Isn't it amazing what the NSA can do with a billion dollars in computer equipment?"

"If we had that kind of a budget, we wouldn't need the NSA because we'd catch the spies before they had time to send a message!"

"Now, now. We all have to work together, or as Congress is fond of saying, play together nicely. I'm interested to see if the content of this message helps identify the source of the leaks for us. Do you think it will?"

"If that Army colonel was able to do his part, we should be able to get close enough to see the traitor's shadow."

Director Sanders said, "Since we're already up, why don't you go to your office and I'll join you there as soon as I have the message in hand. Then we can talk about the next step."

"That's a good idea. In fact, I'll call the duty officer and have him call our team together so we can all review the message at the same time. You probably heard that the President is giving a briefing to the intelligence committees on Monday, so I'd like to be able to advise him how to proceed."

"That Army colonel you referred to, Lieutenant Colonel Johnson, is briefing the National Security Council later today. I've been invited, so I'll try and talk with him and see if he was successful in planting any of the information we gave him. Of course, we may already know that answer based on the content of the message."

"Okay, Harm. I'll see you in . . . Ow! What?" A brief pause and then, "Sorry, my wife just hit me and told me to get out of the bedroom. I'll see you in the office later. Bye." He heard the CIA Director laughing as he hung up.

Ninety minutes later, FBI Director Hansen was in his conference room idly chatting with members of the special counterintelligence team when his cell phone rang. He was expecting the call, so he answered after the first ring.

The caller said, "I'm downstairs, but they won't let me come up."

"I'll send an escort right down." He then motioned to the team member nearest the door, who was already out of her chair, to go get the CIA Director. They all knew who it was because they had been excitedly discussing what the message he was carrying might contain. In just a few minutes, they were both back in the conference room.

Director Sanders sat at the far end of the table from Director Hansen, and after introductions were completed, began the discussion with, "Well, as you might expect, I have good news and bad news. The bad news is, we still don't know who the spy is. But the good news is, with Colonel Johnson's help, we've narrowed the search for the traitor to one of the intelligence committees. So we have positively ruled out the White House and the Pentagon as the source of the leaks, at least in this case.

"The message specifically said, and I quote, 'My informant says the President will brief the committee on Monday and his boss will be in attendance.' There's more in the message but that's the part that helps us narrow our search.

"We know the President will actually brief both the House and Senate committees, but that language excludes anyone from the Pentagon or the White House." Looking at his notes, he continued, "So that narrows our search down to the 21 members of the House committee and the 15 members of the Senate committee – or more accurately, a staff member of one of those 36 committee members."

At this point, FBI Director Hansen took up the conversation. "That may sound like a lot of work, and it actually is a lot of work to check on almost three hundred people, but we can bring a tremendous amount of resources to work on this investigation. As soon as this meeting breaks up, we'll start running soft background checks on all of the staffers for those 36 committee members." Looking at his team, he said, "That's only nine offices for each of you. As soon as we have staff in the office you can delegate a lot of that work to them." Looking back at the CIA Director he condescendingly said, "A soft background check looks into bank accounts, trips they've taken, unusual purchases, newspaper reports, telephone records; in other words, anything we can discover without leaving the office." He smiled and said, "We've learned to really love cell phone records!"

Seeing the questioning look on Director Sanders' face, he continued, "Although it'll take a little longer, we'll get the telephone records for the last 90 days for each of those staffers and let the computer start cross-checking telephone numbers. You, as well as most of America, might be surprised at how much we can find out about people just by going to the Internet."

Director Sanders' response as he stood elicited a chuckle from everyone at the table. "Thanks for the reminder. I'll go to my office now and close my Facebook account and throw my cell phone in the incinerator!"

After the CIA Director left the conference room, FBI Director Hansen looked at his counterintelligence team and said, "We're coming down to the home stretch, so it's time to expand our team. Each of you knows someone in this building who would be an asset to us on this case. Think about it for a few minutes and give me some names. I'll call their supervisors and have them reassigned as quickly as possible.

"Based on the content of the latest message, it's obvious that we have a congressman or senator who is talking out of school. Let's find out who they are having lunch with, who they are spending time with, and who they are sleeping with." Looking at one of the team, he said, "Jack, grab 10 support staff and let's get started on the court orders for the telephone records. Let's start with the congressmen and senators and their top three staffers."

Looking at another of the team, he said, "Jessica, you concentrate on the financial records for the same group of people; let's see if we can find anything unusual or suspect.

"Paul and Henry, you guys start checking social media for any deviation from the norm. Each of you grab three support staff to help you with that.

"I'm going to talk to the IT people and let them know we're going to need a 24/7 effort on this case." Thinking for just a moment he said, "I need to back away from the details so that I can keep the big picture in mind. Henry, you're the senior agent so you are now the team lead. Congratulations!"

"Thanks, Director. My wife already wonders what I'm doing 12 hours a day. Last week she asked me about retirement and I told her that we'd retire as soon as there was peace in the Middle East! She wasn't very happy."

And with that, the five of them left to attend to their duties.

Chapter Thirty-Six

As the C-37B, which is what the Air Force calls the Gulfstream G550, taxied up to the ramp at Andrews Air Force Base, I glanced out of the window and was not surprised to see a staff car waiting for us. I was surprised, however, to see Admiral Harrison getting out of the car as we deplaned.

As the three of us walked up, he looked at Sergeant Garcia and without a greeting turned to me and in a gruff voice said, "Who is this, Colonel?"

Sergeant Garcia dropped her bag and stood to attention as I responded, "Admiral, this is Master Sergeant Garcia. She works in my office at the Pentagon and is the NCO you authorized to assist us at SOCOM. She helped prepare the briefing paper for today."

He turned to her and said, "Sergeant, everything you've heard or seen or speculated about while on this TDY assignment is classified top secret, need to know. You will not discuss this with anyone, I repeat anyone, including your commanding officer or anyone in your office. Is that understood, Sergeant?"

What else could she say! "Yes sir, understood, sir!"

He turned back to me and said, "The President has decided to convene a meeting of the National Security Council to hear your briefing. The meeting starts in just a little over two hours. What do we need to do to be ready on time?"

I thought for a moment and then said, "Admiral, I think I should give my briefing in my Class A uniform, not my Army Service Uniform. Let's drop Dr. O'Brien off at her apartment and Sergeant Garcia at the Pentagon, so she can put her laptop in a secure safe. While at the Pentagon we'll make copies of the briefing paper for everyone. Then we'll go to my condo where I can change my uniform and then I'll be ready for the White House."

"Okay, let's go. We'll just make one change to that plan; we'll make copies of the briefing paper at the White House. Everybody in the car." I hadn't noticed until then that the driver had already taken our bags and put them in the trunk.

The Admiral sat in front next to the driver, not usually where a flag officer would sit, while I sat in the back between the ladies. I wasn't really the right size to sit in the middle of the back seat, but that's the way it turned out. They had decided it was easier to drop them off if they were sitting next to the doors.

After a few minutes it occurred to me that I was sitting close – really close – to Vivian. I glanced to my right at Sergeant Garcia who just smiled and said, "It's nice to be chaperoned by a flag officer, isn't it?"

I sighed with my arms uncomfortably in front of me as we continued. Shortly, we arrived at Vivian's apartment complex in Alexandria. As she climbed out I followed her and pulled her bags from the trunk. While we were at the back of the car, I leaned closer and said, "I'll call you as soon as the briefing is completed. Perhaps we can have dinner together."

She smiled in return and said, "I'd like that." And then she walked away.

After I got back in the car, Sergeant Garcia said, "It was nice of you to help Dr. O'Brien with her bags," as she gave me a big smile. I smiled in return and said, "It's what a gentleman would do."

As we continued toward the Pentagon, I reached in my pocket and pulled out two $20 bills and handed them to Sergeant Garcia. When she asked, "What's this for?" I replied, "It's to help with the taxicab to your daughter's soccer game."

With an impish look she said, "Is this also what a gentleman does?"

As I reached to grab it back, she giggled and quickly put her right hand behind her back. I guess there's a little girl in every woman!

We soon dropped her off at the Pentagon and were on our way to my condo. I wanted to wear my Class A uniform for a couple of reasons. First, I knew that wearing my Battle Dress Uniform around civilians would emphasize that I was a soldier ready to do battle, an image I did not want them to have for this meeting. Second, although I don't normally emphasize my ribbons, for this occasion, I wanted the National Security Council to see that a professional soldier who was wounded in battle and had been awarded the nation's second-highest military medal was giving the briefing.

I knew that many of the men and women at the meeting would have no idea what all the colorful ribbons meant, but the two who mattered most, the President and the Chairman of the Joint Chiefs of Staff, would. The President would make the final decision and would ask the advice of the chairman. Interestingly enough, by law the Chairman of the Joint Chiefs of Staff, although the senior uniformed officer in the U.S. military, commands no soldiers, sailors, or airmen; his only job is to advise the President. The others in attendance would ask questions and offer advice, but I suspected the President had already made up his mind.

As an intelligence officer, I had given hundreds of high-level briefings. While I knew that what I told them was important, the way it was presented would be crucial. That was one of the reasons I had taken out most of the details of our mission. The fewer details there were, the less opportunity there would be for nit-picky questions.

I knew the chairman would want to know more about the mission than what I was going to share in this briefing, so I expected to be invited to another meeting where I would be grilled about some of the details. That was okay with me, because we needed the support of the JCS to get all the resources it would take to pull this off.

I was thinking about all this and was rushing out my door when I remembered the briefing document was on the flash drive sitting on my kitchen table. I mentally chastised myself and quickly returned and retrieved it, where I also discovered the lanyard with my ID on it. I wouldn't have gotten very far without that! Maybe I wasn't as calm, cool and collected as I thought I was. I stopped and took a deep breath and mentally recomposed myself.

I walked slowly to the stairs and down to the ground floor. By the time I reached the parking lot, I was mentally ready for what lay ahead.

When I returned to the car I saw that Admiral Harrison had moved to the back seat, a place more befitting a flag officer, so I went around to the other side and sat beside him. As we started for the White House, I asked, "Admiral, on the flight here I had the feeling that I needed to minimize the amount of detail in my briefing, so I'm going to paint broad strokes for the National Security Council. If they ask questions about details, I'm going to tell them we aren't that far along in our planning. This is technically correct, since we haven't developed a written operational plan yet. Do you see any problems with that?"

He chuckled and said, "Colonel, that's the only way to give a briefing to the National Security Council! Of course, General Underhill will want a more detailed briefing, so when the President asks for his advice, he'll have a better idea of what your whole plan is." He looked at me and said, "I presume you do have a plan that has a reasonable chance of success?"

"Yes sir, we have a plan. There are lots of details to work out, and plenty of resources to gather together, but we believe it is the only plan that will work. Especially with the President's demand that nothing points back to the United States."

"I think you'll discover in this meeting that he'll reemphasize that point as the number one requirement of any operational plan. I think you'll also find that he is also going to tell the National Security Council that the reason for this preemptive strike is to ensure that North Korea cannot launch a nuclear weapon toward the United States. You might want to mention that in your briefing as well."

I started to ask a question when he continued, "Yes, I'm aware we don't even know if they have that capability yet, but we don't want to learn they do have it by a rocket landing in San Francisco. Just stick to your plan; be brief and sit down. That's why it's called a briefing!"

Another one of those what-else-can-I-say moments! "Yes sir, can do!"

When we arrived at the White House parking lot, I reminded the Admiral that I still needed to make copies of the briefing paper. He said, "The Situation Room has a photocopier with a USB port for your flash drive." Apparently we were not the first to have that need.

I made 22 copies as quickly as I could, and the Admiral and I collated and stapled them. There were two baskets at the workstation with single pages containing the words SECRET or TOP SECRET; I looked to the Admiral and he handed me a stack of sheets with the top-secret designation, which I attached with a second staple to each report.

We walked into the large conference room joined to the Situation Room with five minutes to spare. Fortunately, we were not the last to arrive. After we were seated in the second row of seats, Henry Williams, the Secretary of Homeland Security, and Harmon Sanders, the CIA Director, arrived at the same time. As soon as they sat down, the President said, "Ladies and gentlemen, let's get started."

He then proceeded to explain his concern with two issues from North Korea. He explained that while we had no evidence that North Korea had yet been successful in miniaturizing a nuclear payload for their rockets, we had to imagine they were making progress. He said he was gravely concerned with their latest public boast about sending a ballistic missile across the Pacific toward our West Coast.

He answered a few questions of little consequence and then got everyone's attention by standing up. When everyone else started to stand, he motioned them back into their seats. He started by saying he did not want to learn that the North Koreans had been successful by hearing about it on CNN. He said he was even less willing to hear about it when a rocket landed in Los Angeles.

And then he dropped the bombshell I knew was coming. He said he was going to borrow a page from the Israeli playbook by ordering a preemptive strike. You could've heard a pin drop on the large oak conference table. He waited a few moments while it sunk in and then said, "I've invited Lieutenant Colonel Johnson, a decorated Army intelligence officer, to brief us on the plans to make that strike." He turned to me and said, "Colonel Johnson, you're up!"

I walked to the end of the table opposite the President and started my presentation. "Ladies and gentlemen, the President's assignment to us contains three elements. First, and the highest priority, whatever we do we can leave nothing that points back to the United States or our ally South Korea. That means we cannot use any of our high visibility assets, such as bombers, cruise missiles, a Marine landing force, or anything with USA stamped on it. Second, to return a sense of stability to that area, we are to ensure the North Koreans do not launch a long range ballistic missile of any kind. And third, we want to ensure we do not start another shooting war between North and South Korea.

"As you can appreciate, or are beginning to appreciate, ladies and gentlemen, this is a daunting challenge for us. We have collected some of the best tactical minds in the American military to draft a plan that will accomplish these goals. We have met, and I am here to tell you, Mr. President, that we believe such a plan can be developed. We now await your orders to continue."

Before I could continue, the President's Chief of Staff, Jefferson Jackson, spoke up. "Surely, Colonel, you don't expect us to believe that you can successfully accomplish those three elements, as you call them; the political implications of failure would be horrendous! We haven't even tried a diplomatic solution to this challenge."

I responded immediately with, "Mr. Jackson, I'm not saying we shouldn't attempt a diplomatic solution; however, we know from previous experience that diplomatic solutions take a long time, especially with the Hermit Kingdom. And time is on their side; if we give them enough time they will develop a nuclear delivery system capable of reaching our West Coast. And the political implications of a ballistic missile launched at us, even if it lands a few hundred miles short, will be even more horrendous."

"Mr. President," said Roberta Quinonez, the Secretary of State, "As you know, we don't have an embassy in North Korea. However, we could ask the ambassador from one of the friendly nations who has diplomatic relations to carry a message inviting the North Koreans to secret discussions. We could at least get a diplomatic solution started."

"Thank you, Roberta. We should certainly make the attempt." Then the President looked at Michael Gonzalez, his Secretary of Energy, and said, "Mike, you've been working with the CIA to try and discover what progress the North Koreans have made on reducing the size of their nuclear weapon to fit on a missile. What can you tell us?"

"Mr. President, getting information out of North Korea is extremely challenging. We're monitoring their efforts via satellite imagery, and we're also watching their imports for clues on their progress. But we don't have any human intelligence assets in North Korea to draw on. Just as an example, there is a large Korean population in the U.S., any one of which could be an agent for them without our knowledge, but there is virtually no Western population there. And no, Dennis Rodman doesn't count!"

Interrupting the chuckling, the President quietly said, "So it's likely the first time we will become aware of their progress is when they actually use it; is that what you're saying?"

"Yes sir, that's a possibility."

"Wait a minute here." When he had everyone's attention, the Secretary of Defense, Hiram Burt, continued, "Are we talking about a long-range ballistic missile or are we talking about a nuclear package?"

The Secretary of Energy answered, "I was referring specifically to a nuclear package, but I suppose the same principle applies to a long-range ballistic missile."

Before the infighting and posturing could continue I spoke up. "Ladies and gentlemen, let me bring us back to the focus of today's meeting. As we all know, North Korea has announced to the world that they have developed a large ballistic missile capable of reaching the West Coast of the United States. So far, we have not been able to confirm the validity of their statement. What the President has asked us to do is develop a plan to neutralize that specific threat.

"If we complicate this assignment, it reduces our chances of success. Besides, if they do have such a missile and we destroy it, it doesn't really matter if they have a small nuclear package; they won't have any way to launch it."

The President's Chief of Staff, who was apparently still smarting from my earlier rebuff spoke up, "Colonel, all you've given us are generalities without any details. How are you going to accomplish such a seemingly impossible task?"

I turned and gave him my best smile and said, "Mr. Jackson, as I mentioned earlier, we've only just met and decided that such a task is achievable. Because significant resources will be required, we're now waiting for the President, our Commander in Chief, to give the go-ahead for additional detailed planning."

The President spoke up before anyone else could and said, "Ladies and gentlemen, the question before the National Security Council is this: Can the United States launch a preemptive strike against a country with whom we are not at war but who has brazenly threatened us?" He turned to his legal advisor, the White House Counsel, and asked, "What is the legal position, counselor?"

"Mr. President, if there is a clear and present danger to the security of the United States, and in this case there appears to be one since they've publicly threatened us, you need only publish a finding to that effect to authorize preemptive action. Of course, it would be better if we had substantive proof that they had such a long-range ballistic missile."

"I agree; we shouldn't do *anything* until we have that proof." This comment came from the president's Chief of Staff.

There seemed to be a murmuring of agreement with that statement from around the table. Then the Chairman of the Joint Chiefs of Staff spoke up. "Mr. President, if we wait until we have that proof to begin planning, then the only viable plan at that time would be to send bombers and cruise missiles into North Korea. That would have significant political consequences, and could potentially begin another shooting war on the Korean Peninsula. And this time, our Japanese ally would probably come under attack, as well.

"I recommend you authorize Colonel Johnson to continue our planning so when we have that proof we can proceed immediately with a viable alternative."

Another murmur of approval came from around the table. The President looked at me and said, "Thank you, Colonel Johnson. Please be seated while we take care of the technicalities." I started to return to my chair and noticed I had not handed out my briefing papers. I paused a moment and then picked them up and carried them with me as I sat down.

The President turned to his legal advisor and said, "Draft a Presidential finding for my signature that there is a clear and present danger to the security of the United States posed by the Democratic People's Republic of Korea. The recognition of this danger is based on the public statement of the President of the Democratic People's Republic of Korea that they will soon launch a ballistic missile at our West Coast, and on satellite surveillance that supports his threat. Put today's date on it."

He turned to Harmon Sanders, the CIA Director, and said, "Director Sanders, continue working directly with the Department of Energy to see if we can learn more about their progress on that missile-sized nuclear package."

Next he turned to General Underhill and said, "General, I want you to support Colonel Johnson in developing a comprehensive plan for neutralizing the North Korean threat of a long-range ballistic missile." He turned to me as he said, "Lieutenant Colonel Johnson has a good start, so let's not lose momentum by burying this in the bureaucracy at the Pentagon." He turned back to General Underhill and said, "Remind everyone that we will take no offensive action until you have specific orders from me."

He looked around the table and asked, "Are there any other questions or comments?"

Although I saw several who looked apprehensive, it appeared his assertive action had quelled any further discussion.

He ended the meeting by saying, "One last thought; I better not read about any of this in tomorrow morning's newspaper. Am I clear on that point?" He looked at everyone and then he stood and left the room, with his Chief of Staff in tow like a puppy dog following its master.

Chapter Thirty-Seven

I had started to stand when Admiral Harrison put his hand on my arm; when I looked at him he nodded to the other side of the table. Admiral Underhill was motioning for us to join him. We waited for most of the others to leave, then walked around the table to where Admiral Underhill was sitting.

We sat down, Admiral Harrison next to the general, and me next to Admiral Harrison. Everyone had gone except CIA Director Sanders, who walked over and stood next to me. He looked down at me and asked, "Any progress on that topic we discussed down south?"

I looked up and said, "I had only one unexpected phone call this past week and it was of no consequence. But I gave him the story we talked about. Oh, and here is the number of the cell phone he used." I wrote the number on the bottom of the cover sheet on my briefing paper and handed it to him.

"Okay, we appreciate your help. Stay on your toes; the President will be conducting another congressional briefing on Monday." And then he left the room with everyone else.

General Underhill stood up and said, "Hold on just a minute." He walked to the door, opened it, and we could hear him tell the Marine guard, "Sergeant, no one comes in." He took one step back toward us and then turned around and went to the door again; he leaned out and said to the sergeant, "Unless it's the President!" Then he came back to the table and sat across from Admiral Harrison and me.

Looking me right in the eyes, he said, "Colonel, Admiral Harrison has led me to believe that you are further along in your planning than you indicated in this briefing. Perhaps you should bring me up to date. Are you further along?"

"General, I think the proper way to answer your question is that we are further along in our thinking, not necessarily our planning. That said, we think we have a plan that solves the middle part of our dilemma, the part about the rocket not being launched. We still have to get our team, or teams if that turns out to be the case, into position to be able to do that. And then we have to extract them after they take care of the rocket."

The general raised his eyebrows and asked, "Are you telling me you expect to put Americans on the ground in North Korea? And not get caught? What kind of crazy people do they have down at SOCOM?"

I chuckled and responded, "Well, General, if they're crazy, they're crazy smart! The tasking ended up in the hands of the Navy SEALs, and they have a lot of experience getting into and out of unfriendly places without being noticed.

"Back to your original request, General; we do have the beginnings of a plan. In fact, I had intended handing everyone a copy of our watered down plan." I stood up and handed him one of the printed briefing papers. "I purposely left out most of the details, because . . ." I sat down as it suddenly dawned on me that the Chairman of the Joint Chiefs of Staff might be out of the loop regarding the search for a traitor. I looked up and said, "General, it suddenly occurs to me that you may not be aware that someone is leaking information to the North Koreans. In fact, the FBI has asked me to assist in ferreting out the traitor."

Giving me a steely gaze, the general said, "Colonel, you amaze me! One day you're a humble lieutenant colonel working in an out-of-the-way office in the Pentagon. The next day you're working for the President's National Security Advisor; and the day after that you're working directly for the President. Now you tell me you're working for the FBI? Tell me, Colonel; as the highest-ranking Army officer in the United States, how do I fit into your schedule?"

I started to answer when the General waved and said, "Never mind, Colonel. I just had to get that off my chest. I happen to agree with the President that switching horses in midstream is not a good idea. I've also looked into your personnel file; it's possible, just possible mind you, that he may have made a good choice."

He looked over at Admiral Harrison and said, "With respect, Admiral; why don't you keep me more in the loop from this point forward."

Now it was Admiral Harrison's turn to have one of those what-else-can-you-say moments. He simply said, "Yes sir!"

The General turned back to me and said, "You heard the President's orders; what do you need from me?"

I thought a moment about the best approach to take with the general, and then decided the direct approach was best. "First and foremost, we need all the resources that Commander Throckmorton listed at the back of that briefing paper. He also said it would be nice if the CNO would sign a general letter tasking subordinate commands to respond to our needs so we didn't have to bother him every time we need something new from the Navy."

I paused while he glanced at the list and then continued. "We need to continue to use the assets we're using from the National Reconnaissance Office, but I think the National Security Advisor, Dr. Richardson, can make that happen. Current satellite imagery is going to be vital to the success of this operation.

"Next, we need orders cut sending the top two or three long-distance sniper teams from the Marine Corps and the top two or three from the Army to MacDill as soon as possible after the first of the year. We think we know who the top two snipers are, but we want to hold a competition to confirm our information. When I say long-distance, I mean a marksman who can hit a 10-square-foot target a mile away."

I pulled out the list of weapons that had been compiled and handed it to the general. "This is a list of the resources we think we're going to need; however, as planning continues our requirements could change. What we need from you General, is a letter signed by the Chief of Staff for each service so that we can draw these resources, and any others we deem necessary, without being questioned." The general nodded and made a note.

I thought for a moment about how to address the next ticklish issue. Again it seemed the direct approach was best. "General, I'm going to continue to need air transportation between here and MacDill; what I've been using, by the way, is just great!"

Before I continued, Admiral Harrison jumped in and said, "General, when the President ordered me to take care of Colonel Johnson, and to see that he had transportation to visit South Korea, I commandeered the Air Force C-37B at Andrews." Sheepishly continuing, he said, "I sent you a memo saying that I had used your name." When General Underhill didn't say anything he continued, "In any case, the President thought it was a great idea." He then nodded to me to continue.

"When the time comes, we're going to need some serious Air Force transport, first to Hawaii for some specialized training and then to Japan to embark upon the submarines that will carry us to the two coastlines of North Korea." I looked down and paused a moment and then looked up and said, "General, I may have inadvertently created a little problem with this." I paused to see his reaction but he merely said, "Son, at my level there are no *little* problems!"

So I continued, "While coming back from South Korea we stopped in Alaska for refueling and a change of crew. When I re-boarded, I was surprised to see an Air Force Major General sitting in the first section. When he challenged me for being on board what he called a senior general's aircraft, I may have offended him when I told him that he was on board my aircraft but he was welcome to ride with me. He was surprised by my answer and didn't take kindly to it. He sat alone for the whole trip and didn't say a word to me.

"When we landed at MacDill, he asked for my unit and commanding officer's name. I may have offended him again when I told him he wasn't authorized to know that information. He stormed off the aircraft and I haven't seen him since. I've recently discovered this general has recently been appointed the deputy commander of the Air Force Airlift Command."

The general leaned back and said, "It turns out I'm acquainted with Major General Burton. I won't give you the details, but he's the *deputy* commander for a reason." His emphasis on the word deputy spoke volumes. "Just make sure when you work with the Air Force that you cross all your T's and dot all your I's. You might even consider delegating the work with the Air Force to someone else.

"Colonel, let me take a moment to talk about the big picture here. You've already seen that the President is being pressured not to do anything that might be politically disadvantageous to his run for reelection. While he has told me privately that he supports this operation 100 percent, remember that the winds of politics are pretty fickle. If you pull this off, you'll get those shiny silver Eagles for your uniform and a pat on the back, along with orders to your next duty station. If it blows up in your face, you're going to be standing all by yourself and you can kiss those Eagles goodbye." He looked at me for a moment and said, "Make sure you're okay with that before you continue."

What he didn't say was that if I didn't continue, I could also kiss those Eagles goodbye. But that wasn't the reason I accepted this assignment. I took an oath when I became an officer and it didn't say anything about picking and choosing my assignments. I looked him straight in the eyes and said, "General, I'm an Army officer with legal and lawful orders; I intend on carrying them out."

"In that case, Colonel, follow your orders. Admiral Harrison will continue to be your point of contact for my office, and I expect to receive regular reports." He stood up and paused a moment on his way to the door, and then he said, "I think you're only going to get one chance to do this right. Let me pass along a piece of advice my father gave me a long time ago – measure twice and cut once."

As he reached the door, he turned again and said, "Regarding you working with the FBI, I think it best if you clear all your actions with Admiral Harrison before you undertake them. I thought the Army was a complicated bureaucracy, and yes, it is, but as I've risen higher in this bureaucracy,

I've discovered that every federal agency is a complicated bureaucracy, and the FBI is right up there at the top of the complicated list."

He opened the door and said, "Colonel, you have our blessings and our prayers." He then turned and left the Situation Room.

After rapidly tapping his fingers on the conference table, Admiral Harrison turned to me and said, "Well, that didn't go quite the way I expected, but all's well that ends well. Let's get organized. First, call Morty today and tell him to continue planning first thing Monday morning. Next, the two of us should meet in my office on Monday and flesh out the requests you've made; that might take a couple of days.

"I'll ask Dr. Richardson to relate to us the gist of what the President tells the two intelligence subcommittees on Monday. I'll also ask her to let the NRO know that we're going to continue to require the services of Dr. O'Brien." Of course, I couldn't help but smile when he said this!

"I think we should visit with the Chief of Naval Operations, perhaps on Wednesday, and confirm the full participation of the Navy. Your request for two submarines that can carry the new advanced SEAL delivery vehicle will have to be coordinated at the highest levels.

"Next, we need to put the Air Force on notice that we'll require a C-17 for transportation. They like to receive those requests as far in advance as possible.

"As far as the FBI thing goes, I agree with General Underhill. The FBI can be quite demanding! Don't get so tied up in their business that it impacts your ability to properly manage this mission. You've got my cell phone number, so use it anytime day or night should the FBI call.

"Any questions?"

I finished making some quick notes and looked up to ask, "I haven't heard him called Morty, so I presume you are referring to Commander Throckmorton; is that right?"

He smiled as he said, "No need to repeat this, but I consider Commander Throckmorton one of the brightest tactical minds in the Navy. He's on a fast track to flag rank, even though he won't like it a bit to be pulled from the field. You would be wise to give him as much latitude as he requires."

He gathered his things together and stood. He turned to me and said, "Well, Colonel, I don't know about you, but I'm going to take the rest of the weekend off! See you in my office Monday morning at 9 AM. I have early meetings that will last until about then." He started to walk away and then turned and said, "By the way, there's a shredder out in the work area; be sure to shred those briefing papers you didn't use." And then I was left alone in the White House Situation Room to ponder my future.

Chapter Thirty-Eight

I gathered my things together and walked out where I found the Marine still guarding the Situation Room. When I asked him, he pointed to the shredding machine. I figured there was no time like the present to complete the first item on my to-do list.

It was early afternoon and I hadn't had lunch yet. When I finished the shredding, I noticed a phone, but when I picked it up there was no dial tone. I figured the Marine guard outside would know how it worked. When I asked he explained, "Sir, that is an internal phone only. If you need to make a call, dial zero and tell the operator the outside number or White House extension you want."

Armed with that information, I dialed the operator and heard, "White House operator; how may I help you?"

I fumbled for a moment and then said, "I need an outside line, please."

"Sir, if you give me the number I'll dial it for you. Do you need a secure line?"

I thought for a moment and realized I could tell Commander Throckmorton everything he needed to know while saying almost nothing. So I said, "I do not need a secure line and the number is 813-555-1793." I heard nothing for several seconds and then, "Sir, this is Commander Throckmorton, sir."

I wondered if his caller ID said White House before I said, "Hello, Morty; this is Robert. We have a green light."

"That's great news! What about all the supplies we need?"

"We'll start filling your requests next week, so I'll be here for several days helping with that. I hope to be back there the following week. Your additional staff should start arriving at the beginning of January. That gives you about a month to pull everything together before leaving for . . . your destination."

"Don't worry, I'll see to their room and board. By the way, there's only one person who calls me Morty, so say hi to the Admiral the next time you see him."

I chuckled and then said, "I'll do that! Talk to you soon; bye." I replaced the phone in its cradle and was surprised when it immediately rang. Looking around and seeing no one else, I picked it up and said, "Colonel Johnson."

"Sir, this is the White House operator; have you completed your call?"

"Yes, I have. Wait! I have another call to make. By the way, do you just connect the call or do you announce it in some way?"

"Sir, we announce all calls by saying, 'This is the White House operator; please stand by while I connect you to a call.'"

I stifled a laugh and said, "Okay, thank you. Here's the phone number." I gave him Vivian's telephone number. It never hurts to impress a girl!

When she answered the phone, I told her that my business at the White House was completed and wondered what her plans were. I was surprised by her answer!

"I've eaten lunch, I've done my laundry, and now I'm going to spend the rest of the weekend with you. What are your plans?"

I must admit, I was at a loss for words. When I didn't respond right away, she said, "What's the matter, cat got your tongue?"

I chuckled out loud and said, "Yes, I think he does! I haven't eaten lunch and I haven't done my laundry. On the other hand, I think it's too early in our relationship to do laundry together." At this, she laughed out loud. I continued, "It turns out that I'm actually free this weekend, but I'd like to start with clean clothes."

"I think that's a good choice. By the time you finish, it's going to be suppertime. Do you suppose we could get a meal someplace other than Denny's?"

I laughed out loud, then said, "What do you think about dinner in a nice place in Baltimore, and then a romantic walk around the harbor?"

"That sounds dreamy!"

"Okay then. Let me get my laundry done, then I'll rent a car and come pick you up. Will you text me your address please?"

"Oh goodness! You don't have to rent a car; I have one. I even think you'll like it. In fact, I may even let you drive it."

"I can drive most anything, even a girl's car."

"Who said anything about a girl's car! I have a bright orange Ford Mustang with lots of muscle! Why don't you text me your address and I'll pick you up in two hours?"

"This I have to see! I'm still at the White House so make it three hours and I'll be ready for you."

"It's a date! See you then. Bye-bye."

"Goodbye." But I think she was already gone. I texted her my address and repeated that I'd see her in three hours. She texted back a simple okay.

Three hours later, my laundry was clean, folded and put away, and I was clean, dressed and standing on the curb. She was right about the muscle! I heard her arriving before I saw her; and it *was* a bright orange car!

She pulled up and pointed to the passenger door, so I climbed in and threw my coat in the back seat. As I did, I saw that she had a coat on the back seat as well. Although a stroll around Baltimore harbor can be romantic, it can also be a chilly walk in the evening. I noted that she waited for me to buckle my seatbelt before driving off.

As we did, I heard Neil Diamond's voice singing *Brother Love's Travelling Salvation Show*. She had a CD of Neil Diamond's hits, and she told me later that his songs relaxed her. Since we lived on the south side of Washington, D.C., I knew we had a bit of a drive to get all the way to Baltimore. I sat back and relaxed as we both listened to Neil Diamond. All in all, we spent a very pleasant hour talking about everything and nothing as we meandered toward Baltimore. Vivian turned out to be a careful and safe driver, notwithstanding the muscle under the hood.

We found a parking spot just off the inner harbor, and after putting on our coats, walked to the Thames Street Oyster House, where I had made reservations. It was rumored to have the best fresh seafood in Baltimore. We were seated upstairs with a great view of the harbor. Since the sun was already down, we enjoyed watching the lights flickering on the surface of the water.

We agreed on the Lobster Mac N' Cheese for an appetizer, while we both asked for water with a lemon twist. Vivian ordered the Gulf of Maine Hake with a spicy tomato sauce, some kind of sausage, fava beans and Maine potatoes. Being less adventurous, I ordered the fish and chips, served with coleslaw and French fries.

We enjoyed a leisurely dinner where Vivian told me she didn't get out much in the area surrounding Washington, and she was enjoying seeing Baltimore. I'd been here with Beth and the children, but I elected not to tell her that. I told her we'd have to come back in the daytime and tour Fort McHenry, which was the inspiration for Francis Scott Key to write his poem that became *The Star-Spangled Banner*.

We finished dinner, and as we walked out I reached for her hand; she turned to me and smiled, and she also moved close enough that our shoulders were touching. Although the wind had been blowing when we entered the restaurant, it was now calm and although chilly, it was not uncomfortable. It was turning out to be a very pleasant evening indeed!

As we walked, we were disappointed to find the National Aquarium closed, but we both commented that it was a beautiful building. We also saw the submarine USS Torsk tied to the pier, which we learned from a bronze plaque has the distinction of having sunk the last Japanese ship in World War II. We walked around the inner harbor and were excited to see the brilliantly lighted USS Constellation, the only Civil War ship still afloat.

We sauntered back and stopped at one of the pavilions and found a place where we could sit on a bench and take in the complete view of the inner harbor. I put my arm around her as we sat close together, and after a moment, she said, "If I were a cat, I would be purring."

After a few minutes, she sat up and turned to me, and softly said, "I have a confession to make." She paused, and the range of possibilities sped through my mind. Was she secretly married? Was she gay? Was she moving to California? Did she have cancer and was dying next week? I knew it was too good to be true; she's really an alien and she's been called home! I couldn't believe how many crazy thoughts went through my head before she continued.

"Before you were brought on board, during a previous meeting in Dr. Richardson's office, Admiral Harrison shared your background with us. I already knew a lot about you before you even showed up. I knew where you went to school, I knew about Beth and what happened, and I knew you're a real American hero with medals and all. The reason I bring this up now is, I know you went to the Mormon University and that you take religion seriously, so I know you're not going to ask me up to your place. That's why I am so relaxed and at peace! I thought you should know. So . . . what fun and exciting things are we going to do tomorrow?"

She sat quietly while I thought about this. Now I knew why when she looked at me with that big bright smile, she sometimes looked like the cat that ate the canary. It took me a moment to process what she had said, but I finally concluded that it didn't change my feelings for her. This wasn't like it is in the movies where the actor would get upset and walk off feeling betrayed and lied to; there was no script here! I looked down and saw that we were still holding hands. I looked up and said, "Vivian, as long as I'm with you, anything would be okay." I continued to look at her eyes as I said, "I just had a thought; let's drive up to Gettysburg and spend the day together."

I hadn't been paying attention to her expression, but now I could see that she had been holding her breath and had an anxious look on her face, which melted into a broad smile when she heard my answer. She threw her arms around my neck, kissed me quickly on the cheek, and whispered in my ear, "Yes!" And then she held me tight.

We stood and hugged each other, and then I kissed her again, but not so quickly! Hand-in-hand, we walked back to the car where she asked, "Would you mind driving?" I nodded my head as she reached into her pocket and handed me the keys to her bright orange Mustang. It felt like a pivotal moment in our relationship.

We were both quiet as I drove back to my condo, but we held hands for almost the entire trip. I drove up to the entrance of my complex where we both got out of the car. Before she got back in to drive home, we hugged each other again and gently kissed once more.

I didn't know about Vivian, but I knew I was going to sleep soundly that night!

Before she drove off she looked up and asked, "How about 8 o'clock for breakfast?"

I smiled and said, "I'll be waiting right here."

"I have a similar philosophy. We can choose a life based on fear or a life based on faith; why would anyone choose fear?"

We were quiet for a moment and then I continued, "What I said earlier about you being like Beth . . . You remind me of her, but that is not the reason I'm attracted to you. I was attracted to her, and now I'm attracted to you for some of the same reasons. You are intelligent, upbeat and positive, self-assured, unafraid, and you possess an unusual amount of common sense." I turned to her and continued, "And to top it off, I find you, and I'm sure it would be true in any society, a strikingly beautiful woman."

Although my bold statement seemed to put a damper on our conversation, when we arrived at the restaurant a few minutes later, she grabbed and held my arm as we walked across the parking lot. She grabbed it again once we were inside waiting to be seated.

I had my usual hearty breakfast and she had Belgian waffles and a small glass of orange juice this time. She looked at my breakfast and said, "I see you're a creature of habit."

"When I find a good thing, I don't give it up easily." I looked at her until she realized the double entendre, then we both concentrated on our breakfast.

Although I don't normally eat quickly, I think we both wanted to be on our way, so we ate without conversation. After I paid the bill, she once again grabbed and held my arm as we walked across the parking lot. I was beginning to like that!

The 90-minute drive to Gettysburg seemed to pass rather quickly as we talked about likes and dislikes and things we'd like to do if we only had time. We also played a game of conversation that started with, "When I was a little girl, I wanted to be . . ." and then she finished the sentence, or "When I was a little boy, I wanted to be . . ." and then I finished the sentence. It was a delightful conversation, and we were learning a lot about each other.

When we arrived in Gettysburg, I immediately headed to a gas station. Not so much for the gas as for the restrooms we both needed! As we were walking out, Vivian pointed and said, "Oh, look at that! I've always wanted to ride a Segway." She had spotted an advertisement for a guided tour of the battleground on Segways. I thought it was a grand idea! We saw that we had enough time for a quick lunch at the Wendy's across the street. It would have to be a quick lunch because at this time of year, 12:30 was the last tour of the day, and the advertisement warned that late arrivals would not be permitted on the tour.

We arrived at the Segway location about 15 minutes early and as luck would have it, we were able to rent the last two Segways available, so we easily fell in to the tour that was about to take place. The first 30 minutes was spent learning how to drive the Segway; it turned out to be pretty simple, but only after several minutes of practice. Vivian picked it up pretty quickly and laughed as I had to learn not to over control my mount!

The tour lasted about two and a half hours after we got started. We drove, if drove is the right word for a Segway, along both Union and Confederate lines and visited many of the most famous sites. We saw Seminary Ridge and Cemetery Ridge, Union General Meade's Headquarters, the Lutheran Theological Seminary, Pitzer Woods where Confederate General Longstreet had his headquarters, and several other points of interest.

We learned that the three-day battle ended with the largest number of casualties of the entire Civil War. On the third day, there was a dramatic infantry assault by 12,500 Confederate soldiers against the center of the Union line on Cemetery Ridge, popularly known as Pickett's Charge. The charge was ultimately not successful, at great loss to the Confederate Army. Although both sides had over 23,000 casualties each during the three days of fighting, General Lee led his battered army back to Virginia after the battle. Some considered this to be the turning point of the war.

The battle took place during the first three days of July, 1863, and later that year, on November 19, President Lincoln was there to honor the fallen Union soldiers, and in what we now call his Gettysburg Address, he redefined the purpose of the war.

We finished this tour around 3:45 and decided to walk through the museum. There were many artifacts on display, including period-specific cannon, firearms, and uniforms. We were especially intrigued with the oil painting of Pickett's Charge by a French artist; this amazing painting is 42 feet tall and 377 feet long. We even walked through the gift shop, and while we enjoyed looking at all the items for sale, we didn't buy anything.

We did stop in the restaurant in the visitor center, which they referred to as a Refreshment Saloon. We tried the beef stew and cornbread, which was advertised as one of the *Tastes of the Period*, and possibly because we were hungry by this time, we both found the selection quite tasty.

After our supper, we sat for a few minutes and talked about the evils of war. For a relatively new nation to be engaged in a Civil War, over what was essentially an economic issue, where over 600,000 American lives would be lost, seemed pretty senseless to both of us.

Although slavery had been one of the major issues that led to the Civil War, it was more an economic issue than a moral issue. In fact, President Lincoln's desire at the beginning of the war in 1861 was to simply keep the Union together.

However, as the war proceeded, slavery became a larger issue. We both agreed that as it turned out, the American Civil War had far-reaching effects on the topic of slavery, not only in the United States, but in Europe as well. Although it would take many more years to overcome the prejudices based on skin color, the American Civil War would stand out as the pivotal event in human history to achieve this end. Both Vivian and I agreed that this goal had not yet been fully achieved.

Vivian looked at her watch and said, "If we leave now, we could go to my apartment and watch a movie before the day ends. I'll even provide the popcorn!"

I readily agreed, so we left the restaurant and walked hand in hand to her car. I was still trying to get accustomed to a bright orange Mustang. As we walked, I wondered what kind of movie she would pick. Although Beth had tried to expand my interests, I generally steered away from girly movies. Truth be told, I really enjoyed a good action flick.

The drive back took longer than I expected; it seemed like everyone who had gone away for the weekend was now headed back to the D.C.

Metro area. Oh well, I was in the company of an intelligent and beautiful woman, so why should I mind?

Following her directions, we finally ended up at her apartment. I asked her why she lived here when the NRO was up in Chantilly; her answer told me more about her.

"I used to live just five minutes away from the office but soon discovered that whenever there was a question or a problem, I had a tendency to jump in my car and drive to the office. Pretty soon I felt like I was living there! So when my lease was up, I moved down here. I live near the freeway, so if I have to I can go to the office after hours. But now it has to be a pretty darned good reason for me to do so."

Her hand reached for mine as she led me to the main entrance and then she walked right past the elevator for the stairs up to her second-story apartment, a nice two-bedroom apartment, with the smaller of the bedrooms furnished as a study.

She noticed my surprise when I saw the very large big screen TV in her living room. "I often use a magnifying glass at the office to see the details of an image; I didn't want to have to use one at home too."

I couldn't help but notice that everything in her apartment seemed to have a place, and everything was in its place; her apartment was spotless. It could've been used for an advertisement in *Better Homes & Gardens*! My condo was clean, but I didn't mind having a few things thrown about. And it definitely wouldn't qualify for an advertisement in a magazine.

I saw that she had a small collection of DVDs, all still in their original cases by the way, so I returned to wondering what movie she would choose. As if reading my thoughts, she turned to me and said, "I don't have a large collection, but they are movies I enjoy. Come help me choose one."

As I looked at her collection, I saw that they were mostly older movies, not only popular in their day but still popular today. As I looked through the titles, it suddenly dawned on me that they were in alphabetical order. As I confirmed this, I looked up and she said, "Yes, they are in alphabetical order. It makes it so much easier to find one that way. Do you see one you like?"

"Actually, it looks like I would enjoy any of them. How do you suggest we choose?"

"Well, in that case, we'll just start at the beginning!" And she reached over and pulled *The African Queen* off the shelf.

My enthusiastic response was, "That's a great choice. I love it when the good guys win!"

While she inserted the DVD in the player and started the movie, I turned toward the sofa and was trying to decide where to sit when she solved that problem for me. While the sofa was large enough for three, she chose to sit in such a manner that I could choose to sit on her right side with our hips virtually touching and with the right arm of the sofa to my side, or to her left, leaving plenty of room between us. I don't think she was testing me but she did leave me a choice.

I smiled at her and said, "Vivian, when you give me a choice, I'll always choose to sit close to you." I sat down to her right and reached for her hand. As if on cue, the movie started before she could say anything.

Just over halfway through the movie, she untangled her hand from mine and used the remote to pause the movie. She stood up and said, "I almost forgot; I promised popcorn."

While she busied herself with the popcorn, I excused myself to use the bathroom. Like the rest of the apartment, it was spotless! Though I admit I was tempted, I did not look in her medicine cabinet to see if the items were in alphabetical order! When I came out, the microwaved popcorn was divided into two bowls she was holding, and she had resumed her spot on the sofa. She held out both bowls to me inviting me to choose one.

As I sat down she used the remote to restart the movie. She turned to me and said, "I hope you like buttered popcorn! Here's a napkin because you're going to need it!" She was right; it was buttery, and it was delicious!

We had just finished our popcorn when she reached for my hand and held it tightly. This was the scene in the movie where Katharine Hepburn was helping to pull the leeches off Humphrey Bogart's torso and legs. This seemed like the ideal opportunity to put my arm around her, so I took her hands in my right hand and put my left arm around her shoulders; she moved closer and seemed very comfortable in my embrace. We stayed that way through the rest of the movie.

When the movie ended she looked up with an expectant look on her face so I leaned over and quickly kissed her. We held each other for a moment longer and then she quietly said, "I know, it's time for you to go."

I was full of emotion, but I stood up and said, "It's late; there's no sense you driving me home and then having to come back here. Why don't I call a taxi and save you the trip?"

She stood and said, "I don't mind driving you, but I'll take you up on your offer. Why don't you make the call while I clean up the popcorn mess? Then we can wait downstairs for the taxi." There was certainly no mess from the popcorn, but she did have to move the bowls to the kitchen and throw away our used napkins. I didn't think she was a neat freak, but she was tidy!

I made the call while she washed the popcorn bowls, and then we walked downstairs together to sit in her lobby. I turned to her and asked, "I'm not certain of my schedule, but I expect to be in town all week long. Are you busy tomorrow night?" And before she could answer I said, "And Tuesday night, and Wednesday night, and Thursday night, and Friday night? And what are you doing next weekend?"

She laughed in a delightful way and said, "I don't know; I'll have to check my social calendar!"

I saw that there was a pen and a small notepad on the desk in the lobby, so I excused myself and went to the desk and used the pen to write quickly on a sheet from the notepad. I tore off the sheet, folded it in half and carried it back to her and said, "I think I found your social calendar." She laughed out loud when she unfolded the paper and saw the one word I had written on it – *Available*!

The taxicab arrived in a few minutes, and after she gave me a parting kiss on the cheek, I was alone in the back seat thinking that the world was a wonderful place and life a wonderful adventure.

Chapter Forty

Monday morning, while I was waiting in Admiral Harrison's office for him to return from his earlier meetings, my cell phone vibrated. I pulled it out and saw I had a text message from Major Green that read: *call me!* I was about to call him on his office phone but thought better of it and called him on his personal cell.

He answered not by saying hello but with, "There are rumors you are in the building; could that be correct?"

I responded with, "I'm not sure I'm allowed to answer that question! But just in case the rumors are true, what did you have in mind?"

"I don't want to be a gossip, but I do have some office intel you'll be interested in. As Sergeant Garcia explained it to me, when Colonel Jacobs got here this morning, he called her into his office and asked where she'd been for the past week. He wasn't happy when she told him that her TDY assignment was classified. Then he asked her if she knew where you were. When she responded that he wasn't cleared for that information, he about had a conniption fit!

"But wait, there's more; it gets even better. While Garcia was in his office, she talked with his sergeant. Guess what she learned from her?" When I didn't answer he continued, "Okay, since you asked, I'll tell you. She told Garcia that on Thursday last week a copy of your orders came in detaching you for TDY of an indeterminate period of time in the office of the National Security Advisor. She told Garcia that he stormed out to visit with our general. When he came back, he had a grin like the Cheshire cat.

"Wait, you haven't heard the rest of the story; would you like to?" Again, I didn't answer, and after a moment he continued. "All right, since you asked again, I'll tell you the rest of the story. Friday morning, Colonel Jacobs came to my office and handed me orders appointing me section chief; they were countersigned by the general. Not acting, not temporary, but the actual section chief. You know what that means don't you?"

"Well, to start with, the section chief is an O-5 billet. You can thank me later if your oak leaves change color."

"You're right about that, but he had that topic covered. It turns out that a new section chief can be one grade below the billet for up to six months. But that's not what I'm referring to. What that really means, Robert, is that when your TDY assignment is finished, there is no place here for you to return to."

"Hmm, I'll have to ponder the implications of that. There's another piece to that puzzle. Since I'm technically still assigned to his office, he's responsible for writing my annual performance review. But since he just did that last month, he doesn't have to write one till next year. If I move on from this TDY assignment before then, there could potentially be a missing performance review in my personnel file. That's not good for one's career."

"You're beginning to understand how the Pentagon works. But there's one more piece to this puzzle that you're going to love. He called Sergeant Garcia in and told us both that since you are no longer assigned to this office, you're not authorized access to any of the information we process. He gave us a direct order that if you called we were to hang up on you!"

"David, you are just full of good news!" I pondered all of this for a few moments and then said, "For the health of your career, this should be the last conversation we have for a while. But David, don't be surprised if you get a request for information from the Office of the Joint Chiefs of Staff."

"So that's where you are today! By the way, it was one of Sergeant Garcia's sergeant friends who saw you earlier. Now that I think of it, is it possible that Jacobs will mess with Sergeant Garcia's career?"

"I wouldn't put it past him. I'll see what I can do." I looked up as Admiral Harrison walked in, so I said to Major Green, "I have to go now; thanks for the info." I put the phone away before he could answer but I hoped he knew me well enough to know I wasn't being rude.

The rest of the day was spent refining the requests that our planning team had put together, with an emphasis on getting orders out to the sniper teams we wanted to invite to the competition at SOCOM. To do that expeditiously we had to involve the Commandant of the Marine Corps and the Chief of Staff of the Army. By the end of the day, they had not only our requisition, but had also received a hand delivered letter from General George Underhill, Chairman of the Joint Chiefs of Staff, acting for the President, ordering them to comply.

In a couple of weeks, there would be six sniper teams arriving at MacDill Air Force Base. I made a note to call Commander Throckmorton with the news first thing in the morning.

The Admiral asked me when I would have an outline of the support staff we would need, along with proposed reporting dates. Because I wanted to consult with Commander Throckmorton, I told him I could have that Tuesday afternoon.

Not that I had anything else on my mind, but at around 5:30 PM I asked if he had a moment to discuss an issue that was only tangentially mission oriented. He invited me in and I described the situation with Sergeant Garcia. He leaned back and said, "Colonel, I'm an admiral in the United States Navy. What do you expect me to do about a potential problem with a master sergeant in the Army?"

I smiled and said, "Admiral, I've already discovered that you're not *just* an admiral in the United States Navy. You work for the chairman of the Joint Chiefs of Staff and you have a permanent pass to the White House. You know people, you meet people, you influence decisions.

"I wrote Sergeant Garcia's last performance review and I know she's eligible for promotion early next year. She has a home and family here in the D.C. area; I think she'd opt for retirement rather than take a career move. It would be a shame for the Army to lose her talents. Especially because of a narrow-minded, egotistical commanding officer."

"First, Colonel, I'm going to ignore your disrespect of a senior officer, but don't make it a habit. Second, I'm too busy to be your errand boy. On the other hand, if you had a reason to visit the Deputy Army Chief of

Staff's office tomorrow, you could keep your eyes and ears open for yourself. I suggest around 10:30 or 11 o'clock."

He then changed the subject by saying, "By the way, I had a phone call from Dr. Richardson. Apparently two boxes with your name on them arrived at her office from the Pentagon. When she had one of her staff call about them, she was told that since you were never coming back to your job at the Pentagon, they boxed up your things and sent them to you.

"It seems your CO has crossed you off his Christmas list! It also appears he plays the bureaucratic game better than you do. But don't worry, there'll be a slot for you somewhere. Anything else?"

"No sir, I'll see you in the morning."

"In case I forget to tell you later, we have a meeting in Dr. Richardson's office at 7:30 next Monday morning." And with that he turned his attention to the stack of papers that were covering his desk.

I returned to the closet-sized office they had let me work in during the day and texted Vivian. No response!

As I worked my way toward an exit that I knew Colonel Jacobs would not use, my iPhone beeped. A text message from Vivian said: *in traffic almost home movie your place? I bring movie you bring popcorn.*

I smiled and wondered what movie she would bring, then texted back: *it's a date.* In my rush to be accommodating, I forgot about Jacob and Susan! I realized my dilemma in a few minutes and came up with a quick solution. I texted both of them and told them I was bringing a coworker home and would they mind studying at a friend's house. Not unexpectedly, they both replied in the affirmative. I know I was being disingenuous, but it wasn't a lie.

I rode the Metro toward my home, and by the time I walked to my condo from the stop, the orange Mustang had already arrived. We walked arm in arm to my door, where she immediately took control of the DVD player. While she was loading up the movie, I went to my bedroom and changed out of my uniform. When I walked out, she gave me a big smile from the sofa. We sat on the sofa in the same relative spots we had in her apartment; it's an arrangement I could get used to!

About halfway through, she paused the movie *American Beauty*, and gave me an expectant look. So I leaned over and gave her a kiss! After a moment, she said, "That's very nice and I like it, but where's my popcorn?"

I chuckled as I jumped up and headed for the kitchen. After a moment, she asked where the kids were, so I told her they were studying at a friend's house. After I started the microwave, she joined me and asked where the bowls were. It looked like this would be a team effort! I handed them to her, and after she placed them on the countertop, she reached around my head and pulled us closer for another kiss. We gently hugged each other to the sound of popcorn popping and didn't let go until the microwave dinged to indicate the popcorn was ready.

To make a short story even shorter, we ate our popcorn as we watched the rest of the movie. At its conclusion, she turned to me with her dreamy eyes and said, "I don't have to leave right away; what have you been doing at the Pentagon?" We talked about work for a few minutes and then switched topics and talked about her movie collection. I haven't talked that long with a woman for a long, long time, but pretty soon she pushed away from the sofa and quietly said, "I better get my movie now and head for home."

I tried not to sound disappointed as I said, "Okay, I'll walk you out to your car."

Just before we got to the door, Jacob and Susan walked in. When they saw Vivian, Susan's eyes went wide open and Jacob almost tripped over the sofa as he walked into the living room. When I returned from walking Vivian to her car, Susan said, "She's your coworker?" And then I spent several minutes describing her job at the National Reconnaissance Office and how it related to my new assignment in the White House.

And that's how the rest of the week went; we both worked during the day and then ended up at her apartment to watch a movie, munch on popcorn and talk for a few minutes after the movie. She selected a new movie each time from her collection, all in alphabetical order. We had already watched *The African Queen,* and after *American Beauty* on Monday, we watched *A Beautiful Mind* on Tuesday, *Braveheart* on Wednesday, *Casablanca* on Thursday, and *Groundhog Day* on Friday.

On Saturday, we drove down to Mount Vernon and explored a little bit and then drove back to her apartment to watch *The Lion King* late that afternoon. We went out for supper and then drove to her apartment to watch another movie. This time I selected one out of my small collection; it turned out to be a movie she had never seen before, titled *Lost Horizon*. This was the version with the Burt Bacharach music and was a favorite of mine.

Before I left her apartment Saturday evening, I told her that on Sunday I would be attending church in the morning with my children. I was surprised when she asked if she could go with me, but of course I said yes. We attended church and then came back to my condo for lunch, after which we all watched another movie from my collection. I selected *Mary Poppins* and was surprised when she said she had never seen it. She also told me that she had never been to a Mormon Church service before and was fascinated by it. She even commented that everyone seemed so friendly.

Our pattern continued on Sunday afternoon, with the exception that we had two teenagers watching the movie with us! We all watched the movie to about the halfway point and then popped popcorn and watched the rest of the movie as we munched on our popcorn. I think my kids watched me almost as much as they watched the movie.

However, Vivian broke our after-movie routine when at the end of the movie she stood and said, "This has been an exciting week for me; I've enjoyed every minute we spent together. But as you once said, I'd like to start tomorrow with clean clothes. Will you walk me out to my car?"

With that she turned to Jacob and Susan and said, "I'll see you guys later."

In the absence of facts, I decided not to read anything into her somewhat abrupt departure. So I walked her out to her car, where we shared a somewhat chaste kiss and she drove off.

As I walked back to my condo, it occurred to me that I also needed to get some laundry done. But laundry would have to wait a few more minutes! Just as I closed the door, I was waylaid by my two teenaged children. Jacob was especially curious.

"Dad, you said she was a coworker, right?" I nodded, so he continued. "Are you allowed to date coworkers?" At which point, Susan jumped in with, "She's more than a coworker; I see the way she looks at you – and the way you act around her."

I interrupted with, "We're just friends." Before I could continue, they looked at each other and said in harmony, "Right!" Then they both giggled and went to their rooms.

Shaking my head, I went and gathered up my laundry. While my clothes were being gently beat to death in the washing machine, I thought about what they had said. I don't know why I said that Vivian and I were just friends, because I knew we were more than that. If my kids could see it, I wonder if we were that transparent at work?

Taking a deep breath, I decided to ponder that question another time. I wanted to move my thinking back into my comfort zone, so I mentally reviewed what I had accomplished this week on the mission.

As planned, I had called Commander Throckmorton Tuesday morning and gave him the good news about the sniper teams' orders having been cut. We had talked for almost an hour about support staff requirements and proposed reporting dates so that I could draft the outline we would need for Admiral Harrison; this took the rest of Tuesday.

On Wednesday morning, Admiral Harrison and I met to discuss the support staff requirements. He told me that to forestall any inter-service rivalries, the support staff would be drawn from all four major services. We needed meteorologists, communications specialists, real-time satellite image analysts, armorers, aircraft dispatchers and schedulers for all the transportation that would be necessary, and equipment specialists. We broke for lunch and then I spent the rest of the afternoon in my little closet office drafting the orders to the appropriate service commanders.

I hadn't realized the extent of the bureaucracy in the Pentagon until I had to spend all of Thursday and most of Friday answering and making phone calls responding to inquiries about the personnel levies from the

JCS. Friday afternoon, Admiral Harrison and I met again to discuss what still needed to be done and to develop a plan to attack those needs on Monday.

He also agreed with me that I should head back to SOCOM on Tuesday or Wednesday at the latest. I wanted to be there to pick up on all the little things that needed to be done, just in case we needed Admiral Harrison's influence. I also wanted to be involved in in the decision-making process about where the operational practice would take place and how much practice would be necessary.

I wanted to visit in detail with Lieutenant Commander Cromwell regarding the advanced SEAL delivery vehicles that would be used for our landings and extractions in North Korea. While the SEAL teams were familiar with their operation, the Army and Marine Corps members of the two teams would need at least a little practice. Our initial planning team had been convinced our landings could take place without being discovered, but they were not as positive about the extractions. It was vital we accomplish our mission without implicating either the United States or South Korea, so we wanted the landings and the extractions to go off without a hitch.

My laundry was washed, dried, folded and put away before my thoughts returned to Vivian and her abrupt departure that evening. We spent a lot of time together this past week, and I was not unfamiliar with the concept of a person needing time to ponder. After reaching for my iPhone several times, I decided not to intrude beyond a simple text message wishing her a good evening. Her response was a simple thank you.

Although I had been married for several years, I was still not comfortable with my understanding of the complexities of the female mind. I remember someone once said that a woman is like a mystery wrapped in an enigma. I finally fell asleep wondering if there was something I'd left undone.

Chapter Forty-One

I was surprised as I was preparing for work Monday morning when my iPhone sounded an alarm. The alarm reminded me of the meeting in Dr. Richardson's office at 7:30, which I had completely forgotten. Although I had pulled out my Army Service Uniform, I decided instead to wear my Class A uniform. Since I didn't know what the agenda for the meeting was, I opened my small briefcase and confirmed that all my notes about the upcoming mission were there.

Probably because it was way above my pay grade, I had also forgotten that the President was going to brief the House and Senate subcommittees on intelligence last week. I made a note to ask Dr. Richardson how that briefing had gone.

Since the White House was further away than the Pentagon, I had to leave in time to catch an earlier train. I was in a rush, but I caught myself at the door and took time to turn around and check the dining room table to make sure I hadn't forgotten anything. Satisfied, I closed the door and ran down the stairs.

At about the same time, in Congressman Paul Singleton's crowded office, a full staff meeting was taking place. He and his wife had only arrived back in Washington the previous evening from a short but successful four-day campaign fund-raising trip. He had just finished telling his staff that he was excited to get back to real work, when he excitedly added that the chairman of the Democratic Party had assured him that he had their full support for the upcoming election.

After the polite applause died down, he chased them from his office but called to his Chief of Staff to remain. After the office door had been closed, he said, "Mike, I haven't had time to brief you on the President's presentation early last week to the two intelligence committees." The congressman sat in his favorite loveseat as Mike settled into the well-used office sofa.

"The President spent several minutes rehashing the threats North Korea has made about sending a ballistic missile our way. He went on to tell us that current intelligence gathering methods had not been able to determine whether they had that capability or not. He also said that conversations with the South Koreans had not thrown any new light on this topic.

"Then he changed subjects slightly and spent several minutes rehashing the capability of the North Koreans for reducing a nuclear package to a size that would fit on such a missile. Then he again told us that our current intelligence gathering methods have not been able to determine whether they had that capability. He told us the South Koreans didn't know either.

"It was obvious he was setting the stage for something more dramatic. And sure enough, he was!

"He told us that he had authorized the Special Operations Command to formulate plans for sending a SEAL team into North Korea to obtain first-hand intelligence. When he told us this, the committee room just exploded!

"He waited for the hub-bub to quiet down, then reminded both committees that in March 2013, North Korea had invalidated the 1953 armistice and was therefore in a state of war with South Korea and that the United States was obligated by treaty to continue our military support.

"He then essentially threatened all of us by saying that if we didn't approve of his intelligence-gathering foray, he would be compelled to tell the American people that Congress was not supporting his efforts to defend against North Korean threats. That caused another series of angry replies from committee members.

"He finished by telling us that he wasn't rushing to take irresponsible action and that he anticipated a lengthy and detailed planning period, probably resulting in a SEAL team operation next spring. He told us he would give a further briefing before sending the SEAL team into North Korea."

The Congressman continued his story. "The next hour was taken up with committee members throwing out questions and making statements; the Senators were especially vociferous toward the President! I sat and listened to everything he had to say and was glad I was not in his shoes. If he doesn't do something and the North Koreans make good on their threats, he'll be skewered by the press. If he does do something and it goes wrong, same result!"

While the congressman caught his breath, his Chief of Staff spoke up and said, "It sounds like the odds are against him. It's curious that he would use a SEAL team for that surveillance; wouldn't it be better to use an agent from South Korea to gather that intelligence? At least they'd fit in better with the general population."

"In fact, one of the Senators asked him why the South Koreans weren't willing to help. His response was, that they had sent someone into North Korea earlier this year and he had been captured almost immediately. Apparently the North Koreans took them to task about it and they weren't willing to be embarrassed again so soon. And to top it off, they summarily executed the South Korean agent!

"In any case, the President told us that SEAL teams were accustomed to getting into and out of places that others couldn't; like we didn't already know that! He went on to tell us that he had someone from the White House providing oversight of the operation, apparently the same Lieutenant Colonel Johnson he told us about before. He told us that no action would take place until he was absolutely certain it could be done without incriminating the United States, or South Korea for that matter."

The Chief of Staff asked, "As a President running for reelection, he's in a tight spot. Do you suppose the North Koreans are trying to influence the election by forcing him to take action?"

The congressman leaned forward and said, "That's precisely what Senator Bollinger asked after the President left our meeting. As chairman of the Senate intelligence committee, he tries to stay on top of the politics involved in any military operation. He even suggested that embarrassing the President was exactly the North Korean plan."

"Did the combined committee decide on any action at this point?"

"No; we're taking a wait-and-see attitude. This is where you come in. I want you to call this Army officer and see if you can learn any more about their plans. Congressman Hoag even suggested, after the President left, that perhaps he wasn't telling us all he had in mind. It would improve my standing on the committee if we discover something the President hasn't told us. Don't rock the boat, but see what you can find out."

Mike Fontana chuckled as he said, "The colonel was surprised when I called him on his personal cell phone the first time; I'll give him another call this morning and see what I can find out."

They both stood up and the congressman gave his Chief of Staff a man hug before he returned to his desk and his Chief of Staff left to return to his own small office.

As he walked toward his office, he nodded to Mrs. Endicott who followed him. While the congressman's office door was a solid and substantial wooden door, the Chief of Staff's office door was flimsy and contained a window in the upper half. He sat behind his desk as Mrs. Endicott took a chair in front of it. Although he was certain no one was listening to their conversation, he still turned on a small radio he kept in the office for just that purpose – that of masking any conversation in his office.

Before he spoke, she asked, "Did he brief you further on the success of his campaign fund-raising trip?"

Fontana laughed as he said, "He never mentioned it! What he did talk about was the briefing the President gave to the house intelligence committee." Looking down and fumbling with some papers on his desk, he continued, "We can talk about it after work tonight." With a condescending smile on his face he asked, "You are free tonight, aren't you?"

She gave him a coquettish look as she stood, and then said, "Well, let me go out and check my social calendar!" And with that she left his office, but left his office door standing open.

She knew enough about Michael Fontana at this point she was certain her departing words would leave him struggling with his self-importance the rest of the day. Nonetheless, at the end of the day after everyone else had left, they were the only ones in the office.

When Michael came out of his office, she stood and walked to the main door and made a big show of locking it. She turned and smiled at him as she walked toward the Congressman's office. She knew how to use the sofa to her advantage.

Seven minutes later, the congressman's Chief of Staff was telling her everything he had just learned about the President's briefing. And three hours later it was being decrypted in the basement of the North Korean intelligence service building in Pyongyang.

Chapter Forty-Two

Half a world away, General Kim Hyun-woo, Director of the North Korean intelligence service, was taking an early phone call at home telling him a new message from their agent in the United States had arrived. He ordered that a courier be dispatched immediately to his home with the message.

It is remarkable that the North Korean Director of intelligence would learn about the President's intelligence briefing almost as quickly as Colonel Johnson.

The courier arrived within 15 minutes, which pleased General Kim, and after he read the message, he knew he would have to inform General Gae as soon as possible. General Gae would want to know immediately that the Americans planned to send their Navy commandos to spy on their research facility early next year.

It would be unusual to call General Gae at his home, but the commanding general had ordered General Kim to notify him immediately of any additional news. General Kim smiled as he realized he would be interrupting General Gae's dinner.

And that's exactly what happened. When General Gae's military aide answered the phone, he told General Kim the general couldn't be disturbed because he was just sitting down to dinner. He insisted, and in a few moments General Gae angrily answered the phone. "Is it your intent to be obnoxious, or do you have important news?"

"General Gae, it was you who asked that I notify you immediately when we received important information. We have received another important message from our hero in America." He paused for effect, thereby eliciting an angry response from General Gae; "Yes, yes! Why do you make me wait? What is the report?"

General Kim smiled as he responded, "The American President has briefed his politicians and in doing so gave them a date for sending his Navy commandos to spy on us." He paused again, eliciting another angry response from General Gae. "Kim, you try my patience! What is the full report?"

"General, the report is that they will send Navy SEALs to invade our country to learn more about our efforts to place a nuclear weapon on top of our ballistic missile. They are in the planning stages now and will be ready to invade us early next year, perhaps in March or April."

"That is excellent news; your source must be very good. By the way Kim, you have never told us, are you using a spy or have you found an American traitor?"

"As you know general, this is a closely held secret. I would prefer not discussing it on the telephone. Perhaps we can discuss my success the next time we meet."

Obviously seething, General Gae responded, "You are a presumptuous man, General Kim. However, I should meet with General Lee Gun-woo and tell him he must launch our new rocket in February before the Americans can spy on us. Notify me immediately if you learn anything more." And with that he summarily hung up.

General Lee Gun-woo was the commander of the North Korean Army Rocket Service and responsible for launching the new ballistic missile that would surprise the world. It had been decided at the highest levels that they would launch the rocket as soon as possible and announce to the world that they had a nuclear package they could use whenever they wanted. That this was not yet true didn't bother the North Korean leaders.

The scientist who had failed to achieve this goal had already been sent to greet his ancestors and his deputy put in his place. But even this had not generated the scientific breakthrough necessary to place a nuclear weapon on their new ballistic missile. While the scientists at the research laboratory reported that progress was being made on reducing the size of the nuclear package, they had not yet been successful.

After General Kim concluded his conversation with General Gae, he sat and pondered what he should do next. After a few moments, he reached for his phone and called his aide, Major Yuh Min-soo. When Major Yuh answered, the general told him that they had received another message from their spy in America and then said, "Major, send a message to our hero in America and tell her that she must find out how the Americans plan to invade our country. We must know this so we can prepare a proper reception for them."

General Kim knew that if he was personally responsible for capturing the American invaders, his career would receive a substantial boost. Then General Gae would have to show him proper respect! His smile grew as he walked to his dining room; he sat and told his servant he was now ready for his breakfast.

Chapter Forty-Three

Meanwhile, 6,900 miles east of Pyongyang and half a day earlier, Colonel Johnson had received a phone call from Dr. Richards' secretary advising him that their meeting had been postponed until 4:30 PM. Delighted that he would be able to take care of more details about the mission, he directed the cabbie to head for the Pentagon.

After nearly a full day of work, Colonel Johnson left the Pentagon in time for his 4:30 meeting at the White House. A few moments after he arrived, Admiral Harrison walked in, and shortly after that Marty Packard, the CIA IT specialist, arrived. As they were exchanging pleasantries, the President's Chief of Staff, Jefferson Jackson, also walked in.

He didn't waste any time preempting the meeting by saying, "Dr. Richardson, thank you for bringing us all together once again. Director Sanders met with the President earlier this morning and convinced him we should give additional consideration to a cyber-warfare solution. Mr. Packard is here to describe their plan in more detail." And he nodded to Marty Packard who stood up.

Before he could start, Dr. Richardson's office door opened and in walked Dr. O'Brien, who said, "Sorry I'm late; two accidents on the Beltway." Although she sat in the empty chair next to me, she didn't look my way.

Dr. Richardson spoke up and said, "Go ahead, Marty; the floor is all yours!"

While I listened to Mr. Packard's description of the CIA proposal to put a virus in the North Korean research laboratory's computer system, I was very aware of Vivian's presence. I had been in hundreds, if not thousands, of meetings with women present since Beth had caught my attention, but I had never been this preoccupied before; I found myself completely distracted by Vivian's presence in that small office.

Marty was continuing his monologue as I considered whether I was in love with Vivian or was suffering from the effects of puppy love. It had been many years since I was this twitterpated, and I wasn't sure I could tell the difference.

I was awakened from this reverie when I noticed that everyone was looking at me and Marty had taken his seat. I felt my cheeks redden as I said, "Sorry, my mind was traveling down a different path for a moment."

Dr. Richardson, with a knowing smile, said "Marty was suggesting that they put into motion the resources necessary to conduct their cyber-attack on the research laboratory at the same time you continue your plans for a physical attack. He was suggesting the two of you work closely together to coordinate your attacks. What do you think?"

Now that I was fully engaged in the conversation, I realized the CIA knew more about our plans that I expected. I looked to Dr. Richardson and said, "Now that we're talking about an additional attack, a cyber-attack if you will, I agree that coordination will be vital. My immediate reaction is that the cyber-attack should take place 24 hours *after* our mission is completed.

"The goal of our mission is to take action without the North Koreans realizing we've been there. But if they've already been put on alert because of a problem at the research labs, security could be increased to the point where our mission would be compromised."

Admiral Harrison now spoke up, "Marty, how much time do you need to put your plan into action?"

"We've been able to monitor their Internet search activity and discovered they are conducting research into university databases here in the United States and in Europe and China, as well. We have a team working on the design of a non-memory resident virus that can be inserted into their system when they download some real research data on a fake website. We won't be able to control when they actually find our website, but we can control when the virus is made available. Our plan is to send an agent into China, perhaps Shanghai where they have two dozen universities, so it appears the virus came from them."

Admiral Harrison patiently asked, "Yes, Marty; but when will you be ready to do all that?"

"Oh, sorry! I forgot to answer your question. With our current level of progress, we should be ready in February."

I spoke up and disingenuously said, "We don't have a specific date yet for our mission, but I'm certain it won't be before February."

At this point Dr. Richardson said, "So we're all agreed then, that neither group will take action without notifying the other. Any questions?"

There was some headshaking but no one said anything so she continued, "All right, thank you, Marty. We'll excuse you now while we continue another discussion." At which point, Marty stood up and left the office.

After he left, Admiral Harrison turned to me and said, "Colonel, based on my previous experience working with the CIA, you should touch base with Marty at least once a week. Even then, don't expect him to be too forthcoming with their progress. They like to hold their cards pretty close to their chest."

I nodded to the Admiral and then turned to Dr. Richardson and asked, "Can you tell us how the President's briefing to the intelligence committees went?"

As she was beginning to answer, the President's Chief of Staff interrupted and said, "Let me handle that, Sarah." He faced the three of us and said, "The President met with both the House and Senate subcommittees on intelligence and briefed them on his plan to send Navy SEALs to North Korea to learn more about their progress on reducing the size of their nuclear weapon. He did not, repeat did not, say anything about the real mission being planned.

"He doesn't plan to tell them about the real mission until the day before. He did tell them that he had assigned someone from the White House to provide oversight of their planning; that would be you Colonel Johnson. As you might imagine, not everyone on those two committees is excited about sending a SEAL team into North Korea.

"In fact, not everyone in the White House is convinced the plan can work. That's partly the reason the CIA suggestion has resurfaced. In any case, continue your planning and you can expect to brief the President on the detailed plan sometime after the holidays.

"Only after you brief the President will he decide if the mission will proceed; until then it's just a proposed plan. The political implications if it should fail may be too great to overcome, but that is not your concern." He then stood up and superciliously said, "I must be going; there are a million things that need to be done today." He nodded to Dr. Richardson and left the office.

After the door closed, she quietly said to all of us, "It's been my experience that he often speaks for the President, as a Chief of Staff should; but sometimes he speaks before the President has spoken." She smiled and turned to Dr. O'Brien and said, "Vivian, is there anything new to report from the NRO?"

Vivian spoke without hesitation, "There continues to be increased activity at their primary rocket manufacturing facility – trucks and trains arriving and departing more often than we've seen in the last two years. Either something important is going on, or they're doing a very good job of letting us think there is.

"We also note slightly increased activity at both the Sohae and Tonghae launch facilities. The single track railway ends at each facility's assembly building, and that is also where the trucks are stopping. Again, we can only speculate that they are preparing to assemble a rocket for launch. It is very unusual for this activity to occur at both launch facilities at the same time."

Looking directly at Vivian, Admiral Harrison interjected, "It's vital that we not only continue the satellite surveillance, but that top-notch analysts continue to review the imagery. That may be the only clue we get as to the timing of their activity, whatever it might be."

He turned back to Dr. Richardson and said, "May I suggest we send Colonel Johnson back down to SOCOM to confirm the planning is proceeding as we expect. Commander Throckmorton is an excellent planner, but sometimes he loses the big picture when he's down in the weeds concentrating on the details."

I was intrigued with this statement since he and I had already decided that I would fly down tomorrow or at the latest on Wednesday. But now that I think about it, my orders assigned me to the Office of the Assistant to the President for National Security Affairs, not to the Pentagon. I could see he understood the political bureaucracy better than I did!

My expression must've given me away, because Dr. Richardson smiled when she said, "I agree." Turning to me she asked, "Colonel, when can you get away?"

I thought for a moment, and caught myself before I looked at Vivian, and then said, "There are a few more details I'd like to follow up on at the Pentagon; how about I plan Wednesday morning?"

Dr. Richardson responded, "Sounds like a plan!" She turned to Admiral Harrison and said, "Admiral, will you take care of the transportation?"

"If you'll authorize it, we'll continue to use the same airplane we have been using."

To which she responded, "Sounds good to me; I'll send an email to Andrews right now."

While she was clicking her mouse and typing, Admiral Harrison turned to me and said, "Why don't you head back to the Pentagon while I discuss a few other issues with Dr. Richardson." That didn't seem to leave much room for discussion so I stood, gave a little wave of my hand to Dr. Richardson who nodded, and left her office.

After the door closed, it dawned on me that Vivian was still inside. I waited a few minutes to see if she would follow me into the hall, and when that didn't happen, I shrugged my shoulders and headed for the exit. Apparently the other issues referred to involved her as well.

It wasn't long before I was settled into a taxi cab on my way back to Admiral Harrison's office at the Pentagon. There were a few more details I wanted to finish up before the end of the day.

On the way, I decided to call the pilot of the Gulfstream. Although I couldn't remember his name, I had it stored in my iPhone directory under

"Pilot," so a quick search discovered Major Guthrie. I gave him a quick call because I wanted to know what time we could leave Wednesday morning.

When he answered I said, "Hello Major, this is your favorite Army Lieutenant Colonel." To which he responded, "Well hello, I wondered if we'd be hearing from you again. You know, Colonel, there's an Air Force General who doesn't take kindly to you. In fact, he gave us orders that the next time you are a passenger on our Gulfstream, we're to notify him before we take off. And now that he's our boss, my hands are tied."

I thought for a moment and came up with a solution to that dilemma. "Major, you or your immediate commanding officer are about to get an email from the White House tasking you to provide transportation for me. So let me untie your hands! My travels are classified top secret, need to know – and the general does not have the need to know! In fact, that information is restricted to you and your crew and the National Security Advisor, Dr. Richardson.

"Anyone in your chain of command who questions that can be politely referred to Admiral Harrison in the office of the Chairman of the Joint Chiefs of Staff or to the White House." I may have stepped out on a limb with this last statement, but I was pretty certain that Admiral Harrison would back me up.

I waited for a response and when none was forthcoming, I said "You're pretty quiet, Major."

"I mean no disrespect, Colonel, but do you have the authority to do that – to untie my hands, that is?"

"Let me put it in perspective for you, Major. This past week my time has been filled with drafting orders and tasking assignments to the Chief of Staff of the Air Force, the Chief of Naval Operations, the Commandant of the Marine Corps, and the Chief of Staff of the Army. In addition, I recently attended a meeting of the National Security Council, where the President gave me very specific marching orders. So yes, I have that authority!

"Now, Major, what I just told you is also classified top secret, so that information is for your benefit only."

I paused and then continued, "Now that we've got that out of the way, the reason I called is this. I need to travel to MacDill again and would like to leave Wednesday morning. What would be an ideal time for us to take off?"

"Well, Colonel, since you're giving me a choice, 9:30 would be a good time. That allows the congested airspace caused by early morning flights from Reagan to dissipate. Can you tell me when we'll be returning?"

"That's still up in the air, pardon the pun, but I'm thinking after work on Friday. Will that work for you?"

Laughing out loud, Major Guthrie responded, "Colonel, we're accustomed to being told when we're leaving, not asked! Sure, that works for me; we'll even bring supper!"

By this time my taxi was pulling up at the Pentagon, so I closed our conversation with, "Okay, we'll see you Wednesday morning."

I paid off the cabbie and walked into the Pentagon to take care of a few last-minute details with our tasking orders. Once again, I was surprised by the bureaucracy that awaited me. There were literally 50 to 60 emails waiting for me, plus a dozen phone calls to return. All this was generated by the four relatively simple tasking orders that had gone out last week.

Although I had selected Wednesday for my departure to SOCOM for other, purely selfish, reasons, it was a good thing I had. I was beginning to understand more and more why there were so many people working in the Pentagon. Somewhere there's a phrase that says the devil is in the details; I don't know how the devil got involved, but I was learning there are lots of details in this work!

Chapter Forty-Four

It was 6:30 before I decided it was okay to leave the office; I figured I would be able to take care of the few remaining emails tomorrow morning, thus leaving the afternoon to handle any new questions that arose. The 12 telephone calls turned into twice that number, but at least I had taken care of them.

I sat back in my chair and after pondering a moment, sent a text message to Vivian. It was brief: *dinner and a movie?*

I leaned forward and put my iPhone on the desk as I took a deep breath and awaited her response. I was getting a little nervous when she hadn't responded for several minutes, but when I looked closely, there were the three little flashing gray dots on the screen indicating that a reply was being composed. I shook my head as I realized I was behaving like a lovesick teenager; what was the matter with me?

I put the phone back down, took another deep breath, and waited for the message to be completed. In a few moments, my phone chirped to indicate the new message had arrived. With trepidation I reached for my phone and pulled it closer without looking at the screen. I took a deep breath and looked at the screen. I let out my breath as I saw her reply: *I'll bring the movie, you make dinner.*

So there I was, a single man with two teenage children and with an almost empty refrigerator, making a date with a beautiful woman who expects a decent evening meal. What do I do? Although she didn't say so, I didn't think take out was going to be adequate! So I sent her another text: *7:30 okay?* To which she replied: *It's a date!*

Whether she intended it as I took it I cannot say, but her use of the word *date* brought a smile to my face. So now all I had to do was catch the next Metro, walk to the little grocer two blocks away from my condo, buy all the fixings for dinner, and then walk home and change. Oh, let's not forget, I had to fix a great meal!

Fortunately, Jacob and Susan prefer to eat early, so I can bribe them with some cash for fast food and ask them to visit friends. Not a perfect solution, but I wanted to be alone with Vivian.

As I rode the Metro to my stop, I considered what to make for dinner. I finally decided I didn't want something complex that could turn out a failure, so I bought boneless and skinless chicken thighs, because they take less time in the oven, a box of shake and bake mix, one of those little microwave cups of mashed potatoes, and a can of sweet corn. I also bought a six pack of root beer and a gallon of vanilla ice cream; my kids would enjoy the leftovers. I was going to break from our traditional popcorn snack with homemade root beer floats!

I think Vivian was as surprised by my choice for a dinner menu as I was by the movie she brought. I most definitely did not expect *Mr. & Mrs. Smith*! But I enjoyed her holding my arm as the almost nonsensical action scenes unfolded. And she seemed to enjoy the fried chicken supper before the movie and the root beer float about midway through.

I was surprised, though, when at the end of the movie she moved to the other side of the sofa and softly said, "We have to talk." My heart started racing as I responded, "Okay," and waited for her to speak. If a man never heard those words – *we have to talk* – from a woman he cared for, men might live as long as women do!

I refocused my attention as she continued, "Robert, I told you I grew up pretty much a tomboy, and that's oh, so true, and that I generally rebuffed male attention. Well, not generally, always! At first I wasn't interested, and then later on I guess I was afraid. And because I didn't have the experiences with men that other girls typically had, you know, during dating and other activities, I'm not sure how to handle my obvious attraction to you. Plus, it's obvious you're attracted to me as well!

"How do we know if it's real or just a passing infatuation? And what's really confusing to me, you don't behave at all like men I've heard described by other women." And then she looked at me with her big green eyes and waited for my response.

I paused for a moment as I tried to collect my thoughts, and then said, "Vivian, I don't want to compare you with anyone else, and although I did not recognize it at first, I can tell you that I fell in love with you the first time we talked. It may not have been love at first sight, but it was darn close! And now that I think about it, I've been here before emotionally and I recognize my feelings as love, not infatuation.

"If you're still working through your emotions, I can be as patient as you need me to be."

She gave me a weird look and said, "I don't need to work through anything; I just want to understand what's going on! When you walk into a room, I smile. When we're close to one another, my heart races. When you put your arms around me I feel contented. When we're not together, I miss you. Is this what love is?"

"Those are all symptoms! Love is that and much more. When you talk about me being different from other men, that's probably only true in two areas. First, I was raised in a culture that actively taught boys and young men to respect and honor women; not all men are raised that way. Second, I've been married and widowed, and I'm finding I am hesitant to develop a new and meaningful relationship, so I am taking baby steps with you.

"Having said that, though, let me assure you that I am not anywhere close to being a perfect man. I have made and will continue to make mistakes, and when you gently point them out, I will ask your forgiveness and try to do better."

"Funny man!" After a brief pause, she continued, "How do we behave around one another in public?" And more quietly, "How do we behave in private?" And with that question she looked again into my eyes. We seemed to do a lot of looking into each other's eyes!

"I don't think it's a secret to anyone that we're attracted to one another; so, in public, I suggest we behave in such a way that others can see that we are no longer *available*. In private, well, in private we need to continue to show respect for one another, to become real friends, to continue falling in love."

With that she broke into a broad smile and hopped back to my side of the sofa and linked her arm with mine. In a moment her head was resting on my shoulder. We stayed close for several minutes and then she looked up and said, "I know it's early, but I've lost a lot of sleep the last few nights thinking about things, so tonight I'm going to get caught up! Thank you for talking with me, and especially for listening!"

So I walked her down to her bright orange Mustang, gave her a warm kiss and said good night. As I watched her drive off, I thought that I, too, would sleep well tonight.

Chapter Forty-Five

Work on Tuesday went as predicted; the morning was spent making and receiving telephone calls clarifying the tasking instructions issued earlier. The afternoon was similar, but late afternoon activity actually slowed down to the point that I was pondering leaving the office at 4:30.

A quick text to Vivian confirmed that she was eager to begin our evening together. She reminded me that it was my turn to choose the movie and that she would provide supper. I thought about this and then called her. When she answered, I said, "How about we eat out; there's a small Italian restaurant in Old Town that makes great spaghetti. Then we could stroll down to the boat harbor for dessert."

Her response was immediate. "Sounds like fun! Shall I pick you up?"

"Let me go home and change first. I'll walk to the restaurant. How about we meet at the corner of King Street and Payne Street; you can park on Payne. Say sixish?"

"Okay. You sure I can park there?"

"Guaranteed!"

"Okay, see you there."

I was standing on the corner when shortly after 6:00 she turned the corner and parked in a spot just three stalls away from the corner. As I opened her door, she picked her coat off the passenger seat and handed it to me. I helped her into her coat and then gave her a quick hug.

As we walked back to the restaurant, she asked, "Have you been here before?"

Without thinking, I Immediately said, "Oh yes, we've been here many times before."

She stopped so quickly it took me a moment before I realized she was no longer beside me. I turned and took a couple steps toward her as I asked, "What, did you forget something?"

She gave me a look that would have turned melted butter into solid rock!

Looking me right in the eyes she very quietly said, "You bring me to a restaurant where the two of you used to come?" And with that she turned around and stomped back to her car.

Since I was thinking about the many times Susan and I came here, it took me a moment before I realized she thought I was talking about Beth. I ran ahead and stepped in front of her just as she was opening the car door. She gave me another cold look so I quickly said, "Wait, you misunderstand. I mean I wasn't very clear. Beth and I never came here. This is Susan's favorite restaurant; we come here for daddy daughter dates."

It took her a moment to process what I had said. Then she visibly relaxed and said, "Oh, I'm so sorry; I shouldn't have jumped to conclusions. It was just the way you said it."

"I know; I wasn't very clear." Not really knowing what to say next, I said, "They really do make great spaghetti!"

So we walked to the restaurant, enjoyed a delicious spaghetti dinner together, and then strolled down to the boat harbor. It turned out to be colder than I thought it would be, so we didn't spend much time there, but it was enjoyable being together.

We walked back to her car rather briskly, as the cold was starting to be uncomfortable. We were both rather subdued as she dropped me off at my apartment; she knew I was going out of town and we wouldn't see each other until the weekend. All in all, a nice evening, but nothing to write home about.

I guess my mind was on the mission, and not on her. It was a real conflict for me; one minute I was enjoying her company and the warmth of her hand in mine, and the next I was wondering how far the team had gotten in writing the detailed operational plan. As I ponder this, it occurs to me that since the loss of Beth, I had grown accustomed to only thinking about work. Now I had to allow for thoughts about Vivian. It also occurred to me that I could be more involved in the activities of Jacob and Susan. Wow, the thoughts that go through a man's head.

In any case, the next morning Vivian was only a fleeting thought as I packed for my trip to SOCOM. I was once again the only passenger on board the confiscated Gulfstream G550. The ever-present Sergeant Mitchell welcomed me aboard, and off we went!

I brought copies of every tasking order I had written, and during the flight I reviewed each of them so they would be fresh on my mind as I met with Commander Throckmorton and his planning team. I knew they would also want to review each of them to ensure we hadn't forgotten some small detail.

I was reminded of a story my father had told me about paying attention to details. Apparently in the early 70s, an airplane crashed in the Florida Everglades killing more than half the people on board. The cause of the crash was determined to be the inattention of the flight crew. They were focused on a burned out light bulb for one of the landing gear, which had extended properly, and failed to notice the autopilot had been inadvertently disengaged. While they were fixated on the light bulb, the aircraft crashed into the Everglades.

I didn't want our mission to fail because of a 25-cent piece of equipment!

For lunch I ate a delicious roast beef sandwich that Sergeant Mitchell offered and was therefore able to join the planning team in the tiny conference room immediately upon my arrival. Everyone was there, including Senior Chief Aloysius O'Hara, who would take detailed notes of our discussions.

I have to admit, although I've seen hundreds of operational plans in my career, both large and small, I had never seen anything this detailed! We eventually took the operational plan and divided it into sections that we laid out on the conference table. Then we took my copies of the tasking orders and attached them to each of the appropriate individual plan sections. This helped us see that I needed to modify one tasking order and make two additional tasking orders.

It turned out that my tasking order for the Air Force C-17 that would transport all the team members from SOCOM to Japan left them stranded there after the mission. I modified the order to require the aircraft to re-main in Japan to transport the team members back to SOCOM after the completion of the mission.

The two new tasking orders had to do with the submarines that would carry us up into Korea Bay and the Sea of Japan. I had assumed that Commander Throckmorton would use his connections at SOCOM to ar-range for the two submarines. He told me that without orders from the CNO, the Navy might at the last moment decide to do something else with those two submarines.

So I painstakingly wrote out task orders for the USS Dallas, a Los Angeles-class submarine, and the USS Florida, an Ohio-class subma-rine, both fitted with the super-secret dry-dock shelter. These would be critical to the success of our mission, as they would be the transport for the advanced SEAL delivery vehicles we would use.

The tasking orders for the two submarines were complex because the combined Army-Navy-Marine Corps teams would need to practice with these vehicles in Yokosuka, Japan, where the U.S. Seventh Fleet was based, without drawing attention.

By the end of the day, the individual pieces of the operational plan had been reviewed and confirmed as complete. We all agreed that a compre-hensive tabletop exercise tomorrow would be a further review of the plan. It would also allow me to see the mission in more detail – an important aspect of my responsibilities as the White House liaison. When I say end of the day, it was truly bedtime when we finally left the conference room.

Commander Throckmorton gave me a ride to the BOQ, so I took the opportunity to ask if he had any reservations about the mission. He said his only misgivings were because of the co-mingling of SEAL teams with Army and Marine Corps snipers. He would feel better if everyone was a Navy SEAL. But he went on to say that he understood the importance of using snipers who were experienced shooting at targets almost a mile away.

He went on to say, "I'm also concerned about the mud flats leading up to the mountains near Sohae; if they are wet and soft they'll not only be difficult to travel over, but they'll also make it impossible to hide our tracks. One thing in our favor, however, is that the North Koreans have restricted access to the mud flats near Sohae, where people used to harvest fish and crabs. In any case, we're still looking at the satellite imagery to see where the best place for landing is."

I reminded him that I had asked Dr. O'Brien to make a detailed examination of the west coast of North Korea to find the best place. I was hoping she would come up with a suggestion that would resolve his concerns.

I had a hamburger and French fries for a late supper at the officer's club and then retired to my room at the BOQ. I called Vivian to say good night and realized that she had already retired and I had awakened her, so I said a quick good night and hung up! I fell asleep as soon as my head hit the pillow.

The tabletop exercise took two whole days to complete, but at the end of the day on Friday I had a much better understanding of how the mission would proceed. We tweaked the mission plan at several points as we walked through the exercise, and several pages of questions were recorded by Senior Chief O'Hara. It would be up to Commander Throckmorton and his planning team to find answers for those questions over the next few weeks.

The mission plan called for Commander Throckmorton to lead the team going to Tonghae and Major Denton to be in charge of the team at Sohae. In addition, Lieutenant Williams and Lieutenant Rogers, of SEAL Team 2, the Arctic warfare experts, tossed a coin to see which team they would go with. It was decided that Master Chief Petty Officer O'Shaughnessy, the SEAL team weapons specialist, would not go on the mission. Although disappointed, he knew he would have difficulty keeping up with the younger members of the SEAL team in the rough mountainous terrain of North Korea.

Late Friday afternoon, we all decided it would be acceptable to enjoy the Christmas holidays and return to work after the New Year. The additional SEAL team members would be selected in early January, and the best Army and Marine Corps snipers would be invited to a competition in mid-January to determine who would be selected for the mission.

I felt I had a pretty good handle on the details of the mission, and I was completely satisfied that Commander Throckmorton and Major Denton were up to the task. Since we had worked so late on Friday, I flew back to Washington, D.C., Saturday morning, completely satisfied that we were on track to meet the President's requirements for the mission.

Although I didn't know it at the time, having gone through the table top exercise would prove more than just informative.

Chapter Forty-Six

I actually took a nap Saturday morning on the flight back to Washington, D.C. It was the first time I remembered taking a nap for, well, a long time! I was still a little groggy when Vivian picked me up at base operations. She gave me a nice hug when I walked in from the ramp; when we separated she gave me a great smile. It was nice to be home!

As we approached the car, she squeezed my arm, looked up into my eyes and said, "What would you like to do for lunch?"

I returned her look and said, "How about we pick up a couple of sandwiches at Jason's Deli, and then go to your apartment and play dominoes?"

She wrinkled her face and said, "Dominoes? Where did that come from?"

I gave her a smile and responded, "Actually, what I'd like to do is talk about your plans for Christmas. Dominoes was the first thing that popped into my mind that allows us to talk while we're doing something together."

"We don't need an excuse to talk! How about this? Let's eat our sandwiches at Jason's Deli and then we'll park somewhere close by and we'll walk around the Jefferson Memorial." She looked up at me with an impish smile and said, "You can walk and talk at the same time, can't you?"

I returned her impish smile with one of my own and said, "Did you know that several of the quotes in the Jefferson Memorial are taken out of context? Franklin D. Roosevelt took advantage of his position as President to have Jefferson's quotes appear to support his New Deal politics."

She looked at me again, serious this time, and said, "I did know that, but I choose to look at the Jefferson Memorial with a broader perspective. He was a great man with great ideas for his time, and many of his ideas are still valid today. His political perspectives should be required reading for every politician that comes to Washington!"

We had reached her car, so I took her hands into mine and said, "Vivian, I'm happy to see that our political views are the same. But what I'd really like to talk about is, what are your plans for Christmas?"

She laughed out loud and said, "Okay! We'll talk more about politics another time. I think we'll also have to talk about religion, but that conversation can also wait.

"Why don't we get in the car and turn the heater on."

She dug in her small purse and handed me the keys, so I jumped in the driver's seat while she ran around and climbed in the passenger seat. I had the engine and heater running before she fastened her seatbelt! As I started driving toward the restaurant, she said, "My original plan was to spend a few days with my parents for Christmas. But now that I've met you, I'm open to other suggestions. What did you have in mind?"

She had given me the perfect opening! "My original plans are also open to other suggestions; I'd now very much like to spend Christmas with you." We were both quiet for a couple of minutes and then I said, "Assuming we don't have any problems meeting each other's parents, let's do both! How about we spend Christmas day and a day or two before, with your parents, and then spend a few days after Christmas with my parents." I looked at her and asked, "How does that sound?"

She looked at me as she thought for a moment, and then quietly said, "That sounds like a pretty big leap in our relationship; are you sure that's what you want to do?"

I didn't hesitate as I said, "Absolutely! You will soon learn that I am a buyer, not a shopper!"

She laughed out loud and then said, "I think I understand what that means, but just remember, I am not something you can buy!" And then she tenderly said, "But I am available." She was quiet for a moment and then said, "I appreciate your offer to spend Christmas day with my family; they are really expecting to see me. This will be the first time in a few years that our entire family will be together at the same time. But, what about Jacob and Susan? And are you sure your family won't be disappointed?"

"Quite the contrary! They will definitely be disappointed that I'm not there for Christmas day. However, since I wasn't sure how much time this new assignment would give me for celebrations, we've already made arrangements for Jacob and Susan to spend Christmas with their grandparents in Arizona – with or without me." I turned and looked at her and softly said, "And when I tell them I'm bringing a girl home, it will soften their disappointment. The kids seem to like you, and it will certainly generate some conversation before we get there." We were both quiet again for a few moments, and then I said, "Would it be all right if I make the arrangements for us to fly to Arizona?"

"As long as you're making arrangements, why don't you schedule the flight from here to Boston on the 23rd and then from Boston to Phoenix on the 28th, and then back to Washington, D.C., after New Year's. That way we can spend New Year's Eve with your family."

She was right; we did not need an excuse to talk together. I felt very comfortable with her, and it appeared she was comfortable with me. If I had any doubts about how brilliant she was, she removed all doubts by how quickly she had worked out our travel itinerary. I must say I was impressed!

"Okay. I'll take care of it as soon as I can get in front of my computer. Oh, I'll need your middle name to make the reservations; and when you get a chance, text me your frequent flyer number."

As I moved into the left turn lane waiting to turn into Jason's Deli, she said, "Erin." Since I was watching the traffic and wasn't paying attention to her, I said, "What? What did you say?" And she said, "Erin; my middle name is Erin."

So that's how we spent Christmas and New Year's. Her parents were charming and helped me feel right at home, while her brothers kept a wary eye on me. Although I struggled with what to get her for Christmas, I finally settled on a nice conservative silver necklace with a not too large diamond pendant. I could tell it was a home run when she gave me a hug in front of her family on Christmas morning.

I was completely surprised when I opened her gift to me. It was a book titled, *The Real Thomas Jefferson* by Andrew Allison, an author I'd not heard of before. I was surprised because, even though we had discussed him briefly, I had not had the opportunity to tell her that Thomas Jefferson was my favorite of our country's Founding Fathers. I looked forward to reading the book!

We spent the next two days enjoying each other's company, even taking an evening sleigh ride on an old sleigh pulled by a pair of very large Clydesdales with real sleigh bells attached to their harness. It was the best Christmas I'd spent since Beth's passing; I'm not afraid to admit that I was looking forward to many more Christmases with Vivian.

It turned out that her brothers were leaving the same day we were, so we all headed for the airport where she cried, and her mother cried, and the men gave each other manly hugs. Even though I had just met her family, I too felt a trace of emotion as we left.

It was a long flight from Boston to Phoenix, and we were both happy after we arrived to be able to stretch our legs! We rented a car and began the 90-minute drive north to Prescott, where my parents had retired just the year before. For some reason, they had bought an acre and a half of land and built a barn on it where they were raising chickens. Mom told me they sold fresh eggs to some of the local restaurants.

When we arrived, dad stoically shook my hand and nodded his welcome; some things never change. On the other hand, mom made a big fuss about Vivian and immediately guided her into the house. Jacob and Susan were out in the barn collecting eggs, but when they heard us drive up they came into the house. After I gave them both hugs, I started to introduce everyone to Vivian; I was embarrassed as I realized I hadn't decided on how to introduce her. Was she simply a friend? Was she a girlfriend? Was she a close friend?

Then I remembered how she introduced me to her parents, simply as Robert. So, I followed her model. I didn't refer to her as my friend, or my girlfriend, or a coworker; I introduced her to my parents simply as Vivian. And that seemed to satisfy everyone.

We all enjoyed a warm dinner that evening, and on subsequent evenings as well. During the days, we enjoyed hiking around Lynx Lake and canoeing on Watson Lake. We even took a quick tour of historic downtown Prescott, where we learned that it had once been the capital of Arizona. But mostly we hung around home and enjoyed each other's company.

On New Year's Eve, it was a family tradition that we shoot off fireworks on the front lawn, or actually we sat on the front lawn and ignited fireworks in the street in front of the house. It was not as warm in Prescott as it was in Tempe, where I grew up, so we quickly moved back indoors after the fireworks were finished.

Mom had earlier made an apple pie from a scratch recipe, so we sat at the kitchen table and munched on homemade apple pie and played dominoes. When dad pulled out the box of dominoes, Vivian looked at me and said, "Now I know where the dominoes idea came from!"

I was confused for a moment, and then I remembered our conversation while walking to her car from base ops at Andrews Air Force Base. I merely smiled and nodded.

At midnight, mom stretched up on her tip toes and kissed dad on the cheek while Jacob and Susan watched me to see if I would kiss Vivian. I looked her way and saw she was smiling, so I leaned over and kissed her as well, but not on her cheek! Happy New Year!

The next day, Dad led me into his office and after we sat down, asked, "Robert, what are your intentions with Miss O'Brien?" I'm not sure subtlety is a concept my father ever learned.

After a moment, I looked at him and said, "Dad, I'll never stop loving Beth, but Vivian fills that empty spot in my heart. Although we've only known each other a short time, I know we both have warm feelings for each other. We haven't talked about it, but I'd like to spend the rest of my life with her as my companion."

"I see the way she looks at you, Robert; don't make her wait too long!"

And with that bit of sage advice, he stood up and left me sitting alone in his office. After a moment, I walked out and found Vivian on the front porch and put my arms around her. She seemed all too willing, so I held her longer than I had originally intended. We broke apart when Susan came through the outside door of the enclosed porch. She smiled, but didn't say anything as she walked into the house.

So we had a wonderful time together over the holidays; the first few days with her parents and these last few days with my parents and children. And I hadn't thought about work once! But all good things must come to an end, and so on January 2nd we drove down to Phoenix and caught our flight back to Washington, D.C.

And work finally made its way back into the active part of my brain.

Chapter Forty-Seven

Back on the hillside in North Korea, I have slept off and on throughout the day and am now fully awake and notice the sun falling in the west. Because the sun was below the ridge line and already hidden from those in the valley, I can see a significant amount of light glowing in the fog and coming from the valley floor, presumably from around the launch gantry.

If the briefing we received from the NASA engineer was correct, we had about 12 hours before the rocket would be ready for launch; that means the earliest they could launch was the next morning. I give this a little more thought and realize it had taken them longer than I anticipated to move the rocket from the assembly building to the launch pad. Maybe it would take them longer to prepare the rocket for launch, thus allowing enough of the fog to burn off tomorrow morning to give us a clear shot.

As I pay even more attention to the valley below us, I can tell the mixture of light snow on the ground and fog is amplifying the sounds coming from the valley. I try to identify the cacophony of sounds that were reaching my ears, but even as I am listening, the valley floor falls silent.

For a moment I'm concerned they have stopped working for the night, which means they would finish preparations sometime tomorrow, thus forcing us to spend another night on this cold and dreary hillside. But even as I have this thought, I realize the light glowing in the fog has not diminished. I also realize there are still small sounds coming from the area of the gantry, which suggests they are continuing their preparations.

I take a deep breath as I realize I am worrying about things over which I have no control. I can't control the speed of their work in preparing the rocket for launch, and I can't control the weather. I recall a conversation with Lieutenant Carrollton where he said the one quality that all Navy SEALs had to possess was patience.

I don't know how they do it. My legs are cramped, my back is aching, my hips are probably bruised, and they are definitely cold from lying on the ground. He also said that Navy SEALs could go three days without a regular meal and not lose any of their capabilities; as he said this he handed me some high-protein and high carb bars and told me to stuff them into my outer jacket pockets. As I had this thought, I also realize I am hungry again! So I pull one out and eat it.

As I slowly chew the high-protein bar, I think about the last time I was trying to be patient.

I was sitting on a bench near the Capitol building late one afternoon in mid-January while I waited for a call from an FBI agent. Earlier in the week, I had received a phone call from the Director of the FBI who told me they had narrowed the list of suspects to four and they wanted my help in narrowing it even further.

I was here because he had a hunch, and as he told me, in his business, hunches were sometimes as good as solid information. He couldn't say why, but he felt certain the information was being leaked from Congressman Paul Singleton's office, and most likely through a Korean-American woman who was one of his aides.

The original plan he suggested was that I meet with the congressman, pass along a piece of seemingly sensitive but in reality innocuous information, and then see if that information turned up in an email box the NSA was monitoring. If it did, they would have the congressman dead to rights and would be able to turn all their investigative capabilities to the woman. He felt certain that if the congressman was indeed the source of the leak, they would find incriminating evidence in the woman's possession.

But as it stood right now, even with national security at risk, he couldn't get a court order based on a hunch with no evidence. And that's where I came in.

Even as he shared his plan with me, my mind was devising a plan to use this opportunity to mislead the North Koreans about our mission. Our original plan called for a distraction that would direct attention away from our landings at Tonghae and Sohae. One of the reasons General Chang, the deputy commander of the South Korean Army, had been against our plan was he felt it unduly exposed South Korea to risk and condemnation – risk of a new land war on the Korean Peninsula and condemnation by the world community.

But his Commander in Chief felt the risk was worthwhile, especially if we could hinder the progress of North Korea's nuclear program. During my meeting in Seoul, Major Kim had suggested a diversion – winter exercises for their Army could be announced at two locations in South Korea, one south of Kaesŏng and the other south of Kosŏng. Both cities were in the southern part of North Korea. Kosŏng was on the east coast of North Korea, and a few ships of the South Korean Navy could hover on the horizon to emphasize their participation in the Army exercises.

Now I realized we could use the leak in the congressman's office to send confirming information that Navy SEALs would cross into North Korea at their southern border. By mispronouncing the names of the two towns, Kaesŏng and Kosŏng, we would further confuse the North Koreans about our intentions. We could also make them believe that we would brazenly use their highway system to travel to their nuclear research facility near Pyongyang. This plan would be foreshadowed by the movement of military equipment by South Korea toward those two locations but still south of the DMZ.

Director Hansen was initially fearful that my desire to plant false information would compromise his efforts to uncover the spy. He was swayed when I convinced him that the information I proposed sharing would appear to the North Koreans as daring and arrogant – just what they thought of the Americans anyway!

After a brief meeting with Admiral Harrison where I explained what the FBI wanted me to do, and my modification of the plan to include the misleading information, Admiral Harrison gave the go-ahead for me to continue.

So there I was sitting on a bench in civilian clothes waiting for the FBI agent inside the capitol to telephone and convey to me that both the congressman and his aide, Mrs. Endicott, were in his office. The plan was that I would then call the congressman, tell him I was in the neighborhood and ask if he had a few minutes that I could meet privately with him to answer questions about my assignment. I felt this ruse would work since I had told his Chief of Staff that I was unwilling to discuss it with anyone other than the congressman, and that I would personally meet with him in the near future.

I was beginning to get uncomfortably cold when my cell phone rang. The FBI agent told me that not only were the congressman and Mrs. Endicott in his office, but his Chief of Staff was there also. I thanked her and hung up.

After only a few minutes, because it really was cold, I called the congressman's office, and after identifying myself, I was told the congressman could see me in 30 minutes. I immediately walked to the Capitol building because I didn't want it to appear that I'd been waiting outside for the last hour; at the very least I wanted my handshake to be warm.

I arrived at his office a fashionably five minutes late, but with warm hands, and was immediately ushered into his office. He stood and walked around his desk and shook my hand as he greeted me, "Colonel, it's a pleasure to finally meet you. Please, have a seat."

"Thank you, Congressman. I appreciate your seeing me on such short notice."

"Nonsense, Colonel. I've only just returned from a boring committee meeting and was wondering what I would do next when you called. By the way, first let me thank you for your service; it's a pleasure to meet a real American hero." And he shook my hand again!

I would be lying if I said I wasn't impressed with the sincerity of his greeting. I was becoming every day more accustomed to smooth talking politicians, but he seemed honestly sincere. I responded with, "I don't know about being a hero, I was simply at the wrong place at the right time." I looked him squarely in the eye as I shook his hand and said, "Thank you." Then we both sat down in front of his desk.

I started with, "You realize, Congressman, that I really can't discuss any details with you, especially here in your office." As I said this, I reached down with my left hand to adjust my chair. The congressman never noticed the bug I attached to the arm of the chair at the request of the FBI.

He gave me a politician's smile and said, "Completely understood! I just want to make sure I understand everything the President told us in our last briefing." And with that, he moved his chair much closer to mine and said, "The entire country is concerned about the latest North Korean boast that they will soon be able to launch a nuclear weapon all the way to our West Coast. We all agree that we need to know more about their capabilities.

"As you know, I'm a member of the House intelligence committee, and the President is required to brief us on covert intelligence missions." As I started to interrupt, he continued, "Yes, I know he has done that and has promised to brief us again as your plan comes together." He leaned closer and continued in a quiet voice, "Do you really think we can send a SEAL team into North Korea and discover their nuclear capabilities without being discovered?"

I leaned closer and answered in a similarly quiet voice, "Congressman, I can tell you this only because you've been cleared for sensitive top secret information as a member of the House intelligence committee; you should not share this conversation with anyone. The Navy has two SEAL team members of Korean descent who speak the language fluently. Because the North Koreans would never expect us to be so bold, we're going to insert these two SEAL team members through a town in the south of North Korea called Kasong, and then brazenly use their new highway to drive into central North Korea where their nuclear research facility is."

I had purposely mispronounced the name of the North Korean city to further confuse the issue. "Our friends in South Korea are even going to hold Army exercises on their side of the DMZ at the same time to distract the North Koreans."

I used my bragging voice and continued, "Our satellite surveillance is so good that we'll be able to tell if there are any unexpected roadblocks on the highway. Then I excitedly but quietly added, "This is so bold the North Koreans will never expect it!"

The congressman sat back in his chair and gave me a stunned look. "You can't be serious! Even if they're lucky enough to get into North Korea, they will never be able to safely get back to South Korea. And if they're captured, the United States will be the laughing stock of the world."

I gave him a smug look and said, "That's the beauty of our plan! We don't plan to have them come back the same way; after their surveillance is complete, they're going to drive due west to the coastline where a Navy submarine will pick them up."

He gave me a sly look and said, "Just as you said earlier, that is a bold plan. The President said you would be ready in early spring; is that still correct?"

"Based on other intelligence gathering methods, we believe that's the best time to launch our reconnaissance mission. We're also hoping that the worst of the winter weather will be over by that time, as well." I gave him my most severe look and said, "Congressman, that's really all I can tell you at this time."

He stood and reached for my hand as he said, "Colonel, you've been most helpful in clarifying what the President has already told us. Thanks again for spending a few minutes with me."

Although a rather abrupt end to our meeting, I knew when I was being dismissed. I shook his hand and allowed him to walk me to his door; I quickly crossed his lobby and left his office.

As I walked away I thought to myself, whatever else happens now, at least the bait is set. Now it was up to the FBI to see if this information turns up in an email to the North Koreans.

Although politicians are not typically anyone's favorite people, with the possible exception of lobbyists and contractors, I came away thinking that he wasn't the traitor. But I suppose that's what makes a good traitor, the ability to fool people.

Chapter Forty-Eight

It wasn't 90 seconds later that Michael Fontana, the congressman's Chief of Staff, was standing in front of the congressman's desk asking a question. "That wasn't a very long meeting, Paul. Was he willing to tell you anything?"

Congressman Singleton walked around his desk and the two of them sat in the same two chairs used in the previous meeting. Shaking his head, the congressman said, "Mike, for an Army intelligence officer, Colonel Johnson is an extremely naïve man, maybe even a little arrogant. After swearing me to secrecy, he proceeded to tell me the outline of their plan.

"Here's the gist of it. They're waiting for winter to die down and then they plan to send two Korean-speaking Navy SEALs into North Korea. Apparently they think they can cross the DMZ near a town he called Kasong, or something like that, and then travel north on the highway without being discovered by the North Koreans.

"They're going to spy on the nuclear research facility near Pyongyang and then head west to the coastline where a Navy submarine will pick them up." Shaking his head again, he continued, "He called it a bold plan; it sounds to me like it borders on foolishness!

"Apparently they've convinced the South Koreans to conduct some military training at the same time on the other side of the country from where the two Navy SEALs will enter, hoping to distract the North Koreans. Knowing the difficulties that still exist between those two countries, I'm surprised the South Koreans would agree to help.

"I think most of the committee members, including the Senators, are upset with the President for not sharing more details. In any case, now that I know the basic outline of the plan, I'll be able to ask intelligent questions when the President next meets with us. If I can outshine Congressman Hoag, my status on the committee will be greatly enhanced." He stood and smiled and then said, "We need to figure out a way to use this in my reelection campaign; start giving that some thought, will you?"

The congressman returned to his desk and his Chief of Staff to his office, both of them with Cheshire cat smiles on their face.

As he passed Mrs. Endicott's desk, the Chief of Staff said, "Mrs. Endicott, we have a new project from the congressman; please come to my office so we can discuss it."

She smiled as she looked up, and then dutifully followed him into his office, quietly closing the door behind her. Before she could speak, he lifted his desk phone and punched a speed dial number. He waited a moment and then said, "Hello sweetheart; I wanted to let you know that Paul has given me a hot new project to work on so I'll be late getting home tonight." He listened for a few moments and then said, "Yes, I know it's getting to be a habit, but you know the reelection campaign is in full swing now. I'll be home as quickly as I can. And don't worry about supper for me. I'll stop on the way home."

Reading between the lines, Mrs. Endicott smiled outwardly but was groaning inside. She had a good idea where he was going to get his supper, and supper would not be his highest priority! But she maintained the best smile she could manage.

She had watched him enter the congressman's office and suspected there was additional news that she would need to wheedle out of him, and there was only one way to do that. She physically shivered at that thought, but gritted her teeth!

The evening turned out just as she expected. He arrived at her apartment a bare couple of minutes after she had. He swept her into his arms and carried her into the bedroom where, after a few minutes, he shared everything he had learned from the Congressman.

As they lay there talking, she asked, "Are you sure he said Kasong? I don't remember a town by that name near the DMZ."

"That's what he said, Kasong. You can look it up tomorrow on the Internet." Then he looked at his watch and said, "I have to be going soon; did you have something planned for supper?"

Groaning inwardly at his continued presumption that she would invite him to join her for supper, she had a flash of inspiration. "It's been a long day, so I'm going to fix some macaroni and cheese. Would you like some?" She knew full well that he was a meat and potatoes kind of guy, and would not look forward to macaroni and cheese.

Sure enough, he said, "Ah, Julie, that's not my kind of thing; I'll stop and get a Big Mac on the way home." And with that, he jumped up and was soon gone without even saying as much as a goodbye.

His hasty departure from her apartment, however, was noted by a young woman in the apartment on the opposite side and just a door closer to the elevator. In his hurry, he didn't notice the peephole was larger than others on that floor. In fact, it was not really a peephole at all; it was a lens attached to a computer inside the apartment where a perfectly clear picture of Michael Fontana, Chief of Staff to Congressman Paul Singleton, was captured. In the bottom right corner of the screen was a date/time stamp, forever noting when he had departed her apartment.

Julie quickly got up and locked her apartment door and then pulled out her laptop and turned it on. While it booted up, she ran back to her bedroom and got dressed. She pulled on a pair of sweatpants with the Georgetown logo on one leg, a purple T-shirt, and a pair of well-worn slippers.

In North Korea, women are required to style their hair in one of 14 government-approved styles, all of which are relatively short. However, Captain Pak had been authorized by General Kim Hyun-woo, Director of the North Korean intelligence service, to let her hair grow in preparation for coming to the United States on this mission. It was presumed that American men preferred long hair on their women, especially attractive single women. Her lustrous, raven-black hair now hung below her shoulder blades. Before coming back to her computer, she gathered her hair into a loose bun at the back of her head.

She searched the Internet for the city in North Korea that sounded like Kasong, but the closest she could find was a word used in the Philippines. However, after looking at a map, she discovered two cities in southern North Korea that had similar pronunciations. They were on opposite sides of the peninsula, but they both had access to the newly built freeway system in North Korea.

She quickly composed an email message containing the information shared by the congressman's Chief of Staff. She knew her general preferred reports that contained only facts, but she offered her opinion that since the Americans had difficulty pronouncing Korean words, she felt certain that the mention of Kasong most likely referred to one of the two cities in southern North Korea near the DMZ.

Within minutes, her message was encrypted and on its way to the crowded communications room in the basement of the North Korean intelligence building. And by 8:30 in the morning in Pyongyang, General Kim Hyun-woo was reading about the American plan for spying on their nuclear research facility – at least the plan as it was related to Congressman Singleton. Unknown to her and her general, her message also ended up at the NSA data center in Utah, where it would shortly be decrypted and sent to the Director of the FBI in Washington, D.C.

FBI Director Hansen wasn't surprised to learn that it was not the congressman who was observed leaving Mrs. Endicott's apartment. Just minutes before he received that report from the agent in the neighboring apartment, he had received a report from other agents who had followed the congressman directly to his home, where he was enjoying dinner with his wife.

Now all they had to do was wait for a report from the technology division to confirm that information had been transmitted to North Korea. That would take some time because they had to wait for the NSA to intercept and analyze the email transmission.

◆ ◆ ◆

Meanwhile, 6,900 miles west of Washington, D.C., Major Yuh Min-soo, military aide to Colonel General Kim Hyun-woo, knocked on the general's office door and after a moment entered without invitation. When the general looked up, he said, "General, we have received another message from Captain Pak." When the general held out his hand, Yuh handed him the message.

Major Yuh stood quietly and patiently as his general read the new message. After a moment, the general looked up with a smile and said, "It appears we now have three of the four pieces necessary to embarrass the Americans; we know who is coming, we know where, and we know approximately when. We just don't know how they plan to do it.

"Based on the outline of their plan, I agree with Captain Pak about where they will initiate their illegal entry into our country. Those two cities are where two of our new freeways begin; they are an obvious choice, even if the Americans cannot pronounce our Korean names! Because one of our spies in South Korea has informed us about the Army exercise, we now know from Captain Pak that this is an attempt to distract us at the time of their attempted infiltration. This gives away the approximate date of their operation."

After pondering for a moment, he looked up at Major Yuh and said, "Major, I want you to personally travel to both cities and examine the geography between each town and the DMZ. Talk to local commanders about any attempts by the South Koreans to cross the DMZ. Ask them if they have identified any areas that may lend themselves to use by agents."

After pondering for another moment, he continued, "In addition, examine the highway north of each town and identify possible chokepoints where we can place roadblocks to catch the Americans. Don't do or say anything that would arouse suspicion; pass your travels off as simply routine inspections. In fact, there is no need to rush your inspection; we have plenty of time to prepare. It might even be best if you made two separate trips."

"A good idea, general; I will make one trip this month and schedule the other trip for the middle of next month. Perhaps I should take one of our unmarked vehicles, one that cannot be traced back to us."

"A good idea! I don't want General Gae to get wind of our plan to capture the Americans. In fact, I want him to be very surprised when we make the announcement that we've captured two American spies." With a broad smile on his face, he dismissed his aide with a wave of his hand.

He played with a pen on his desk as he pondered whether to notify General Gae of the latest message. He finally decided that he should for two reasons; first it would keep the general from calling him! And second, it would further emphasize that he was doing his job very well. But he would keep to himself the locations mentioned in Captain Pak's message.

He used his intercom to ask his secretary to call General Gae's office, and when the general was on the line, told him clearly and concisely that he had received another message from his agent in America that confirmed the information in the first message but this time from a second source. He also told him the American weaklings were waiting for the end of winter to begin their operation. He told the general he would inform him immediately if he learned anything new. He smiled as he thought it almost seemed like a race to see which of them could hang up first!

His next call was to General Lee Gun-woo, Commander of the North Korean Army Rocket Service, to ask about progress with the new rocket. As Director of the North Korean intelligence service, it was his job to ensure that no foreigners learned of their progress with this new large rocket. General Lee told him that all the technological challenges had been overcome and that they were on schedule for a launch in the spring, or perhaps even sooner.

When General Kim heard this, he thought to himself how ironic it would be if they launched their new ballistic missile toward the American West Coast at the same time he was capturing their spies in North Korea. As he thought about this, an American idiom occurred to him, one he had learned on a recent trip to China: Everything's coming up roses!

Chapter Forty-Nine

As General Kim was thinking how wonderful his life was turning out to be, FBI Director Hansen was smiling at the news he had just received. When he arrived early in his office at FBI headquarters the next morning, his secretary told him there was a courier from the NSA to see him. The courier had him sign for receipt of a top-secret message and then left without waiting for a response.

He was smiling broadly as he read the message a second time.

Translation of encrypted email message sent to unidentified destination intercepted at 1923 hrs. EST:

> *Regards to my father. Confirmation of previous information. Today, White House liaison, U.S. Army Lieutenant Colonel Robert Johnson, personally briefed U.S. Congressman Singleton on nature of mission to DPRK. Two American Navy SEALs of Korean ancestry will enter DPRK near "Kasong" (this could be either Kaesŏng or Kosŏng) and travel openly on highway to research facility. They will not return to DMZ but will travel west to coastline where American submarine will pick them up. They wait for our winter to end before sending their spies. Assignment continues. Pak*

The Director reached for his phone and called Jefferson Jackson, the White House Chief of Staff. When he answered, he said, "Jeff, I need to meet with the President. We know who it is!" He didn't want to be open with any details on a non-secure line, but he was sure the Chief of Staff would understand.

"The President will be pleased to hear that. Today's schedule is full, more than full really, and tomorrow he's flying out to Ohio for a very important fund-raising meeting, so how about day after tomorrow in the morning? I can get you the exact time after I check his schedule."

"That will be fine; we're keeping everyone under close surveillance from this point forward. You should also invite Director Sanders and Dr. Richardson so that we can coordinate our efforts."

In a condescending voice, the Chief of Staff responded, "I could invite them if you believe it's necessary."

Shaking his head, the FBI Director calmly responded, "Yes, Jeff, I believe it is necessary; please invite them."

"Very well. I'll text you the time once it's set. Gotta go! Bye-bye."

Two days later in the Oval Office, the President greeted Harmon Sanders, Dr. Sarah Richardson, and Ernest Hansen. The President had also asked his Chief of Staff to attend this meeting.

The President invited them to sit in the informal meeting area across from his desk. In that rectangular space were two sofas and four comfortable chairs. The President always sat in the chair nearest his desk while the others sat on the sofas and his Chief of Staff sat next to him in one of the other chairs.

He turned to the FBI Director and said, "Ern, you have news for us?"

"Yes, Mr. President; with the help of Colonel Johnson, and a little bit of luck, we've been able to identify the source of our leaks. After thousands of man-hours of mind numbing research, we . . ."

The President interrupted by raising both hands and said, "Ern, please, spare us the gory details; we know your people work hard."

"Er, yes sir. Colonel Johnson had previously given us the telephone number that Michael Fontana, who is the Chief of Staff to Paul Singleton, a member of the house intelligence committee, had used to call him. It turned out to be a throwaway cell phone that had not been thrown away!

"That same phone number was used on numerous occasions to call a staff member of Congressman Singleton whose name is Julie Park Endicott. It turns out that she is of Korean ancestry; we're starting to look into her background now. We got a court order to tap that line, and it appears Mr. Fontana and Mrs. Endicott have been having an affair. At first, we thought that's as far as it went.

"Meanwhile, we asked Colonel Johnson to help us by meeting with Congressman Singleton. The original plan was that he would give the congressman a piece of information that only he would have. And then we would look for that piece of information to show up in an NSA surveillance operation that was previously authorized."

He looked around the room at the others, as he said, "Isn't it ironic that a surveillance operation authorized by the House subcommittee on intelligence would point back to one of its members!"

After a grim chuckle, the President said, "Ironic isn't the word I would use!"

The Director continued, "In any case, when Colonel Johnson visited with the congressman, he was able to leave behind a short range transmitter in the congressman's inner office. Almost immediately after he left, Mr. Fontana entered the office, and even though he had been warned not to, the congressman told his Chief of Staff everything that Colonel Johnson had told him.

"We discovered the congressman and his Chief of Staff go back a long way, and the congressman shares almost everything with him. While Congressman Singleton is indeed the source of the leak, he thought he could trust his friend to keep confidences.

"But it turns out his friend has a propensity for bragging about what he knows, particularly, it seems, to pretty young women. Unfortunately for us, he's been bragging to a woman we now believe is a North Korean spy." He paused a moment as if considering what he should say next, and then said, "Mr. President, it's obvious that Mr. Fontana likes to chat after sex; we heard him tell Mrs. Endicott virtually everything that the congressman had told him."

Before he could continue, CIA Director Sanders asked, "Ern, did you have a court order to bug her apartment?"

Looking somewhat embarrassed, the FBI Director answered, "Harm, that seemingly easy question has a complex answer." He could see that he had everyone's full attention, so he continued, "We have a court order to monitor the activities of Michael Fontana, and we are interpreting that to mean not only all of his physical activities but also all of his . . . verbal activities.

"We had one team of agents engaged in monitoring Mr. Fontana and a second team of agents monitoring Mrs. Endicott. Because this is a national security issue, we are taking this very seriously. The team monitoring Mrs. Endicott asked the tenants in the apartment next to hers to temporarily move to a rather nice hotel room. Then we moved in some really sophisticated technology; it turns out the two bedrooms are next to one another. To their common wall we attached an infrared imager and a very sophisticated transducer to pick up sounds. We'd only been in there 24 hours when the other team followed Mr. Fontana to her apartment. We also have an agent in an apartment across the hallway with a video camera monitoring all the activity in the hallway.

"I have to tell you, I was somewhat embarrassed for him when I watched the replay on the infrared imager of their time together. We were all surprised by how short a time they spent together, but while they lay together afterward he told her everything the congressman had shared with him. Every stinking word!

"After he left, we heard her moving about the apartment, and possibly using a computer, but learned nothing new. However, when I compared the timestamp on the audio recording of the possible computer sounds, it corresponded almost exactly to the time shown on the NSA intercept."

When he paused, the President asked a question. "It sounds like you've got enough to round all three of them up. What's your next step?"

Before the FBI Director could answer, Dr. Richardson spoke up, "Mr. President, before he answers, I'd like to point out that we still have our mission to North Korea to consider. The information that Colonel Johnson gave the congressman and the congressman gave to his Chief of Staff and his Chief of Staff to Mrs. Endicott . . . Well, it's a red herring about our mission.

"If we move too quickly, it may spook the North Koreans into taking action prematurely." She looked at Director Hansen as she asked, "Is it possible to keep them under surveillance while we complete our mission? It's only a few weeks away."

Before Director Hansen could respond to her question, the President spoke up and said, "Let's keep in mind that I'm obligated to brief the two intelligence committees before the mission sets off. Can we ensure my briefing doesn't make it into the hands of Mrs. Endicott?"

At this point, CIA Director Sanders spoke up. "Mr. President, if I may, this looks like an ideal opportunity to insert our new virus into their computer system. We all know the CIA cannot operate on U.S. soil, but if we provide IT support to the FBI, they could put the virus on her computer.

"There's clearly enough evidence to get a court order to enter her apartment and search for tools of the trade, the spy trade, that is. Our IT specialist could go along with the FBI team as an advisor and help examine her computer. Since she works all day at the congressman's office, we'd have plenty of time to check it out.

"If you give your briefing the day before the SEAL teams enter North Korea, it's possible the whole North Korean Army computer system could be compromised by the time they get there." He finished with a smug look on his face!

Dr. Richardson asked, "If we use her computer to do that, won't they be able to trace that back to us?" The President leaned forward to hear this answer.

With a wide smile, Director Sanders answered, "Only if they have her computer to examine. Otherwise the virus just suddenly appears in their system. It really is a beautiful plan!"

The President turned to FBI Director Hansen and asked, "Ern, how certain are you that you can keep her under surveillance?"

"Mr. President, as of today I've assigned three additional teams to keep track of Mrs. Endicott, and because we don't yet consider him a flight risk, I've only assigned one team to monitor Mr. Fontana's activities."

With a grim look on his face, he continued, "Right now, we consider Congressman Singleton a victim of his own misplaced trust. Our initial background check shows he is generally a good guy! He's never cheated on his wife; in fact, he watches old movies with her when they are at home together. He's publicly acknowledged the service of men and women in the military, and he seems sincere. Of course, at some point he will have to face up to the fact that he violated the conditions of his security clearance. That's a violation of federal law, and he'll have to pay the penalty."

Everyone was quiet as they watched the President consider those thoughts. After a moment, and without looking up, he said, "I know he holds a position of trust, and I can personally tell you how lonely it is holding high office. His lack of judgment in trusting a longtime friend can almost be forgiven."

He looked up then with a stern expression on his face, and said, "But only almost." He looked at FBI Director Hansen and said in his official voice, "Mr. Director, on the day I brief the two intelligence subcommittees, I want you standing outside the door. When Congressman Singleton shows up to attend, take him into custody." The President stood up as he continued talking. "Take him to FBI headquarters and tell him that his naïveté and his unwise trust of a friend has resulted in top secret information landing on a desk in North Korea.

"Have a confession already typed up and put it in front of him. Tell him he has two choices: He can either sign the confession and immediately and publicly resign as a congressman, and I mean resign the same day, or he can go through a public trial and federal prison.

"As for his Chief of Staff, have your agents arrest him at the same time and throw the key away!

"As for Mrs. Endicott, if I understand correctly, it doesn't matter what message she sends, the virus will be effective. So let her go to her apartment and use her computer; as soon as she sends a message, arrest her on espionage charges.

Pointing his index finger at the FBI chief, he said, "And Mr. Director, don't let them slip through your fingers!"

FBI Director Hansen firmly responded, "Mr. President, you have my word! We'll be attached to them like ticks on a dog."

The President returned to his seat and continued, "Dr. Richardson, I'm convinced now more than ever that our incursion into North Korea is a necessity. The General Counsel's office sent me the official text of the Presidential finding yesterday; if you will wait a moment, I'll sign it so you can have a copy."

The President looked at each of the others, and said, "I appreciate everything you've done, but let's not drop the ball before we get to the end zone." He stood up and dismissed everyone with a brief, "Thank you."

Dr. Richardson stood in front of his desk as the President signed the lengthy Presidential finding. As he handed her a copy he quietly said, "Sarah, you'll notice that not only is their nuclear program mentioned in this Presidential finding, but so is their threat of launching a ballistic missile at us. I consider that threat just as dangerous. This authorizes both the CIA and our Special Operations Command to take whatever action is necessary to reduce that threat. Share this with the JCS and with Director Sanders and caution them all that it is not to be shared with anyone else without my express permission.

"Any questions?"

She shook her head and said, "No, sir; your instructions are clear."

He smiled and said, "Let's all pray that it comes off without a hitch!" He dismissed her with a "Thank you."

Chapter Fifty

Senator Jack Bollinger, Chairman of the United States Senate Select Committee on Intelligence, and Congressman Barry Hoag, Chairman of the United States House Permanent Select Committee on Intelligence, were both alone in their offices when they received the notice from the White House Chief of Staff that the President wished to formally brief both committees on the Democratic People's Republic of Korea issue.

Each was equally excited when they read that the briefing was requested for three days hence at 2 PM, as that gave them time to properly prepare to meet and quiz the President. Both politicians asked their Chief of Staff to properly notify other members of their respective committees.

In due time, Michael Fontana notified Congressman Paul Singleton of the meeting. As part of his preparation, the congressman met privately with his Chief of Staff on the morning of the meeting and reviewed all the material they had collected, especially what they had learned from Colonel Johnson.

The congressman asked one more time, "Mike, are you certain we aren't able to discover the start date for this covert operation? It would really be nice to know that before the President's briefing."

The Chief of Staff was sitting in one of the side chairs which he had pulled in front of the congressman's desk, behind which the congressman was sitting. He responded with, "All we know, Paul, is what Colonel Johnson told you in that private briefing he gave you. I've called him several times this week. Each time my call goes to voicemail, and he has not called me back. I even called my source at the Pentagon, and they don't know where he is."

"Okay, we'll just have to go with what we know. I've reviewed the notes I made from my meeting with Colonel Johnson, and have committed the details to memory. For what it's worth, I've made small talk with some of the other committee members, and I'm pretty certain I'm the only one who knows those details. I have to tell you, I'm actually a little nervous about this upcoming meeting. If the President doesn't tell us everything, I'll have to be very careful as I put him on the spot."

"Don't worry, Paul, you'll do just fine! Since the briefing is in the Hart Building, why don't we walk over so you can relax on the way? In fact, let's leave early and have lunch in the cafeteria in the Dirksen Building?"

"That's a great idea, Mike!" He glanced at his watch and then said, "Let's leave in about 30 minutes; I wouldn't want to be late!"

Thirty-five minutes later, Mike was standing next to Mrs. Endicott as the congressman appeared from his office. Before turning to join him, he leaned over and whispered to her, "I'll text you when the committee meeting is over, and we'll meet at your apartment later."

As he turned away, she visibly shivered.

While this interchange was taking place, three FBI agents and one CIA technician were searching Mrs. Endicott's apartment. It didn't take long for them to find her laptop, and they were soon delving into the depths of its operating system. It wasn't long before they discovered the secret encryption program attached to her email software, and it took them even less time to upload the virus from a flash drive to that program. The laptop was back in the kitchen drawer about three hours after they started, and the agents left the apartment just as they found it.

As the congressman and his Chief of Staff left the Capitol building, they ignored the out-of-town visitors who were a constant nuisance walking up and down the hallways; they even ignored the two women who were chatting outside the congressman's office door. As was customary, neither the congressman nor his Chief of Staff paid any attention to the people who were wandering up and down the sidewalks outside the Capitol. They had grown accustomed to the tourists who were gawking at all the government buildings. They would have been surprised to learn that six FBI agents were mingling amongst the dozens of tourists, including the two women just outside the office door.

They took a leisurely pace as they left the U.S. Capitol and crossed Constitution Avenue on their way to the Dirksen Senate Office Building. They enjoyed an unhurried lunch in the Senate cafeteria as they sat unrecognized amongst the hundred or so diners; this cafeteria was one of the few that was open to the public. About 20 minutes before the briefing was to begin, they began their short walk to the Hart building.

They walked together toward the committee meeting room on the second floor, where they found a large gathering of reporters and news cameras. When one of the reporters noticed him, she started throwing questions at Congressman Singleton, which he chose to ignore. A few cameras then turned toward him, which automatically triggered his politician's smile! When they were stopped at the metal detector about 20 yards from the entrance to the meeting room, the congressman observed to his Chief of Staff, "That's Ernest Hansen, the FBI Director, up by the door; I didn't realize he had been invited."

Because Mr. Fontana had not been invited, he moved to one side as the congressman entered the queue for the metal detector. As he did so, the FBI Director started walking toward the metal detector. The two men met after the congressman was through the metal detector, and about halfway to the committee room doors, where the Director stepped directly in front of him.

"Hello Director Hansen, it's a pleasure to see you again."

It couldn't be helped! The arrest of Congressman Singleton was going to take place in front of a whole gaggle of reporters with bright lights and cameras. "Congressman Singleton, with respect sir, you are under arrest. If you agree to come quietly, we can dispense with the handcuffs." As quickly as it was said, there were two large and intimidating special agents at either side of the congressman.

Although the Director spoke quietly, it was inevitable that someone would hear what he said. There was an immediate increase in noise from the reporters, and an exponential increase in camera lighting and the flashing of multiple lights as cell phones and cameras captured the moment.

The expression on Congressman Singleton's face showed he was clearly dumbfounded by Director Hansen's statement. So much so, in fact, that he didn't know what to say; so, he said nothing and just stood there, as if frozen in space.

At the same time, his Chief of Staff, who had also heard Director Hansen's words, moved as quickly as a gazelle and, because of the press and clamor of the news people in the hallway, was able to race down a nearby stairway several steps ahead of the FBI agents. At street level he quickly flagged down a taxi-cab and raced away as the two agents exited the Hart building.

While those two agents were running for their car so they could follow the Chief of Staff, his boss, Congressman Paul Singleton, was escorted from the Hart building.

While Congressman Singleton was being driven to FBI headquarters, Michael Fontana was on his cell phone talking with Mrs. Endicott. "Julie, the FBI has just arrested Congressman Singleton. I can't believe it! Why would they arrest him?"

She may have been a young and rather inexperienced spy, but that didn't mean she was stupid! But instead of panicking she said, "Michael, I have no idea! What do you want to do?"

"I'm in a taxi on my way to the office, so I'll see you in a few minutes." He paused for a moment and then said, "On second thought, the press is going to converge on the office pretty quickly. Let's not meet there. Let's meet at your apartment; if you leave now we can get there at about the same time." The Chief of Staff still had no idea that he was being pursued by the FBI, albeit far enough back that they had lost sight of his taxi.

Likewise, as she left the congressman's office, she didn't notice the two agents following her. Captain Pak Ji-woo was well trained as an agent, at least by North Korean standards, but she simply lacked the experience to pick out the two skilled female FBI agents.

As she crossed Constitution Avenue and began looking for a taxi, one of the agents ran for their car as the other stood on the curb nearby. Mrs. Endicott in a taxi and the two FBI agents in their car were soon headed toward her apartment. The agent in the passenger seat, whose name was Olivia, used her cell phone to let the task force lead agent know they were moving. During that call, she was told the congressman had been taken into custody and the Chief of Staff was in a taxicab.

Also a well-trained agent, and having been previously briefed on their relationship, Olivia wondered if the Chief of Staff and the spy were going to meet. As time passed, it became a clear possibility that Mrs. Endicott was headed toward her apartment, so she called one of the agents assigned to Michael Fontana. As they discussed that possibility, it became clear they were also headed to her apartment and the agents behind the Chief of Staff would arrive a few minutes after Mrs. Endicott and Olivia and her partner.

Mrs. Endicott was walking quickly into her apartment building as the two FBI agents arrived and parked in front of the building. Moments after they entered the building, Michael Fontana arrived. And three minutes after that, the two FBI agents on his trail parked illegally in front of the building.

Like a carefully choreographed dance, Mrs. Endicott entered her apartment, Olivia and her partner entered the FBI apartment across the hall, Michael Fontana, after a knock, was invited into Mrs. Endicott's apartment, and the two agents who followed him up the stairs also entered the FBI apartment.

In her apartment, and under the watchful but curious eye of Michael Fontana, Mrs. Endicott pulled out her laptop computer and powered it up. He asked, "What are you doing?" As she sat down at the kitchen table in front of her computer, she said to him, "Please, Michael, sit down and let me take care of one small task." She pointed to the chair directly across from her. Confused, he pulled out the chair and sat down. He sat for a moment and then agitated, got up and pulled a beer out of the refrigerator.

He watched as she quickly typed at her computer. She raised her head and gave him a quick smile and then quickly typed a brief message:

Regards to my father. Mission is compromised. Beginning evasion plan Alpha. Pak

When she hit the send button and looked up, he asked, "What was that?"

She thought for a moment and then said, "Hold on a moment; I have to get something from the bedroom."

As she was walking to her bedroom, there was a knock at the door. She stopped for a moment and then hurried into her bedroom. He asked from the kitchen, "Do you want me to get that?"

Without answering, she walked back into the kitchen with a grim look on her face. He stood up abruptly when he saw she was holding a gun at her side. He came around the kitchen table and grabbed her arm, and after a brief struggle he took the gun from her just as her apartment door burst open.

When he turned at the sound of the door breaking, the gun was in his hand and pointed at the floor. Olivia was the second person to come through the smashed-in door, and when she saw the gun her excellent training took over. She yelled, "Gun! Gun! Gun!" and dropped to one knee with her gun pointed at the Chief of Staff.

When he heard her yelling, he looked down at the gun in his hand and intuitively raised it as he looked, at which point Olivia fired her Glock 19 twice, both bullets striking him high in the center of his chest. His uncomprehending eyes were wide as his lifeless body slid to the floor.

Captain Pak Ji-woo merely stood there with her arms at her side and a neutral expression on her face as one of the agents said, "Julie Park Endicott, you are under arrest for espionage!" In a moment, she smiled as she realized they were too late; her message had been transmitted. She looked down at the body of Michael Fontana lying at her feet and quietly said, "What a fitting end for a foolish man!"

She would've groaned with great anguish had she known about the computer virus she had transmitted.

Chapter Fifty-One

The brief message Captain Pak Ji-woo managed to send arrived in the North Korean intelligence service communications room just mere minutes after the confrontation in her apartment. As soon as the communications technician enabled the decryption program, however, her computer screen flickered several times and then went dark.

While it appeared their bug was working, the CIA would've been dismayed to learn that the North Korean IT people had made allowance for the possibility of a message containing malware programs, such as an embedded virus. While the virus operated exactly as designed, it infected only the one machine on which Captain Pak Ji-woo's message had arrived.

Although the technician was surprised when her screen went dark, she calmly followed the established protocol and notified her supervisor. The supervisor's instructions were simple: He was to notify Major Yuh Min-soo if there were any irregularities in any message from this particular agent. However, the supervisor was not calm as he followed his instructions; he knew that Major Yuh Min-soo was the military aide to the commanding general of the intelligence service, Colonel General Kim Hyun-woo, who would not be pleased.

As he related the circumstances surrounding the arrival of the latest message from their spy in America, he was very much surprised when the general's aide merely acknowledged his call and hung up. Still anxious about possible repercussions, he ordered his technician to complete the additional steps in the written protocol. This required them to disconnect the computer immediately and move it to the computer antivirus research branch on the second floor.

Meanwhile, Major Yuh Min-soo moved from his bed as quietly as possible so as not to awaken his wife. He glanced at his watch and saw that it was only 4:30 AM. After pondering his options for several moments, he decided he would shave and shower and go to his office. He was not willing to wake his commanding general based solely on a single telephone call.

By the time he arrived in his office, the computer antivirus research branch had already determined that the incoming message had contained a very potent virus. In fact, they told Major Yuh that the only way the virus could have been placed on Captain Pak's computer was if a technician had physical access to the laptop.

Even though the brief message from Captain Pak could not be retrieved, this report told Major Yuh everything he needed to know about their mission in America – it was compromised.

He left the second floor laboratory and took the elevator to the top floor where his office was located next to the general's office. He hesitated only a moment before reaching for his telephone and dialing General Kim's home. He was not surprised when the general told him he would be at his office in 30 minutes.

Only 27 minutes later they were together in the general's office. General Kim asked, "Has there been any additional information received?"

"Yes, sir; rather significant news. While waiting for you, I searched the Internet for recent news from Washington, D.C. There are several news reports that their Congressman Paul Singleton was taken into custody by the FBI and that his Chief of Staff has died from wounds received during an FBI raid on the apartment of a suspected spy.

"While the reports did not give the name of the spy, who was arrested by the way, I believe it is safe to assume that Captain Pak Ji-woo has been captured.

"Of greater significance to us, General, the reports say the congressman was taken into custody just prior to attending an intelligence committee briefing by the President. You may recall that Captain Pak's last report said their President would brief the committee just prior to their operatives entering North Korea."

At this report, General Kim became more animated. "Yes! But have we been able to discover where they will enter our border?"

"Not yet," Major Yuh replied, "But as you know, the South Korean Army is conducting what we consider to be minor exercises at the two locations referred to in the previous communication – near Kaesŏng and Kosŏng. I have pondered this and have developed a strategy.

"The highway from Kaesŏng to Pyongyang is 170 km of four-lane highway, while the highway from Kosŏng to Pyongyang is over 300 km, about one-third of which is single lane and very slow from Kosŏng to Wŏnsan. Furthermore, there are numerous checkpoints around the port of Wŏnsan, making the risk of discovery too great. I cannot believe they would choose this highway! If I were them, I would minimize my time in our country and choose the shorter route. The most logical course of action seems to be to focus our attentions on Kaesŏng.

"My plan is this: North of Kaesŏng, near Sariwŏn, the highway makes a sharp turn; this is an ideal place to establish our checkpoint. We can make it look like a normal army checkpoint, but staff it with our people. The spies will of course have made arrangements, including forged travel documents, to get through the Army's normal roadblocks, but there is so little traffic on that highway, we can afford to stop and inspect every person and vehicle in much greater detail. They will not escape us!"

The general was firm when he said, "That is a good plan, Major; alert our teams now! Send two vehicles with two squads each. The first vehicle is not to stop until they establish our inspection point near Sariwŏn, while the second vehicle will stop and inspect every vehicle traveling from Sariwŏn to ensure the agents haven't already entered our country."

After a moment's consideration, he continued, "While I agree with your assessment, let's ensure our success by sending a third vehicle toward Wŏnsan; they can establish a checkpoint at the bend in the highway about 60 km from here. Be sure this vehicle also contains two squads of our people. Go now!"

As Major Yuh was leaving his office, the general added an additional comment. "General Gae will certainly hear about our activities; I will call his office and inform his staff that we are conducting training exercises for our counterintelligence agents. That should satisfy any curiosity that arises!"

General Kim was generally considered a competent commanding officer, but in his desire to impress his superiors, he accomplished two things that were of great detriment to their efforts. First, he sent six full squads of counterintelligence agents, virtually all of the experienced agents in Pyongyang, in the opposite direction from where the Americans would be; and second, by failing to inform the Commanding General of the Ministry of the People's Armed Forces that American operatives were likely entering their country, he gave the Army no time to prepare a proper response.

In fact, his actions diverted the attention of the Army, thereby accomplishing the very purpose of the American ruse. When he called Army headquarters and left his message, it was immediately brought to the attention of General Gae.

"General Gae," his aide began, "we've just received a message from General Kim that units of his Counterintelligence Corps will be conducting routine training on the highway between here and Sariwŏn and the highway between here and Wŏnsan."

General Gae didn't even look up as he said, "Thank you, Colonel." Then before his aide could close the office door he called, "Colonel, come back." As his aide came back and stood before his desk, General Gae said, "Has General Kim ever notified us previously when they were conducting training exercises?"

"No sir, we typically find out about it when one of our roving units comes across them on the highway. Now that I think about it, it is unusual to be notified, especially by General Kim himself."

"Colonel, something else is going on here! Send a squad with an officer in charge to observe their training. Have them report immediately if they see anything unusual." After a short pause, he continued, "Has there been any additional news regarding his spy in America?"

"Only a brief report that their mission was continuing and there was no additional news."

Thinking out loud, the general said, "So, General Kim calls me personally to brief me on their mission when there is virtually nothing to report. Then he chooses to leave a message without talking to me. That is unlike him! Now he conducts what he calls routine training, and he personally calls to tell us this. I repeat, something is going on here!"

After a moment's thought, he ordered, "Colonel, alert the 1st Home Battalion immediately! I want units patrolling every mile of both highways; they are to stop every vehicle and search it thoroughly. It may not be a coincidence that South Korea is conducting military exercises near the DMZ; it's possible they are masking something else. Alert all units along the DMZ and place them on high alert. General Kim is keeping something from us, and I want to be ready when he fails."

When his superiors analyzed General Kim's actions afterward, the act of sending the bulk of his Counterintelligence Corps on training maneuvers at the same time was considered a foolish action. However, he would be more severely criticized for failing to inform General Gae of the American plans to infiltrate across the DMZ. For this, he would be demoted to the rank of colonel and retired from the service. Although his retirement was publicly announced, he was never seen again.

Chapter Fifty-Two

At about the same time on the other side of the world, Vivian and I were enjoying a late dinner at my condo when I heard my cell phone make that irritating buzzing sound, the sound it makes when it is set to vibrate. I walked over to the table in the living room where I had left my phone and saw the call was from Admiral Harrison.

I answered with a cheerful, "Good evening, Admiral; I hope you're home enjoying an old classic movie with your wife!"

Without preliminaries, he said, "I'm not! Colonel, we have a problem and you've been elected to fix it."

My inward groan must've escaped through my lips, because he said, "No sense complaining, Colonel, your country needs you, and it needs you right now!"

He went on to say, "Our favorite lieutenant commander has been in-jured in a training accident; his left arm is broken. When I got the news I called Dr. Richardson, and after discussing it for several minutes, she said she'd call me right back and hung up. Well, she called back in a bit and told me she'd discussed it with the President.

"I don't know how they came up with your name, but it could have something to do with the fact that you were fully briefed on the mission, so the President wants you as Morty's replacement. Your favorite airplane will be waiting for you at Andrews, and after a stop in Alaska it will deliver you to Atsugi, Japan. From there, arrangements have been made to get you to Yokosuka where you can join up with the other members of your team. How soon can you pack your bags and get out to Andrews?"

I looked over at Vivian and then said, "Admiral, you really know how to ruin a beautiful evening!" Hearing this, Vivian stood and walked over next to me as I continued my conversation with the Admiral. "Did he lose any gear? In other words, do I need to take any replacements with me? Do I need to go to SOCOM first?"

"Hold on a minute, let me read that section again." I heard some paper shuffling then it was quiet for a few moments and then he said, "There's no report of lost equipment, gear or weapons. Just that silly broken arm!"

"Admiral, you asked how soon *I* could get to Andrews. Have you already notified the Air Force flight crew?"

"I called them just before I called you. They said they could be ready in about two hours."

"Hold on a minute, Admiral." I muted the phone as I turned to Vivian and said, "I'll explain the details in a few minutes, but can you take me out to Andrews in about 90 minutes?"

She made a pouty face but said, "Yes, I can."

I turned back to my phone, canceled the mute and said, "I can be at base ops in about two hours, Admiral. And Admiral, since Commander Throckmorton was assigned the primary, send a message to Major Denton reassigning him to the primary; I'll go to the secondary."

"Thank you, Colonel. I'll do that. And say hi to Dr. O'Brien!" And he was gone!

I turned to Vivian again and said, "Admiral Harrison says hello. How did he know you were here?"

She smiled and said, "They say that love is blind; but he's not the one in love with me."

I was momentarily thrown off balance with that comment but quickly regained my composure and said, "The bad news is, Commander Throckmorton has a broken arm from a training accident, and the admiral says the President tagged me to take his place. You attended our early planning meetings so you know what our mission is. I'll be gone about a week or 10 days."

She took a deep breath as she sat on the sofa and said, "I know enough about the mission to know that it's not as simple as you leave tonight and then you're back in a week; it's not the same as a business trip."

My first thought was, uh-oh, our first stretch of rough road. Although it hadn't been a major problem between Beth and me, I've watched other families be torn asunder as the soldier marched off to war and the spouse stayed home, always wondering if they would ever see their loved one again.

I sat next to her and said, "I don't know exactly how you're feeling right now, but I can tell you that I'm no more happy about my leaving than you are."

The next 90 minutes seemed to pass so very quickly. We talked about inconsequential things as I pulled my bag out of the closet and started to pack. Her only physical reaction came when I pulled my Glock out of my computer bag and placed it in with my other things.

She was quiet as I drove to Andrews Air Force Base. She was right about one thing; I did enjoy driving her bright orange Mustang!

She stood near me as I pulled my bag out of the trunk and then gave me a hug after I set it on the curb. She kissed me for a long minute and then with a pout said, "It's just like a man to make a woman fall in love with him and then run off to do battle with dragons; it's just not fair!"

It was all I could do to keep from laughing as I kissed her again. Dragons, indeed!

And that's how I ended up on a cold wet hill in North Korea.

Chapter Fifty-Three

I must've dozed off again because the next thing I remember is someone screaming in my ear! I lie there a moment as I try to clear the fog from my brain; that task is made easier when I move abruptly and knock a little more cold, wet snow into my face.

I suddenly realize it is morning and I had slept most of the night. My first thought is that I most definitely would not be a good candidate for a Navy SEAL! My next realization is that two men in gray parkas are standing in front of me pointing their rifles at me. It's at that point I realize the screaming voice hadn't been in my ear, but is standing right in front of me!

All of a sudden I am wide awake!

I look at the two North Korean soldiers, one older and one very much younger, with what I hope is a blank expression on my face. As the older soldier continues to yell at me, I realize there is significant noise coming from the rocket gantry down in the valley. It looks like my worst dream is coming to fruition; at the exact time we need to be concentrating on the rocket, we have been discovered by a North Korean patrol.

Then I realize that is not quite true; the two soldiers have only discovered me, not the rest of the team. I see the old soldier reach for the microphone that is clipped to the outside of his parka, so I look up at him and smile and say in Korean, "Good morning, Grandfather." His hand quickly moves back to his rifle, but I can see that I confused him by speaking in his native language.

While still smiling at the older soldier, I squeeze my push-to-talk switch with my left hand and say out loud, calmly, but in English, "SEAL team, I've been discovered. Come help now." I then speak again to the old soldier in Korean, "What a beautiful day we have before us; come, join me for breakfast."

My attempt at delay and confusion, although feeble, appears to be working. The old soldier takes a step back and gruffly tells me to stand up. As I move to do so, the young soldier suddenly gets a look of stark terror on his face. He is just starting to say something when he drops his rifle and suddenly falls to the ground. The old soldier is quick to recognize the new danger, but not quick enough. As he turns his rifle to meet the threat to his left, I jump up and push his AK-47 into the air just as he fires. I then scream "Cease fire! Cease fire," just before I tackle the old man.

I can't ever remember hearing the sound of a suppressed handgun before, but as I turn to my right, I see Lieutenant Carrollton coming toward me with his Glock 17 still in his hand and the distinctive sound suppressor attached to the muzzle. It was only now that I fully recognize what had happened. Lieutenant Carrollton had shot the young soldier, wounding him as it turned out, and was just about to shoot the older man, as well, when he heard my scream to cease fire.

I look down at the old man and softly say in Korean, "Please don't move or he will kill you."

I look up at the Lieutenant, and I'm sure he's having the same thought I am; the two-man patrol had walked past the two SEAL team members on my left and also past Sergeant Parker and Sergeant Harris without seeing any of them. I could see it in his eyes. I was the new guy, a desk soldier, and I may have just blown the whole mission.

Right then a funny thought occurs to me: In Hollywood movies, the newest character to be introduced in the plot is typically the one who dies when there's a problem. Well, even though I am the new guy, I'm not a Hollywood character and I'm not going to die!

Lieutenant Carrollton looks up at the sound of boots crunching on the snow as another SEAL team member, it was Lt. Williams, approaches from the other side of the hill. He too has his Glock out and ready to use. The two of them talked for a few moments, and then Lieutenant Carrollton says to me, "Colonel, when they don't show up, I'm guessing there'll be a whole bunch of people out here looking for them."

My heart is still racing from watching two men almost killed right in front of my eyes, and can only nod at Lieutenant Carrollton. Finally catching my breath, I say to him, "We can't leave them here, and I'm not willing to kill them!"

Before he can respond, the young soldier groans as he reaches feebly for his AK-47. Lieutenant Williams easily kicks it out of reach. The soldier then clutches at his bleeding arm as he rolls onto his back and glares at Lieutenant Williams.

Lieutenant Carrollton replies, "What else is there?" A brief pause as he looks at me, and then he says, "Wait, you want to take them home with us?"

Just as he says this, there is a tremendous noise from down in the valley in the direction of the rocket gantry. We all turn that direction to see flames dancing in the fog! In a split second, I recognize it as the exhaust of the rocket. I turn and yell at Sergeant Parker to start shooting, but he is already way ahead of me. His first shot rings out as I'm still yelling at him. The M107 Barret sniper rifle, chambered for the .50 caliber BMG round, makes a substantial crack when it is fired; the sound literally hurts my ears. The two Navy SEALs and I quickly jump behind the muzzle of the booming rifle with hands covering our ears, as two more shots ring out. The two soldiers quickly clamp their own hands over their ears as they lie there on the ground in front of us.

When the meteorologists told us back at SOCOM that we could expect early morning fog, the plan we developed was that the snipers would shoot at the sound of the engine exhaust and just above where the fog was being rent by the rocket exhaust. In the pre-mission practice, a well-controlled environment, the snipers were only able to make two hits out of five shots. The success of the mission is literally now in the hands of fate.

Even as I am thinking this, the slowly climbing rocket appears above the fog layer. From my left I hear Master Sergeant Parker's spotter, Sergeant Harris, scream just one word, "Yes!" as another shot rings out from the sniper rifle. Still the rocket climbs! Another shot rings out!

What happens next is almost indescribable! The rocket exhaust is clearly visible below the rocket as another shot rings out from Sergeant Parker's rifle. One moment I'm watching the rocket climb ever higher into the sky, thinking that our mission and my career are both about to become dismal failures, when all of a sudden it seems the entire sky is obliterated by the explosion of the rocket. Even though we are over three-quarters of a mile away, we still feel the warmth of the explosion and the tremendous change in air pressure created by the exploding rocket fuel.

It takes us a few moments, even the Navy SEALs, to recover our senses. As the noise dissipates, I hear Lieutenant Carrollton calling the other SEAL team members to join up. As they continue running toward us, I hear Sergeant Harris say to Master Sergeant Parker, "Pop, you made five shots, I have five shells! We're good to go."

And indeed that was the plan! As soon as the rocket was destroyed, or it was no longer a viable target, we were to start running for the coastline. I turn to Lieutenant Carrollton and say, "Get us out of here, Lieutenant! And yes, these two are coming with us."

His response is an immediate, "Aye, aye, sir!" He tells one of the other SEAL team members to quickly bandage the young soldier's gunshot wound so he can travel. He then takes a couple of moments to police up the area where I had been sleeping; apparently he trusted everyone else to police their own area!

The plan was that he and his SEAL team partner would lead off, followed by me and the sniper team, and then the other two SEAL team members would bring up the rear. We would now insert the two North Korean soldiers just ahead of the trailing SEAL team duo. We are not going to leave the cold North Korean Hills the same way we had arrived, so Lieutenant Carrollton heads off in a southwesterly direction. This was Plan B. Remember, I don't like plan B!

All of a sudden I remember the rest of my responsibility and call for everyone to stop. First, I pull out the satellite phone and hit speed dial number two. When someone answers, I say, "Team two, normal extraction, location Bravo. Plus two additional passengers." I had almost forgotten to call for our ride home! After they repeat that back to me, I hit the end call button and then quickly hit speed dial number one. This will connect me with Major Denton, in charge of the team at Tonghae. There is no answer! I think for just a moment and decide to make another call after we are well away from this ridge line. I turn to Lieutenant Carrollton and say, "Carry-on, Lieutenant!" And away we trotted!

A short time later, I'm able to call Major Denton and confirm the status of his team. He reports their success and both teams continue their retreat toward their respective coastlines and waiting submarines. I know we won't talk again until after we're back together in Yokosuka, Japan.

Chapter Fifty-Four

My mission report would detail the rest. We followed our extraction plan without a hitch. We reached the coast in good time, without encountering any North Korean patrols. Perhaps they assumed the team traveling with us was actually out looking for us!

From the coast, our submarine took us on to Yokosuka, Japan, to rendezvous with the Tonghae team. It was there we learned the reason Major Denton didn't answer my first call was because his team was in the process of taking shots at the missile being launched there. Although their missile launch site was not covered in fog, it still took Marine Corps Gunnery Sergeant Henry Patterson three shots from his M107 rifle to destroy the rocket. It too exploded just above the gantry.

From Yokosuka, the Air Force C-17 flew us all to MacDill Air Force Base in Florida for debriefing, just as we'd planned. In fact, the only change to the established Plan B had to do with our new North Korean soldier friends. We made a slight detour on the way to Yokosuka to drop off the two soldiers at Yeongjongdo Island, just a few miles west of Seoul, where Major Kim met us and took delivery of them. A few weeks after I returned home, Major Kim let me know that they were very happy to be in South Korea, and the young soldier was recovering nicely from his wound.

My mission report didn't mention, however, my relief that it all came off as well it did. I was glad to know my career was secure, but more than that, it was gratifying to see a plan come together to accomplish an important mission. While solid planning combined with good intelligence and skilled officers were key, I still can't discount that fact that we got a little lucky, too!

Also not in the mission report was my own rendezvous with Vivian. She met me at Andrews when I returned from MacDill. Until I saw her standing there, I hadn't realized just how much I had missed her bright green eyes and her permanent smile. I also hadn't realized just how much I missed feeling that indescribable way I feel around her. She melted into my embrace when we met, and I pulled back only enough to kiss her smiling lips. Boy was I glad to be back!

One afternoon about two weeks after I returned to the Pentagon, Admiral Harrison shared the following report with me:

> The Democratic People's Republic of Korea state news service, Korean Central News Agency, reported today that a fast-moving freak winter thunderstorm had damaged the launch facilities at both Sohae and Tonghae. The central ruling committee in Pyongyang stated that the effect of the storms was magnified by defective electrical grounding systems. It was reported that commanders at both facilities were relieved of their duties and summarily executed for their gross dereliction of duty. Repairs have begun, and it is expected that both facilities will be operating at 100 percent in the very near future, according to the news service.
>
> In another announcement, the state news service reported the death of General Lee Gun-woo, who was commander of the strategic rocket forces, sometimes known as the Missile Guidance Bureau. A previous news item reported he had just returned from conducting a routine inspection at the Sohae launch facility. His death has been attributed to complications of pneumonia.
>
> The state news service also reported that another high-ranking official, in a bizarre coincidence, had also died. The state news service reported the death of General Gae, Commanding General of the Ministry of the People's Armed Forces. General Gae's death was attributed to a lingering illness.

It would be a long, long time before North Korea would again be able to threaten the United States with an intercontinental ballistic missile! Months later, the NRO reported that both launch facilities were still a mess of tangled metal. In fact, this later analysis of satellite imagery would indicate the rocket destroyed at Tonghae was probably a Taepodong-2 rocket. It is rumored to have a range of approximately 6,700 km or about 4,100 miles – well short of our West Coast. So much for North Korean threats!

Epilogue

Paul Singleton, the former Congressman from New Jersey, and his wife moved to a condominium in Vail, Colorado, near their children, and he is rumored to be writing his memoirs.

Captain Pak Ji-woo, known in the United States as Julie Park Endicott, was found guilty of espionage and is serving a life sentence at the Leavenworth, Kansas, federal prison facility.

After moving back to North Bergen, New Jersey, Karen Fontana, former wife of Congressional Chief of Staff Michael Fontana, grieved his death for all of 60 days and then married her former high school sweetheart, a used car salesman also from North Bergen, New Jersey.

Olivia McCarthy, the FBI special agent who shot and killed Mike Fontana, was promoted to Supervisory Special Agent in charge of the Cleveland, Ohio, field office.

Colonel Jacobs, who had been my commanding officer in the Pentagon, was transferred to Wiesbaden, Germany, to command the 66th Military Intelligence Brigade. A few months later, he was passed over for promotion to Brigadier General and submitted his retirement papers.

In late spring, I received my promotion to full-bird Colonel and a new assignment with Army Intelligence. I am now the commanding officer of my old unit in the Pentagon, replacing Colonel Jacobs. I moved Master Sergeant Garcia to my new office and confirmed Major Green, soon to be Lieutenant Colonel Green, as the permanent head of the Far Eastern desk of military intelligence.

Vivian and I continue our habit of eating dinner together as often as we can, sometimes with Jacob and Susan, and often combining dinner with a movie on Friday or Saturday evenings.

Next Sunday after church, I'm going to follow my father's advice. I plan to take Vivian to the Jefferson Memorial and, in the shadow of a great man, ask her to be a June bride. I shared my plan with my children just today, and they are excited to soon have a woman around the house!